# YARRICK

## THE PYRES OF ARMAGEDDON

*More tales of the Astra Militarum from Black Library*

YARRICK: CHAINS OF GOLGOTHA
A Commissar Yarrick novella by David Annandale

HONOUR IMPERIALIS
An omnibus edition of the novels *Cadian Blood* by Aaron Dembski-Bowden,
*Redemption Corps* by Rob Sanders & *Dead Men Walking* by Steve Lyons

STRAKEN
An 'Iron Hand' Straken novel by Toby Frost

## • THE MACHARIAN CRUSADE •
By William King

BOOK 1: ANGEL OF FIRE
BOOK 2: FIST OF DEMETRIUS
BOOK 3: ANGEL OF FIRE

## • GAUNT'S GHOSTS •
By Dan Abnett

### THE FOUNDING
BOOK 1: FIRST AND ONLY
BOOK 2: GHOSTMAKER
BOOK 3: NECROPOLIS

### THE SAINT
BOOK 4: HONOUR GUARD
BOOK 5: THE GUNS OF TANITH
BOOK 6: STRAIGHT SILVER
BOOK 7: SABBAT MARTYR

### THE LOST
BOOK 8: TRAITOR GENERAL
BOOK 9: HIS LAST COMMAND
BOOK 10: THE ARMOUR OF CONTEMPT
BOOK 11: ONLY IN DEATH

### THE VICTORY
BOOK 12: BLOOD PACT
BOOK 13: SALVATION'S REACH

*Visit* blacklibrary.com *for the full range of Astra Militarum novels, novellas, audio dramas and short stories, as well as many other exclusive Black Library products.*

# YARRICK

## THE PYRES OF ARMAGEDDON

DAVID ANNANDALE

BLACK LIBRARY

*For Margaux, always, as we stand together, in all ways.*

## A BLACK LIBRARY PUBLICATION

First published in Great Britain in 2015
This edition published in 2016 by
Black Library
Games Workshop Ltd
Willow Road
Nottingham NG7 2WS UK

10 9 8 7 6 5 4 3 2 1

Produced by Games Workshop in Nottingham

A CIP record for this book is available from the British Library.

UK ISBN 13: 978 1 78496 172 5
US ISBN 13: 978 1 78496 173 2

See Black Library on the internet at

# blacklibrary.com

Find out more about Games Workshop
and the world of Warhammer 40,000 at

# games-workshop.com

Printed and bound by CPI Group (UK) Ltd, Croydon, CR0 4YY

It is the 41st millennium. For more than a hundred centuries the Emperor has sat immobile on the Golden Throne of Earth. He is the master of mankind by the will of the gods, and master of a million worlds by the might of his inexhaustible armies. He is a rotting carcass writhing invisibly with power from the Dark Age of Technology. He is the Carrion Lord of the Imperium for whom a thousand souls are sacrificed every day, so that he may never truly die.

Yet even in his deathless state, the Emperor continues his eternal vigilance. Mighty battlefleets cross the daemon-infested miasma of the warp, the only route between distant stars, their way lit by the Astronomican, the psychic manifestation of the Emperor's will. Vast armies give battle in His name on uncounted worlds. Greatest amongst his soldiers are the Adeptus Astartes, the Space Marines, bio-engineered super-warriors. Their comrades in arms are legion: the Imperial Guard and countless planetary defence forces, the ever-vigilant Inquisition and the tech-priests of the Adeptus Mechanicus to name only a few. But for all their multitudes, they are barely enough to hold off the ever-present threat from aliens, heretics, mutants – and worse.

To be a man in such times is to be one amongst untold billions. It is to live in the cruellest and most bloody regime imaginable. These are the tales of those times. Forget the power of technology and science, for so much has been forgotten, never to be re-learned. Forget the promise of progress and understanding, for in the grim dark future there is only war. There is no peace amongst the stars, only an eternity of carnage and slaughter, and the laughter of thirsting gods.

# CHAPTER 1
# TEARS OF THE EMPEROR

## 1. YARRICK

The return to Armageddon was a hard one. As we made our way back from Basquit, the warp convulsed. Waves of insanity slammed against the *Glaive of Pyran*. The Lunar-class cruiser was a good ship, strong in hull and crew. Even so, cries echoed down its length. Some were the wailing of tocsins as the Gellar field's integrity was strained by the currents and tides of the immaterium moved to anger. Others came from the *Glaive's* astropathic choir and navigator. In the troop holds, we felt the cruiser shake as its reality came under assault and the certainty of its path eroded. At one point, the walls reverberated with a groan that was too deafening to be human, and too agonised to be metal.

And yet this was not the storm. This was the storm building. The *Glaive of Pyran* held true to its course, and when it exited the warp, we were in the Armageddon System.

'A rough passage, Commissar Yarrick,' Colonel Artura Brenken said to me in the shuttle that carried us from the cruiser towards Hive Infernus. There was a jolt as we began re-entry. My grav-harness held me in place as the fuselage shook.

'Very,' I agreed. I raised my voice over the violent rattling caused by the atmosphere's turbulence. 'I doubt many more ships will be able to enter or leave the system until the storm passes.'

Brenken gave me a sharp look. 'This storm worries you.'

'All warp storms do.'

'This one more than others.'

I gave her a crooked grin. She knew me well. She should, after so many decades. We had first met shortly after my initial mission as commissar. After serving on Mistral, I had been seconded to the Armageddon Steel Legion for the first time. She had been a sergeant, then a captain, and had been a colonel now for over seventy years. She would have made a fine general, and in my more cynical moments, I sometimes thought that was precisely why she had never reached that rank. She was a superb soldier, but a poor politician – an officer who became more uneasy the further she was from a battlefield.

She wouldn't make general now. She was near the end of her career. We both were. We were old. Juvenat treatments had kept us physically viable, but her face, like mine, had been moulded by the decades upon decades of war. The unnatural smoothness of her augmetic lower jaw stood out in stark contrast to the landscape of wrinkles and scars on the rest of her clean-shaven skull.

No, colonel would be the peak of her ascension in the ranks.

But she had ascended. I was still a simple commissar.

We both had debriefings to attend. She, as commanding officer of the 252nd Regiment of the Armageddon Steel Legion, would be due for official commendation, following the success of the campaign against the ork raiders. My day would be less pleasant. Seroff would see to that.

Brenken prodded me. 'What is it about this storm?'

'Nothing definite,' I admitted. 'I don't like its conjunction with what we found on Basquit.'

'Orks...' Brenken began, but was interrupted by turbulence.

I was sitting next to the viewing block and looked out at our descent through the cloud cover of Armageddon. The air was dense and filthy as an oil slick, lightning flashing between roiling fists of brown and yellow. Then we dropped below the cover. The air was still far from clear. I looked out through the eternal layers of grit and banks of sluggish, low-hanging smog. Corrosive rain streaked the viewing block, blurring my first view of Infernus. At this distance, the spires of the hive were indistinguishable from its chimneys. It was a hulking mass of black, filth-crusted iron and rockcrete surging up from the planet's surface, forever surrounded by the choking aura of its industry. It was nestled between two mountain chains – the Pallidus to the west, and the Diablo to the east. The winds of the Season of Fire buffeted the shuttle, but did nothing to clear away the smog. The bowl between the mountains held the poisoned air trapped over the city.

Brenken tried again. 'Orks are a threat, but hardly an uncommon one. And we purged them from Basquit.'

'But what were they doing so deep into Imperial space?' I asked. 'And where did they come from? There aren't any ork-held worlds in any proximity to the Armageddon sub-sector. And then there is what we heard.'

She looked troubled at that reminder. 'You think there's a connection?'

'I don't know. I hope not.' I tried to imagine what a link

between orks and warp storm could mean. My failure did not reassure me.

The shuttle brought us to a landing pad that nestled at the base of the cluster of spires that housed the government of Infernus. The uppermost reaches were also, at this time, the residence of the ruler of Armageddon. Brenken and I disembarked. A staff officer stood on the pad, waiting to escort her to the debriefing. When she saw who was waiting for me, Brenken gave me a sympathetic nod. 'We'll speak later, commissar,' she said.

'Until then, colonel,' I answered. I walked across the pitted rockcrete to where Lord Commissar Dominic Seroff stood at the edge of the landing zone.

'Sebastian,' he said. The familiarity was an expression of contempt.

'Lord commissar,' I answered. I kept my tone neutral, greeting formally correct. I would not begin the hostilities. I left that to Seroff.

His once-blond hair had turned a blind white. It had receded from the top of his head, but the fringe that ran from ear to ear still had pronounced curls. There was something a bit comical in its refusal to be tamed. More than a century ago, Seroff's eyes had shone with a sense of the comic too, but they hadn't for a long time. They were cold. His face was pinched with bitterness. I was in no small way responsible for the officer Seroff had become. I did not regret the decisions I had made, or the actions I had taken. They were necessary. They were correct. But I had been suffering their consequences for much of my life. Seroff was one of those consequences.

'The 252nd returns in triumph,' said the lord commissar.

'It does.'

'Congratulations are in order.' His mouth, pursed, tight-lipped, twitched in the right corner.

'Thank you.' I had just seen what passed for a smile on Seroff's features. The day was going to be worse than I had expected.

Behind me, the shuttle lifted off again. Seroff said nothing while the roar washed over us. Even after the sound of the ship's engines had faded into the distance, we stood in silence. The rain pattered against my cap. It ran down my greatcoat. I felt the faint tingle of its acid as it dripped from my hands. Seroff was savouring the moment. I did not grant him the satisfaction of showing impatience or confusion.

'Your actions on Basquit have received the attention they deserve,' Seroff said at last. 'Overlord von Strab wishes to see you.'

Ah. Light began to dawn. I had a good idea which of my actions would have drawn the interest of von Strab. 'I am at his disposal,' I said.

'Yes,' Seroff said. 'You are.'

My formulation had been an expression of civility. Seroff had underscored its brutal truth. I was not, strictly speaking, under the authority of the overlord. I was, though, under Seroff's, and he had just told me that he would see von Strab's wishes concerning me carried out.

'When, lord commissar?' I asked. Still neutral. Still correct. Did Seroff seriously hope to see me worried? If so, that was disappointing. He knew me better than that.

'He's waiting for you now,' Seroff said.

I nodded. I almost thanked him for delivering the message, but there was nothing to be gained with the slight. I had no interest in the trivial games of personal pride that were consuming Seroff's energy. They were another source of disappointment. I understood why Seroff hated me. But I had once believed he had more discernment. I had once believed he would have made a superb commissar. Instead, he had become an excellent politician.

I made the sign of the aquila and walked towards the spire doors. Seroff remained where he was, preferring to stand in the rain than appear to act as an escort. No doubt he imagined himself a forbidding figure, alone on the landing pad in the rain. I'm sure he was, for the rank and file. But we wore the same uniform. We had come up through the schola progenium together. The more he tried to intimidate me, the more he diminished himself.

I didn't look back. 'Throne, Dominic,' I muttered. 'Have a little dignity.' We were much too ancient for such sad games.

I had never met von Strab, and I had never been to the overlord's Infernus residence. My dealings with all of the governmental bodies of the hives had been limited. I knew who the governors were, though. And I knew my way around the administrative centres. I had been attached to the Steel Legion long enough now that Armageddon was as close to a home as I had ever known. Seroff in his animosity kept me from the centres of the decision-making, but he had not prevented me from learning where those centres were, and who inhabited them. My first duty was to the Emperor, and the more I knew about Armageddon, the better I could serve the Father of Mankind.

I had learned the cost of ignorance long ago, on Mistral. Lord Commissar Rasp, my mentor and Seroff's, had warned us that what we did not know of a world's political currents could be deadly. He had been correct. Even forewarned, we had stumbled. Our ignorance had almost killed us all. I had taken the lesson to heart.

So I had come to know Armageddon. Over the years, I had come to know its spires and its depths. And they knew me.

I navigated the halls, stairs and lifts that would take me to von Strab's quarters with confidence. I would not appear at his door like a lost supplicant. I had my pride, too, no matter how much Seroff worked to trample it in the mud.

The higher I went, the more luxurious my surroundings became, though the grime of Armageddon was always present. Even scrubbed by the ventilation system's filters, the air tasted of grit, and had the faint smell of sulphur. The stained glass windows were darkened by the smoke and ash of the atmosphere. They also bore other, more symbolic stains. They paid tribute to the accomplishments of the planet's ruling families. There was a grim continuity to the lineages pictured. On the surface, Armageddon's politics had been characterised by remarkable stability for centuries. The same families had governed the hives for generations, and the von Strab dynasty's rule of the planet had been unchallenged for as long. Beneath that surface was a history of rivalries, assassinations, treachery and corruption. The von Strabs embodied that tradition better than any of the other families, which was another reason they had ruled for so long. Their line of succession was neither patrilineal nor matrilineal. It was homicidal.

The corridor I was in branched. To the right was the gateway to the quarters of Erner von Kierska, Governor of Hive Infernus. I went left. The hall ended after a few metres at an ornate iron desk. Behind it sat a serf in the livery of the von Strabs, and behind her was a bronze door engraved with the family's coat of arms: eight spears, one for each of the great hives of Armageddon, held by a mailed fist. I presented myself to the serf, who ushered me to the door. She pulled the lever beside it, and it slid open, granting me access to the lift to the final reaches of the spire.

For all the luxury on display, this was still Armageddon, still an industrial world. The machinery of the door was not smooth. It ratcheted with age and rust. The lift's cage was unadorned, and it shook and screeched as it carried me upward. It sounded like the leavings of industry and the blood of politics had caked its gears. The bangs and mechanical stuttering lasted several minutes, and then the door opened again.

I entered the vestibule to the overlord's quarters. At this height, the rockcrete of the walls, floor and ceiling had been given a cladding of gold-veined marble. The impression created was that here, thousands of metres up, was where the construction of the hive had begun. Despite the taste of the air, the stone was clean. The windows were larger and more elaborate than those below, though just as darkened by the outside ash. They suggested, without actually tipping into the heretical, that the von Strabs had been given explicit dispensation from the Emperor to rule over Armageddon in perpetuity. The chamber was a large one, and empty except for another desk. It was made of the same marble as the cladding, and appeared to grow out of the floor. There was nothing else in the vast space. The excess of luxury was ridiculous. It radiated vanity and waste. It was very difficult to take the power behind this lavish display seriously.

Failing to do so, however, would be a mistake. One that others had made. Fatally.

The serf rose from his desk as I approached. His expression was a smooth sculpture of servility and superiority. 'Commissar Yarrick,' he said before I could speak. 'Thank you for coming.' As if I were waiting on his pleasure. 'The overlord is expecting you.' He barely repressed his amusement.

I couldn't help myself. 'You mean he won't be surprised?' I said as I walked over to the desk.

The serf paused, blinking, his hands on the gold-leaf-encrusted double doors in the centre of the far wall. He looked back at me, confused. I was not showing the required anxiety upon meeting the Great Man. I stepped forward and returned his stare. He swallowed, looked away, and pushed the doors open. He announced me and withdrew, closing the doors behind me as I stepped through. The boom of the doors bounced around the chamber in which I now found myself. I assumed the intended effect was more deliberate intimidation.

The overlord's Infernus throne room was twice the size of the vestibule. It occupied the entire width of the spire. The east and west walls were gigantic stained glass windows. Mirrored heroic portraits of von Strab in military uniform towered above the room, a colossus with his feet planted on the diminished orb of Armageddon. There was far more gold in the marble cladding. It twisted around pillars, exploded in convoluted webs from the keystones of the vaults, and covered the throne itself in such a profusion of leaves that it looked like a disease. At regular intervals around the periphery of the chamber stood the honour guard clad in black armaplas and ceramite armour. Over the heart on the carapace was the von Strab coat of arms, but otherwise there was little adornment. The soldiers were equipped in an attempt to resemble the Tempestus Scions, the resemblance enough to cow the citizens of Armageddon. Only the effort involved impressed me. Well protected from standard-issue M-35 Pattern rifles, they were only exceptional as a piece of theatre.

On the throne, Overlord Herman von Strab presided in all his glory. The fourth son of Overlord Luther (deceased), younger brother of Anton (deceased), Otto (deceased) and Vilhelm (deceased), he was a squat man, almost as wide as he was tall, fat enough to look stronger than he was. He wore the same uniform as his image on the windows, darker than the dirty ochre of the Steel Legion trench coats, though its cut was similar enough to declare von Strab as the supreme commander of the regiment. He was bald, with a heavy brow that shadowed his sharp gaze. A bionic monocle sat over his right eye. A thin mechadendrite ran coiled from the lens around his skull and rose over his pate to bury itself in his forehead. Information boosts to his frontal lobe, I guessed, amplifying his ability to foresee consequences. All the better to plan and scheme.

Given what happened to Armageddon, the widespread belief is that the monocle was a spectacular failure. Given what happened to von Strab, I'm not so sure. I think the device could only have strengthened what was already present in that devious mind.

On that day, however, I was less concerned with the function of von Strab's lens than with doing what I could to prise something useful out of this meeting. I didn't know what von Strab had in mind for me. My duty, at this moment, was to express my concerns. I knew in my gut that something was coming. But if I wanted von Strab to listen, I would have to find a better way of communicating a sense of urgency than intuition and foreboding.

'Commissar Yarrick,' von Strab said. 'Welcome. I've heard many startling things about you. Very busy on Basquit, weren't we?' The voice that emerged from his thick lips was deep and nasal. It was oiled with a self-satisfied attempt at charm, but edged with a perpetual, defensive petulance.

'We were,' I answered. 'The 252nd distinguished itself in heroic combat.'

'So I've heard. So I've heard.' He drummed the fingers of his right hand on a data-slate perched on the arm of the throne. He didn't look at its screen. 'A great victory, you would say.'

'I would. The orks on Basquit have been exterminated. However–'

He cut me off. 'Be that as it may, the victory was not without sacrifice.'

'No war is.'

'Basquit lost its overlord.'

'True. But Albrecht Meinert wasn't killed by orks.'

'No. My cousin was murdered by his successor.'

Ah. I began to see where I stood. 'I heard the rumour,' I said, non-committal.

'And you let such treason stand.'

The remarkable thing was von Strab spoke without a trace of irony. I responded in kind. 'My duty was to rid the planet of orks, not to police its internal politics.' All of which was true, but I was allowing myself the small pleasure of being as disingenuous as the overlord. Meinert had been an active hindrance to the Basquit campaign. He had insisted that the bulk of the troops be held in the defence of land and homes of the agri world's ruling families. Lord Berthold Stratz had shown himself to have a much more realistic grasp of military necessities. He had also had designs on Meinert's throne. While Brenken turned a blind eye, I had met with Stratz. We had spoken in bland, unobjectionable circumlocutions, and Stratz had departed convinced that the Imperium would welcome a new regime on Basquit with himself at the top. Within a day, Meinert was dead, Stratz was overlord, and the 252nd had been freed to bring the battle to the orks.

'Your duty was to protect Basquit,' von Strab said. 'The orks were defeated, but there were incalculable losses of land and property.' By which he meant the nobility's holdings. Those lush valleys had become the battlefields where we had trapped the orks and exterminated them.

'I did whatever I felt was necessary in the service of the Imperium.'

Von Strab smiled. 'Of course you did. As do I.'

He meant the last statement as a threat. I used it instead as an opening. 'Good. Then I must inform you that I am greatly concerned that the ork raid on Basquit was just the first sign of a much larger threat.'

'Oh?' Von Strab leaned back on his throne, signalling just how ready he was to take me seriously.

'An ork incursion this deep into Imperial space is already one thing, but we have no adequate explanation for how they arrived there. We had no warning of any sort of approaching fleet. There were no ork vessels in orbit over Basquit.'

'The greenskins travel the immaterium too.'

'Indeed. And the reports I gathered on Basquit imply they fell planetside in a space hulk. But it was a small one, just large enough to hold the force we encountered. It may have come out of the warp, but it would have been too small to survive there for any length of time. I believe it was a fragment of something larger.'

'I didn't know you were given to such unsupported speculation, commissar.'

*Not as much as I am given to hopeless tasks*, I thought, but I forged on. 'There is more. During the battle, I heard the orks chanting.'

Von Strab was looking more and more amused. 'And what was it they were chanting?'

'It sounded like *Ghazghkull*.'

'You speak greenskin, don't you, commissar?' He spoke as

if that made me as contemptible as the orks. 'What does it mean?'

'I believe it is a name.'

Von Strab shook his head. 'So the brutes shout the name of their warlord. Please tell me you don't believe that to be unusual.'

'What was unusual was the depth of their fervour.'

'Their fervour? You read the greenskins' minds now? Are you a psyker, commissar?' He laughed, pleased with his joke. An appreciative, dutiful snicker did the rounds of the honour guard.

I knew how this would end, but I did not give up. I would see my duty through. The odds against its success were irrelevant. I ignored von Strab's jibe and summarised my position. 'Orks attacked a planet in a strategically critical sub-sector. They were, I believe, united in their fervour for a single warlord. They must have emerged from the warp. There is a warp storm brewing. The conjunction of these factors should not be ignored.'

Von Strab regarded me for a few moments. 'Are you done, commissar?'

'I am.'

'Then I thank you for this diversion. I hope you don't mind if I turn to the reason I sent for you.'

My jaw clenched. I swallowed my rage. It would serve no purpose. 'You are taking no action at all?'

'About what you have just told me? Of course not. You are aware that the Feast of the Emperor's Ascension is almost upon us? You know the scale of the celebration. I have enough to think about without indulging in surmise and fantasy.'

The fingers of my left hand twitched. The movement was

very slight. I was barely conscious of it myself. Von Strab saw it, though. The monocle whirred faintly, and his eyes narrowed. He smiled again, much more broadly than before. 'What are you doing, commissar? Are you reaching for that bolt pistol? What are you thinking? That I am guilty of dereliction? Shall I be executed? By you?'

I said nothing.

He laughed, enjoying himself. 'We have much in common, don't you think?' He paused just long enough for my silence to turn into an insult. 'No?' he continued. 'It's true, though. We are both willing to do what is necessary. Without exception. Well, almost. I believe you are betraying your own principles at the moment. If I should die, why am I still speaking?' The smile grew broader yet. I could see his teeth. They were yellow.

Whatever else von Strab was, and whatever his catastrophic weaknesses, he was a superb politician. A politician of the most leprous sort, but a brilliant example of his species. At this moment, he was demonstrating the skills that had made him overlord of Armageddon, and had kept him alive. Not only was I stymied, it was all I could do to keep my temper and not have myself gunned down.

In the years to come, I would ask myself if I made the right decision by staying my hand. I would wonder if events might have turned out differently. The questions still come to me during sleepless hours. If I had drawn my pistol, I would have been dead in the next second. But might I have been fast enough? Could I have killed von Strab then and there? Would my sacrifice have been worth it? Was there any chance it would have saved billions of lives?

I believe I made the right choice. The coming agony of Armageddon cannot be put down to the incompetence and venality of a single man. The Enemy racing our way was far too strong.

Even so, the questions still come.

I didn't answer von Strab. I clasped my hands behind my back and waited.

When he saw I wasn't going to be goaded, von Strab chuckled. 'Well then,' he said. 'Well then. Enough of that.' As if the conversation had been nothing more than banter between old friends. 'The reason you are here, commissar, is to reap the rewards of your efforts on Banquit.' And he had already made clear what he thought of those efforts. 'Indeed, the rewards of your exemplary career.' His bottom lip glistened with contempt.

'I see.'

'You have earned your retirement, Commissar Yarrick, and I have wonderful news.' A pause and a quick, pursed grin. 'I have intervened on your behalf with Lord Commissar Seroff. He has generously acceded to my request that we retain your services here on Armageddon. For the remainder of your service, you will have the honour of overseeing recruitment in Hades Hive.'

So he was ignoring my concerns, and putting me out to pasture. There was a role for political officers in the process that led to the formation of regiments. New recruits needed reminding of the singular purpose of their lives. Whether from the more privileged strata of society or from the depths of the underhive, they had to feel the impact of the commissar before the battlefield. They had to fear someone more than their sergeants.

But the role von Strab was assigning me was one normally reserved for commissars convalescing from war wounds. Officers temporarily unfit for combat. Such tours of duty rarely lasted for more than a few months. I didn't believe the narrative von Strab was presenting, but I did believe he and Seroff had contrived this punishment together. Between them, they would ensure that I would spend the rest of my days in the most menial fashion possible.

I gave von Strab a crisp nod. 'I see. Will that be all, overlord?'

'You are dismissed.'

I turned on my heel and left the chamber. I was supposed to feel humiliated. I was enraged, but not because of my punishment. I was sure that something infinitely worse was coming to us all.

## 2. MANNHEIM

He woke with thoughts of burning. A single, fading image from his unconscious lingered before his mind's eye: a flare of suns.

Princeps Kurtiz Mannheim of the Legio Metalica Titan Legion sat on the edge of the bed, waiting for his head to clear. He cursed the softness of the mattress. He was, at the insistence of Herman von Strab, quartered in a guest chamber one level down from the overlord's residence. Von Strab wanted all the senior military currently stationed on Armageddon to be on hand for the feast day. Mannheim despised the posturing spectacle. But it would be over in two more days.

He stood and walked to the half-circle window in the east wall. The stained glass was black with night. He could see nothing out of it. Even if he could, the staging grounds of the Legio Metalica would not have been visible. His Iron Skulls had a base on the outskirts of Infernus many kilometres to the west. He hadn't had sight of *Steel Hammer* for three days now. The absence of connection to the Imperator-class Emperor Titan was an acute spiritual pain and growing weakness, like a slow loss of vitae. The implants at the base of his skull had no surface feeling, yet he experienced a phantom lack. That was a distress he expected, though. It began whenever he uncoupled from *Steel Hammer*. Something more had jolted him to consciousness. His frame tingled with a sense-memory of pain and an anticipation of disaster.

He moved to the footlocker beside the bed. He had no choice but to accept the overlord's hospitality. That did not mean he had to indulge in the decadence of too many members of Armageddon's ruling class. He would not insult his uniform by placing it in the chamber's armoire. It was a bronze monolith, its size dictated, as far as Mannheim could tell, by the need to support the heraldry of both the von Strabs and the von Kierskas. The more Mannheim had to do with the nobility, the more disgusted he became, and the more fervently he clung to his faith in the Imperium's structure. The chain of command and the oaths that held it together were stronger than the unworthy leaders who weakened individual links. Mannheim had no respect for von Strab, but he would give his life for the order that dictated he obey the overlord's commands. The Emperor was at the top of that order. Mannheim would rip out his implants before he challenged a state of being dictated by the Father of Mankind.

He opened the footlocker and began to dress. The unease of his awakening refused to fade. It lay over his thoughts like a slick of promethium. He could not ignore it. So he would seek clarity. There was someone he could consult.

He wondered if her sleep had been as broken as his.

\* \* \*

## 3. YARRICK

The librarium was a few dozen levels down from the peak of a spire just to the south of the one housing the overlord's and governor's residences. It was still above the thick of the hive's population cauldron, though there was little of the luxury here that surrounded von Strab. The librarium was clean enough, but its air was stale with neglect. The shelves had grown shabby with age, the rockcrete floor webbed with hairline cracks, and the stacks of volumes and scrolls smelled musty. It was not a place many went. This was not surprising. Armageddon was not a planet where life was conducive to study, and this librarium was not connected to any of the major chapels in the hive. It was almost forgotten.

Meeting here felt clandestine. That worried me. It had since the morning, when Brenken had found me and asked me to attend the gathering.

I was greeted at the door by a scribe as faded and mildewed as his archive. He didn't speak. He bowed, gestured down the main aisle for me to proceed, then withdrew into the shadows.

The others were waiting for me in the small rotunda at the centre of the librarium. With Brenken were Kurtiz Mannheim and a woman I had not met before. Her red robes, trimmed in yellow, white and black, declared her service to the Legio Metalica. She was a psyker, with a serpent coil of mechadendrites around the back of her skull. The use of her powers had withered her physical form. Her skin was tight against her bones, thin, brittle, a translucent yellow. Her eyes glittered with the intensity of her vision. She sat at a small reading table just behind the two officers.

Mannheim nodded in greeting. 'Thank you for meeting us,

commissar,' he said. 'Colonel Brenken spoke to me of your concerns.'

'She said you share them.'

'I do. Especially after last night.'

'What happened?'

Mannheim turned to the psyker. 'This is Scholar Arcanum Konev. I consulted her after I experienced…' He searched for the words, then admitted, 'I don't know what I experienced.'

'The tempest in the immaterium is growing worse,' Konev said. Her voice rasped like sand over bones. 'The ripples are reaching many.'

'I asked Scholar Konev to draw from the Emperor's Tarot,' Mannheim said.

'And?'

'The Great Hoste, reversed,' Konev recited, hoarse tones taking on the rhythms of a chant. 'The Despoiler, reversed. The Shattered World.'

I felt the sickening tightness in my chest of the worst being confirmed. I was no psyker, and I was no reader of the Tarot. But I had a rudimentary knowledge of the cards, and I could tell that what Konev had read was nothing good.

'A great enemy is coming,' she said. 'His forces are overwhelming. This is a foe such as the Imperium has rarely seen. What lies in his path will be smashed, and we are in his path.'

Konev would be choosing her words carefully. A great enemy, she had said. Not *the* Great Enemy. The dark forces from the Eye of Terror were not on the march, then, at least not here. But that was little comfort.

'Can this still be orks we're talking about?' Brenken asked. 'Their threat isn't exactly rare.'

'This one must be,' I said. 'We must never underestimate the orks. There's a good reason we have been forced to fight them on so many fronts: they are very successful in spreading their plague. But in this case...'

'Would you tell me what you told the overlord?' Mannheim asked. And after I had done so, he said, 'If you're right that we face a greenskin threat, then it must be incredible for it to be of an order to generate this reading.'

'The warp storm is part of this,' I said. 'I'm sure of it.'

'A worrying conjunction,' Mannheim admitted.

'What is our course of action, then?' Brenken asked. 'Other than to increase our level of preparedness.'

The question fell into a silence leaden with our own powerlessness. The threat was still too vague. There were no countermeasures to take against it.

Mannheim sighed. 'Scholar Konev and I will speak with von Strab. Perhaps this reading, and a reframing of Commissar Yarrick's points, will convince him at least to build up the defensive posture of the hives.'

'Warn the other senior officers too,' I said. 'Before the overlord explicitly forbids doing so. And what about the Navy?'

'I have an acquaintance with Admiral Isakov,' Mannheim said. 'I'm sure the warp storm is already a point of concern for him. I'll speak with him.'

The actions felt inadequate, but I could not see much else to be done at this point. 'We should also send out an alert beyond the system,' I said. 'If the warp storm grows much worse, we will be cut off from the rest of the Imperium. If no one thinks to look this way during that period...' I left the thought unfinished.

Mannheim nodded. 'I'll see what I can do.'

'There is something else that concerns me,' I said. 'Why did we meet here?'

'For discretion,' said Brenken. She gave me an apologetic

shrug. 'Word of how you stand in von Strab's eyes has spread quickly.'

'I imagine he made sure of that.'

'If the overlord knows we've had this conversation, he is less likely to listen to Princeps Mannheim.'

'Of course.' To Mannheim and Konev, I said, 'I wish you luck. I hope my toxicity doesn't prevent your message from being heard.'

The precautions were futile. Von Strab had no more time for Mannheim's warning than he did for mine. I sought out Brenken in the barracks of the 252nd later in the afternoon. The regiment was preparing for the march through the streets of Infernus the following day as part of the observance of the Emperor's Ascension. I found Brenken on the parade grounds, inspecting the companies. The losses on Basquit were already being filled out with new recruits. Brenken spotted me at the entrance to the barracks. The slight shake of the head she gave me told me what I needed to know.

Disgusted, I left the barracks, plunging into the streets of Infernus. I pushed my way through the crowds. The streets at ground level were fifty metres wide, and too narrow for the flow of foot traffic. Vehicles moved at a crawl. On either side, the monolithic slabs of manufactoria rose for hundreds of metres. The air was grey with smoke and exhaust. Tomorrow, this and other major thoroughfares would be cleared for the marches and religious processions. All the quadrants of Armageddon's hives would pause in their industry to observe the solemn day. This was true of even some regions of the underhive. Von Strab's enforcement of the Feast, however, had more to do with emphasising his authority than his piety, such as it was.

I pushed my way forward, walking with energy but no direction. I was trying to burn off frustration. Inaction before a threat was unacceptable, yet it was the position in which I found myself. My vision was filled with the smug features of von Strab. I barely saw where I was going. It was several minutes before I realised that something had changed in the foot traffic. More and more people were moving in the same direction. Over the snarl of vehicle engines and the deeper rumbles from within the manufactoria walls came the rising murmur of distress and wonder.

I snapped to alertness. My hand brushed my holster, but there were no sounds of combat. And the people were heading towards the source of the disturbance, not fleeing it. I let myself be carried by the current of bodies.

Whatever the rumour was, it had travelled far, wide and quickly. Hours passed. The collective anxiety around me intensified. People were swept up in anticipation and ignorance. The perpetual twilight of the lower streets of Infernus was darkening towards real night when I reached the square outside the Cathedral of Infinite Obeisance. It was one of the principal houses of worship in Infernus. It was gigantic, its portico alone almost half the height of the flanking manufactoria. Two Warhound Titans could have passed side by side through the open doors. The massive flying buttresses appeared to have shouldered aside the manufactoria to make room for the great bulk of the cathedral.

The people flowed through the doors. The volume of the wailing and prayers I heard coming from inside could not be explained solely by the acoustics of the blackened stone.

I moved forward with the crowd. Once past the threshold, it took a few moments for my eyes to adjust to the deeper gloom, and it was still another half hour before I had gone far enough into the cavern of the nave to see the cause of the anguish. Behind the altar was an immense pict screen, worthy of a battleship's oculus. It had been erected as part of von Strab's determination to have all of Armageddon celebrate as one on the following day. All of the major chapels would be linked by vox, and the congregations in the pews and in the streets would see their fellow celebrants by pict feed.

The screen was active now, a day early. It showed a single exterior view, the colossal statue of the Emperor in Hive Helsreach.

The statue was weeping blood.

Crimson streaks ran from the corners of both eyes and down the noble visage. As I watched, a thick tear formed then trickled down from the right eye. It hung suspended for a moment from the statue's lower jaw before falling into space. The crowd gasped when it dropped, and the wailing surged once more.

I approached the screen, mesmerised. When I was level with the altar, a voice at my left shoulder said, 'Overlord von Strab will ignore this omen too. You know he will.'

I turned my head, tearing my eyes away from the pict feed. Canoness Errant Setheno stood beside the altar, towering over the shuffling crowd. The people flowed around her like a stream parted by a pillar. When I first encountered her, on Mistral, she had been a Sister Superior of the Order of the Piercing Thorn. We had both changed much since then. Her power armour was the most visible alteration. Once black, wrapped in a fine, rising spiral of red, for some time now it had been the grey of tombs. Her cape was grey too, instead of its former gold. There was no longer an Order of the Piercing Thorn. All trace of it, down to the heraldry on her armour, had been expunged. By her command, and at her hand.

The change in the armour, though striking to the few of us who had known her since those early days, was a surface transformation. The most profound alteration was in her face. Her eyes had been an unnerving, uniform gold since our struggle against the daemon Ghalshannha on Mistral. That was the first of the deep changes. They had continued, slowly, but inexorably, reaching their climax in the wake of the tragedy of the Piercing Thorn. Her face had been blasted of emotion as completely as her armour had been of colour. It was immovable as stone, cold as the void. Instead of altering her features, time and darkest experience had hardened them, like metal folded and hammered and refolded in a forge of war. There was more forgiveness in the faces of the sculpted saints in the cathedral.

Setheno was a powerful ally in combat. But I could not say her presence was welcome. It was yet another omen of disaster. After the destruction of the Piercing Thorn, she had become the canoness without an order. I wasn't sure if the journey she had embarked upon was penitence or a crusade. Perhaps both. The experience was certainly a penitential one for those who crossed her path, or that of her ship, the Cobra-class destroyer *Act of Clarity*.

'Canoness,' I said. 'I hesitate to ask what brings you here.'

She watched the statue weep. 'Signs and portents,' she said. 'A disturbing reading of the Emperor's Tarot aboard my ship, among others.'

'We have had one here, too. When did you arrive?'

'At dawn. I was very nearly lost in the immaterium.'

'The storm is worse, then.'

'No vessels have translated in-system after mine.'

'So we are cut off.' I hoped Mannheim's alert had been sent in time. 'You have met with Overlord von Strab?' I asked.

'Briefly. He was not receptive to what I had to say.'

Von Strab's will was impressive. I could think of very few individuals capable of being dismissive of Setheno. I cursed. 'You're right. He will find a way to rationalise the omen of these tears.'

'It may be that the Emperor weeps because of von Strab's intransigence.'

I sighed. 'I've been unable to think what our course of action must be.'

'If anyone could find a solution, commissar, it would be you. You are unable because there is none. Overlord von Strab is immovable. What is coming is inevitable. We cannot stop it. All we can control is how we respond when the enemy arrives. But the first move belongs to the foe.'

I thought about the chant I had heard on Basquit. *Ghazghkull, Ghazghkull, Ghazghkull*. Then, the word had meaning only for the orks. Now my dread was that it would soon have terrible meaning for the Imperium. We had lost the initiative. I knew this with the certainty of faith. I met Setheno's cold, golden stare and said, 'Then we must pray that the first move is not the decisive one.'

# CHAPTER 2
# CLAW OF DESOLATION

## 1. ISAKOV

The battleship *Reach of Judgement* was a cathedral of war. Over ten thousand metres long, and two thousand abeam, it may have been more the size of a city, even supporting its own chapel rising from the stern end of the superstructure. And yet, it *was* a cathedral. Every weapons battery, every Fury interceptor, Shark assault boat and Starhawk bomber in its launch bays, every member of its crew of one hundred and fifty thousand, even every bulkhead and rivet – they made up a whole whose immensity was devoted to a single, sublime act of worship: war in the Emperor's name. Along its length, above each gun port, statues of saints stood guard, each thirty metres high. Its great arches and its stained armour-glass were one with the cannons. No city could boast such unity of force and purpose. It was the massive embodiment of sacred war.

It also had the gravitational force of command. The cruisers and escorts that made up the battle fleet moved in concert with it. Together they were a collective fist that could smash civilisations to ash. The *Reach of Judgement* was a ponderous vessel. It was slow to turn and to accelerate. But once it was set on its course, nothing could stop it. For Admiral Jakob Isakov, his vessel travelled along the straight line of the Emperor's will.

And now, at the centre of the fleet, it manoeuvred to create an impassable barrier against the enemy heading for Armageddon.

On the bridge of the *Judgement*, Isakov sat on the command throne in an elevated pulpit set against a massive pillar in the the rear of the bridge. The pillar rose to meet the point of the Gothic vault forty metres above. Levels upon levels of work stations surrounded the deck in arched galleries. Over a thousand crewmembers and servitors powered the nerve centre of the battleship.

'Mistress of the Augur,' Isakov said, 'what are the readings?'

'Increasingly unreliable, sir,' Eleza Haack answered. 'But the displacement is unmistakeable and growing.'

'Can you extrapolate its size?'

'It is massive. We can say nothing more precise.'

'Very well. Orders to the fleet: maintain formation. Weapons free. As we have no information of an Imperial force approaching the Armageddon System, our visitors are presumed hostile. When they translate, open fire.' He thought for a moment, then said, 'Vox, send a message to Princeps Mannheim. Tell him he was right.'

## 2. YARRICK

Mannheim turned from the vox operator to me. 'The credit is yours, commissar.'

I shook my head. 'The effort was collective. And there is no credit to be had before the enemy is stopped.'

We had been in the augur station of Infernus's spaceport, at the western edge of the hive, since before dawn. It was a circular space occupying the peak of a tower overlooking the landing pads. The stained glass of the lower floors here gave way to an armourglass dome sprouting antennae like spines. The tower was far from the tallest in the hive, but the transmissions were received through the sludge of cloud cover clearly enough. That was more than could be said for astropathic messages. The choir of Infernus was located in the midpoint of the tower. I had stopped there before joining Mannheim and Setheno in the station. They had attempted to send the Princeps' message. Master of the Choir Genest was doubtful about their success. What little they were still receiving was so fragmented and distorted by the storm that it caused psychic wounds without being interpretable. Genest looked worn, even by the withered standards of an astropath. His face was wary too, as if he guessed that he was being used to go behind von Strab's back, and very much hoped not to have confirmed that suspicion.

My presence in the augur complex was not official. I was there thanks to Mannheim's invitation and under the auspices of Setheno's unofficial but powerful authority. It would take the direct intervention of the overlord to counter any demand she made.

And while we waited for Isakov to confront the enemy, each of his messages taking hours to reach us from the edge of the system, the Feast of the Emperor's Ascension was under way across Armageddon. I could guess with what fervour and solemnity the rites were being observed this year, as the statue in Helsreach continued to weep blood. While the processions and prayers filled the streets and chapels of the hives under constant reminders of the overlord's beneficence and vigilant eye, von Strab was using one of the most sacred traditions of the Feast to his own benefit. It is said false judgements are impossible on this day. The practical result of this belief is the irreversibility of pronouncements made during the Feast. My faith in the Emperor is absolute, but I have seen too many crimes committed in his name. Von Strab used the tradition of infallible justice to settle scores real and imagined. His grip on the planet was so strong it could hardly be consolidated even further. But he still used the day to underscore the futility of challenging him.

At least he was busy. His attention elsewhere, we had some room to act.

The vox operator reported that the fleet had completed its manoeuvres. It was in position at the Mandeville point.

I became conscious of Setheno's gaze. 'You don't believe this will be enough, do you?'

'No. Do you?'

She shook her head. To Mannheim she said, 'Have you long been acquainted with Admiral Isakov?'

'I consider him a friend.'

'Then I am sorry.'

'He isn't lost yet,' Mannheim said, though there was little hope in his voice.

Setheno didn't answer. I watched the banks of augur stations. I willed the news to reach us faster.

Though I dreaded what it would be.

## 3. ISAKOV

In the *Reach of Judgement*'s great oculus, Isakov saw the void tear. The wound was greater than any he had ever seen. No single ship could cause such a rift. No fleet would need one. It slashed across the real space, jagged and blazing with the blood of the materium. The flesh of the void peeled back, and the raging non-light and anti-colours of the warp burst across the blockade. And still the wound widened.

Isakov winced. He clutched the arms of the throne, his fingers whitening with tension. Cries shook the bridge as a wave of pain crashed through it. It was a torment of the soul, a response to a greater agony. The warp itself was screaming, as if the thing that had traversed it wounded even that infernal realm, and must be expelled. There was a final blast, a final shriek of tortured materium and warp, and the enemy had arrived.

The space hulk was immense. A moon had appeared before the fleet, dwarfing the warships. It was a world of twisted metal, forged of uncountable vessels. Freighters, colony ships, cruisers and transports had been fused into a mass that was graveyard and fist. The ships were barely recognisable, but portions of superstructure and shattered bows emerged from the conglomeration, fragments of identity drowning in the mass. The hulk looked as if a great fleet had been caught in the grip of a terrible gravitational force, and the moment of collision had been frozen in time. The surface of the misshapen behemoth was a patchwork of mountain ranges and canyons, all of them metal. The ship carcasses had been twisted by the warp into melted, writhing shapes. But the hulk itself was not dead. Furious energy boiled out of canyons. New constructions, crude but indestructible, pushed upwards between the iron ruins. Barbaric icons with snarling, fanged visages thousands of metres across gaped in hunger at the Imperial fleet. It was a thing of creative destruction, all of its grand deaths transformed by a savage vitality.

'Orks!' someone called out.

'Orks…' Isakov muttered, transfixed by the icons. He had never seen a hulk like this. More than the size chilled his blood. In those icons, he saw signs of an ambition and ability many orders of magnitude beyond what he knew of the greenskins. He had the unshakeable conviction that these orks had not just traversed the warp, they had enjoyed it.

And now they came for Armageddon.

'Uncatalogued space hulk detected,' came the dead voice of a servitor slaved to a cogitator. 'New designation to be assigned.' There was a brief pause as the cogitator combed through databases and arrived at the correct nomenclature for the monster. 'Space hulk designated *Alveus Alpha Alpha Sextus*.'

Isakov grunted. So dry a name. So harmless. It was a serial number. It did not reflect the horror he saw closing in on the fleet.

*Alveus Alpha Alpha Sextus* was so huge, Isakov did not realise at first how fast it was moving. There was a slight impression of increasing size, but it filled the void as if it were a planet. Then the tocsins blared, and the shouts came from stations across the width and height of the bridge. Calls of horrifying readings of mass, of dimensions, of speed, of proximity, of direction. The portents of doom.

'Fire,' Isakov roared. 'Fire, by the Emperor!'

The order was unnecessary. The fleet was already acting on his prior command. Every forward-facing battery on every ship had opened up. A swarm of torpedoes streaked towards the hulk. Isakov listened to simultaneous countdowns. One marked the progress of the ordnance towards the enemy. The other tracked the shrinking gulf between the beast and the fleet.

Seconds to go before the shells struck. High explosives many metres long, hurled in such profusion that they would have gutted any capital ship. *Kill it*, Isakov willed. *Kill it now, and I will rejoice at the consequences.* The destruction of something so vast would take out much of the blockade too. Perhaps all of it. There would be no evading the cataclysm. But the sacrifice would be worth it.

'Vox,' he said, 'remain in constant communication with Infernus. Let them know everything that happens.'

The cannon fire hit *Alveus Alpha Alpha Sextus.* A few seconds later, so did the torpedoes. Hundreds of explosions peppered the surface. The holocaust that erupted was of a scale that beggared comprehension. The firestorms would have wiped great cities out of existence. Thousands upon thousands of tonnes of metal melted and vaporised. The bones of once-proud vessels spun off into the void, torn free of the space hulk's gravity. This was not destruction: it was cataclysm. An entire Imperial Navy fleet had fired on a single target.

Some of the fires spread and kept burning. Others winked out. The space hulk kept coming.

The fleet kept up its barrage. The bridge of the *Reach of Judgement* shook with vibrations so deep they rang like thunder.

The space hulk reached the forward elements of the blockade: the Dictator-class cruiser *Cardinal Borza* and two frigates. There was no possibility of evasion. Isakov even saw the engines of the *Borza* flare brighter, Captain Hella von Berne turning the vessel into a five-thousand-metre battering ram. *Alveus Alpha Alpha Sextus* hit the cruiser a few moments before the frigates. The *Borza*'s bow disintegrated. Its midsection broke in half. Its engines burned a moment longer, slamming the stern of the ship forward into its own immolation. The warp drives ruptured, and the void was torn again by the light of absolute destruction.

Isakov looked away from the oculus, dazzled, as the flare reached into the bridge, stabbing eyes and soul. 'Full power to forward shields!' he called, and braced for the shockwave. It came, and there was another flare, this time from the *Reach of Judgement*'s void shields. They stood for a full second against the *Cardinal Borza*'s death cry. Then they collapsed, their failure cascading back along the length of the battleship. The *Judgement* shook like a city in an earthquake. A chorus of flat servitor voices began reciting damage reports. Something exploded in the corridor leading off the main doors to the bridge. Isakov smelled smoke, and the sharp jab to the nose of ozone.

And the fleet kept firing. Shells and torpedoes were launched into the searing white curtain of a plasma and warp drive fireball. That anything could survive being at the centre of the cruiser's destruction seemed impossible, but the barrage must continue until either the enemy or the last hope was no more.

The light faded. The space hulk stormed through fire and death. It was shrouded by flame, a comet of fire. It was shedding fragments kilometres long. The *Borza* had inflicted massive damage, but the blow was meaningless. The hulk was too huge. Nothing short of a planetary mass would halt its journey.

Seconds had passed since the initial impact between the hulk and the blockade. Seconds remained before the end. *Alveus Alpha Alpha Sextus* filled the oculus. This close, it was doom the size of a world.

There was nothing left to try. There could be no victory. There could be no flight. All that remained was the gesture, to seek honour in death, and curse the monster with a new name.

'Full ahead!' Isakov ordered. Von Berne had shown the way.

Isakov and his hundreds of thousands under his command would shed more ork blood as their own boiled into the void. 'Vox, tell Armageddon. Tell them the *Claw of Desolation* reaches for them. Tell them to fight hard. In the name of the Emperor.'

Then he stared at his killer as if his hate itself could stop it. Through smoke and flame, he saw its surface draw near. A graveyard with tombstones the size of hive spires rushed forward to surround his ship.

He saw Death.

Kilometres distant from the bridge, the bow of the *Judgement* struck the ruined superstructure of an embedded colony ship. The two vessels melded in a storm of wreckage. Then the great explosions began.

Isakov saw the end come in a triumph of fire. The moment before agony was full of awe. But his final thought was bitter, because the sublime destruction meant nothing.

## 4. YARRICK

The sudden silence from the fleet was followed by silence in the augur station. It lasted almost a full minute, beginning with the final transmission from the *Reach of Judgement* until the augur operator called out that all contact with the fleet had been lost.

'What about the *Claw of Desolation*?' I asked. I honoured the admiral's last gesture. What had entered the Armageddon System must be known for what it was, not hidden behind a cogitator's cataloguing designation.

'Still a unique, coherent signal,' one of the augur operators said. 'The space hulk is intact and moving deeper into the system.'

'Its course?' Setheno asked.

We waited as trajectories were recalculated.

'No deviation.' The operator's voice was awed. He was an old veteran, younger than I was but someone who had never had juvenat treatments. He had lost his legs, and his upper body was fused with a mobile plinth. He had seen much. But nothing like this. 'Its course will intersect with Armageddon's orbit in less than twelve hours.'

'So fast,' I said. I looked at Mannheim. 'You must warn the hive garrisons.'

'He will not,' said a voice behind me.

I turned. Flanked by two of his honour guard, von Strab stood in the entrance to the station.

'I am surprised to see you here,' Setheno told him. 'Shouldn't you be presiding over the celebrations of the feast?'

Setheno was the only one present who did not fall under von Strab's authority. The only one he couldn't order shot for the insult. So he pretended to ignore the slight and responded as if her question had been a genuine inquiry. 'I am where I need to be. Word has reached me of a crisis. Despite the efforts of those who do not appear to have a proper respect for the chain of command.' He strode into the centre of the station. His voice echoing beneath the dome, he announced, 'Let this be understood by all. There will be no operations undertaken without my authorisation. I am the supreme commander of all forces on Armageddon. The defence of our world is in my hands.'

And with those words, the agony of Armageddon began.

# CHAPTER 3
# PLANETFALL

## 1. KOHNER

'Our orders are to make ready,' Sergeant Hugo Kohner of the Tempestora Hive Militia announced. 'So make ready we shall.' He led his squad at a quick march from the barracks towards the hive's outer wall.

'Make ready for what, sergeant?' Bessler asked. Of course he did. He couldn't just take an order and shut up about it. He was older than Kohner by a good decade and he had resented the younger man's promotion over him for at least that long.

'If you're not told, you don't need to know,' Kohner snapped. 'You do as you're told. Clear enough? Or do I have to ask a commissar to come calling?'

'Clear, sergeant,' Bessler said.

'Good.'

In truth, he was venting on Bessler his own irritation with the vagueness of his orders. He'd asked the same question of Captain Wendlandt, who had been more forthcoming than Kohner could afford to be. 'They're not telling us,' he'd said. 'An enemy landing of some kind. Nothing more specific than that.'

'So what are we supposed to do?' Kohner had asked.

'Stand vigil on the walls.'

The order lacked shape, but it was still an action to be taken. So Kohner led his squad with the other soldiers of the militia towards the wall. There were two regiments of militia: twelve companies, over four thousand troopers. They marched through streets reeking of burned excess promethium and coated in the perpetual rain of ash sent up by the Tempestora East and Morpheus manufactoria complexes. They were slowed as they ran into masses of celebrants still marking the Emperor's Ascension.

A step behind Kohner, Bessler grumbled, 'Why are all these civilians still out here?'

Kohner said nothing, but he agreed. More signs of conflicting messages coming down from on high. Prepare for an enemy. Honour the Feast. Was no one stopping to think how those two commandments interfered with each other?

His jaw set in frustration, he bulled through the crowds. A preacher cursed him when a jostled procession almost overturned the idol of the Emperor they transported over their heads. Kohner twitched at the near miss with blasphemy, but he kept going.

The outer wall was less than two kilometres from the barracks, but it was an hour before Kohner began to climb one of the iron staircases that zigzagged up its surface, taking him the hundred metres to the parapets. He was out of breath when he reached the top. So were the other squad members. He envied the Steel Legionnaires their rebreathers. The militia troopers took the unfiltered air of Armageddon into their lungs, cutting down on their stamina as well as their life expectancy. Their uniforms were the same ochre as those of the Steel Legion, but lacked the greatcoats. The militia troopers wore the reminders of what they should aspire to become, but were not yet.

Kohner looked east over the parapet. This was not the Ash Wastelands to the north of the hive, though the land was harsh enough. It was a dry, poisoned plain broken up by gullies that had run dry centuries before, and the topsoil had blown away not long thereafter. The few rivers that still flowed north towards the Boiling Sea were sluggish and brown with contaminants. Thorny scrub grew along their banks. The only vegetation stubborn enough to cling to its hold in the region, it was tall and sharp enough to disembowel the unwary. Even through the ashfall and overcast, Kohner could see dozens of kilometres into the grey distance. The land was empty. No enemy approached.

Two hours later, Bessler came and said, 'So? What now? How long do we stare at nothing?'

'Until there is something, or we are commanded otherwise,' said Kohner. He turned his head to glare at the militiaman. 'How is this so difficult for you to grasp?'

Bessler didn't answer. His head tilted up and his eyes snapped wide. His face, always pinched in resentment like an arthritic fist, went slack with awe and paled. Light seemed to shine from it.

No, that was wrong. The light shone down on it from the sky.

Kohner looked up to see the fire descend.

## 2. YARRICK

*Claw of Desolation*'s arrival was visible across Armageddon Prime, and as far east into Armageddon Secundus as Infernus.

I remained in the augur station after von Strab took over the operations. He withdrew to his quarters, summoning Mannheim and the commanding officers of all Steel Legion regiments to attend his pleasure. He had no use for me. So I stayed to bear witness to the coming of the space hulk.

As the augurs tracked the *Claw of Desolation*'s trajectory, a terrified quiet descended on the station. Since the warp storm had begun, the flights to and from the spaceports had been reduced to a fraction of their usual rate, being limited to in-system traffic only. Now all ships were grounded, and vessels in near orbit were ordered to maintain their positions unless they were in the path of the hulk. Many of the monitoring servitors lapsed into quiescence, their particular stations having gone dark. The sentient technicians gathered around the augurs that followed the voyage of the intruder. The old veteran at the augur called out the shrinking distance. His gravelly voice rang through the air of the station like the countdown to an execution.

I stood at his shoulder and watched his pict screen. The figures dropped steadily towards zero. As the final hour began, the fear around me turned the air sour. The operator opened his mouth to announce the *Claw of Desolation*'s latest position and I interrupted him. 'What is your name?' I asked.

'Kovacz, commissar.'

'You served with the Steel Legion.'

'I did. Gunner in the 158th Armoured.'

'Then you've killed your share of greenskins.'

He grinned. His teeth were stained yellow from lho-stick use. 'I have, commissar. They didn't get my legs cheaply.'

'I don't think they've finished paying for them. Do you?'

'No.' The grin became tight-lipped. His gaze hardened.

'No,' I repeated, raising my voice. I looked around the

station. The sounds of other activity had diminished even further. Attention was centring on me. 'You are citizens of Armageddon,' I said to the entire station. 'Remember what that means. The steel of this world's legions does not come from lasguns and tanks. That is common to all regiments of the Astra Militarum. The steel is in the soul of its heroes. I say that that steel is the birthright of every son and daughter of Armageddon. Will you contradict me?'

A few shouts of 'no' answered me.

'No,' I said again. 'And that is the steel the enemy will encounter. If I had room in my hate, I would feel pity for the xenos mad enough to set foot on the sacred soil of this world.'

A servitor jerked to life. 'Orbital defences acquiring target,' it announced in flat tones.

'Perhaps they'll stop it,' said another operator from across the room. He was much younger than Kovacz. He sounded more frightened than hopeful.

'No, they won't,' I said. 'Not if the Imperial Navy failed. The *Reach of Judgement* alone had several times their fire-power. We must have no illusions. The enemy will come. The xenos will not be stopped on our doorstep.' I waited, giving them no comfort in my gaze. Nothing but the coldest truth would serve. There had been too many lies. I had to pierce through von Strab's veil of self-serving confidence. If the people of Armageddon believed he knew how to deal with orks, then the planet would fall. As yet, I had no true measure of the might of the enemy, other than immensity. Between the omens, the energised orks of Basquit and the devastation of the fleet, I expected a challenge unlike anything we had ever encountered.

I was naïve in my optimism.

'Our test,' I resumed, 'is in our response. Will you despair before the battle has even begun? Will you surrender Armageddon out of fear?'

'No!' The answer was staggered, a mix of desperate bravado and hesitation.

'Will you yield to the greenskins?'

'No!' Stronger now, more unified.

Good. 'Then make ready to fight,' I said. 'And prove yourselves worthy of the Emperor's protection.'

There was fatalistic determination in the faces around me. That was a start. I concealed my own sense of helplessness. There was nothing more I could do until the enemy's first move.

'Atmospheric entry,' said the servitor.

We all looked up through the armourglass dome of the station. We stared at the turgid, discoloured sky. There was nothing to see at first. A minute later, the fire came. It streaked across the zenith, a sword of flame blazing through the overcast, the hulk itself still concealed behind the clouds. I squinted, dazzled by the glare. A wide swath of the sky burned, but there was no sound for several seconds. The *Claw of Desolation* was still in the upper reaches of the atmosphere, the great fire the sign of its distant passage, the flames streaking to the west and disappearing beyond the horizon.

The thunder came now. It reached us through the armourglass and the rockcrete of the tower. It was the deep howl from the throat of a beast as big as the world. It came in a rapid crescendo. It beat at the dome, at our ears, at our souls. It was an endless rage. It was both the shriek of the wounded planet, and the hungry snarl of its tormentor. The entire tower vibrated. I felt the thrum in my bones. People were screaming, but I couldn't hear them.

I did not cover my ears. I walked to the west side of the

augur station, keeping my stride steady even though the floor shook and the structure swayed. I set the example. I glared at the enemy in the sky. I knew my role. I had played it for well over a century. I presented the image of the will to fight.

From the distant west came a still-greater thunder. Then night rose to the clouds, and reached out for us.

## 3. KOHNER

The fire and the great shape it enveloped fell to earth just beyond the eastern horizon. Kohner screamed 'Down!' as he threw himself flat. His warning came too late for anyone who wasn't already taking shelter behind the parapet. The blast wave hit Tempestora. It came ahead of sound, and it banished sound. It was a wall of heat and force. It was a thing beyond wind. It slammed into stone and rockcrete and shook them to their foundations. The air filled with glass as every unarmoured window in the hive city exploded. The troopers too slow to duck, who were foolish enough to stand and watch, were flicked off the battlements like insects. Their uniforms were blasted from their flesh. Their bodies splattered against the higher walls behind.

Sound returned, and it was the boom of a planet being struck with a hammer. Blood flowed from Kohner's ears. The hurricane tried to lift him from the wall. He curled tighter against the parapet, clutching at the rockcrete. He heard a sharper, shattering rumble and he looked up. A few hundred metres from the outer wall, a towering hab block collapsed. It fell in on itself at first, and then toppled to the west. It brought other structures down with it, destruction rippling across the streets of the hive.

The winds and the thunder went on and on. Kohner lost

track of time, but when the darkness came, it was too soon. Night fell in a rush, and it was choking. Millions of tonnes of pulverised rock, had been kicked up to the clouds on impact. A blanket of dust spread across the sky. In the lower reaches, it sandblasted the stones of Tempestora. It mingled with the ash. It stung eyes and smothered lungs. Kohner coughed up thick, blackened phlegm.

When the wind at last dropped to a mere gale shriek, he rose. He leaned into the rage blowing from the east. There was a glow in the distance, a burning dawn that would never become day.

The troopers of the Hive Militia regained their footing. Shouting over the wind, Bessler asked Kohner, 'That must have come down close to Uffern?'

Kohner nodded. Uffern was a minor hive, more of an industrial satellite to Tempestora. Its population was a mere ten million.

'What now, sergeant?' Bessler asked. He was not complaining now. He wanted guidance.

So did Kohner. Already hundreds of his comrades lay dead. 'We'll know soon enough,' he said.

He was right. Almost as soon as vox communication was restored, the order came to march.

## 4. YARRICK

I left the spaceport right after landfall. Overhead, the dust turned the clouds black. When the next morning came, I was sure, no corner of Armageddon would see a true day. With the coming of war, the world had fallen into a cycle of twilight and night.

I made my way by maglev train back to the barracks. When

I arrived, the parade grounds were full of mustering troops. The regiments of the Steel Legion present in Infernus were making ready. I was puzzled, though, as to why the tanks were still in their hangars. There did not appear to be any mobilisation of heavy armour at all.

I found Brenken in the officers' quarters. She was in her chambers, sitting on a metal stool, staring at a map of Armageddon on the table before her, but not looking at it. A muscle in her cheek twitched as she clenched and unclenched her jaw. She was lost in anger.

I rapped on the doorway. 'What mad order has he given now?' I asked.

She blinked and focused her attention on me. 'Our only mobilisation is defensive.'

'What?' Von Strab overseeing the efforts against the orks filled me with dread. I could foresee only disaster in his leadership. But I hadn't imagined even he would order that nothing be done. He was many things, but he wasn't a fool. Or so I had believed until this moment. 'He wants us to wait for the orks to come knocking?'

Brenken's grin was ghastly. 'Not quite. He's ordered Hive Tempestora Militia to mount the offence.'

'They're leaving the hive to fight the greenskins?'

'Yes.'

Von Strab's decision was mad on such a colossal scale that for a few moments, I couldn't shape a question capable of dealing with it. At last, I could muster nothing better than, 'Why?'

'He believes most of the orks must have died on impact. He thinks this is a mopping-up operation.'

Put thus, I could see the overlord's logic. The entire planet had felt the reverberations of that blow. It was difficult to imagine any being inside the space hulk having survived such a landing. 'He thinks the militia is going to find a crater and nothing else,' I said.

'That's right. You don't believe that, do you?'

'No. This hulk is gigantic. It destroyed the fleet. It came straight for Armageddon. What are the odds against such a direct hit being due to chance?'

'Astronomical,' said Brenken.

'The statue of the Emperor was not weeping over dead green-skins. The Tarot did not warn of a simple disaster.' I shook my head. 'How was von Strab's theory received?'

'Mannheim thinks it's ridiculous. The other colonels are doubtful, and definitely not happy about being held back.'

'But the hive governors fell into line,' I guessed.

She nodded. 'And they're happy at the prospect of having their territory protected.'

'What about General Andechs?' He had overall command of the Steel Legion regiments on Armageddon, though his authority was limited by the overlord's supremacy over all armed forces. He was also a member of Armageddon's nobil-ity, and his family had a long history of political alliance with the von Strab dynasty.

'He is cautious on both sides of the issue.'

'In other words he's equivocating,' I said. Brenken had to respect her commanding officer. I had to follow their orders unless they were derelict, and I enforced the chain of com-mand. But I didn't have to grant my respect to anyone who hadn't earned it. Andechs was a competent officer, but a better politician, and his elevation to general owed more to the latter quality than the former. 'So what do you plan to do?' I asked.

'I can't do much more than what has been ordered. We pre-pare to defend Infernus.'

'I think you should make ready to head for Armageddon Prime. We'll be sent there soon, whatever von Strab believes right now.'

Brenken stood. 'Agreed,' she said. 'The militia is going to be slaughtered.'

'No,' I said. 'It will be exterminated.'

## 5. KOHNER

Uffern was gone. The space hulk had come down only a few hundred metres from its eastern edge. Entire neighbourhoods had vaporised and in their place were the sloping walls of the huge crater. The blast had flattened the rest of the city. Where spires had stood, there was only rubble. A few shapes reached upwards like broken fingers. They were fragments of towers, hollowed-out shells, a brittle trace of the city that had been.

The Tempestora Hive Militia skirted the southern edge of Uffern's grave. The land over which the columns marched had been scraped bare to the bedrock, and the new surface was rippled and cracked. Kohner had to watch his footing. It would be easy to break a leg in one of the jagged crevasses.

True night had fallen during the march from Tempestora. Whatever dawn could still come to Armageddon was still a few hours away. The militia's advance was limited to the speed of the infantry. Though there were Chimeras and Tauroxes in the field, the militia had no heavy tanks, and its artillery consisted of fixed emplacements at the hive. The militia was not the Steel Legion. Its function was defensive, and it had not left Tempestora to engage in battle for centuries. Kohner didn't even know what its last campaign had been. There were rumours that it had been expunged from the historical record.

Defensive or not, the militia was on the attack now. It was

the largest mobilisation Kohner had ever seen. As far as he could tell, the entire force was marching with him. *No*, he thought. *We aren't the Steel Legion. But we know how to fight.* They were disciplined, well-armed, and numbered in the tens of thousands. *We know how to fight*, he thought again. Then he called to his squad, 'Are you ready to show the greenskins a proper Tempestora welcome?' The shouts that came in response were picked up by other squads. The sound was a good one. He needed the reassurance as much as anyone else.

Beyond the city, a monster loomed. From a distance, in the night, it resembled a new mountain. Its flanks still glowed from the heat of its passage through the atmosphere. There were many dark patches, as if portions had fallen away. Or had opened. The wind was no longer the wrath of a wounded planet, but it still blew from the east. It carried the sounds of a great clamour. Voices and machinery, guttural and savage, blended together into the low grumble of xenos thunder. The stench of ork bodies and smoking engines squeezed Kohner's lungs.

'Purge the alien!' Captain Wendlandt cried. He was riding in the top of a Chimera a short distance to Kohner's right.

'Purge the alien!' Kohner echoed.

'Purge the alien!' Thousands calling for blood now. Thousands united in their determination to defend their world. Thousands shouting to drown out the unclean snarl from the east.

For a few moments, they succeeded. Kohner was surrounded by human rage. He was buoyed by the collective power it represented. He was hungry for the clash. The Tempestora Hive Militia would exterminate the greenskin survivors, and for once the glory of victory would not belong to the Steel Legion.

He was still shouting when the orks roared. They swamped

the human cry. The roar was huge as a wall, crushing as a fist. It went on and on and on, louder and louder, hideous in its eagerness and joy. It was not the sound of the battered survivors of a disaster. It was the triumphant exhilaration of millions.

Kohner's mouth went dry. The rallying cry choked off in his throat. Terror sank fangs of ice into his gut. The roar was something monstrous, beyond his comprehension. The thunder of the space hulk's impact had been shattering, but he had understood what it was. This was something else again. It was exultation, an emotion rare enough on Armageddon. Kohner had a vision of bestial jaws opening wide, wide enough to swallow the sun, about to snap down and devour everything human.

Caught by the headlamps of the Taurox following close on the Chimera, Wendlandt's face was a skull, a thing of stark light and deep shadow. He was shouting something, but Kohner couldn't hear him over the orks. He was gesticulating, waving forward with his laspistol, a desperate marionette. The order was clear: advance, attack.

In the name of the Emperor, attack.

Kohner tightened his grip on his lasrifle, but there was nothing to shoot yet. How far were they yet from the enemy? He didn't know. The space hulk was kilometres distant, but the roar had seemed close, a beast's breath on the back of his neck.

He picked up his pace. He shouted, and couldn't hear his own voice, but his squad joined him in the charge forward. The thousands of the Tempestora Hive Militia rushed to meet the foe. To think was to despair, so the only choice was to attack with speed, with ferocity, with desperation.

The orks were faster. More ferocious. Even more consumed with the need to engage. The roar became the clash of arms and the snarl of heavy vehicles. Kohner was a third of the way down the columns from the front ranks, far enough away that at first he didn't know why the advance had stopped, why he could no longer run because the man in front of him had stopped running too. Then he made out the sounds of war. In the near distance, las flashes strobed in the night. The ork guns barked, so many of them that their reports blurred into a long rattle. Kohner could just make out hulking shapes and flashes of xenos hide. The beasts were taller than men, and wider. They were easy targets to hit, hard ones to drop. They walked into las fire and punched forward, eating into the column, stopping it dead.

Kohner aimed high, firing over the heads of his comrades. He got off four shots, and four hits. He knew this because he could see the ork he was aiming at more clearly with each pull of the trigger. The orks had hit the front ranks so hard they barely slowed in their charge as they cut down Tempestora's warriors. They were close enough for Kohner to see the viscous saliva drooling from their tusked maws, to see their corded muscles, and to feel his blood chill before the wave of greenskins. The blades they brandished were as massive, crude and varied as their armour. Some were defended by nothing more than a few pieces of scrap metal attached to their rough leather clothing. Others, much larger, advanced in massive suits, terrifying patchwork constructions of plates and spikes. The orks had draped themselves with trophy skulls of humans, eldar and other races. Raised above the horde was a forest of iron hacked into icons of horned bulls, serpents, blazing suns and more.

Kohner's target fell, and he took heart in the knowledge that the orks were mortal. 'They can die!' he shouted, though only he could hear. 'They can die!'

The orks died, but they seemed immortal, and for each one that fell, the rest came on with greater frenzy. With the militia's advance halted, Kohner took the time to steady his aim, and place each shot carefully into the skulls of the greenskins. The nearest brutes were only a few dozen metres away from him.

The ork engines drew closer. There were two registers: the deep clanking of heavy armour, and the furious, giant insect rasp of bikes. Kohner looked to the right. Along the edge of the militia formation, ork bikes screamed past. Flames shot out of their exhaust, and from the muzzles of their forward-mounted guns. Their engines spewed dark, noxious clouds over the militia. Kohner choked, his nose and throat raked by the smell of burned, barely refined promethium. The riders butchered at high speed, scything through the human flanks, and they kept going. If it weren't for the sheer number tearing past, Kohner might not have known what hit them. The warbikes disappeared towards the rear of the column.

'Where are they going?' Bessler was wide-eyed. He fired pointlessly at the bikes before shooting towards the front again. He wasn't aiming, wasn't thinking. He was a single shock away from panic.

'To the rear,' Kohner told him. 'They're going to surround us.'

The battlewagons followed the bikes. The war's flames leapt higher, and Kohner could see further into the dark. The ork tanks were an unending stream of metal, a bellowing, clanging, booming sea of destruction. They jostled against each other, too many huge vehicles fighting for the privilege of smashing the humans. The Chimeras and Tauroxes moved outwards towards the flanks, bringing their guns to bear against the ork machines, using their armour to stop the massacre of the flesh. The ork cannons dug huge furrows into the lines. The ground beneath Kohner's feet vibrated with the impact of ork shells and solid rounds. A massive volley smashed into the side of a Taurox twenty metres to the rear of Kohner's position. The hits were a series of rapid concussions, a doom-doom-doom-doom-doom punching through the armour, tearing it open, pulverising the soldiers inside. The Taurox exploded, and the fireball washed over the infantry surrounding it.

Wendlandt's Chimera blasted the driver's compartment of one battlewagon. Still moving fast, the enemy vehicle veered wildly, grinding militia troops beneath its spiked wheels before it collided with another ork tank. The two were moving fast, and they were top-heavy with armour and guns. The first battlewagon flipped onto its side. The other, its front built up into a battering ram, drove into its chassis. The two vehicles fused. Metal scraped over rock, becoming a single burning scrap heap. The battlewagons came to a stop, blocking the path of the vehicles behind them. The flow of the ork monsters slowed as the other tanks manoeuvred to pass.

Kohner experienced a surge of crazed, irrational hope. The destroyed battlewagon meant nothing beyond a minor inconvenience for the orks. Ten killed tanks, twenty, fifty… all meaningless. The army that roared past the militia column defied counting. Kohner knew how this must end. But for a few moments, he managed to push that knowledge away.

The human ranks became more serried. There was no question of an advance. As the warbikes and battlewagons receded towards the rear of the lines, retreat became impossible too. The struggle now was to hold the orks back.

Crackling green lightning blew the wrecked battlewagons apart. All along both flanks of the column, salvoes of the green energy struck. The orks had set up artillery beyond the path of the vehicles, and they unleashed the guns now. A storm of explosions fell on the militia. The barrels of the cannons were long, tapering conglomerations of coils coming to a three-pronged end which created a blistering nexus. The guns were not accurate. They weren't even stable. Several blew up as they fired. The orks' self-inflicted casualties didn't matter. The power and the volume of the salvoes were overwhelming.

Kohner's senses were battered by the energy gale. His comrades became silhouettes backlit by searing green flashes. The explosions came from all sides. The incinerated corpse of a militiaman knocked him down. When he staggered up, he had lost all sense of direction. He was surrounded by destruction. He tried to locate Wendlandt. He spotted the captain, still riding in the hatch of the Chimera, just before a direct hit disintegrated both.

To Kohner's right, three ork cannons exploded in quick succession, leaving a gap in the artillery line. He could see a glimpse of the night through the emerald maelstrom. 'This way!' he shouted. He didn't know if anyone could hear. He had no reason to believe his action would serve any purpose. But he saw a gap, and he took it. He would fight the greenskins. He refused to wait for their gunfire to come for him.

Whether his comrades heard him or saw him, or acted on the same desperate instinct, he was not alone as he made his run. His squad and others followed him. They charged over terrain littered with charred corpses and smoking wrecks. Kohner clambered over a slag heap that had been a Taurox. At the top, he fired into the dark. Dazzled by the bombardment, he could see no targets. He knew they were out there, though. And they would know he was here.

Ahead of him, more of his comrades were making the same rush. He started moving again, and he was part of a concerted attempt to escape the noose the orks had thrown around the Tempestorans. To the east, the ork infantry continued to press forward, heedless of the danger as they headed into the region being hit by their own artillery. To the west, the battlewagons drove over the militia, their siege shields grinding the humans to bloody smears on the ground, their guns blasting the rear-guard defenders apart. In the south, the energy cannon's barrage went on unbroken.

The column bulged to the north. In a matter of seconds, the struggle to break out involved thousands of combatants, backed up by the armour that yet survived. The Tempestorans shouted their rage as they stormed into the night. Kohner's voice was part of the great shout. He ran faster. Over death and the rubble of a devastated land, he ran. He fired. His hatred was such that he could smash through the ork lines alone, and he was far from alone.

At his left, he saw Bessler, as driven and enraged as himself, his mouth wide in the shout.

*Are you ready for this, xenos?* Kohner thought.

They were. Just as Kohner began to wonder about the enemy's silence in this one area to the north, just as he began to suspect the sudden hole in their lines was too good to be true, the orks struck. They had been waiting behind the destroyed gun. They were an army larger than they had appeared to the east. They had been standing in silence, weapons up, letting the humans run forward and take the bait. Before they fired, they roared again. Kohner was suddenly running against a sound so huge it was physical. Hope drained away, leaving only horror.

How could orks show such discipline? The question tormented him even as the orks attacked. They fired, and the rounds were another storm, destruction so concentrated that there was no longer any air to breathe. There were only bullets and shells. Then the orks came on, an unbroken mass of brutal muscle and armour.

The Tempestorans fell. The rout was beyond massacre, beyond extermination. The orks stampeded over the humans without stopping. The eastern and northern infantry were battering rams. They came together, annihilating the Hive Militia. The artillery bursts died down as the human force vanished.

Kohner saw the slaughter before him, but he kept moving forwards. There was nowhere else to go. He drained his rifle's power pack firing into the unstoppable tide. He reloaded, and looked up to see a giant heading his way. At the head of the orks attacking from the north was a warlord almost twice his height. The beast wore a horned helmet, and from its back rose a towering icon of iron, also horned, a crimson bull, almost as tall again as the ork. The monster wielded a power claw and a handgun whose barrel was as thick as Kohner's arm. The warboss barely glanced at Kohner's squad as it waded through. It clamped the claw over Bessler's head and torso. The trooper's blood sprayed over Kohner's face.

Kohner fired up at the ork's head. It looked down at him and shot him once, hitting Kohner in the chest. It felt like a pillar of burning stone, and he stopped running, unable to feel his legs. His head rocked forward and he saw the hole in his body – his core was now gone.

His legs folded and he fell. He lay on his back. His arms flapped on either side, dragging his splayed fingers over the jagged bedrock. The ork stopped to watch. Its minions held their position, awaiting its pleasure. It raised and lowered its arms, mimicking Kohner's movements. It laughed, a braying, savage noise. The other orks joined it. The sound of mockery travelled across the battlefield, a contemptuous farewell to the dying humans.

Somewhere beyond Kohner's fading sight, a voice barked an order. The voice was gigantic. It had to come from a chest as big as a mountain. It silenced all the orks.

The warboss turned around. It looked back. It looked up. It growled an acknowledgement, and when it did, Kohner understood he had heard something new in human experience: an ork expressing awe. Kohner knew he was dying. He was moving beyond pain. And still he was terrified.

There was an ork out there much larger than the monster that had killed him. An ork whose existence made him weep. He wasn't crying for himself, or even for Armageddon. He wept for the Imperium. He prayed for mercy. He prayed the darkness would take him before this terrible being came into sight.

His prayers went unanswered.

# CHAPTER 4
# THE RACE

## 1. YARRICK

I stood up from my seat in the forward area of the heavy lifter's troop compartment and joined Setheno at a small viewing block in the port side of the fuselage. Most of the Steel Legionnaires travelling with us were seated. The few who moved around the compartment gave the canoness a wide berth. We could speak without being overheard.

Below us, the terrain of Armageddon Prime rolled past. The Equatorial Jungle was far behind us. Our air armada of lifters was less than an hour from Hive Tempestora.

Setheno nodded at the lifters visible off the port wing. They were fat-bodied beasts, their hulls disproportionately large, making their wings seem stubby despite their hundred-metre wingspans. Each lifter carried a full company, the ones that weren't transporting our heavy armour. 'Half a regiment,' she said. 'We fill the sky.'

'Are you suggesting the response will be sufficient?'

'Hardly. I was making an observation of scale. We fill the sky, and that is not enough.'

'You think we are flying to our doom?'

It is not possible to shrug in power armour, but the slight tilt of her head suggested the gesture. 'It is our duty to ensure that we are not.'

'I agree. I will not let Armageddon fall while I draw breath. But Overlord von Strab appears to be doing everything in his power to engineer our defeat.' I shook my head. 'A single regiment as a response.'

'Are his actions treasonous?' Setheno asked.

Her question was not an idle one. I thought carefully before I answered. 'I don't believe so. They are ill-judged. I think he's motivated by a combination of over-confidence and excessive political calculation. He still doesn't believe the orks are the threat we know them to be.' Before our departure from Infernus, Brenken had played for me the few vox transmissions we had received from the Tempestora Hive Militia. We hadn't been able to glean many details about the disaster. We had a rough idea of where the *Claw of Desolation* had landed. We didn't have anything that even approached an estimation of the size of the greenskin army. What we had were recordings of panicked screams and pleas to von Strab and to the Emperor. And we knew the timeline. We knew how long it had taken the orks to obliterate the entire Hive Militia.

Not long.

Not long at all.

In response to the massacre, von Strab had ordered the 252nd Regiment to deploy. The orks were most likely making for Tempestora, but Volcanus was also within reach. Brenken was leading half the companies there. Dividing our already inadequate strength troubled her, but we could not leave either of Armageddon Prime's principle hives undefended.

'The overlord's sense of the situation is either naive or delusional,' Setheno said. 'In the council, he remarked that no matter what happens in Armageddon Prime, the Equatorial Jungle will prove an impassable barrier for the orks, especially since we are on the eve of the Season of Shadows.'

I snorted. 'I wonder if even he is that stupid. He might have been speaking for the benefit of the hive governors.'

'I'm sure he was. The defensive measures he has ordered suggest his confidence in the jungle is not absolute. Even so, he is determined to remain in Infernus.'

If the orks reached Armageddon Secundus, Hive Infernus would be the first major centre in their eastward march. 'If he leaves now, he shows weakness,' I said. 'And keeping the other regiments stationed in the hives will keep the governors in line.'

'Herman von Strab is a skilled politician,' Setheno said. She spoke as if she were proclaiming his death sentence. 'He should have been dealt with before now.'

'True,' I said. I thought again of that moment when I had considered putting a round through von Strab's head. I grimaced at the possibility that the missed opportunity had led to the present pass. Though I have come to terms with my decision, and believe that it was, in the end, the correct one, I had no way of taking the long view in that moment. In the short term, von Strab's survival was one of the greatest tragedies of Armageddon's history. As we flew to Tempestora, I sensed the curtain rising on that tragedy, and I knew I had to accept the role my decision had played in bringing it about. 'The overlord is beyond our reach now,' I said. 'He is running the campaign. It falls to us to make it a successful one.'

'You speak without irony.'

'Because what I say is true.'

She bowed her head once in acknowledgement. She glanced back at the ranks of steel benches where the company sat. 'You have seen Captain Stahl in combat,' she said. 'I have not. Your evaluation?'

'A skilled officer.' Brenken had given Stahl the overall command of the companies bound for Tempestora.

'Not the most senior, though.'

'No. But the right choice, I think. He doesn't avoid hard decisions, and he can think well on his feet.'

'I saw resentment in the faces of some of his fellow captains. The older ones.'

'We might need to reinforce his authority.'

'If he proves worthy.'

'If he proves worthy,' I agreed.

Emerald lightning lashed upward. It sheared off the starboard wing of the lifter closest to us. The aircraft went into a spinning dive and veered our way. Setheno and I remained motionless at the viewing block as the collision loomed. Thousands of tonnes of high-velocity metal rushed together. Our engines screamed as the pilot, Rhubeck, pulled us up. The stricken craft dropped beneath us and spiralled towards the ground.

More lightning reached upwards for the fleet. Two lifters took direct hits to their fuel tanks and exploded. I was thrown against the fuselage wall as Rhubeck tried to manoeuvre defensively. The effort was pointless. The lifter turned slowly, and the energy beams came in such profusion and in such wild arcs that there could be no anticipating them. I staggered back to my seat and strapped myself in. Setheno followed. The weight of her armour gave her greater stability as the lifter rocked back and forth.

'We are under fire,' I called out. 'Prepare yourselves! We will be hit, but the Emperor protects!'

We had need of his protection. Our turn to be hit came a minute later. There was a green flash to port that shone through the viewing block with the intensity of a sun. Metal shrieked. A blast close at hand, and then we were going down.

The drop was fast. My feet rose from the deck and I was weightless for several seconds. We tilted sharply to starboard as the dive steepened. It neared the vertical, and I felt the sickening momentum of a spin building. The engines screamed, and they rushed us still faster towards the ground. I bit back a snarl of rage that the end should come in so pointless a fashion. I kept my face impassive. Beside me, Setheno stared straight ahead, her eyes cold as the fate before us. I prayed to the Emperor that I would yet be allowed to fight in his name. This death would be wrong. Plucked from the sky, trapped in the giant, tumbling sarcophagus, this end was tantamount to dereliction of duty.

The Emperor protects. There was a great shuddering, and the lifter's dive began to level off. We came out of the spin. The engines whined even higher, and there was a second explosion, this time on the port side. The aircraft jolted, but its nose continued to even out. Over the din of the howling lifter, from behind the door to the cockpit, I heard a scream, as if Rhubeck were dragging us out of the plunge through will alone.

He did well. We were almost horizontal when we hit the ground.

The impact shattered my perceptions. Time broke into a jumble of splinters. Blows hammered me from all sides. Reality was a tumbling, rolling blur of thunder and metal and pain. The lifter slammed belly-first into the ground and ploughed a furrow through earth and rock. I heard the cracking of rock, the disintegration of steel, the cries of the dying, the blank roar of fire. I don't know if I lost consciousness. The line between awareness and oblivion vanished. There was only the crash, the great rending of the world, the smashing and hurling of my body. My restraints tore and I flew.

I knew nothing, but I still knew pain.

And then it stopped. The stillness was so sudden, it was its own form of trauma. I lay on my back, blinking through a haze of confusion and agony. Everything was motionless. Everything was silence.

But no, that was a lie. I grunted. I tried to sit. I succeeded. No bones were broken. The ringing in my ears and the fog before my eyes faded. The violence of the world returned. The silence gave way to the hiss of leaking promethium, the crackle of flame, and the earth-shaking pounding of more and more aircraft hitting the ground.

I managed to stand. My left leg tried to give out beneath my weight. I allowed myself to stagger a single step, no more than that. The Emperor had heard my plea, and my duty to him called with a voice louder than the white noise of our catastrophe.

I had been thrown free of the lifter in the last moments of the crash. The wreckage was strewn across a thousand metres of ground: smashed engines sat in pools of burning fuel, the wings had broken off on impact and the fuselage had broken into three large pieces. They had more or less held their shape, though there were huge rents in their sides. The one I had been in was twenty metres long. The nose was crushed. No one in it could have survived, but Rhubeck had saved many of us. As I gathered my scattered thoughts and took stock of the situation, Setheno emerged from the fuselage, followed by Steel Legionnaires. Her forehead was bleeding, but she moved easily. The troopers who stumbled out behind her were in much rougher shape, but they were mobile. That meant they could fight.

To the east, the orks' green lightning still streaked to the sky, felling the armada. There was such a concentration of fire, across such a wide area, that it was impossible to avoid. We had flown into a wall of devastating energy. I had encountered this form of ork artillery before. It was volatile, inaccurate, but devastating. I had never seen it deployed in this kind of strength. The greenskins had the means for a massive invasion, and the cunning to use them well. The ground shook, and shook again as more lifters crashed. Some managed to land without disappearing into balls of flame. Others disintegrated, leaving nothing behind but tracts of blackened metal and unrecognisable flesh.

Setheno joined me, along with Captain Stahl. His face was turning purple and black from a mass of contusions. One eye was swollen shut, and he was favouring his left arm. He gazed eastward in horror.

'A powerful enemy,' Setheno said. 'Von Strab is not alone in underestimating them.'

'We are guilty too,' I agreed. As we would be again. And again. No matter how desperately we struggled against making that mistake.

His voice cracking with awe and despair, Stahl said, 'They've finished us before we even started.'

'What do you mean?' I snapped.

He looked at me in surprise, puzzled that I couldn't see the scale of our defeat. 'They countered our response,' he said. 'They've taken us out before we could even reach Tempestora.'

'Are you dead?' I asked.

'I don't understand, commissar.'

'You're still drawing breath.' I pointed to the soldiers still emerging from the fuselage, and then at the survivors I could see gathering outside the other pieces of the lifter. 'So are they. We are only defeated when we are dead. If even then.'

I glared at him until I saw determination take hold once more. He nodded and marched towards his troops. He began to call out orders, and the dazed crowd took steps towards becoming a military force once more.

'You're thinking of a run to Tempestora?' Setheno asked.

'Yes.' I looked towards the ork lines. The enemy was not coming for us yet. The orks were content for the moment to shoot us out of the sky. The gauntlet had taken almost all the lifters now. The crashes covered a wide area, but many aircraft, including our own, had still travelled many kilometres as they fell. We had a lead on the orks. Perhaps enough to win the race, if we started soon.

'We cannot save Tempestora,' Setheno said. I would have punished any soldier who spoke those words before an engagement. Coming from the canoness, however, they were nothing more than cold-eyed clarity. And she was right.

'I know,' I told her. 'But we can damage the enemy. And the longer we hold the orks there, the better Brenken can prepare Volcanus.'

'Agreed.'

Over the course of the next hour, we worked with Stahl and the other officers still alive to re-forge the companies into something coherent and capable of fighting. We had lost almost all our vehicles in the crashes, and at least half the troops. We were still many hundreds, and as we started the march to Tempestora, we were an army, not a rabble. The Steel Legion trenchcoats bore the burns of the disaster. Many of the rebreathers were damaged or unusable. But this was a regiment that had fought well for its colonel, its home world, and the Imperium. It would not stop now, especially when the home world itself was under threat.

We gathered the companies for as long as the orks continued to fire at the sky. When the green energy bursts ceased, we were out of time. Some of the lifters had come down too far for us to reach. I saw one near the northern horizon that looked remarkably intact. There could be more survivors there. But we could not afford the delay in hooking up with them. To the west, Tempestora's silhouette bulked towards the clouds. To the east, a dust cloud was rising. The orks were on the move.

Stahl voxed orders to all survivors to make for the hive. Some answered his call. Perhaps there were others who heard and could not answer. There was no way to tell. And there was no choice.

In the clammy heat of the Armageddon Prime day, we began the forced march to Hive Tempestora.

## 2. SEROFF

In the reception hall of von Strab's quarters, Dominic Seroff savoured his amasec and waited for the evening to end. The reception was a show of confidence. Under the pretext of honouring the Feast of the Emperor's Ascension despite the recent events, von Strab was reassuring the hive governors of Armageddon Secundus that the situation was well in hand. The reassurance was also reinforcement. The overlord's authority was absolute. Even now.

The amasec was good. Too good, Seroff thought, for Armageddon. The taste had a nuance of flavours, a subtlety at odds with the industrial brutishness of the world. Von Strab must have it imported from elsewhere. The bottles, though, bore the overlord's family crest. Vanity, pretence and power came together in that lie. Seroff shrugged and took another sip. The amasec's provenance was irrelevant. What was true of the vintage was true of the overlord. Von Strab was powerful, effective, and his grip on Armageddon unchallenged. His corruption and venality were irrelevant.

His competence as a war commander was a question. Seroff was sceptical about von Strab's assertion that the Equatorial Jungle would stop the orks. But if the overlord was wrong, then a strong defence of the hives was paramount. He understood why Mannheim was upset about the size of the force sent to defend Tempestora and Volcanus, but he also understood the expediency behind von Strab's decision. He didn't like the idea of Armageddon Prime already being as good as lost, but the possibility was a real one. It had to be faced.

Seroff finished his amasec. He signalled a passing serf for another drink, and then found von Strab at his elbow. The overlord had been in conference with Governor von Kierska a few moments before. His movements could be stealthy for a big man.

'I hope you're enjoying the evening, lord commissar,' von Strab said.

'I appreciate its necessity and execution.' He had no reason to play the toady. His remit extended far beyond Armageddon itself. Von Strab was a useful political ally, not his master.

Von Strab smiled, unoffended. 'I just received some news about the 252nd. The airlift to Tempestora has been lost.'

Seroff looked at von Strab for a long moment. 'Lost?' he asked. 'Completely?'

'We're waiting for more news. But all the lifters have fallen off the augurs.'

'You don't seem overly concerned.'

'We don't know everything yet.' He made a show of sighing. 'Losses are inevitable in war. Regrettable. But there we are.'

'You aren't worried,' Seroff repeated.

'I have no reason to be. If the orks had landed on the eastern side of the jungle, I would be concerned. They did not.'

'We may yet lose Prime.'

'We'll reclaim it in time.'

Seroff couldn't decide if von Strab was more naïve or more pragmatic than anyone he had ever met. The thought that he might be both was chilling. Seroff dismissed it.

'There is something I wanted to ask you,' von Strab continued. 'I've been wondering why you raised no objection to Commissar Yarrick being part of the expedition against the greenskins. You made it very clear that you wanted him sidelined after Basquit.'

'Was he part of the Tempestora contingent?'

'I don't know.'

'If he was, I haven't done him any favours by allowing his participation in the campaign.'

Von Strab smiled like a happy predator. 'Pure conjecture, lord commissar. And you haven't answered my question.'

'Sebastian Yarrick has no conception of loyalty,' Seroff said. He bit off the syllables of the man's name. Speaking it left a foul taste in his mouth. 'He deserves the worst humiliation, and a dishonourable death.' Wounds more than a century old bled as freely as the day they had been inflicted. 'But he's skilled. He's strong in the field. Which is why that should be taken away from him. Unless he's useful.' He drank from his refilled goblet. The amasec was bitter now. 'Today he's useful,' Seroff finished.

'I see,' said von Strab. 'And there's the chance he could die being useful.'

'You said it yourself. There are losses in war.'

\* \* \*

## 3. YARRICK

The warbikers came for us. I heard the high-pitched growl of the engines and looked back through the dark grey of Armageddon's new form of day. The sound grew louder, redolent of brutish speed. I saw dots at the horizon, pulling ahead of the main ork force, whose trace was still just the dust cloud. Warning shouts rang out along the length of the column.

Setheno and I were in the front ranks, leading the way forward with Stahl. He cursed when he heard the bikes. The walls of Tempestora were still kilometres away. The orks would be upon us in under a minute. Stahl looked at the broken plain before us. 'We have no defensive position,' he said.

'We cannot afford one,' Setheno told him.

'If we let the bikes stop us,' I said, 'they'll hold us until the rest of the greenskins arrive. They will destroy us in the open and then take Tempestora unopposed. We must keep moving.'

I saw the implications of our position sink into Stahl's eyes. A running battle on open ground against warbikes would exact a heavy toll. But he had to understand that a defensive response would do nothing but buy a little more time before a worse disaster. He looked to the west, where a befouled river flowed on a parallel course to ours. The bikes would not be able to follow us there, true, but we would be handing high ground to the orks, who would not find it difficult to push us into the water.

I was pleased when Stahl shook his head. He was thinking his decisions through. He wasn't about to lead us to oblivion.

'Vox!' he called, and a trooper ran up with a field unit. 'Double-time march,' Stahl ordered. 'We're about to be raided on both flanks. Heavier weapons to the edges. Take out the enemy vehicles.'

'Sir,' the trooper responded, then spoke into the handset.

Setheno nodded to me before she donned her helmet and moved towards the right flank. We would have need of someone with power armour against the ork vehicles. I headed left. I belonged wherever fighting would be most intense.

A long line of warbikes raced up the length of the column. The orks strafed us hard. Their bullets blew apart troopers on either side of me. Rounds dug up the ground as I jogged, and something hot and lethal burned through the left sleeve of my greatcoat and grazed my arm. The bullet was so big, even that glancing blow was almost enough to knock me down. I kept my feet and fired my bolt pistol. 'Aim for the lead bikers!' I shouted, and then led by example when one of my shots took off the head of a rider. The ork's bike cartwheeled end over end. The greenskin coming on behind jerked right so fast that its nearest brother went out of control trying to avoid the collision. That brute went into a long skid. It rose and started to right its bike, but now it was an unmoving target. Concentrated lasfire burned it where it stood.

The stream of bikes streaked past the fallen riders and reached the front of our column. They cut in close, their guns punching holes into our ranks. The bikes from the left and right flanks joined up. They didn't slow down.

We ran into a thresher of metal and gunfire.

## 4. SETHENO

This was not the battle that had drawn her to Armageddon. This was not the disaster foretold by the Emperor's Tarot. This was a skirmish, a mere prologue. Armageddon's true ordeal had yet to begin. That was when she would understand her purpose here. The forces that would shape the war were still gathering, still aligning. The war was embryonic. When it had grown to its full storm, she would see how best to use her strength. She would see with the clarity that had been her gift and her curse since Mistral, so long ago. It didn't worry her that she had no definite role yet. Recognising the early, rapid unfolding of battle as an avalanche of contingency and accident and randomness was another form of clarity. The fools were the ones who thought they could foresee and control the outcome.

Her immediate path was clear: reach Tempestora, and ensure that the sacrifice that followed was as damaging as possible for the orks.

As the warbikes screamed up the right flank of the Steel Legion companies, she charged out of the column. She brandished *Skarprattar*. Saint Demetria's relic sword was a daemon bane. It would end xenos abominations just as well.

An ork biker veered towards her, the brute's features stretched wide in the ecstasy of velocity. Setheno braced. The ork rose in his seat, brandishing a shaft of pipe topped by a massive head of twisted, jagged scrap metal. Setheno sidestepped the blow and swung her blade against the ork's back, severing its spine. The bike tumbled away, bouncing over the rocky plain. Setheno turned to counter the next bike. A stream of bullets slammed into her breastplate. The impact knocked her back, though the ceramite held. She raised her bolt pistol and shot the ork through the face. The body convulsed. So did the bike. It remained upright, its course wildly erratic, its guns still blazing. Disorder rippled outward from the bike as the other riders fought to steer around its death-ride.

A gap opened up in the orks' strafing. The Steel Legion poured fire into the breach, and more riders went down. The flow of the bikes stuttered, a river of savage iron running dry. Multiple flamers lit up the bikes that came too close. The bodies of legionnaires were spread on the plain, but the column retained cohesion, and kept moving forward.

Setheno pounded over the earth to intercept a bike that was charging straight at the column. Focused on the humans it was mowing down, the rider didn't see her until she brought *Skarprattar* down in an overhead arc. The blade's aura shone blue as it cut through the bike's front wheel. Setheno leapt back, out of the way of the wreck as the bike flipped over and crushed the ork beneath its weight.

Then there were no more bikes coming from the east. But the forward movement of the Steel Legion had slowed. Setheno ran to the west, towards the front of the lines once more, towards the snarl of butchery.

## 5. YARRICK

A biker came too close and ploughed into the column. It ground troopers beneath its wheels. The crush of flesh slowed it down. The bones of dead and dying comrades crunched beneath my boots as I launched myself forward and plunged my blade through the driver's throat. The ork gurgled, blood jetting from its neck and mouth. It tried to beat me away. I dragged the sword back, sawing through muscle. The ork's head flopped backwards and the bike fell over.

Stubber rounds from more bikes beat against our ranks, and I had to duck behind the vehicle I had just stopped. We were moving at a crawl. Two clusters of warbikes kept crossing each other's paths ahead of us. The strafing was continuous. I could hear Stahl shouting to be heard over the hammering of the guns. He was urging the troops forward, but that wasn't enough. Advance was impossible. The orks were putting up a fast-moving, lethal wall.

Multiple flamers opened up from the captain's position. They sprayed burning promethium over the nearest orks and punished them for their approach. Troopers at the front dropped to a crouch so their comrades behind them had clear shots. Sheets of las reached out for the orks. Our attack was disciplined and relentless, but it wasn't enough. The smog of exhaust and the speed of the bikes made them difficult targets. Vehicles and riders were resilient to las, soaking up damage. We were still stymied. Rocket launchers had taken out a few of the bikes on the flanks, and we needed them now at the front.

A fireball bloomed to my right when ork rounds punched open a trooper's flamer reservoir. A second tank went up. Our response faltered. A rocket launcher team arrived at my left. They loaded the weapon but were cut down before firing.

I dragged the launcher away from the bodies. I checked that its payload was a krakk missile, and then looked over the mound of the wrecked bike. The two streams of orks had finished crossing. There would be a slight pause as they reversed direction, and then we would get their redoubled fire once more, coming in at a murderous cross-hatch of angles.

I saw a chance.

'Grenade launchers!' I shouted. 'Lascannons! To me now! To victory!'

Three troopers carrying launchers and a brace of two-man teams converged on my position, crouching low.

'Fire at my target and on my signal,' I said. 'Not before.'

I coughed on the choking air. On either side of me, rebreather-clad heads nodded.

The strafing started again. The warbikes converged.

'Lead bike on the left,' I said. I shouldered the missile launcher. I stayed low. The ork bullets passed just over my head. 'Grenades, now!' I shouted.

The grenades arced towards the point where the two streams of bikes would meet. As they came down, I launched the rocket and said, 'Las now!'

Grenades, missile and las burst hit the lead bikes at the same moment. The explosion took out three ork vehicles instantaneously, and ferociously. Their ends were more blasts, heavy shrapnel flying out at eviscerating speed. The chain reaction was huge. The orks were going too fast, and there was no way to avoid the growing collision. The view ahead of me disappeared in a maelstrom of metal carnage, flame and roiling smoke. I heard Stahl shouting, and though I couldn't make out the words, I saw the effect. The companies poured their firepower into the spreading devastation.

There was sudden movement to the far right. Setheno led a charge straight at the stalled orks. Her towering figure in grey armour was the inevitability of death coming for the enemy. She was followed by the roar of soldiers hungry to carve their vengeance into the flesh of the foe. The orks didn't wait for their arrival. Some turned bikes around to fire at the rush, and others mounted a counter-charge.

But now we had the advantage of firepower.

Stahl kept up the punishing las volleys. He pinned the orks and gave some cover to Setheno's run.

The greenskins tried to regroup to meet our right flank. They moved away from the burn we had created. They weren't paying attention to our left.

I seized on their mistake. I raised my sword high and vaulted over the wrecked bike. 'For Tempestora!' I shouted. 'For Armageddon! Our path is over the bones of the greenskin!'

We charged, our numbers counting for something now. We had the momentum, and the orks were caught in the middle of our twin hammers. The rebreathers turned the men and women who ran with me into identical creatures, a legion of predators with insectoid skulls. A wave of ochre hurled itself against the green tide.

The orks fought as long as they could. The bikers were not the biggest of orks, but they were big enough. They were brutal masses of rage and muscle. A single blow from their axes or clubs or machetes imploded skulls and shattered spines. But we hit them harder, and we hit them more. I brought my sword down on the skull of one brute. My blade was embedded in his forehead, but he swung at me with his axe. I dodged the blow and finished him off with a bolt shell to the neck. I pushed the body down, yanked my sword free and rushed forward to the next one. I killed as fast as I could. I was drenched in xenos blood. I fought as if the annihilation of this small band of the enemy was the key to victory.

I knew this was not true. I knew we were fighting simply for the chance to fight again, to do something more than retreat from the orks' march. But at a more profound level, there was a darker truth to how I fought, and I knew it too. If we didn't attack the orks as if every struggle was the turning point of the war, then we would be defeated.

I killed each ork with the energy built up from a lifetime of hate. And it still wasn't good enough, because I still didn't realise what led them. I did not know what *Ghazghkull* meant, though these orks were chanting it too, and I sensed its great importance.

We cut the orks down. A few escaped. They tore off on their warbikes, filling the air with their guttural curses. I knew orkish. The howls were threats of retribution and return. So common that I paid them little attention.

There was one sentence, though, that chilled me to the bone. The clouds of exhaust had faded, and the way to Tempestora was clear. The battered companies of the 252nd cheered our first triumph against the enemy. I nearly missed what the last ork snarled as it retreated.

As we regrouped and moved forward again, I thought about what I had heard. I said nothing to Stahl. But Setheno saw. She always did.

'What did you hear?' she asked, keeping her voice down.

'The ork said the Prophet will wear our skulls.'

I was precise in my translation.

Not warlord.

Prophet.

# CHAPTER 5
# TEMPESTORA

## 1. YARRICK

The governor of Tempestora, Lady Ingrid Sohm, was at Volcanus, being hosted by von Strab and reassured that nothing would threaten her hive. We were met by her lieutenant, Relja Thulin. I was prepared for the worst as we marched through the main gates, into the huge, rockcrete-paved square beyond, and Thulin walked forward to greet Stahl. Setheno and I followed a pace behind the captain.

'He is tired,' Setheno said, observing Thulin.

'Yes,' I agreed. I was relieved. Thulin's robes were excessive finery, out of place in the ashy grey of Tempestora, but they were filthy. They looked as if they had been slept in. Another good sign. I took the corruption and venality of Armageddon's ruling class for granted. No honest administrator would have survived the first year of von Strab's rule. The question that concerned me was Thulin's realism. And what I saw in the thin, greying nobleman before us was a man who fully expected to die.

'You are most welcome, captain,' he said to Stahl. 'We feared we had been abandoned, and when we saw the fleet brought down…'

'The Steel Legion is a ground force, Count Thulin,' said Stahl. He gave the viceroy as confident a smile as his exhaustion permitted. 'The foe who shoots us out of the air is just calling down our anger on his head.'

Setheno's eyes narrowed slightly. The captain's bravado did not please her.

Stahl glanced up at the battlements behind us. There were no patrols on the parapet. 'What defensive capabilities do you still have?' he asked.

'Our guns,' said Thulin. 'The ones in fixed emplacements, that is. But we have no one to fire them.'

'No one?' I asked. I had hoped von Strab's mad order hadn't been followed down to the very letter.

'No one,' Thulin repeated. 'We lost the entire militia.'

Stahl winced. The twitch in his eye was subtle, but I caught it. 'I see.'

Thulin hesitated, then asked, 'The greenskins are heading this way?'

'They'll be here before nightfall,' I said.

'Will you have enough time to prepare?'

'For what must be done, yes,' Setheno said.

'Praise the Emperor,' said Thulin. 'I was…' He trailed off as the ambiguity of the canoness's words sank in. 'What must be done?' he asked, barely whispering.

'Tempestora has a hard task ahead,' Setheno told him. 'Sacrifice.'

'Sacrifice.' Thulin spoke the word as if he was unsure of its meaning, but the shape of its syllables hurt his tongue. He swallowed. 'What kind?' And then, his voice whipped away by the wind, 'How large?'

'We will have the answer to that shortly,' I said. I wanted to speak with Setheno before she announced Exterminatus for later that afternoon. The situation was desperate, but I rejected her instant fatalism and apparent willingness to throw Tempestora to the orks. Stahl looked distressed as well. He had no more illusions about the capacity of our reduced companies to hold off the orks than I did. But we still had orders. We still had a mission. We still had a duty.

Setheno gave a slight nod.

'We need to inspect the defences,' I said.

A few minutes later, the three of us stood on the ramparts, alone except for the other surviving captains. Gunzburg, Boidin and Mora were the only other company commanders to have made it through the fall of the lifters. In the east, the dust cloud of the ork army drew nearer.

'Tempestora will fall,' Setheno said.

'Its walls are strong, canoness,' Stahl began. 'Breaching them won't be easy.'

'Your lack of confidence in the enemy's means does you no credit, captain.'

He coloured. 'You have none in the Steel Legion?'

I was impressed. I had seen very few individuals brave enough to challenge Setheno's position so directly.

'I have every confidence in it,' Setheno answered. There was no anger in her voice. Only the calm of the sepulchre. 'But even without knowing the full strength of the enemy, I can see where we stand. We cannot defend Tempestora. The siege will be a brief one.'

'You are asking a great deal,' I said to her. 'You are asking soldiers to abandon their mission.'

'In the service of a greater one,' she said. 'It is Armageddon that must be preserved, not an individual hive.'

'Defeats have a way of accumulating.'

She cocked her head. 'You surprise me, commissar. Do you believe we can hold the orks here?'

'No,' I admitted. The admission caused me physical pain. I had seen battles lost before. I had been on worlds that had fallen to xenos threats or the Ruinous Powers. Each defeat was a stain on my soul, and to concede the end before the battle began was abhorrent. Every clod of earth lost to the Imperium goaded me to fight ever harder for the preservation of the whole. The word *no* was a stiletto jab to my gut. But the canoness was right. The regiment, cut in half, and then in half again, deprived of all its heavy armour, might be able to delay the orks a short while. Nothing more. I could accept the necessary sacrifice. It was the pointless one I rejected.

Setheno had spoken of sacrifice. But not the Steel Legion's. Tempestora's.

'What is the city going to give up?' I asked.

'Everything,' she said. 'You already know that, commissar.'

I did. 'Then its sacrifice must be a true one,' I said. 'One with meaning.'

If Tempestora was going to die, it would be for the salvation of something real.

## 2. BRENKEN

The outer defences of Hive Volcanus gave Brenken hope. They were incomplete, but work was progressing quickly. Count Hans Somner, the lieutenant of Lord Otto Vikmann, was a veteran of the Steel Legion, a former colonel himself. He was a grox of a man, and walked with such a wide gait that he seemed broader than he was tall.

Brenken waved to take in the network of trenches and

earthen barriers that stretched for thousands of metres beyond the main wall. 'How much of this is recent?'

'The basics were there already. Disused canals, old fortifications. But we've been working hard since the warning came.'

'At least Vikmann took it seriously.'

Somner snorted. 'I made sure he did. The old toady was swallowing Herman's swill, believe me. I just frightened him more. Told him some good stories. Voice of experience and all that.'

'I wish the overlord was open to that voice.'

'Only one he hears is his own.'

Brenken grinned. 'You aren't shy about giving your opinion. You aren't worried I'll relay it up the chain of command?'

Somner started to laugh, then broke into wracking coughs. He spat a wad of blackened phlegm and blood on the ground. He tapped his chest. 'He'll have to move fast if he wants to kill me before what's in my lungs does. Anyway, I know a real soldier when I see one. I'm a politician now, and we all have to swim in Herman's mucky swamp, but a good fight will make honest soldiers of us, wait and see. We shoot straight or we die. That simple.'

Brenken smiled, but she didn't share his optimism. She had seen plenty of corruption strong enough to survive the most unforgiving of wars. Somner's confidence surprised her. Instead of agreeing, she said, 'How close are the defences to being complete?'

'Still some work to do. Need to link up and reinforce some trenches. Some of the barriers are just dirt. We have rockcrete blocks on the way. Don't worry. We have all the workers we need. The job will be done. Now that you're here, we'll show the greenskins what it means to attack one of our cities.'

Brenken heard it this time: the brittleness of Somner's bluff certitude. He was clinging to the belief in easy victory because the alternative terrified him. He was working too hard to keep up his façade. He wasn't lying, though, at least not to her. He couldn't afford to have the slightest doubt about what he was saying.

'We'll teach the orks a few things,' she said. She could promise that much. She could not promise that six companies would be enough for more. Three companies of armour and three of mechanised infantry had raced across the wastes of Armageddon Prime without rest, crossing the Plain of Anthrand and reaching Volcanus in two days. They had seen no sign of the orks, confirming that the landing point had been far closer to Tempestora. No ork forces had yet been detected outside that hive's vicinity.

That much was hopeful. But in the first day of the run to Volcanus, the six airborne companies had gone down. Contact had been lost for several hours. She had feared the worst. The news of their condition, when it reached her, was better than the worst, but not by much. And now Somner's boasts were making her uneasy. There was a difference between determination and delusion. If Somner hadn't lost the ability to make that distinction, he was well on the way there.

'We'll set up our tanks and artillery outside the main gate,' she told Somner.

'Good, good,' the old soldier said. 'And we'll have so many guns in the trenches that we'll shred them before they even reach the walls.'

That was a good dream, Brenken thought. It was the best plan available. She didn't think it was a realistic hope.

Kuyper, her vox operator, came pounding down the path that zigzagged over the rims of the trenches. 'Colonel,' he called. He held up the handset. 'I have Commissar Yarrick for you.'

'Thank you,' she said, and accepted the unit from Kuyper. Her tone was clipped, but she was relieved to be able to speak to someone who had a clear-eyed view of where the regiment stood. 'Commissar,' she voxed, 'where do things stand with Tempestora?'

*'Not well. We have a few hours at best before the orks are at the gates.'*

'And?'

*'The siege won't be long.'* The old war-dog's voice rasped with frustration, and Brenken knew how much it cost him to admit a battle could not be won. *'What is your situation?'*

'Uncertain but better. I hope we'll be ready in time.'

*'We will buy you a few hours,'* Yarrick told her. *'Perhaps as much as a day.'* His tone was clipped, matter-of-fact.

Brenken sensed something terrible behind the words. 'How?'

*'We'll hold the orks' attention. We can do that much. And we'll bloody them too.'*

'At what cost?' Brenken asked, though she already knew.

*'Tempestora will be lost. But if its sacrifice can save Volcanus, then its fall can have meaning. Tell me you'll be ready, colonel.'*

'We will be.'

*'What about the Hive Militia there?'*

'At full strength, and Count Somner has ordered weapons distributed to all citizens.'

Somner nodded, happy to be part of the good news. The manufactoria of Volcanus produced rifles for export across the Imperium. Supplies were limitless. If the preparations could be completed, the orks would encounter a civilian army tens of millions strong.

*'That's good,'* Yarrick said.

'Commissar, is part of Tempestora's sacrifice going to be half my regiment?'

'*No. We will hold the orks, and then we will reinforce you.*'

'Even better would be to catch them in a pincer attack.'

'*That is our intent.*'

Brenken thought about how it would be possible to delay a much-larger army, and still be able to move quickly over the distance between the hives. There were many details she didn't have, and they were unnecessary. All that mattered was how Yarrick's plan would affect Volcanus. Even so, she could see the cost that would be paid. There was no choice, but they would all have blood on their hands before the next dawn. She accepted the necessities of war, but she did not revel in them. 'The overlord will have much to answer for,' she said.

'*Quite,*' Yarrick replied. He sounded as if he planned to put the questions to von Strab himself.

## 3. YARRICK

I knew Tempestora well. I knew all of Armageddon's hives. I had served long enough with the Steel Legion that the planet was the closest thing I had to a home world. I had learned from the beginning of my career as commissar, as far back as Mistral, the value of being familiar with any world to which duty called me. I knew Tempestora's geography, its industrial capacity, and its particular strengths. I knew exactly how best to kill it.

I had Thulin bring me to the northern docks. Great tankers sat in their berths. They might be useful, but I was more concerned with the pipelines. Wide enough for a Leman Russ to drive through, there were twenty of them, emerging from the Boiling Sea to then split into a network of smaller pipes. They carried the one great resource of the scorching, uninhabitable land mass to the north, beyond the sea. The promethium deposits of the Fire Wastes were among the greatest of any in the Imperium. Lines fed the manufactoria of Tempestora, ran outward from the hive towards the other industrial centres of Armageddon, or flowed to the spaceport where orbital lifters would carry huge reservoirs up to the waiting mass conveyors, which would take it out to the endlessly thirsty Imperium.

'We will have to open all the valves,' I said. 'And where there are none, the pipelines will have to be breached.'

'Ah.' Thulin's grunt didn't mean anything. It was an expression of pain. He was pale with horror. Disbelief had robbed him of speech.

I sympathised. But there was no time to manage him. If his ability to listen fled as well, I would have to make sure Tempestora had a functional acting governor.

We were standing on a pier, its rockcrete stained black. We were in the perpetual shadow of the pipelines over our heads. I looked up and traced their path back to the hive. I thought about the most comprehensive way to accomplish our ends. I had accepted the necessity of Tempestora's sacrifice. Doing so before the first shot had been fired still rankled, but there was no point kicking against reality. Having committed to this course, I would make it count. I would do whatever was necessary to give Volcanus a fighting chance. And I would hurt the orks to the greatest extent possible, by whatever means necessary.

'We'll need a greater distribution of the promethium,' I said. 'We'll need a team of welders.'

'You want to divert some of the flow from the pipelines?'

The deputy governor was articulate again. Good.

'Yes,' I said. 'To the Khatrin complex.'

Thulin managed to grow even paler. 'If we flood the water purification plant with promethium...'

'Yes,' I said. 'We'll be sending promethium instead of water throughout the hive. That is my intent, Count Thulin. That is what must be done.'

'But the damage... If it should ignite...'

He wasn't thinking clearly.

'Of course it will ignite,' I told him. 'That is the point. The damage is the point.'

Thulin stared into an absence in the middle distance. He could already see the flames. He tried again. 'The people...'

It was the first time since the *Claw of Desolation* had been detected that I had heard such a concern expressed. I tried to remember when I had last heard any politician on Armageddon worry about its citizens. I failed.

I blinked, surprised. Then I showed him how misplaced his priorities were. 'The people will be fighting, or they will be dying, and nothing that we do here will change the end result. The fate of Tempestora's citizens is secondary to the strategic situation. That is how it must be, count. I take no pleasure in this truth, but that doesn't make it any less valid.'

He said nothing. He stared at the spires of the hive, no doubt already seeing the smoke. He didn't dispute what I said. He didn't even question why a commissar was ordering him to burn the city under his charge, and why he should give my words the force of law. Stahl had command of the military operations in Tempestora. But he had looked to me when Setheno had begun to speak of the sacrifice. I did not have the seniority of rank. But I did have well over a century of experience. That came with its own weight of authority. It was not a formal one, but it was felt.

So many wars. So many sacrifices.

At length, Thulin said, 'We don't have enough weapons. Not nearly enough for the population.'

He looked at me, hoping for something. He had, in effect,

abdicated in my favour. What was coming was beyond his competence, and he knew it. I suspected that his pliability made him well-liked by those higher in the hierarchy of Armageddon's ruling class. But today that made him one of its more valuable members. If he was not quite willing to do the unspeakable thing, he was willing to let others do it.

Right now, though, he was desperate for anything at all that might give him the hope of sleeping again at night. Even if he had little hope of seeing another night.

'Tell me what you want to do,' I said.

'Order an evacuation.'

'Of fifty million people? And to where?'

'Away from the orks.'

I didn't bother to tell him that if the orks were not stopped, there would be nowhere to fly from them. In the meantime, though, that meant heading north. 'Into the Ash Wastelands?'

He nodded. 'As many as there is time for.'

I stared at him. 'Do you understand what you will be telling them to do?'

'Yes. And so will they. They will still prefer to run, commissar.'

'Very well,' I said. If we hadn't already committed ourselves to a path that meant the loss of the city, I would have given him a different answer. I would have made every inhabitant of the hive fight to the last drop of blood. They owed the Emperor that and more. But any further sacrifice there was pointless. If the people of Tempestora preferred a slower death in the Wastelands, I would not stand in their way.

Thulin was right. The word went out, from the spires to the underhive, that the orks were coming, and the decision to be made was death or flight. The choice was a false one, but I let it stand.

The Steel Legion companies spread out, at squad level, across Tempestora to oversee the sabotage of the pipelines. Some of the Tempestoran work teams resisted the destruction they were ordered to prepare. They did not accept the coming sacrifice. And the legionnaires had to move from overseers to enforcers. Setheno and I divided the key points of the pipeline between us.

We oversaw the enforcers.

I encountered the greatest reluctance at the Khatrin plant. The foreman of the shift raged against the desecration of his sacred trust. At the far end of a vaulted enclosure a thousand metres long, he stood on a dais before the primary controls, unarmed but calling a mob of workers to his side. The idea of turning the hive into a trap for the orks had no purchase for them. All they could understand was that we wished to replace the city's water supply with promethium. When I arrived, a squad led by Sergeant Loxon was positioned at the other end of the room, rifles aimed at the workers. They had not yet fired on the people they believed we had come to save.

I walked down the platform that ran the length of the enclosure. On either side were gigantic reservoirs of water undergoing filtration and desalination. I kept my weapons holstered. I strode forward in silence. I stared at the workers who blocked my path, one at a time, until they stepped aside. In a few minutes, I mounted to the dais and confronted the foreman.

'What is your name?' I asked.

Seeing my uniform, he had hesitated to launch into a tirade. My question further took him aback. 'Heinrich Groete, commissar,' he said.

'Very well, Groete. You believe in duty, I see.'

'Yes, commissar.' He stood taller. He was a big man, wide of shoulder and generous of stomach. His hair and beard were untrimmed. He was so grease-stained, it was easy to imagine he never left his domain of huge iron wheels and levers.

'I believe in duty, too. Mine is to defend the Imperium at any cost. Sometimes that cost is very high.' I spoke so my voice echoed across the space. 'The cost gives me no pleasure, but nor do I have a choice. You do, however.'

'I do?'

'You can help me in the performance of my duty. You can help fight the xenos plague. Or you can perform your duty as it has always been. To the end.'

He swallowed. 'This has been the purpose of my life,' he said quietly.

'I understand,' I said. 'I respect your decision.' And I did. But I really did have no choice. I pulled out my bolt pistol and shot him.

The other workers backed away in fear.

The ruin of the water supply proceeded smoothly.

I was fortunate that on this day I did not have to enact judgement on any troopers.

Later, as the rumble of the orks' approach grew louder, and their stain covered the plains to the east, I stood on the northern ramparts with Setheno and watched the stream of the desperate. They flowed out of the gate, their fear greater than their speed. The gate was hundreds of metres wide, and that was too narrow. The people pressed against each other with such urgency that hundreds were being crushed and trampled to death with every passing minute. The exodus fanned out across the blasted land. Marching feet raised huge clouds of cinders. The twilight into which the *Claw of Desolation* had plunged Armageddon did little to diminish the heat of the day. The Wastelands were a panorama of grey desolation.

Dunes of ash rolled towards the shores of the Boiling Sea. The accumulation of millennia-old industry had smothered all trace of life. The north-west reaches of Armageddon Prime were a shifting, smothering desert, a dead foretaste of the Fire Wastes.

'It is possible,' Setheno said, 'that the evacuation may be of some use after all.'

'They may hold the orks a little longer,' I said. There had been nothing in the Wastelands to draw the greenskins. But now there was an invitation to slaughter.

'The enemy will be amused for a few hours.'

That might help a little. I wasn't convinced it would make a significant difference. 'Perhaps a final struggle in the open will be a mercy,' I said.

'Mercy would be better earned if they ran towards the orks,' she replied.

'I will not ask that of civilians when we will be retreating.'

'Can we afford such a luxury, commissar?'

'I don't believe it is one, canoness.'

She pointed down at the fleeing hordes. Their anxious howls reached up to us. From this height, and in this light, the people were an indistinguishable mass. A swarm of frightened insects. 'Look at the weakness of their faith. They deserve no compassion.'

'They are receiving precious little,' I said.

'You think me too quick to choose the monstrous act, don't you?'

'I think we will all be forced to make that choice soon enough.'

As if in answer, the thunder in the east resolved itself into the enemy's laughter.

# CHAPTER 6
# A SMALL SACRIFICE

## 1. YARRICK

By nightfall, the orks were at the gates.

The companies under Stahl's command stood guard on the east wall. After the crashes and the fight against the warbikes, we were fewer than five hundred strong. Over the length of the wall, we were stretched thin, and our numbers seemed even smaller.

Stahl seemed very conscious of our weakness as he looked to his left and right. 'What kind of defence is this?' he asked me. 'So much of the wall is undefended.'

He was right. Our guns were trained only on a few hundred metres above the main gate. If the orks chose to breach or ascend the wall at another point, they would encounter no resistance. And perhaps they would. Their army was so vast its flanks were invisible in the darkness. Even so, their interest appeared to be the gate. 'Our defence is exactly what it needs to be,' I told Stahl. 'We don't intend to keep them out, do we?'

'No,' he admitted with effort. The nature of the operation offended the officer's soul.

'Remember what we're doing, captain.'

'I know.'

His voice sounded faint, demoralised, even though he had to shout. The clamour of the orks on the verge of attack was tremendous, a constant roar forged from currents of savagery and excitement. It grew louder by the second. There was no room for more orks to arrive, but the ones before the wall were working themselves up to paroxysms of war frenzy.

We held our fire. We would have precious little time to strike the enemy. We would make our opportunity count.

I heard how battered Stahl's morale was. I hoped he was, in the end, worthy of Brenken's trust. The war was only beginning. There were many blows to come.

Though none, I dared to hope, on the scale of the self-inflicted wound we were about to suffer.

Some distance to my left, almost disappearing into the darkness, Setheno stood motionless, a forbidding grey statue. She had expressed no satisfaction as the preparations for sabotage had been completed. Neither did she show regret for the looming cost. We had known each other for over a century and a half, and I still found myself wondering about the nature of her faith. In her youth, it had always been stronger than adamantium. But since the destruction of the Order of the Piercing Thorn, and since she had blasted all colour from her armour, its strength had been so cold I had trouble distinguishing it from despair.

Of us all, she was the one who had the most intimate acquaintance with sacrifice.

The bellowing of the greenskins changed. It continued to grow louder, and now it took on a shape. It ceased to be the roar of thousands upon thousands of savage throats all trying to shout over each other. They found unison. They chanted. The word I had first heard on Basquit resounded once more. It beat against the walls of Tempestora as if those two syllables alone could smash the rockcrete.

*Ghazghkull Ghazghkull Ghazghkull.*

Louder, louder, a chant of praise, of war, of the victory of the green tide. It hammered at my mind. It dug claws into my soul. The ancient pain in my right arm, a legacy of Mistral, began to throb with renewed ferocity. I could not shake the irrational conviction that something prophesied to me long ago was coming to fruition.

*GHAZGHKULL GHAZGHKULL GHAZGHKULL.*

The word was a sound I had never heard from the orks in a lifetime spent fighting them. I recognised it all the same. It was a sound that should never be made by these xenos abominations. It was the sound of faith.

And then it stopped. The quiet that descended was uncanny. A single ork that did not shout was far more disturbing than a thousand roaring brutes. And in this moment, all of them were quiet. I leaned forward, staring down into the night, fruitlessly attempting to see what had silenced the orks.

Then I heard it. The voice rumbled over the plain. As it spoke, it rose from a deep, guttural snarl to bellowing exhortation. This, then, was their prophet. This was our enemy. I listened, conscious of the importance of the moment, and responding to a deeper intuition that the importance was even greater than I knew. The prophet called his forces to conquest, and promised endless spoils and endless battle. He paused, and the horde answered with terrifying unity, and in their violent joy gave me the full name of the prophet.

*Ghazghkull Mag Uruk Thraka.*

I marked the name. This was our target. This is the ork we must kill, I thought.

I peered into the dark. I caught a glimpse of a massive shadow moving through the ranks of the orks. I could make out no features, nothing but a vague, hulking shape that drew the eye with inexorable gravity.

Ghazghkull spoke again, invoking the crude names of the gods the orks worshipped, and raging about a destiny of interstellar conquest. The words chilled my blood. They were not mere bluster. This ork had forged a fanatical unity in his kin. If he was not defeated here, on Armageddon, how far might his influence spread? I had a vision of a monstrous will uniting orks across the galaxy, launching a xenos crusade the likes of which the Imperium had never faced.

*Stop him*, I thought. *Stop him*.

I was the only soul on the walls of Tempestora who could understand what was being said. The only one who heard more than brute growls and roars. The only one who realised that I, too, had underestimated the threat that had come to Armageddon.

And I would still make that mistake. I don't think I truly understood just what Ghazghkull Thraka was until that day, years and billions of lives later, when he spoke to me in High Gothic.

I looked at Stahl. Though he didn't understand the full import of what was happening, what he grasped was bad enough. Even in the poor lighting on the wall, I could see how taut and brittle his expression was.

'Let me speak to the companies,' I told him.

He nodded and summoned the vox operator, Lorenz, who took me to a node next to the nearest gun turret and plugged the unit in to the wall's vox-casters.

'Soldiers of the Steel Legion!' I said. My voice bounced off the façades of Tempestora. It was loud enough to be heard over the ranting of Ghazghkull. 'The enemy is below us, and his numbers are legion. Is this a revelation? It is not. His strength is not a surprise. The surprise will be ours. Can the greenskins possibly imagine what we are about to do to them? Do you not wish you could see their brutish faces when the trap falls on them?' I paused so the troops could hear their own cheers. 'We will not end the threat this night. But the orks will remember what happens at Tempestora. They shall behold the will of the Armageddon Steel Legion.' More cheers. There was iron in them. 'Remember what you fight for: you do not fight for a single hive. You fight for the entire world. You fight for the Imperium. So fight well!'

The cheers were strong, and then kept going. I walked back to Stahl, and he gave me a grateful look. The shouts turned into jeers directed at the orks. We were mere hundreds taunting untold thousands, and that was a triumph in itself.

With a roar so huge it hit us like a wind, the orks charged, stampeding over the narrow strip of plain that separated their front lines from the gate.

'Fire!' Stahl shouted. 'All guns fire!'

The turrets opened up. Autocannons rotated back and forth, strafing the ork lines as they approached. The larger, fixed mortars and modified siege cannons fired into the main body of the greenskin army. The great cannons all fired at once, and a wall of explosions lit the night. Chunks of ork bodies flew high, and a pall of smoke and dust spread over the field.

The orks didn't slow. The gaps in their ranks filled with even more eager brutes. By the time the next round of the barrage began, they slammed into the gates. Over the howling of the infantry, I heard the buzz of more warbikes somewhere off to the north, but almost nothing in the way of heavy armour. It was as if Ghazghkull thought so little of our defences that he didn't care to commit anything more than footsoldiers to take the walls. What chilled me was that he was right.

I didn't know if the tactic was an act of contempt or a gift to the individual orks on the ground, a chance to strike the first great blow of the siege with their own muscle.

Leading the charge was a huge, heavily armoured warboss. It trampled over any subordinate that made the mistake of rushing in front. When I saw its power claw, my right arm gave a momentary throb and I pushed away the distraction of the ache. Our second volley blasted craters in the horde, but the warboss ran through the explosions without slowing. If I didn't know about the still greater monster in the darkness, I would have guessed this beast was leading the army.

The autocannons, now aiming straight down, hammered at the orks closest to the gates. The entire line of the Steel Legion fired at the besiegers. We managed a solid rain of las and bolt shells for several seconds before the orks showed interest in us and responded. A storm of bullets and rockets hit our position. We took shelter behind the battlements. Not everyone was fast enough, and a few of the more powerful rockets disintegrated rockcrete crenellations. One of the siege cannons exploded. An autocannon turret was blown off its base and fell down the outside of the wall. I hoped its gunner would be dead before he landed.

The orks concentrated rocket fire against the gates. A massive drum began to beat as explosive after explosive battered the metal. The wall shook.

We fired a third volley, and sent clusters of frag grenades sailing over the parapet. We were buying seconds. The length of time was irrelevant. What mattered was the show of force and the deaths. We needed the orks driven to paroxysms of violence, uncaring of anything except the rampage and the pursuit of their opponents into the hive. They were an incautious race, but not without cunning. Even they would be suspicious if they entered Tempestora unopposed.

So we fought as if there were a real chance of defending the hive. We drew the orks' attention to the main gate. We kept the huge mass of their infantry concentrated. That was an accomplishment.

At least it felt like one.

Streaks of fire lit the night from dozens of positions. The orks unleashed a barrage of rocket attacks. Deep booms followed. Metal screamed. The thousand-year-old gates, as thick as the body of a Leman Russ tank, fell.

The orks laughed, and though I had expected this moment, though I had counted on it, I grimaced in pain and hate as the fall of a great Imperial city began.

All the while, the streets of Tempestora ran deeper with promethium.

## 2. THULIN

The rebreather was old, and not up to the task. It was clogged with ash. Thulin gasped, his lungs clawing for oxygen. He yanked the rebreather off his head, stumbling forwards as he gagged, coughing up a soggy cud of cinder and dust.

'Count Thulin?' Countess Zelenko asked.

'I'm all right,' he said. 'Keep going.'

He was trudging across the dunes with the rest of Tempestora's nobility. The rich and the powerful looked like neither. Their robes were ragged, soiled and grey. So were their faces. Their eyes were hollows of fear. They had stuck together throughout the evacuation, bunching close during the horrific passage through the north gate. There had been no option but to use the same egress as the lower classes, and Thulin had seen many acquaintances and relatives fall during the stampede and be trampled into the mire of other victims. He didn't think any of his friends had died, but that was because he regarded so few of his peers as his friends.

There was little room for trust under the reign of Herman von Strab.

Thulin had never thought of himself as an idealist. His existence had been an exercise in pragmatism, of establishing himself as useful but unthreatening to those more powerful than he. But without his conscious knowledge, he had acquired a sense of duty. When the threat to Tempestora had become clear, his chest had constricted, pained by the danger to something he loved.

Now he had abandoned the city. He still had a duty to the millions of refugees staggering through the Ash Wastelands. But there was no way to perform it. There was no mechanism of government now. Most of the forces of the Adeptus Arbites had remained to fight alongside the Steel Legion, and those who accompanied the exodus could do little in a movement so gigantic. There was no order. There was only flight. And suffering.

The winds here desiccated and choked. They blew cinders into his eyes, his nose and mouth. Breathing hurt, and his eyes watered constantly. The land swallowed the humidity of Armageddon and radiated heat. Thulin's exposed skin was baking. His face felt as if it would curl off his skull. Every breath damaged his lungs further. He couldn't see more than a few steps ahead. The torches he and thousands of others carried struggled to pierce more than a few metres of night in any direction. They were dying embers of Tempestora's hope, smothered by the dead land.

Thulin crested a dune. He followed the slope down because the people in front of him were doing the same. He climbed the next dune for no better reason. There was no destination. The population of Tempestora travelled north, inching towards the Boiling Sea. There would be nowhere to go from there, but Thulin found it easy not to worry about the decision to be faced then. Making it that far was unlikely. What mattered was to keep going north. He and millions more were alive for now. Far behind, the evacuation continued. He did not expect it to be complete before doom struck the hive. He found that thought harder to suppress.

The Wastelands devoured the refugees. People dropped, overcome by heat and dehydration in a matter of hours. The dunes swallowed others. The ash heaps shifted according to the whim of chance and wind, and rolled over their victims, smothering them with silence. An hour after leaving Tempestora, a man five paces ahead of Thulin disappeared into a crevasse hidden by a thin crust of cinders. Thulin walked more slowly after that. He shuffled, kicking up puffs of ash. He let himself believe he would feel the void beneath his feet in time to leap backwards.

Cannons boomed. Thulin looked back. To the east, white flashes lit the wall of Tempestora. The barrier seemed very small from this distance. Yet the city was a mountain, looming so close it was as if he had been standing still all these hours. The windows of the spires were still illuminated, the lights of the hive another lure for the enemy. Thulin's eye traced the shape of the buildings behind the artificial constellations. He saw the silhouette of the charge he had abandoned.

He turned his back on Tempestora and walked on.

'What's that?' said Zelenko. She was still looking south and east.

Thulin listened. Guns in the distance, hammering the night again and again. The rumour of a multitude of savage throats. And there, coming closer: engines, high-pitched and hungry.

'Run,' Thulin said. He tried to do as he said. His legs were exhausted from hours of walking over the soft terrain of the dunes. He could manage no more. 'Run!' he pleaded with his body. No more thoughts of duty. No empathy for the millions with him. Only the desperation to break through the sluggishness of nightmare.

His fellow evacuees also tried to move faster. Most fared no better than he did. A few found the energy to lunge forward a few metres. Then the cries began. Of terror, of despair and, further away, towards the sound of the engines, of pain and death.

The ork vehicles closed in. Thulin refused to look, but he couldn't block out the sounds of massacre. At the top of the dune, he tripped over his feet and fell to his knees. He whimpered and looked back.

Vehicle headlamps and spotlights illuminated the landscape. Thulin gaped in incomprehension. He could not process the scale of the atrocity.

There were too many vehicles to count. They were battle-wagons, bristling with jagged armour. Lethal metal plates sliced apart anyone who came into contact with their flanks. Mounted on the fronts were bladed siege shields and spiked cylinders. They slammed through the refugees, crushing and gutting, raising a wake of blood and ash.

And that was not the worst. In twos and threes, and even a few groups of four, the battlewagons were linked together at the level of the chassis by tangled nets of barbed and razor wire. As the vehicles advanced, they created a line a thousand metres wide of mutilation and death. There was no escape from the absolute slaughter. The ash turned to mud, soaked by the murder of thousands.

Thulin pushed on, found his footing and stumbled down the dune. The massacre was out of sight now, but he could hear it. He could hear it approaching. He could hear his end close in.

He could run now, finally, when nothing mattered any more. The guns fell silent, and he wondered, bitterly, why he had chosen to die in the wastes. What use was the Steel Legion?

Why had the Emperor abandoned them?

A great light answered.

## 3. YARRICK

The time for retreat had come. The orks were through the gates, into the staging grounds beyond, and pouring through the streets. They were looking for a fight. Against all the urging of our training, we would not give it to them.

We retreated. We ran. That this was the plan did nothing to quell the stab of shame. *Never again*, I thought as I pounded along the battlements, heading south. We had several kilometres to cover until we reached the Morpheus manufactorum. To reach it, we had to rely far too much on luck. We needed the orks to be more interested in the city itself than their defeated opponents on the wall. We needed the right collision of violent elements, one that would give us time rather than cut it short.

Too much left to chance.

Too much shame.

Never again. Never again.

To my right, the orks rioted through the streets. They roared their challenge, and when it was not answered, they laughed at our cowardice. Glass shattered and stone shattered as the plundering began.

The entire promethium output of Tempestora's refineries had been diverted. It flowed back into the hive now, and through perforated pipelines. The crude fuel arriving from the Fire Wastes joined it. Black rivers and fountains filled the streets. Sources that should have provided drinking water delivered more of the promethium. It was everywhere, running down corridors and façades, falling in cascades from walkways, its fumes making the atmosphere almost unbreathable. On the outside wall, the winds blowing towards the Ash Wastelands kept the worst of the poison from our lungs. I hoped they would also spare us from the cataclysm. With every step, I waited for the spark.

So much reliance on luck.

It was several minutes before the inevitable happened. We had made good progress towards the Morpheus plant. The manufactorum and its environs, on the south side of the hive, was the one region we had been careful to spare from the promethium flood. We were still a distance away, but at least we had put space between ourselves and the gate.

The fire began to the north. I guessed the orks had used open flame near the north gate. There were still citizens fleeing the city. Millions still. I reminded myself that they were doomed to brutal deaths no matter what action we took. Setheno would have remarked that their continued presence in the city was useful. They gave the orks something to kill. A reason to use their weapons deep in the city. An invitation to flame.

*Whumpf whumpf whumpf whumpf* behind me. Fire exploded

into being, triggered more fire, and more, and more. Explosions built on explosions. I heard them, and then I felt the heat as the conflagration raced from its origin and reached across the city. Light came. It burned the night away. It spread faster than any being could run, but several minutes passed before the flames drew abreast of my position. Minutes that brought us that much closer to Morpheus.

The roar of the fire reached me. The city came to violent life as it died. On my right, the streets ran with liquid flame as if the upper spires had become a volcano. Fire spewed from the windows of hab blocks. It embraced the towers. It rose higher by the second. The flames reached for the heavens. They became a tortured, roaring, writhing wall. The side of my face burned with a stabbing pain.

The orks howled with rage and pain. So many were caught, so many were dying, that their cries were even louder than the rising thunder of the firestorm. We had bloodied the foe. Our first solid blow.

All it had taken was the sacrifice of an entire city.

The towers were torches now. The conflagration generated its own wind. The city was becoming a vortex, and it pulled at us. A powerful gust hit us, and the trooper in front of me stumbled. Off-balance, he was pushed towards the inside edge of the wall. I reached out and grabbed him by the trench coat before he fell. He gave me a nod of thanks. Like most of his comrades, he had pulled off his rebreather in reaction to the heat, and the fire shone in his eyes. He kept glancing towards the destruction as if it were an act of sacrilege.

'We have done good work on this day, soldier,' I told him. 'The xenos is burning.'

He looked even more grateful now, and we ran on, keeping close to the crenallations.

My lungs were burning from heat and exhaustion. They felt like bags of blood and embers. Augmetic surgery and juvenat treatments kept me in the battlefield, but I was an old man, and every step reminded me of that. I wanted to stop and catch my breath, but there would be no breath to catch. There was only the heat, and if I paused long enough, even on the wall, I would become part of the city's cremation.

Setheno caught up to me just as a massive explosion shook a spire midway up the bulk of the hive. It collapsed into the flames, its rumble lost in the roar of the storm.

'It was necessary,' the canoness said. She kept up a steady pace in her power armour.

'Yes,' I agreed, speaking between breaths. 'It was necessary. But the destruction is ours. We will carry a stain.'

'We have before. Our hands are dark with blood, commissar. That is our lot.'

'We have spread the blood widely.'

'That was inevitable.'

'Yes, but there will be consequences. We must be mindful of them. We can carry the burden. Not every member of the regiment will be able to.'

'Some will break.'

'They might,' I said.

Flames billowed close, and the heat made it too painful to speak.

We ran. On and on. Slower, the distance between us and our destination becoming greater as the fire grew stronger. Eventually none of us could run any longer. There were too many kilometres to cover, and we were trying to flee the rage of a newborn sun.

At least it was only the fire that pursued us. Our retreat from the orks appeared to be successful. There was no way to know how many had been caught in the trap. The numbers were high, to judge from the howls we had heard at the start. But what proportion of the army? And what were they doing now? The fire obliterated knowledge as it did Tempestora.

At last, the wall ahead began to curve. We were almost at the south-east end of the hive. I thought I saw darkness beyond the flames. Perhaps we were fortunate, and our efforts to preserve the Morpheus complex had been successful.

'The Emperor protects,' I muttered.

Then it seemed His eye turned from us. The winds of the firestorm spun with such violence that they formed a funnel of flame. Twisting and sinuous, it filled our ears with the din of a gigantic engine. It passed between towering hab blocks and hurled its wrath against the wall just ahead of me. It swept troopers up with fire and wind. They flew like burning angels. I dropped and rolled against the parapet. So did all the other legionnaires in my vicinity. I turned my face into the rockcrete. Setheno crouched one pace ahead, helmet on, a ceramite barrier. The heat was an agony, shrivelling my lungs. The wall was an oven, cooking me through my uniform.

The great, hollow, raging shriek of the fire vortex came closer. There was nowhere to run. There was no counter to this force we had unleashed. There was only luck now. Or the benevolence of the Emperor.

We were calling too much on his help. We were not serving as we should.

The roar came closer. The agony covered my body. The smoke had the stink of charred flesh. I could believe it was my own. I braced for the greatest pain, and my fists clenched with my own anger. My duty to the Emperor was not yet done. To die so pointlessly, with so much work left unfinished, was intolerable.

If the flames reached me, I would stand and fight. I would not die on my knees.

## 4. THULIN

He waited until he reached the top of the next dune to look back. The light grew stronger, and soon he didn't need his torch to light his way. Ahead, other refugees had stopped to stare. Even with the ork slaughter machine drawing close, they paused. When Thulin turned around, he too was mesmerised. The sight turned him to stone.

Tempestora blazed. The mountain of manufactorum chimneys, cathedrals, hab towers and Administratum spires was alight. Its entire height roiled with flame. The destruction struck Thulin with religious awe. His hand was in this horror, but he saw only divine wrath. The event was too gigantic, a single fire that burned the clouds. The shapes of the city poked through the flame, black on red, like the bones of an immolated corpse. The holocaust dwarfed everything. For a few moments, the massacre became trivial. The orks' vehicles were insignificant objects moving through a carpet of insects. The death cry of Tempestora swept across the Ash Wastelands like a great tide. It washed over Thulin and kept coming. He stared at the end of his city. The event was so huge, it should have stopped time.

But orks smashed that illusion too. The battlewagons kept coming. Their engines made themselves heard over the great fire. So did the screams of the dying. Thulin blinked as the line of vehicles crested a dune less than a thousand metres away. Their approach made no sense. Didn't they see what was happening? How could they still be intent on such meaningless carnage?

The machines came on. Unwavering, unstoppable. They were close enough now for Thulin to see the orks riding on their roofs. They shouted with gleeful savagery. And now the scything line seemed even longer to Thulin. A second tide was racing towards him, a tide of blood and severed limbs, driven forward by the wall of grotesque vehicles and an inescapable net of killing steel.

The flames of Tempestora burned higher. The city was disappearing into the inferno. The orks ignored it. Their casualties must have been high, Thulin had to believe that. He needed some meaning left to his final moments. But the orks did not turn back, and they did not look at the fire. They advanced, celebrating, as they exterminated the population of Tempestora.

Thulin broke free of his hypnosis. The burning hive receded to the background of his consciousness. The grinding machines and the sea of blood were closer yet. There was no hope of escape, no point in running, but he ran anyway. He turned his back on the ork line and fled. He moved with the current of the panic. He was surrounded by fellow refugees, and he was alone. He had lost track of Zelenko while he gazed at Tempestora. She might have been running beside him, but he didn't know and didn't look. The only thing that mattered was his own terror.

As long as he didn't look, he could believe that he would still be alive in the next second. He could believe he could keep running, that as long as he did, the battlewagons wouldn't catch up.

Shadows beside him and before him. They were other people, and they were screaming. He tuned them out. His perception narrowed to the next few metres, and then the metres after that. His world became a small portion of ash. All he had to do was cross it. He sank to his ankles in the grit. Each step kicked up more fine, choking powder. Every step felt like the last he could take. But he kept running. He would run to the shores of the Boiling Sea, and he would swim the waters, because he would never look back, and he would never cease his flight as long as he heard the terrible engines behind him.

Louder. Louder. He could hear the orks shouting to each other. His feet splashed through muck as the blood flowed past him over the ash. Louder. The engines were so close they were in his head.

He would not look back. He must look back.

But they were so loud, and the snarls of the orks were beside him now, and that could not be because he had been good, and he had not slowed down, and he had kept running, but he broke the rule and looked back now.

The shadows of mechanised horrors on either side, rollers puncturing and crushing bodies. And coming at him, so fast, the weave of razored iron.

There was no time to pray. No time to scream. But there was so much time for pain as the taut metal cut through flesh and severed bone.

## 5. YARRICK

The bellow of the vortex faded. I looked up, staring into the blaze. I only managed a second before I had to look away again. The funnel was losing coherence against the wall, the wind blowing inward to the city again. The flames lapped at the battlements, then withdrew. We stood and moved forwards over scorched rockcrete. The fiery tempest had not thrown all its victims into the air. Carbonised bodies lay in contorted positions.

More losses. This time not at the hands of the orks.

I told myself that the sacrifice was not in vain. That the orks had taken heavier casualties. That we were doing what must be done to save Armageddon.

A stretch of the Morpheus river was within the outer wall. On its banks was the Morpheus manufactorum complex. It was a cathedral of industry. A dome sixty metres wide, and one hundred and fifty high rose from its centre. Eight chimneys, almost as tall, surrounded it. There was no smoke from the chimneys, no lights coming from the open bay doors. The manufactorum had its own power plant, but there could be no reason to attract the orks. The Morpheus had gone dark shortly before the greenskins had arrived. The complex was one of Armageddon's main production centres for the Chimera. Tempestora didn't have the means to arm all its citizens, but it could provide its defenders with the means to depart at speed.

This is not a true retreat, I told myself. This is a reorganisation of the battlefield. We do this to hit the orks all the harder. The truth had rarely felt more false. It was brittle, thin. It would gain strength only if it was justified by future events.

The Chimeras were ready. Their drivers had started the engines as soon as the fire had begun. They were lined up on the bridge crossing the river and on the road leading to the south gate. We came down from the wall and boarded the vehicles. After the losses in the lifter disaster, and the warbike raid, and the siege, we finally had a gain. There were enough Chimeras available for every surviving trooper. We had become a mechanised infantry.

I spoke to the companies over the vox as the armoured carriers started forward and our exodus began. I told them what I had been telling myself. I did so with more conviction. 'This is not a retreat. We have struck a first great blow, and shown the enemy there is nothing we will not do to safeguard the Imperium. Now we look forward. Forward to Volcanus!'

I rode in the roof hatch of the second Chimera. Stahl was in the lead one. He was looking back. I shook my head at him and gestured for him to face forward. He hesitated, then did as I said.

He had given the orders, but the stain of Tempestora's death was mine and Setheno's. I would relieve the captain of as much of it as I could. To command, he had to look forward. He must not let the decisions of the past cast a shadow over the choices to come.

I turned around. Setheno was in the next vehicle. She faced forward, a silhouette of dark sanctity. She was shouldering the burden of the fire as though she felt nothing. Many believed that to be the truth. I think, rather, that the burdens she already carried were so great that one more mattered little.

I watched the blaze. I took in its full enormity. I counted the cost, and accepted all responsibility. *Now that you know what it is to destroy a city of the Imperium*, I thought, *do you stand by your choice?*

Yes, I decided.

Yes. It was the only option. We had hurt the enemy. We had bought ourselves time.

But this sacrifice would not be necessary again. We had done this terrible thing to ensure the defence of the other hives.

I stared at the city I had turned into a pyre.

We passed through the gates, onto the plain. The convoy headed south towards Volcanus. A few minutes beyond the wall, we saw a single ork battlewagon by the side of the road. It was quiet, its engine off. It seemed abandoned. Our guns were trained on it, but Stahl ordered fire to be held. We did not want to announce our position by engaging in combat with an empty vehicle. We drew even with the battlewagon, and its crew appeared. They jumped up on its roof. Instead of firing, they did something far more damaging.

They laughed.

The turret of Stahl's Chimera fired its heavy bolter, splattering the orks.

Ghazghkull had struck back, and hit hard. We had burned Tempestora and thousands of his troops. He had anticipated our next move, and sent us a message.

He was amused.

# CHAPTER 7
# PRELUDE TO VOLCANUS

## 1. YARRICK

We rode hard. There would be no rest until Volcanus, and none then either. The troopers slept on their benches. Drivers took shifts. The convoy travelled without stopping. The flames of Tempestora followed us through the rest of the night and were still bright in the dim morning. Before the hive disappeared over the horizon, a cloud of dust rose next to it. The orks were on the move again. Our lead was a small one.

Setheno and I met with Stahl and the other captains in the lead Chimera. We examined the map of Armageddon Prime on his data-slate, and raised Brenken on the vox.

'How are the defences?' I asked.

'*Progressing well,*' she said.

'Will they be finished?'

'*I could do with an extra year. But they'll be as finished as time permits. Your actions bought us several new tunnels and a completed redoubt. That's valuable. You have my thanks.*' She knew there were other soldiers present, and was speaking for their benefit. '*Captain Stahl,*' she added, '*well done.*'

Mora, a florid-faced officer with greying stubble, frowned but held his peace. The rest of the officers did not react to Brenken's reminder of which captain had command. I made a note to watch Mora.

'Thank you, colonel,' said Stahl. 'What are your orders? We are currently making all speed to reinforce your position.'

The vox spat static while she thought.

'*The Chimeras will be welcome,*' she said. '*But given our casualties, we have to consider what will be the most effective use of our strength.*'

'A few hundred bodies added to the main force won't make a significant difference,' I said.

'*I'll rely on your judgement,*' said Brenken. '*Can you slow them down still further with harrying attacks? More time at this end would help.*'

I exchanged glances with Setheno and Stahl. They looked as doubtful as I felt.

'We still don't have a clear idea of the enemy's strength,' the captain pointed out.

'Beyond the fact that it is considerable,' Setheno said.

'The ork warlord held back much of his strength at Tempestora,' I said.

'*He did what?*' Brenken sounded as alarmed as she should be. '*What kind of ork does that?*'

'He is called Ghazghkull Mag Uruk Thraka,' I said. 'We would do well to remember that name. His destruction will be key to ending this threat. The danger he represents is something we have never encountered before.'

'*Then reconnaissance is our best move,*' said Brenken.

'It is.'

*'Captain,'* she told Stahl, *'learn what you can of the enemy heading for Volcanus. We'll decide on our course of action based on what you learn.'*

Surveillance meant giving up our lead. The loss wasn't a great one. We were a few hours ahead of the orks, a few hours that had no clear tactical value, and that could be taken from us if it turned out that the orks had any form of air support.

We were on the main highway linking Tempestora to Volcanus. Though repair crews worked on its length constantly, Armageddon's brutal climate and the heavy volume of traffic that normally travelled it had left its surface cracked, pitted and uneven. The flaws meant little to the Chimeras. Eight lanes wide, the road also served well for the rapid transfer of military force from one hive to the other. The orks would find it to their liking. It would be a gift to the warbikers. We abandoned it to them, pulling off onto the rough surface of the plains. We had to slow down now. The land was rocky, ridged and uneven, broken up by gullies and narrow crevasses. The orks would have no concern about excessive velocity leading to a loss of vehicles. We did.

We moved off at a sharp angle to the highway. We would need enough distance between us and the greenskin army that it wouldn't divert and wipe us out, but not so great a gap that we couldn't observe the enemy force. We were helped by the stoniness of the terrain. As sparse as the vegetation was east of Tempestora, here we were in a desert of rock, scoured bare by millennia of wind blowing over dead earth. We would raise no more dust than if we had stayed on the highway.

We kept going until we hit a wider gulley. Its banks were rounded with erosion. It had once been the bed of a wide river, gone for centuries or more, and it ran more or less parallel to the highway. Stahl sent the other Chimeras on ahead. The command vehicle stayed behind. We left it at the bottom of the gulley and climbed back up the bank. We lay prone and watched. It was morning, but it was twilight. It was dark, but the heat was as suffocating as if Armageddon's sun shone unfiltered by clouds and dust. Stahl had a pair of magnoculars. He passed them around, though we didn't need them to see when the army drew near.

The sound came first, almost familiar now: the blended thunder of engines, boots and brutish snarls. Then the army came into view. Thousands upon thousands of footsoldiers. Uncountable. A tide untouched by the flames of Tempestora. Warbikes and battlewagons, hundreds of them. Mobile artillery and other motorised weapons whose function was obscure from this distance. It was possible that they did nothing at all, or would explode at first use. Ork technology could be as deadly for the greenskins as for their enemies. But it could also be powerful in lethally unexpected ways. The horde was endless. It seemed we could stay here for weeks and never see it all, the rear guard still leaving Tempestora while the front ranks besieged Volcanus.

I took Stahl's magnoculars to focus on the leading elements as they passed us. Riding atop a battlewagon was the same warboss I had seen commanding the assault on Tempestora's gates. The beast had survived the fire, though its armour had been burned black.

'We achieved nothing,' Stahl whispered.

I lowered the magnoculars. I was about to answer Stahl when a distant shadow caught my eye. I raised the lenses again and trained them on the north-east. I was looking in the direction of the *Claw of Desolation*'s landfall. The space hulk was over the horizon, tens of kilometres from our position, and dust it had thrown into the atmosphere reduced visibility. But there was something. It was too far away for details, too far even to be anything more definite than a vague shape in the grey. I saw it again. I fought with the magnification. Stubborn, it remained a blur. But it was gigantic. And it moved. Then dust and distance hid it from view again.

'What do you see?' Setheno asked.

I handed her the lenses and pointed. 'It's gone now.'

She looked for a minute before giving up. 'What was it?'

'Something very large. The size of a Titan.'

Mora started. He peered back along the passing army. 'Nothing like that here,' he said.

'That's the problem.'

'They're still holding back,' said Setheno.

'I think so.'

'Where was it heading?' Stahl asked.

'Impossible to say. Not this way.' I shrugged.

'Then whatever it is, they aren't using it against Volcanus.' Gunzburg was grasping for hope. He was the same age as Mora, but thinner, and more worn. His family was minor nobility, enough for him to hold a product of the manufactoria like Stahl in deep contempt. At this moment, though, he seemed to have little interest in moving up the chain of decision making.

'What they have isn't enough?' Boidin asked. He was the youngest of the captains. Low-born, ambitious, he was a compact brawler. He had led his company well, but he too had been shaken by the siege of Tempestora.

'We did nothing,' Stahl said again.

'Nothing?' I snapped. 'Would you add thousands more greenskins to that mob? Is the time we held the orks occupied pointless? Your colonel's gratitude is empty? Is this what I should understand?' I directed each question to a different officer.

'No, commissar.' Stahl reddened with shame. The other captains shook their heads.

'Safeguard your faith,' Setheno warned them.

The four men eyed us both warily.

'We are outnumbered so badly that our survival alone is miraculous,' I told them.

'The Emperor protects,' Setheno said. Her cold tones made the words truth and threat.

'We have hurt the orks,' I continued. 'And now we know what is heading for Volcanus. That puts us far ahead of where we were even a day ago.'

But a day ago we had not sacrificed a city. The smoke was a huge black cloud rising in the north. 'We did nothing,' Stahl had said. He was wrong. What gnawed at me was the possibility that we had done worse than nothing.

I stamped down my doubts with the same anger I had turned on the captains. What mattered was Volcanus.

We watched the army pass for hours more, and at last it did have an end. The orks were not infinite in number. There were other forces out there, but they were heading elsewhere.

I saw an opportunity.

We spoke to Brenken again as the Chimera caught up to the rest of the companies and we continued to shadow the ork advance. We described what we had seen.

'Hit and run attacks would be pointless,' I said. 'The enemy contingent is too large for us to slow by such means.'

*'But it could be by other means?'*

'Slowed, no. Defeated perhaps.'

*'I'm listening.'*

'Ghazghkull has divided his army. Its full strength is not heading for Volcanus.'

*'What is coming is bad enough.'*

Brenken was careful not to state that we could not defend the hive. The conditions as they stood, however, were not hopeful. 'It is a major assault,' I agreed, 'but your defensive position is much better than the one we faced in Tempestora.'

*'It is,'* she said.

'We just have to hold them long enough for reinforcements to arrive. A strong counterattack, delivered swiftly, trapping the orks between Princeps Mannheim's hammer and our anvil would take out one ork army. The initiative would be ours at last. The greenskins would be forced to react to our moves.'

*'Much depends on the overlord changing his mind,'* she pointed out.

'It will require a strong voice, true. We have one now. Tempestora cries for justice.'

I hoped that cry would be enough.

## 2. MANNHEIM

The *Claw of Desolation* had smashed Armageddon's orbital defences. Some remote augurs still circled the planet, though. What they could transmit of events on the planet's surface was fragmentary. It was tactically insignificant. But the death of Tempestora registered. The fire was visible through the atmosphere as a bright red wound. Mannheim saw the picts in the command centre of the Legio Metalica. He stared at them while he spoke with Brenken over the vox. He transferred them to his data-slate and kept looking at them as he made his way to von Strab's quarters. They were an obscenity.

One that could have been avoided. They must be the goad to preventing other disasters on this scale.

He carried his data-slate because he would not allow von Strab to look away from the results of his military leadership. Mannheim knew the overlord would have seen them. But there would be refuge in a pretence of ignorance.

Von Strab had turned his throne room into a centre of operations. Lithographic tables radiated outward from the throne. Rows of pict screens had been installed on the periphery of the chamber. The hive governors were in attendance, as were the Steel Legion's regimental colonels and General Andechs. The room buzzed with debates and arguments. Ingrid Sohm of Tempestora, looking grim, was speaking with von Strab. The overlord had composed his face into a careful facsimile of sympathy.

Mannheim stopped beside Andechs while von Strab listened to the governor. The general stood beside the largest of the tables. A lithograph of the western region of Armageddon Prime glowed from its surface. It showed the latest reported position of the orks and the companies from Tempestora. The hive appeared as it had before the disaster. 'This map is out of date,' Mannheim said pointedly.

The general sighed. 'We know.'

'And?'

'No one expected anything like this.'

'We should have. Commissar Yarrick tried to warn us.'

'I don't recall his saying anything about the destruction of an entire hive by our own troops.'

'Circumstances,' Mannheim said.

'Yes,' Andechs conceded. His experience in the field was more limited than the princeps considered adequate for an officer of his rank, but it didn't take many battles to appreciate the perversity of circumstances. It usually took only one.

'Princeps Mannheim,' von Strab called out. He left the throne and walked over. 'Dark news from Tempestora, isn't it?'

He did not sound concerned. Mannheim couldn't tell if he genuinely wasn't, or was keeping up a front of absolute confidence for the benefit of the other governors. Perhaps von Strab didn't know either. Appearance became reality. The façade became the soul. Worry might imply doubt in his strategy, and that would be a sign of weakness. Von Strab had not shown weakness once in his adult life. Take note, Mannheim told himself. Be careful how you try to convince him.

'Desperate measures, I agree,' he said, even though von Strab had mentioned nothing of the kind. Mannheim hoped he could lead von Strab to a decision in such a way that the overlord believed it to be his idea. Or at least that others would. 'The enemy surprised the regiment.'

'I expect better from my officers,' von Strab said.

Mannheim fought to keep from grimacing in anger. 'So you should,' he said, half-choking on the words. 'And I have good news. The regiment has found its footing at Volcanus. Colonel Brenken has a plan that, in theory, could turn the tide in our favour.'

'Princeps, you are a welcome presence here!' von Strab exclaimed. He slapped Mannheim's back. 'Tell me more!'

Mannheim's right arm trembled. Striking von Strab would save his honour, but not the planet. His conversation with the overlord was drawing a crowd now. That might help his cause. 'Half the regiment has established a strong defensive position at Volcanus,' he said. 'The remainder is tracking the enemy's advance. The orks have divided their strength. They have left themselves vulnerable to a pincer attack.'

Von Strab nodded approvingly. 'Excellent. Precisely what I would have had our forces do.'

'I'm glad to hear that, overlord. Then shall I tell Colonel Brenken–'

Von Strab cut him off. 'To proceed as planned. Yes. Better yet, I will speak with her myself. She should know that Armageddon thanks her. She will redeem her failure with this action.'

*No*, Mannheim thought. *No no no*. The exchange was slipping from his control. Von Strab had taken the initiative, as if he had guessed what Mannheim was trying to suggest. The princeps tried to reclaim some ground. 'I will prepare the Iron Skulls for immediate departure,' he said. He turned as if the conversation were over and he had been given his orders.

'You'll what?' von Strab said. 'One moment, princeps. You have misunderstood me.'

'I beg your pardon, overlord,' he said. He looked at Andechs. 'And yours, general. It is, of course, only right that the glory of this battle belong to the Steel Legion. Which regiments will you be sending?'

Andechs coughed, buying himself seconds before an answer.

'He won't be sending any,' von Strab said.

Mannheim cursed him, and he cursed Andechs. If the general had committed to more regiments, any number, it would have been difficult for von Strab to contradict him. Did Andechs feel he owed von Strab this much deference? Was he so incapable of initiative? What Mannheim knew of Andechs' record away from Armageddon suggested he knew what he was doing in the battlefield. But so close to the reason for his elevation, he was passive. Von Strab controlled the conduct of the war, but that did not mean Andechs could offer nothing.

Except it did.

Caught between despair and rage, Mannheim played his role in the black comedy to the end. 'None?' he asked.

'I have assured the governors that the Steel Legion will stand guard over the hives of Armageddon Secundus. The regiments have their assignments.'

'But if you're right that the orks will not be able to cross the Equatorial Jungle, why keep the Steel Legion locked down?' He thought von Strab's faith in the jungle was ridiculous, but he tried to engage with the man using the terms of his flawed logic.

'The jungle will keep them from us,' von Strab asserted. 'But we must be prepared for all contingencies. The last few days have brought us some unwelcome surprises, after all.'

'Then we should surprise the orks.'

Von Strab patted his arm with genial condescension. 'And so we shall, princeps. So we shall. You said yourself that the two cohorts of the 252nd Regiment are in the correct positions.'

'Yes…'

'Then Colonel Brenken is to go ahead with the attack.'

'Without reinforcements?'

'From what you have said, her tactical situation is superb. Now is the moment to act. If we ask her to wait, the window of opportunity will close.' He shook his head. 'No, princeps, we cannot delay and risk defeat.'

The reasoning was astounding in its perversity. Mannheim felt numb as he tried to refute it. 'With respect, overlord, the orks outnumber the regiment many times over.'

Von Strab raised his eyebrows in mock dismay. 'You do the Hammer of the Emperor an injustice.'

'I have the greatest respect for the abilities of the Steel Legion.' Mannheim nodded to Andechs, as if there really was a chance he had given offence. He didn't know why he was still playing this charade. He had lost. But he couldn't retreat from any field of battle. Not even this false one. 'I respect them enough that I will not ask them to perform the impossible.'

'Are you so reticent in the demands you make of the Legio Metalica?' von Strab asked.

'I…' Mannheim began, then stopped. He had no good answer. He and the Iron Skulls would fight against all odds until they had won or had shed their last drop of blood. But the idea of defeat when he was one with *Steel Hammer* was absurd. The Steel Legion had tanks, it had artillery. It was a formidable fighting force. But there was a great difference between even a Baneblade tank and the God Machines. And the 252nd was not equipped even with the super-heavies. Courage and determination were irrelevant in the face of the numbers Brenken was reporting. Von Strab was going to abandon the regiment to a slaughter, and with it Volcanus.

That would leave Hive Death Mire. If the expeditionary force failed, Mannheim could not imagine von Strab sending any help to Death Mire. Apart from its militia, the hive would be defenceless. The orks might have full control of Armageddon Prime early into the Season of Shadows.

Von Strab wasn't finished. 'You know what you are about, Princeps Mannheim. But believe me, demanding the impossible of your troops is an excellent way of achieving just that.' He smiled like the veteran commander he most certainly was not. 'Besides, the 252nd will not be fighting alone. Volcanus is an important centre of armament production. Brenken will have more volunteers than she could possibly need.'

'Untrained ones,' Mannheim pointed out.

Von Strab shrugged. 'If they can aim and pull a trigger that will be enough.'

Mannheim looked around the chamber. Otto Vikman of Volcanus and Dirne Hartau of Death Mire were looking at him anxiously, hoping he would carry the day. But they weren't speaking up. The others were very happy to accept the protection von Strab was providing. He was turning Secundus into a fortress, and abandoning Prime. No one was going to stand up against the overlord.

'Have faith, Princeps Mannheim,' von Strab said. 'There is nothing to be gained by sending Colonel Brenken help she does not need that would reach her when the battle is already won.'

'And if Volcanus falls?'

Von Strab looked serious. 'I hope General Andechs's colonels are more competent than you seem to be implying.'

Andechs winced as any defeat that occurred suddenly became his responsibility. Mannheim was disgusted by von Strab's rhetorical strategy, but it was as brilliant as his military moves were dismaying. *You could have spoken up, general,* Mannheim thought. *Too late now.*

'But the fate of Volcanus has no bearing on Armageddon Secundus,' von Strab continued. 'I think I've made that clear.'

He had. His delusion was unshakeable. The overlord's faith in the barrier of the Equatorial Jungle was bizarre, Mannheim thought. He guessed it was a result of his refusal to conceive of a threat to Secundus. Von Strab could not or would not credit the idea of his reign overthrown by orks.

'I understand,' Mannheim said. 'If you'll excuse me, overlord.' The battle was over. There was nothing to be gained here. He took a step away from the table.

'Where are you going, princeps?' von Strab asked.

Mannheim stopped, but he answered without looking back. 'I have duties I must attend.' He had cursed Andechs. Now he cursed himself for his vague answer, and he cursed the need to give one. Von Strab was rotting the soul of every warrior on Armageddon.

Von Strab saw through the evasion. 'You aren't planning to take the Legio Metalica to Volcanus?'

Mannheim turned around slowly. He glared. 'I am.'

Von Strab shook his head. 'No. Your duty is here, at Infernus. You will stay, Princeps Mannheim. That is an order.'

Mannheim would enjoy killing him. War was a duty, not a pleasure, but at this moment he would relish the bloody execution of this ridiculous man. He entertained a vision of *Steel Hammer* unleashing its full power against a single man, vaporising him in an excess of fury. There would be enormous satisfaction in that moment.

It would also be a crime. Von Strab was unworthy. He was dangerous. But he was the ruler of Armageddon. Mannheim's duty was clear: he owed von Strab his loyalty and obedience. He dreaded the path down which von Strab had them all marching, but he could not step away from it without breaking his oaths of service.

'Let me make myself clear,' von Strab said, raising his voice to be heard across the chamber. 'There will be no reinforcements sent to Volcanus. Of any kind.'

Vikman looked ill. Hartau little better. Still they said nothing.

'I think we understand each other,' von Strab said to Mannheim.

'We do, overlord.' Mannheim tasted something unfamiliar and vile at the back of this throat. It was defeat.

# CHAPTER 8
# BETWEEN THE CLAWS

## 1. YARRICK

'*There will be no one,*' Brenken told us.

Stahl blinked. He stared at the vox unit. 'No one until when?' he asked.

Brenken laughed without humour. '*Until we have won, captain. The glory will be ours.*'

Gunzburg had stepped in as vox operator. For now, the only occupants of the lead Chimera's troop hold were the captains, Setheno and me. We had guessed we would have the need to speak freely when we heard back from Brenken.

'This is...' Mora began. He stopped at a look from me before he said the word 'hopeless'.

'It is unacceptable,' Setheno said. 'Though unsurprising. Overlord von Strab is unfit for his office and should be removed.'

The officers cringed. If they had spoken those words, they would have been guilty of sedition. Setheno's moral authority was such that her utterance had the force of holy writ.

I agreed with her. If von Strab had been in our presence at that moment, I would have acted. But he wasn't. And though Setheno could act with impunity, her legal authority was limited. She was a force unto herself. She could no more order an assassination than I could command the Legio Metalica.

But the force of her commands was dangerous. If her words reached Infernus, someone might act. 'There is nothing to be done,' I said.

'You surprise me, commissar.'

'Why? Would you have any of us break our oaths?'

'No,' she said. She did not pursue the point.

I was glad. I was the only one present who could, without rupture to the institutions of the Imperium, kill von Strab. In Infernus, Seroff could do so, though I knew he would not. Even if I were in von Strab's chambers at this moment, I wasn't sure what I would do. Regardless of the legal ramifications of his disposal, creating a power struggle at the top of Armageddon's ruling class in the middle of a war could lead to even greater disorder and catastrophe.

So I thought then. I would hold to that belief for some time to come. Was I right? I'm not sure, and it hardly mattered when I was in no position to act one way or the other. The war would reach a juncture where the desire to preserve order, an order that corrupt, was wrong. But by then it would be far too late for all of us.

We were all silent for a few moments. The Chimera bounced and shuddered over the rough terrain. We were still shadowing the ork army. Volcanus had appeared over the horizon. We were only a few hours from the beginning of the siege.

'What are your orders, colonel?' Stahl asked.

'To act as we planned. Our positions haven't changed, even if we won't have the resources we would have liked. Captain, you

*will attack the orks' rear flank. We will hold them in our defences
and wear them down until there is nothing left.'*

'We look forward to meeting you in the centre,' I said. 'With
the greenskins crushed between us.'

I had no illusions about our chances. But we would allow
the orks no illusions about our will.

## 2. BRENKEN

She could see the orks now in the weak dawn. Snatches of
their barbaric chants reached her ears. Brenken stood on the
roof of her command vehicle, the Chimera *Sword of the Wastes*.
She was forward of the defensive network, along with her
artillery company and three tank companies. Hans Somner
stood beside her.

For the moment.

His eyes were wide as he gazed at the incoming tide. 'How
many...?'

'Plenty. As ever, with greenskins. I'm sure you've fought them
during your years in service.'

'Yes. But...'

Again, he didn't finish. Brenken heard his unspoken words
all the same, *but not like this*. He was right. Most of what they
knew about the enemy was based on the reports from the
Tempestora companies, but even an untrained eye could see
that something massive was heading their way.

Brenken knew she had never faced orks like this either. With
no reinforcements beyond what she could get from Volcanus.
She had integrated the hive's six militia companies into her
infantry, and they were stationed in the trenches and redoubts.
The distribution of weapons to the general population was
still ongoing. There was a corps of volunteers standing by

within the walls. Once she had to call on them, though, the situation would be desperate.

Even so, she couldn't resist poking at Somner. His instincts for the field appeared to have atrophied since he had become a politician. His earlier bluster had withered the moment the orks had come into sight. 'Are you sure you won't join us in the charge, Count Somner?'

He cleared his throat. 'I fear I'm needed back at the wall. The people have to see me. A question of morale, you understand.'

'Of course. Don't let me keep you, count.'

He watched the enemy for a few more anxious seconds, then said, 'The Emperor protects, colonel. May he do so for us all today.'

'The Emperor protects,' she replied, regretting her jab. He was right. Though she had her doubts regarding his ability to galvanise the masses.

Somner retreated. Brenken opened the roof hatch of *Sword of the Wastes* and settled into position with the pintle-mounted storm bolter atop the multi-laser turret.

'Kuyper,' she called down. 'Get me the vox.'

She watched the greenskins draw closer, chanting and growling. Behind her and on either side, the Leman Russ tanks rumbled, the hammer of the Steel Legion ready to be unleashed. Further back, the line of three Basilisk squadrons waited for her word. The fumes of the heavy armour's exhaust stung her nostrils. It was the hard, honest smell of Imperial war.

Kuyper handed her the handset. She gave the word. 'Comrades of the 252nd,' she voxed, 'it's time to punish the greenskins' arrogance. Artillery, commence fire. Armour, advance.'

*Sword of the Wastes* and the tanks lurched forward. They

tore over the gradual downward slope. The engines sounded hungry to Brenken. There were scores to settle for humiliations handed to the other half of the regiment.

The Basilisks opened up, their barrage grouped by squadron, *buh-buh-boom, buh-buh-boom, buh-buh-boom*. Just enough of a stagger so the first squadron was ready to fire again right after the third. *Buh-buh-boom, buh-buh-boom, buh-buh-boom*. A good thunder, vibrating her rib cage with its force. The Earthshaker cannons hammered at the ground twice, first with the report as the huge shells were launched at the enemy, and then again, after the terrible whistle of descent, with the great explosions.

The blasts chewed up the leading ranks of the enemy, and the blasts kept coming, a steady rain of high explosives, the orks running into fire and smoke and earth in upheaval. And they kept running. The ork front was a thousand metres wide. The Basilisks battered the centre, slowing it. The flanks were untouched and they started to pull ahead.

That was a start, Brenken thought. A first disruption, however small, in the ork formation.

*Buh-buh-boom, buh-buh-boom, buh-buh-boom*. Relentless, punishing, the rhythm unbroken even as the ork artillery now returned fire. The blasts were wild. There was no discipline or accuracy to the volleys. There were vastly more ork guns than Basilisks, and the green energy bursts blanketed the Volcanus defence network. Brenken heard explosions. She hoped the walls of the redoubts were thick enough, and that the trenches escaped direct hits. The ork barrages missed the narrow target of the artillery line. The beat of Imperial anger continued without pause, and the two forces raced towards their collision.

'Battle tanks,' Brenken said, and they began to fire. Three companies of armour. Nine squadrons of three tanks each. Every cannon fired at once, and Brenken grinned at the devastation. The explosions were a wall of fire, their force punching deep into the centre of the ork mass. The flanks had come so far forward that they began to move back towards the centre, lured by the narrower Imperial formation. Collisions began as orks ran into each other's path. The formation's advance became more and more confused.

It did not stop, though. It was too huge.

Bullets screamed past Brenken's head. There were countless flashes ahead as the ork infantry fired on the tanks. She hunched low over the heavy bolter and pulled the trigger. The Chimera's multi-laser flashed, incinerating clusters of the foe.

Moments before the collision now. The Basilisks kept up their barrage, the shells now falling deeper into the mass of orks. An entire cohort of greenskins was caught between the charge of the tanks before them and artillery devastation behind them. Battlewagons and armoured trucks were racing forward, but they were hampered by the infantry. The orks were a mob, a pell-mell rampage with vehicles and footsoldiers arranged by chance and enthusiasm. Their vehicles were legion, but they weren't in a position to counter the unity of the Imperial armoured attack.

The ork flanks were on either side of Brenken. A confusion of anger came for the Steel Legion's tanks. But the humans struck first. Cannons blazing, the squadrons slammed into the green tide.

We will hold you back, Brenken vowed, and the muzzle of the heavy bolter glowed red.

## 3. YARRICK

Our signal was the artillery barrage. We heard the stuttering booms, and the horizon flashed with lightning. 'Now!' Stahl yelled into the vox. His cry was unnecessary: every soldier present knew what the cannon fire meant. His cry was vital: it was the call to retribution, the moment for the companies of Tempestora to restore their battered honour.

When Stahl shouted, the Chimeras halted and their rear hatches slammed down. Troopers poured out, and then the vehicles charged across the barren ground to attack the rear of the ork army. Multi-lasers lit up the gloom, attracting the attention of the orks further forward even as they incinerated the last in line.

The rest of us moved diagonally up the orks' right flank. We were the second prong of the rear attack. The tactic was a calculated risk. Rather than engage the orks from a distance, we were going to charge them. The lack of ground cover meant that even with the greater accuracy of our guns, the orks had the numbers to batter us from a distance and regain the initiative with a rush of their own. But if we hit them hard and fast, cutting their ranks, we hoped to crush a large portion of the rear guard between our infantry and the Chimeras. Then we would move forward again, destroying from the rear while Brenken's armour moved in from the front.

That was the ideal, and the last of my illusions about the realisation of ideals on the battlefield had died long ago. It was also the only option that did not guarantee disaster.

As soon as we were close enough, we started shooting. Lasfire and bolt shells cut into the orks. They now had attacks coming from several directions at once. The advance slowed. The green tide became a turbulent river. Currents swirled into vortices as groups of the brutes turned to face a multitude of threats. There was no order to their response. Disorder and anger spread. The shouts and laughter we had heard before gave way to snarls of frustration and rage. Bikes and battlewagons collided. Footsoldiers went under wheels. The confusion granted us precious seconds to draw closer. There was no cover between us and the orks. If discipline asserted itself before we reached them, they could destroy us utterly. But discipline was impossible.

The Chimeras drove into their midst, using their mass as well as their turrets. They moved dozens of metres into the mob, then turned to cut through to the left flank. Most of the orks went after the armour.

We used the time well, sprinting over the gap. The orks were so numerous and so packed together that there was no need to aim. We could sprint while firing, and be sure we never missed.

I was with the forward squads. Setheno took the rear. We split the companies between us so every soldier who tried would be able to see one of us. We were symbols. The soldiers understood what I represented better than what she embodied. By training and by experience, they feared the commissar's uniform, and knew to follow it. By training and by experience, it was the commissar's duty to inspire no less than discipline, to be the spirit of the regiment's hatred of the enemy, and to ignite the fervour to stand with the Emperor. For over a century and a half, my mission had been the perfection of the symbol. No mortal could be the ideal itself, but the closer I could reach that impossibility, the better I could inspire, and the better I fulfilled the purpose the Father of Mankind had given my existence.

For the soldiers who beheld her, Setheno was an unknown. The Adepta Sororitas were a forbidding enigma to the rank and file of the Astra Militarum. The Sisters of Battle embodied a piety that seemed beyond human, a sanctity of ceramite, iron and fire. The Canoness Errant was a further mystery, grey faith shorn of any trace of mercy, the Emperor's wrath turned frozen as the void. She did not fit into what they knew. She was a sign, a terror, an omen, and where she fought, they were driven to redouble their efforts.

Different symbols with the same result: the greater slaughter of the foe.

Setheno's power sword was a firebrand in the morning's gloom. It and her power armour marked her as an inviting foe to the orks as they responded to our flank attack. More fire went in her direction. She ran into the bullets. She was shield and sword. Fewer rounds sought out the troopers with lighter or no armour. The difference was slight but it still mattered. Steel Legionnaires fell, massive rounds punching holes through heads and limbs. The air thrummed with projectiles. But not enough. And so we reached the ork lines.

'For Tempestora!' I shouted. 'For Armageddon!'

We hit with las and bayonet and bolt pistol and sword. The impact was oblique, a diagonal charge through the sides of the orks, stabbing forward and towards the centre. Our formation was tight, every trooper fighting with comrades on either side. We were plunging into a xenos ocean and no one would have to fight alone. At each loss, we contracted, keeping our force concentrated. Our options for attack had come down to a choice of insanities. We had taken the most direct, the most satisfying. The most effective, if it worked.

Survival was not a consideration. Only victory and honour.

Captain, sergeant, trooper – there was no longer a distinction in the solid mass we had become. Our enemy was storm and wall, and whirl of ferocity and terrible density of muscle. They fought with an explosion of violence, corded arms wielding massive cleavers and axes. Even the smallest, most crudely armoured could break a human in half with its bare hands. Some of them attempted to do just that. They failed. Many continued to use firearms at close quarters. Our discipline and coherent formation meant every one of our shots hit the enemy. But the orks killed each other in their fury to get at us. They responded to our multiple strikes by lashing out in every direction. They amplified the wound.

At the centre of our formation, the specialist weapons teams moved up. Flamers washed death over the orks. Burning xenos, screaming rage and pain, were unable to retreat. Their fellows pushed them deeper into the flames. And closer to us. I breathed the sickening sweet, acrid and charcoal smell of bodies on fire. The heat was ferocious. It was an echo of Tempestora's doom. It fuelled other flames – the ones of our rage.

I put two bolt shells into the skull of a brute half again my height. Blood and brain matter slapped against my face. The ork died, but did not fall. I fired to the left and right of the body, taking down a pair of smaller greenskins that squeezed around it. Still the corpse didn't drop. I couldn't see what was holding it up. Then it was tugged away by a cluster of gretchin. It would take much to push the small, verminous creatures to the front. I hacked at them with my sword, and as the big corpse finally went down, I yelled a warning and crouched. Behind the body was the barrel of an energy cannon. The beam flashed over our heads. Searing green lit the world. The air was sharp with ozone. Dazzled, I pulled a krak grenade from my belt and hurled it at the base of the gun.

'Back back back!' I yelled.

We retreated, running and shooting. Orks rushed around the cannon in pursuit. The grenade went off, melting through plating. I could barely see its flash through the mass of the enemy. The gretchen tried to fire the gun again. It exploded. A blinding emerald lightning storm erupted. It took out another cannon nearby, and then nearby munitions. A chain reaction built, feeding on too many unstable weapons in close proximity.

So many storms, so much thunder. Justice falling on the orks.

We were far from done.

We pulled back as long as the explosion grew. I changed my pistol's clip. The instant the glare faded and the fireballs began to contract, I turned and ran at the orks once more. The cohort charged with me. I could hear nothing except blasts and gunfire, but I saw Stahl shouting, and pointing forwards with his blade. His face was contorted by a desperate, hope-filled rage.

Hope. It did not seem mad. Hundreds of orks were dead and dying before us. There were thousands more, but the gap was not filled immediately. Our blows were keeping them off balance, and now the great eruption had come from inside their ranks. More confusion, more unthinking weapons fire. All order, even the ork conception of order, was breaking down.

To the rear, the Chimeras surged forwards in an unbroken line, unleashing a massive stream of las. It burned through the orks. The enemy between our position and the Chimeras dwindled. For the first time since the *Claw of Desolation* had entered the system, an ork contingent was falling.

To the south, the great drumming of artillery and tank shelling went on. I could hear engines, and saw the shapes of ork vehicles ahead in the distance, but they were not heading our way. The ork armour was engaged with Brenken's squadrons, leaving the infantry at this end of the army alone against us. It was a mistake, and we were making the orks pay for it.

A consistent flow returned to the greenskins. They moved south. Away from us, towards Volcanus. Their rear guard was ragged. They returned our fire, but it was defensive.

We had thinned them out. Our casualties were light. We pursued.

The direction of the ork march was towards their goal. But the greenskins in our sights were not advancing. They were retreating.

## 4. BRENKEN

On the left, *Lord Marshal Berrikan* blew up. Brenken didn't see what hit it. The main body of the Leman Russ burst apart. Hurled aloft by flame, its turret flipped over and landed on top of a battlewagon, crushing the orks on its roof. *Sword of the Wastes* was close enough for Brenken to feel the heat of the blast, and hear the laughter of greenskins as amused by their own casualties as they were delighted by the human loss. Cursing, she strafed left with the storm bolter.

Before her, more and more ork armour was closing with the tanks. The infantry scrambled to avoid death by wheel and tread. Many were too slow. A few trucks and battlewagons slammed into wrecked vehicles and became stuck in a tangle of smoking metal. Warbikes circled further out, their access blocked by the heavy vehicles.

'Kuyper,' Brenken shouted. 'Give the signal. We're withdrawing.'

The Chimera jerked hard as the driver, Spira, braked, then reversed. It pulled back in unison with the tanks. The guns never stopped. Shells and las burst against enemy shielding. Another ork truck died, turning into another barrier.

Oily smoke wafted over Brenken. She coughed. Her eyes watered. She blinked away the sting and held her finger down on the heavy storm bolter's trigger. There could be no relenting now, during the most delicate stage of the manoeuvre.

The thrust into the enemy's front had been just the start, a blow to enrage. A goad.

Bait, which the orks took.

The greenskin machines battered their way through and over the wreckage. Their weapons weren't as powerful as the Leman Russ battle cannons, but the volume of their fire was taking its toll. Brenken's squadrons on the left and right flanks now concentrated their efforts on holding off the wave of vehicles as the orks attempted to encircle them. The guns roared, shooting to cripple, blowing away axles and wheels. Many of the targets were top-heavy with armament and shields. The orks drove them at such speed that well-placed shots sent them into shattering rolls.

Some got through. A truck careened into the far right of the Imperial line. The shells from its stubbers and the guns of its passengers bounced off the plating. Rising from the centre of the vehicle was an articulate crane arm. A huge spiked mass hung from a chain at the end of the arm. It swung wildly with every bounce and jerk. The truck slammed into the side of *Lord von Karden*, hard enough to rock the tank up on its side for a moment. The giant flail came down with a colossal crash. It crushed the turret and lodged itself in the tank's armour. *Justice in Hate*, to the immediate left, blasted the truck at close range. The enemy vehicle exploded, but it did not lose its grip on *von Karden*. Human and ork vehicles were locked together. *Lord von Karden* tried to pull away, but it was dragging the truck with it. It lurched back and forth, trying to shake the parasite, and meanwhile other battlewagons were closing in. *Justice in Hate* slowed in its retreat.

Brenken dropped down the hatch and grabbed the vox unit from Kuyper. 'Sergeant Eichel,' she called to the commander of *Justice in Hate*, 'what are you doing?'

*'If we can hold the enemy off* von Karden…'

'Maintain your speed,' Brenken told her.

*'But…'*

'That's an order. *Lord von Karden* is lost. Do not compromise the manoeuvre or I'll blow you up myself.'

*'Yes, colonel.'*

Brenken climbed back up top. She ground her teeth in frustration and resumed firing with the heavy storm bolter. She wished she could kill the orks with rage alone. She had hated giving Eichel that order. Leaving comrades behind while they still fought was abhorrent to her. She had no choice. Any break in the formation could shatter the whole. *Lord von Karden* was an amputated limb. The main body of the tank corps was still intact. So it must remain.

The squadrons moved closer and closer together as they retreated. Behind them, the Basilisks pulled back as well. The width of their barrage narrowed as they moved down the safe channel through the defence network. The artillery and tank shells hit in the same region, turning the gap between the armoured company and the orks into an inferno of erupting earth and flame. The destruction bought the tanks enough time to reach the channel.

The route between the trenches, mine fields and redoubts was wide enough for two vehicles at most. It appeared to run straight back towards the gates of Volcanus, but only the first twenty metres were safe. Beyond that, the first of the turns began, and the direct route was mined.

After the first sharp right, the routes narrowed still further and split. They became a maze of dead ends and choke points. The squadrons split up, tanks taking up positions in support of the earthen-and-rockcrete redoubts. The transition from assault to ambush was complex, and it had to be performed backwards under enemy fire. The channels were deliberately not wide enough for armour to turn around. Brenken had run multiple drills during the preparations, and they paid off now.

Her company moved into the defences faster than the orks could advance. The greenskins collided with each other as they drove towards the lure. The highway from Tempestora passed between two rounded hills. The mounds were hollow, the packed earth a camouflage. A crossfire of multi-lasers cut into the battlewagons. The artillery shelling fell on the same region, cratering the surface, hammering the enemy vehicles to burning scrap.

From her position behind the first line of tunnels, the Chimera stationed just behind a forward redoubt, Brenken dismounted from the vehicle and entered the fixed emplacement with her command staff. The interior was rough rockcrete slabs and packed earth. A pair of heavy bolters on tripods guarded either end of the forward-looking slit. A second entrance to the left led to the trench network. Through the slit, Brenken saw the smoke, fire and dust of the outnumbered Imperium stopping the ork advance. She allowed herself a moment of pride. It was no salve for the loss of *Lord von Karden*. But she took a measure of satisfaction in seeing how they were making the enemy pay.

Stubborn, the orks began to advance into the defences. Enough vehicles kept coming that the bombardment couldn't hold them all back. Infantry stormed the fortifications and silenced the multi-lasers. Battlewagons shouldered through the wreckage and bounced through the craters. The leading ones drove straight into the minefield. They met their end out of Brenken's sight, off to the right. She heard the mines go off in a rapid-fire *k-k-k-k-k-KRAK*, followed by a deeper blast as ordnance and fuel tanks erupted. Smoke filled the defences.

Visibility dropped to metres. The battlewagons became snarling, ill-defined hulks. Easy targets, even in the gloom.

Kuyper was at her side, vox ready. Brenken spoke to combined regiment and Volcanus Hive Militia. 'Constant fire,' she said. 'Any target, take it. Don't give them a chance to get their bearings. This is where we stop them.'

She would have preferred to take one of the heavy bolters in the redoubt, but now the reports were coming in from scores of positions, and she had to concentrate on monitoring the entire battlefield. She stood with Kuyper near the left exit, ready to descend into the trenches and move to the next command point as needed. The air stank of fyceline. It choked with dust and ash. She hardly noticed. The vox crackled with the sounds of vengeance.

The ork battlewagons had come in first. In so doing, they had crippled the greenskin advance. The heavy vehicles were now caught in the web. They could not turn around in dead ends, and ambushes destroyed the following tanks, trapping the leading ones between wreckage and mounds too steep to climb. Reckless drivers overturned in trenches. Collisions multiplied as the battlewagons struggled to manoeuvre and change direction in constricted spaces. The ork tanks became obstacles, blocking more and more of the channels towards the wall. The warbikes would have been able to navigate, but by the time they arrived, every route was now jammed solid. The bikers were deprived of speed. Bolter shells pinned them as they stalled. The infantry had to squeeze through the interstices. The mob was thinned, transformed from a flood into a stream. The militia fired from the trenches. It was the orks who were vulnerable now, exposed to heavy, interlocking las fire. The more vehicles came, the more they slowed the advance, and the infantry added their corpses to the barricades.

Brenken had Kuyper make numerous attempts before they finally reached Captain Stahl's contingent. The captain came on the vox. He was breathless, but excited. *'We have them on the run, colonel,'* he said. *'They're charging your way and we're hitting them hard.'*

'How fast?' she asked.

*'Fast. It's a job to keep up with them.'*

But at this end, the advance had stopped. The implication made Brenken grin. 'Thank you, captain.' She switched to the regimental channel to announce the news – they were doing more than slowing the orks. They were killing them.

The green tide was receding.

## 5. MANNHEIM

He knew what von Strab would say. A glorious day had dawned. His every tactical decision vindicated. The surface import of the latest vox-transmission from Brenken seemed to be in support of the overlord's position. But Mannheim knew the fluidity of war. The situation on Armageddon Prime had changed suddenly. It could do so again. The momentum the Steel Legion had seized was fragile. There was no depth to the 252nd's strength. It had suffered too many losses, and had been an insufficient response in the first place. For this gain to be real, it had to be consolidated immediately.

Mannheim ran through the corridors of the Hive Infernus governmental seat. There was no point speaking to von Strab. But there was Seroff. Mannheim had noticed how the lord commissar appeared to have the overlord's ear. The chance was a small one. It might already be too late.

The chance was still an action Mannheim could take. He controlled a power that levelled cities, but he had been reduced to irrelevance while a xenos warlord stretched his claw over the planet Mannheim was charged to defend. He had to pursue any path that might end the madness.

Seroff's staff directed Mannheim to a study. It was lined with bookshelves, and the worn spines of the volumes suggested heavy use. It was a small chamber, far less ostentatious than anything of von Strab's. Even so, it was unusual. Seroff did not quarter with the Steel Legion. There was an air of permanence to the chambers he occupied. It was not unheard of for commissars to have long postings with a given regiment. Yarrick had also been serving with Armageddon for many years. But by basing himself here, Seroff linked himself with the governing establishment of the planet. It was an effective strategy for the consolidation of personal influence. Mannheim was uncertain what value it had for the actual duties of a lord commissar.

Seroff stood on the right-hand side of the chamber. He had three leather-bound volumes in his arm, and was just pulling down a fourth. 'Good morning, princeps,' he said without turning around. He carried the books to his desk. 'What news?'

'The attack is going well for the moment.'

Seroff looked up. He smiled, and Mannheim thought he looked genuinely relieved. 'I'm glad to hear it. Very glad.'

'You and I both know how tenuous such progress can be.'

'True.'

'Then will you speak to the overlord? He must be convinced to reinforce the 252nd's efforts.'

Seroff hesitated. He drummed his fingers on the top book of the stack. 'You think he'll listen to me?'

'More likely you than anyone else, as far as I can tell.' Why that was, Mannheim could not guess. He didn't care about the reasons today. What mattered was the result. 'This isn't a question of the loss of a single hive,' he insisted. 'This could be a turning point. If we act now, we might secure Armageddon.'

Seroff nodded, and Mannheim's hope flared. 'Does this request come from Colonel Brenken?'

'She has been asking for reinforcements since the beginning. What she and Yarrick have accomplished is miraculous, but–'

'Yarrick?' Seroff interrupted. 'He survived Tempestora?'

'He did.'

The temperature in the room plunged ten degrees.

'I'll speak with Overlord von Strab,' Seroff said. 'I think that you overestimate my ability to persuade him, though.'

'Thank you for trying,' said Mannheim.

Seroff was lying. The words were hollow platitudes designed to satisfy Mannheim and send him on his way. Mannheim was sure that Seroff had been on the point of agreeing with him. He was an intelligent officer. He couldn't have had any more confidence in von Strab's conduct of the campaign than Mannheim did. Yet at the mention of Yarrick, the about-face had been instantaneous.

Defeated again, Mannheim left. Under his breath, he uttered a prayer for the 252nd and for Armageddon.

## 6. SEROFF

The books were treatises on loyalty, honour and sacrifice. These subjects had been robbing Seroff of sleep again, and he had turned to the wisdom of saints for help. He needed support for his decisions. They were correct. They had to be. They placed him opposite Yarrick.

Loyalty. Honour. Yarrick had betrayed both. Which made sacrifice necessary.

Seroff sat at his steel desk long after Mannheim had left. The books remained stacked, unopened. He stared at his folded hands. For the hundredth time, he worked through his choices. He had been truthful with von Strab when he had recommended authorising Yarrick's deployment to Armageddon Prime. He knew what Yarrick was worth. When it came to loyalty, nothing. In the field, much. The limited deployment was a mistake. Yarrick's skills could help mitigate it.

When he had heard of the double disaster of the airlift and Tempestora, he had presumed Yarrick was among the casualties. He should have known better.

And now? Was he letting his hatred for the commissar cloud his judgement?

Where did his own loyalty lie?

It lay with the memory of the great man Yarrick had betrayed. The official memory of Simeon Rasp was a travesty. The lord commissar deserved better from the Imperium and from the officers he had guided.

And his loyalty lay with Armageddon. He believed this to be true. Perhaps he should have tried to convince von Strab to send more regiments to Tempestora and Volcanus. 'Pointless,' he murmured. Von Strab's mind was set. The overlord was a contradictory mix of overconfidence and paranoia. He believed the orks could never touch Secundus, yet he barricaded all the hives this side of the Equatorial Jungle with troops. He was contemptuous of the orks, yet he retreated into a defensive mode. Pointless to try to shift that kind of a mind.

Pointless.

Just as it was pointless to attempt to reinforce Brenken at this stage. The 252nd would stand or fall on its own merits before any help arrived.

He had made the right decision. His judgement was sound. He had no cause to question his motives.

Even so, he pulled the books towards him. He began to read, seeking reassurance from the long dead.

## 7. YARRICK

The victory fever spread. Even those who weren't near the vox could see the difference we were making. We were driving the infantry forwards into a hell of paralyzed armour. Our pincer attack should never have worked. But it had.

We were marching in line with the Chimeras now. We were running to keep up with the armour and the retreating enemy. We had been fighting for hours now, but the troopers around me showed no signs of exhaustion. Their body language was one of exhilaration. They tasted the blood of the enemy. If the orks had not feared the masked face of the Steel Legion before, they would from this day forward.

That was what I told the troopers around me. That was how I fired their ardour even higher. That was what I wanted to believe.

The faster we moved, the more uneasy I became.

I kept firing, but I glanced around for Setheno. She had walked fifty metres to my right. I moved to join her, still shooting, still killing the enemy. The orks' return fire was becoming more and more haphazard as they focused all of their attention on the obstacles ahead of them.

Setheno turned her head towards me. The howling visage on her helmet felt like an answer to my question before I spoke. 'The numbers are wrong,' I said.

'This is not a force on the same scale as the one that took Tempestora,' she agreed.

We would never have been able to whittle that army down as quickly as we did this one.

Yet the army we had been shadowing had been huge. Its length had never diminished. It was only now that it seemed diluted.

Where had the rest of the orks gone?

As soon as I asked myself that question, others arose. It wasn't just numbers that were missing. I knew the greenskin's habits, his foul beliefs, and his way of war. The makeup of the army was wrong. There was not enough variety. The vehicles and energy cannons, and the desperation of our charge had distracted me from this critical truth. The infantry was weak by ork standards. It was composed entirely of the lower castes. Their leaders, though large, were fewer in number than they should have been, and their armour was lighter, less elaborate, less adorned than that of the powerful bosses. Their weapons were mundane.

'Where are all the warbosses?' I asked.

Setheno's helmet turned my way again. She said nothing. I had conjured a shadow too great for an answer.

Still moving forward, I looked behind us. The summoned shadow was approaching.

Looking through my magnoculars I saw a second ork force approaching. It was far enough away that its clamour was obscured by the din of the one we were pursuing. It was eating up the distance quickly, though. Already I could make out some of its shapes. There was no mistaking its nature.

More battlewagons, much larger than the ones Brenken was fighting. Waves of them, stretching out of sight in either direction, an engulfing sea of metal great enough to encircle the hive. Marching with the vehicles were footsoldiers of a very different order. I saw the bulk of heavy weapons and the silhouettes of monsters, their outlines made even more massive and angular by plated armour. Warbosses at last. The infantry had its leaders.

And further back came other shapes, wider than the battle-wagons, towering over the battlefield, rocking back and forth with the slow steps of giants. A hell of myth and iron was shambling towards Volcanus.

We had not caught Ghazghkull in a pincer attack. He had caught us.

# CHAPTER 9
# THE ANNIHILATION BRIGADES

## 1. YARRICK

I heard Ghazghkull's laughter as we ran. It did not resound from any one throat. It was forged from every voice of the hundreds of thousands of orks heading our way, and from the rumbles of every engine of the uncountable vehicles, and from the vibrations of the earth beneath our feet as it trembled under the tread of the invader. It was the sound of an army, but it was still the laughter of a single being. Ghazghkull was laughing at his great joke. He had fooled the weak humans. He had done more than turn the tables on us. He had given us hope. Deliberately. So he could have the pleasure of snatching it away. The move had cost him troops, and the sacrifice meant as little to him as Tempestora was traumatic for us. This was the message: our great sacrifice had meant nothing, while his minor one would tear us apart.

I knew these things with absolute certainty. I knew this was more than just a devastating counter-move, one too far-sighted for any ork. As terrible as that fact was, there was also the laughter. Ghazghkull was playing with us.

How did I know this? It was more than an instinct, more than a hunch. I had studied orks for much of my life. I understood their ways, and the way they thought. Ghazghkull broke from any pattern I had ever encountered. But in breaking from the pattern so radically, he taught me something. I was doing more than realising the danger he presented. I was getting to know the mind of the enemy.

There was value in that. Though I was barely conscious of it as we fled from the advance, and the information would have value only if I survived to put it to use. There was no dignifying what we were forced to do with the word *retreat*. It was flight, pure and simple. There was no dishonour in it because there was no choice. But there was still humiliation. We ran as if from a mountain collapsing into a valley. To pause before the avalanche would mean being crushed beneath millions of tonnes of rubble. To hesitate before the orks would mean the same obliteration.

We pulled away from the retreating ork cohort. We ran in a rough parallel to the advance, rushing for the trenches around Volcanus. The Chimeras did not react at once. They continued to fire on their original targets. Their drivers and gunners did not know what was closing in from the rear.

I found the vox operator. Lorenz was running a dozen metres behind the rest of Stahl's command squad. 'Warn the Chimeras,' I told her. She nodded and voxed the alert without breaking stride.

The effect was immediate. Multi-lasers still blasting the enemy, the vehicles began to move our way. Their rear hatches opened, ready to retrieve us while still in motion. Stahl saw what was happening and waved the companies to the Chimeras.

The air screamed. The green blasts of the ork artillery hit the armoured carriers. The barrage fell on a large area to our left. We were blinded by an emerald storm, deafened by explosions and the crackle of energy. Shock waves knocked soldiers off their feet. I blinked away the dazzle. When my vision cleared, the Chimeras were melted slag.

The companies had escaped the worst of the destruction. We had lost a few more troopers, the ones nearest the blast zone. The others were staggering, stunned by impact and loss. We were losing precious moments. An immense xenos force was coming closer, and we were inviting obliteration from another artillery salvo. 'Come with me,' I told Lorenz. I raised my blade high and strode through the soldiers towards the front. 'I am not done with the greenskins!' I shouted. 'I will fight them yet, and I will find the means to do so! They lie ahead of us, in the trenches and beyond the city gates.'

Only the troopers nearest could hear me, but I was visible to the others. I gave them the image of a warrior advancing, not retreating. A lie covering a truth. We were in flight, but we had to survive if we wanted to strike back.

The lying truth worked. The Steel Legionnaires rallied. They followed me. I picked up the pace. Once again we were gaining distance on the withdrawing orks. I kept my sword high. Lorenz kept pace. I looked at Stahl. He was as focused on the run as any of his troops. He was leading only in the sense that he was in front.

'Captain!' I called.

He glanced my way quickly, a minimal acknowledgement.

'The colonel must know,' I said, giving him the chance.

He took several more steps before reacting. Slow. And I shouldn't have had to prompt him. But he did what was necessary. 'Vox the colonel,' he told Lorenz. 'Let her know we're coming. We need a way in to the defences.'

'Sir,' Lorenz responded, and did as ordered.

I had some doubts about Stahl's leadership. Nothing critical yet, and the other captains weren't shining any more brightly. The situation didn't permit much. But more was always expected of officers. I had never seen Brenken falter in this way.

Behind us, the rumble of the ork army pursued us. The land groaned beneath their treads and boots. The wall of sound came closer, but need gave us speed. After that first salvo, the ork artillery launched its blasts further ahead, targeting Brenken's guns.

At last we saw a flare, before us and to the right. There was a pause, and then two more. Brenken's signal to us. It pulled us forward, gave us energy and the closest thing to hope still possible on this battlefield. Another few hundred metres, and we were at the beginning of the defence network. The flares had come from a camouflaged redoubt. It appeared to be a low earthen barrier, running east and west, for at least a kilometre in either direction. A door had opened in its face. Through it was a short ramp down to a tunnel. A sergeant was waiting at the door, directing us east. I waited with the sergeant while the rest of the companies rushed in. Setheno was among the last to arrive. When she was through, two troopers used plasma cutters to fuse the door shut.

'Colonel Brenken is moving operations back towards the wall,' the sergeant said.

'A fighting retreat?' I asked.

'Yes, commissar, for as long as possible, the colonel says.'

*That won't be long,* I thought. What I said was, 'Good.'

As we hurried along the tunnel, Setheno said to me, 'You know what is coming.'

'I will not accept it.'

'You will not be given a choice.'

'We sacrificed Tempestora to preserve Volcanus.'

'That was always a faint hope. With no reinforcements, it is impossible.'

'You think Brenken's requests have fallen on deaf ears.'

'Don't you?'

I did. 'The Hive Militia is here,' I said. 'And an armed population.'

'Will that suffice against what approaches?'

'It will have to.'

'Your determination is admirable, commissar. It is also misplaced.'

'Is it?' I asked her. 'If Volcanus falls, then the loss of Tempestora has no meaning. What purpose did our actions there have? And if we cut our losses here, what then? Shall we do the same with Death Mire? And then Infernus? Hades? Acheron? Where do we make a stand?'

'Von Strab has prevented us from doing so here.'

I snorted. 'His strategy will prevent us from doing so anywhere. I will not surrender this time.'

'The hive is already lost.'

'I will not surrender.'

'So you do not disagree.'

I couldn't. That changed nothing. I had my fill of defeat. 'I must fight,' I told her.

'As will I. But when the end comes, how will we use it to save Armageddon?'

I didn't answer. If I did, I would already have given up on Volcanus. I had not. I would make the orks bleed for every stone they claimed of the city.

\* \* \*

## 2. VON STRAB

He could speak more freely with Seroff than with any other soul on Armageddon. More freely. That was not the same as being free. He was still careful. He didn't trust the lord commissar. He would never tell Seroff anything that might appear as a weakness. But von Strab found a kinship in the other man, even if Seroff would deny its existence. Von Strab recognised obsession and ruthlessness. They were good qualities. Worthy of respect. He and Seroff could discourse, if not as friends, as two men who understood each other.

They did so now, walking the hall towards the throne room. 'Can they hold?' von Strab asked.

'No,' said Seroff.

'You're certain.'

'You've seen the same reports I have. Armageddon Prime will fall.'

'I thought preserving morale was one of the duties of the commissariat,' von Strab joked.

Seroff ignored him. 'The greenskin threat is severe,' he said. 'Greater than any of us suspected.'

'Even Yarrick?' The old commissar had been tiresome in his predictions of doom.

'I believe so.'

'Then it's a good thing we held back the greatest part of the Steel Legion's strength.'

'The orks will cross the jungle.'

Von Strab sighed. 'None of you will be satisfied unless that actually happens, will you?'

They had almost reached the doors to the throne room. Two guards stood ready to open them. Von Strab paused. He smiled. Never show weakness or uncertainty. Even in situations where only the mad remain confident. The appearance of insanity was another weapon. It created uncertainty in others. Threw them off balance. *Do you know the secret to my long reign?* von Strab was tempted to ask Seroff. *It's very simple: all you have to do is be the only certain human being on the planet.* But the secret was too precious to share. As precious as the other secret he had begun to think about. A much more concrete secret. So he said, 'Lord Commissar Seroff, I do know what I am about. Trust me when I tell you that the only mistake made has been by the orks in invading Armageddon.'

'You know something I don't.'

'I do.' He turned from Seroff and walked the rest of the way to the door. Seroff took the hint and headed off. The guards opened both doors at once, then closed them behind von Strab.

Today, as he had commanded, none of his retinue was in the throne room. It was empty except for the lone tech-priest. Enginseer Alayra Syranax stood motionless, facing the throne, as if waiting for von Strab to materialise in his seat. Her servo-arms were folded against her back, iron insect limbs at rest. Von Strab walked past her and mounted the throne.

'Well?' he said.

Syranax raised her head. There was no flesh visible beneath the hood of her robes. The faceted lenses that had replaced her eyes clicked as they focused on him. The cluster of mecha-dendrites that coiled from the lower half of her skull flexed, stirred by mental impulses. Her voice was an electronic construct, toneless, grating, rusty from disuse. 'The vaults have been opened,' she said.

'The measures will be ready?'

'Ready,' she repeated. 'The term is imprecise. Will you define a time frame?'

'No. How soon can they be deployed?'

'Once proper testing, rituals and triage have been completed–'

He raised a hand, cutting her off. 'Your precautions could take years. That is not what I asked.'

In the silence that followed, it seemed to von Strab that he could hear Syranax thinking. Her frame hummed as circuits opened and closed, and servo motors adjusted to minute shifts in her position. 'Implementation is conceivable within one hour of your command,' she said.

Good. Von Strab settled back in the throne. *You know something I don't*, Seroff had said. Von Strab chuckled. *Very true, lord commissar*, he thought. *Among other things, I know that I can end this war in an hour.*

## 3. YARRICK

Many of the trenches were blocked. They were filled with ork bodies and wrecked vehicles. Even so, we could still travel the defence network. The cumulative work of centuries and the hurried additions of the last few days had created a system both complex and flexible. Enemies trying to use the trenches would be lost in the maze of dead ends and branches. Tunnels ran within the earthworks and underneath the trenches. As the orks had moved deeper and deeper into the defences, Brenken had broken down the Steel Legion and Volcanus Hive Militia companies to the squad level, then unleashed them in the warren. The force was mobile, fluid. Wherever the orks tried to make headway, a counterattack hit them from out of nowhere.

The strategy had eroded the first wave of orks. It would not be able to counter what was coming.

Brenken was still in the forward command redoubt when

Setheno and I reached it. From the bunker's viewing slit, we could just make out the front of the coming wave. 'Is it as bad as it looks?' Brenken asked.

'Worse,' I said.

'They will surround Volcanus,' Setheno added.

Brenken nodded. 'I thought as much.'

'How much are you pulling back?' I asked.

'I had hoped to slow them down,' she said. 'But if they can approach from all sides, there's no chance of that. We need to concentrate our strength.'

'Everyone, then,' I said.

'Everyone.' She shook her head. 'If we had reinforcements coming, we might try to slow them down.'

'Then von Strab said no.' I had expected this. I would have been shocked to hear otherwise. Even so, I felt a new flare of anger.

'Our battles are being chosen for us,' Setheno said.

'This one is not done, canoness,' Brenken told her.

'If we engage in futility, we risk still greater losses.'

'This is not Tempestora,' Brenken insisted. 'We have resources.'

'The population of Volcanus will fight,' I said. A way forward became clear. I knew where my immediate duty lay.

'The longer we fight, the better we will be able to measure the strength of the enemy,' Setheno conceded.

'We will do more than that.' I would not be satisfied with such a paltry victory. Setheno spoke from her position of terrible clarity, not pessimism. Even so, I was determined to challenge the doom she saw coming. 'We have defeated the impossible before,' I told her.

'Yes. But not always.' I saw the pain that flickered through her gaze. It was quick, a fracture that came and went in a blink. I doubt anyone else would have seen it. But I knew its source.

I too remembered the Order of the Piercing Thorn. I remembered her battle sisters. I remembered what had happened.

She was right. Sometimes the impossible was impossible.

'Not always,' I agreed. 'But I will fight for it.' I turned to Brenken. 'We can't slow the greenskins…' I began.

'But we can hurt them,' she finished.

A fighting retreat, then. It involved minimal delay. The orks were minutes away from the outer rings of the defences. It was a question of balance: holding back just enough troops to strike from the tunnels and trenches, and knowing when to pull back completely. We would stab at the belly of the enemy as he advanced. We would make him pay for every metre. Even though the ork force was too vast to slow, we could wound its core. Every blow we landed would count. Every dead ork, every ripple of confusion we could spread through the xenos ranks.

I was thinking in terms of a war of attrition. I was right to do so. But the full truth of that form of struggle was yet to come. Ghazghkull was set on denying me that contest here.

The front ranks of battlewagons hit the defences. Within seconds, they reduced our strategy to ash. Their massive siege blades and battering rams shattered the walls of the redoubts. They hit the earthen barriers with enough force to scrape the ground clear and hurl the debris into the trenches behind them. A huge dust cloud erupted at the edge of the network. The ork engines screamed, pouring more power into the hulking machines. The battlewagons bulldozed their way forward. Through the slit, I could just make out their shapes in the dust. The vox erupted with cries of alarm.

Brenken seized the handset. 'To the wall!' she ordered. 'And hurt them as you go!'

We left the bunker. The rear hatch of *Sword of the Wastes*

was open, the Chimera's engine idling and ready for departure. 'We'll need all the armour we can salvage,' Brenken said.

'Your driver has the skills?'

'She does.'

'Then we'll meet again beyond the walls,' I said. Brenken was needed in Volcanus to hold what strategy we still had together. My place was with the troops.

Brenken nodded. She and her command squad boarded the Chimera.

Setheno and I ran past the tank and dropped into the trench a few metres beyond.

We became a part of a flow of rats. I saw no shame in the comparison. We kept low, we were fast, we survived, and we bit. Squad structure still held. Fire discipline was solid.

The roofs of the tunnels shook and dropped dust as the ork armour thundered overhead. When we were in the trenches, we were rushing through canyons whose cliff faces were moving iron. We did what we could. Heavy weapons teams launched rockets at the battlewagons. The troopers who still had krak grenades tossed them at the wheels and treads. We killed some vehicles, and immobilised others. There was still some infantry from the first cohort that hadn't been destroyed by the initial defence. We killed some of these footsoldiers, but more we had to ignore. Three quarters of the way through the warren, in a trench between two tunnels, I stopped a squad from shooting at a cluster of orks running on the ground ahead of us. They had their eyes on the walls of Volcanus, and weren't looking down.

I seized the sergeant's arm as he was about to give the signal to shoot. Startled, he whirled on me, then stumbled back a step when he realised he had almost struck a commissar.

'Too many,' I said. 'We don't want them in the tunnels with us.'

We could damage vehicles without slowing down. Pitched infantry battles would keep us from the walls, where we would be needed soon enough. I could hear the scream of las and the rattle of ork stubbers some distance from our position. The greenskins were into the network already. I had to hope they hadn't infested it.

Sometimes, small hopes are met. We had a clear run the rest of the way to the wall. Setheno and I were among the last of the troops to make it through before the narrow passages through the rockcrete were sealed. There were still troops out there, and they were fighting. But because they would not make it to the wall before the main force of the orks, now they would never reach Volcanus at all.

The hive was like all the others on Armageddon in that it was as dense with industry as it was with inhabitants. Millions lived to toil, but their toil shortened their lives. The air was filled with toxic grit. Where the atmosphere of Tempestora had been harsh with the stench of promethium, Volcanus was overheated by the abundance of its forges. Its particular specialty was guns – everything from small arms to artillery, lasrifle to Earthshaker. The rockcrete of its walls was stained like those in Infernus, and Tempestora, and Hades. Its gutters ran with the half-molten detritus of the city's production. The streets were narrower than those of Infernus, and the arches higher. Flying buttresses soared from chapels, habs and manufactoria. The density of construction was such that it was difficult to determine which support was part of which building. The honeycomb of walkways further fused the structures together. The hive was a dense maze in three dimensions. Its character might be an advantage.

Most of the regiment's battle tanks had completed the retreat. After the few Chimeras that could be salvaged had arrived, the main gates were shut and reinforced. The barrier was strong. If Volcanus withstood the siege, it would be no small task to open those gates once more. Brenken deployed troops along the ramparts to every point the orks were approaching. The arc of the siege extended over almost a third of the circumference of Volcanus. When Setheno and I joined Brenken above the main north gate, the army stretching left, right and before us appeared infinite.

The minefields were minor irritants. Ghazghkull had so many vehicles that the orks simply rode through the traps, losing as many tanks as it took to clear the explosives. We made sure he lost many. Now positioned on the inside of the wall, the Basilisks added their cry to that of the rampart guns. Shells blanketed the land before Volcanus. Fire and explosions wracked the battlewagons, but the orks continued the operations without pause. The tanks shrugged off all but the most direct hits by the biggest ordnance. They advanced at full charge, destroying obstacles, levelling the terrain.

The advance was relentless. It was also selective. The bulk of the army, a sea of giant shapes and swarming troops, waited beyond the outer defences. For now, the orks attacked the defences with obsessive purpose and alarming specialisation. The battlewagons carrying out the demolition were not troop carriers. Their reinforced armour, their siege blades and their rams made them perfect for this goal. They drew fire and they resisted it. Few of our salvoes reached to the rest of the army. We had no choice but to concentrate on the immediate threat.

'We're doing exactly what they want us to do,' I muttered.

Brenken gave me a sharp look. 'Orks with strategy?' she asked, sceptical.

I pointed. 'The evidence of your eyes, colonel. They're using a specific tool for a specific job.'

As the battlewagons drew closer to the wall, ork footsoldiers moved in behind. Red icons in the crude likeness of a horned bull rose from the black plates of their armour. They wielded flamers. Hundreds of jets of flame pierced the gloom. The orks were purging the trenches.

I swept my gaze over the panorama of eruptions, demolition and fire. And in the distance, the greater strength of the army waited for the first act to be completed. 'They're levelling the ground,' I said.

'And losing armour.'

'Not enough, and they have plenty to spare. They're preparing the terrain for something. When have you ever seen orks mount a siege like this?'

'Never,' she admitted.

I couldn't guess what was coming. I knew it would be devastating. We had limited time to prepare, and doing so involved more than physical reinforcement of the wall. I would prove Setheno wrong. I refused to concede to the inevitability of the hive's doom. But sooner or later, the orks would breach the walls. We had to be ready for that.

'Where is Somner?' I asked.

'Overseeing the distribution of weapons,' said Brenken. 'Getting ready to address the people too, I would think.' She directed me to the Kasadya complex, a manufactorum a kilometre uphill from the main gate. I moved as quickly as I could through a dense crowd of armed civilians. They were pouring out of the bay doors at the base of the building. It was one of the main production sites of lasrifles in Volcanus, and a massive storehouse. Across the hive, the scene was being repeated. The entire population had been mobilised. There hadn't been time in the few days since the start of the crisis to arm every citizen, but millions had been. Many had never held a gun before, though the more desperate knew their way around weapons. I found myself hoping that the dwellers of the underhive had been among the first to reach the armouries, and that they had not been turned away. They had no love for the authorities of Volcanus, but they would have still less for the invader.

The crowd parted. My uniform drove a wedge of fear before me. I reached the base of Kasadya. The aquila spread iron wings fifty metres wide above the vaulted doorways. From the roof, between smokestacks, rose a Departmento Munitorum tower. A wide balcony jutted out, supported by the aquila's heads. Hans Somner stood there, arrayed in the finery of the nobility, now adorned with his medals and seals of service. With him was a tech-priest who was making adjustments to a bank of devices set up on the right side of the balcony. As he worked, feedback whines echoed in every direction.

A mass vox-caster. Good.

I made my way through the frenzied activity in the Kasadya complex and up the tower. The tech-priest had finished as I arrived on the balcony. He stood to one side, servos clicking. Somner was motionless. I thought he was staring at the vox unit on the stand before him. When I reached him, I realised he was gazing beyond the wall at what was coming. The wall seemed smaller from this perspective. Weaker. The ork horde was a massive claw making ready to crush Volcanus.

Somner looked at me. His lips pulled back in a rictus. 'I can't find the words,' he said. The admission was code for a greater failure. He was cracking. The hive was his responsibility. He retained enough instincts from his days as an officer to know his duty, and to realise he was failing it. 'Will you speak?' he asked.

He was ceding his authority to me. Whether that was an act of dereliction or realism was not something I had to decide on at that moment. I gave him a curt nod and took his place.

'Citizens of the Imperium,' I said. My voice, amplified by thousands upon thousands of vox-casters in every corner of the hive. Below, I saw the crowd look my way. 'Today you are the defenders of Volcanus. Today you become heroes of Armageddon!' The cheers began. 'I am proud to stand with you. The Steel Legion is proud to stand with you. You stand with the Emperor, and you will hurl his anger on the heads of the xenos foe.' A great shout answered. For a brief moment, it drowned out the artillery. 'The greenskins dare to set foot on this ground? On a single stone of Volcanus? Will you show them the scope of their folly?' Another shout, louder yet, a massive YES that rolled up the sides of the buildings, a wave ready to sweep away the orks. 'Every street!' I shouted. 'Every doorway! Every window! Every roof! There we will be, with our guns and our wrath. The orks will pay with their blood for every step they take!' I paused. 'I call on you now! By will, by flesh and by faith, transform Volcanus into a great weapon of war! Make it the death trap that ends the arrogance of the greenskin forever!'

The shout, the roar, the wave rose past me. It climbed to the dust-laden clouds. It was a determination born of fear. It was a collective strength forged in a desperate search for hope. The people of Volcanus would fight. They had no choice. But they had each other. And they had weapons.

If there was to be sacrifice here, it would be in battle.

The shout faded, and so did the sounds of battle. Our cannons did not let up, but the ork battlewagons were withdrawing. They pulled back to the edge of the defences.

'We haven't beaten them,' Somner said, hoping I would contradict him.

'No,' I said. The prologue was done, that was all.

For the space of one long breath, the ork army was motionless. Then its war beat began once more. Hundreds of engines snarled with growing anticipation. The earth began to shake with the pounding of monstrous footsteps. The high shadows I had seen before gathered definition as they moved forward and began their ponderous advance towards the city wall.

Stompas. Clanking, grinding embodiments of ork aggression, grotesque expressions of their unholy faith, belching smoke and fire. They were twenty metres tall, and they were squat and wide. They had none of the majesty of Titans, but as they marched, the air cracked with terror. They were taller than the wall. They were monsters come to break everything down.

The stompas advanced along a wide arc. They were separated by hundreds of metres. Each could only be targeted by one of our primary turrets. And they left the approach to the main gate clear for something else.

Far to my left, an Earthshaker cannon struck a vulnerable point in a stompa. The machine burst apart in a fireball so huge I could feel the heat from this distance. The monster's limb weapons tumbled through the air end over end. The crowd below cheered at the sound of the blast. They could not see what was almost upon us.

When the stompas were mere steps away from the wall, a pair of heavily armoured vehicles came up the slope and stopped about halfway to the gates. They were behind the mounds of smashed redoubts, difficult targets for our guns, and the stompas were the more obvious, oncoming threat. What I could make out of the vehicles was strange. Their upper portions were huge, doubling the size of the battle-wagons. They were enclosures, slapped together with welded metal plates.

Brenken must have realised their importance as I did, because shells landed near the tanks. Close hits, but not close enough. And there was only time for that salvo. Then the disaster began.

The attack came on so many fronts I didn't know where to look. Yet it had the unity of a single will. It was a masterpiece of coordination. No ork should have even conceived of it. But this ork achieved it.

The stompas assaulted the wall with wrecking balls larger than Chimeras. With each blow, rockcrete exploded into powder. Cracks became breaches.

From behind the massed ranks of battlewagons, troops shot upward. Strapped to their backs were the ork versions of jump packs – flaming hybrids of rockets and engines. The devices were crude, barely controlled. They should have killed their riders on lift-off. But they worked well enough for the orks, and their howls of glee merged with the shriek of propulsion. The trajectories were high. The assault troops would come down well inside the wall.

A column of battlewagons raced forward. They came for the gate in a straight line. They would hit it at high speed. I had a blessed moment to think Ghazghkull had made a mistake. The gates were strong. They could withstand the ork battering rams, and the chain reaction of collisions would create a greater barrier to the enemy.

The battlewagons drove up between the two stationary vehicles. The covers of these blew off, revealing what had been concealed, and mocked my faint hope. Each vehicle sported a huge rear-mounted turret. The weapon arm was as long as the wagon. It ended in an eight-pronged claw surrounding an energy node.

The weapons were already powering up.

'What…?' Somner whispered.

'Tractor beams,' I said.

The synchronisation of the components of the attack was perfect. In the midst of my horror, I felt the stab of envy. The tractor beams fired. Crackling, coruscating beams lashed out and struck the gates. A foul nimbus enveloped them. Troops on the ramparts scrambled away. Steel ten metres thick screamed. The tractor beams wrenched the gates from the wall.

The battlewagons stormed through the breach, guns blazing.

Once more, the cacophony of war resolved in my ears into a single sound: the laughter of Ghazghkull Mag Uruk Thraka.

# CHAPTER 10
# THE STREETS OF VOLCANUS

## 1. YARRICK

For several hundred metres up the main road from the gates, the only resistance the battlewagons encountered was from the sheer mass of bodies they crushed. They came in such numbers they had to split up. Even the principle thoroughfares in Volcanus were too narrow for a mechanised force on this scale. The lead tanks began to slow, pushing through the corpses of thousands. Others headed up other roads, grinding other crowds into the pavement. Behind the tanks, the infantry rushed in.

In the first few seconds of the flood, the return fire was haphazard, confused. The people tried to retreat from the huge vehicles, their guns and the terrifying, toothed visages of their siege blades. At the wall, the Steel Legion and militia were struggling to respond to the multiple attacks.

And further into the hive, the greenskin jump troops were coming down. They were out of my sight, but I could picture the panic as they began their massacre.

Beside me, Somner was slack-jawed with shock. On the far right, the tech-priest had turned from the devastation, shutting it out, and was adjusting his vox banks with the fixation of a mind whose courses of action have been reduced to none. Instinct urged me to head for street level and engage with the enemy. Reason held me where I was. 'Keep the vox working,' I told the tech-priest.

I used the only effective weapons I had at my disposal: my voice and my mind.

'Get off the streets,' I ordered. Amplified by every vox-caster in the hive, my words were still drowned by the thunder of the ork war machine. 'Get off the streets,' I said again. I repeated the order until I saw movement in the citizens nearest the Kasadya complex. They had heard and were trying to obey.

'Citizens of the Volcanus, you number in the millions, and you are armed. You are more than the orks. You are greater than the orks. From the high ground, in ambushes, from dead ends and byways, you have the strength to turn the streets into killing zones. You will stem the green tide.

'By your numbers, you must stem the tide.

'In the name of the Emperor, stem the tide.'

I had the voice of a god. My commands were heard by every soul in Volcanus. Yet I felt helpless. Below, the battle-wagons were sweeping their cannons back and forth. People ran for the doorways. Bullets and flamers cut them down. Articulated arms swung out from the tops of the vehicles, battering facades and destroying ground floors. I repeated my speech, and then again, and again. For several minutes, all I saw was slaughter and the endless flow of enemy strength into Volcanus.

Then the 252nd Regiment's counter attack began. Rockets and cannon fire cut across the gap in the wall, hammering the flanks of the battlewagons. The miracle began a few minutes later. I heard las fire. For it to be audible over the booming reports of the ork weapons, the roar of the engines and the howling, thundering inferno of the stompa assaults, the las had to be coming from a tremendous number of rifles. The citizens of the hive were fighting back.

My role was clear, then. I stayed where I was. I repeated my call. I summoned the spiritual fire of millions. I sought to inspire the ingenuity of desperation, and the fury of urban warfare. I could only guess at the levels of success. Higher up the honeycomb, the people would have more time to prepare for the orks. Closer to my position, as long as I could hear the bursts of las fire, I knew the fighting was not over, and that was a victory.

I was barely aware of Somner. I hadn't given him a thought since we had last spoken. But now he clutched my shoulder. I blinked. Trying to hear and visualise a battle stretching over many kilometres in three dimensions, I had withdrawn my attention from the immediate area. The orks had been concentrating their fire on the ground level.

Somner was pointing in horror to the right, east of the Kasadya complex. I looked. One of the stompas had broken through the wall, and it was shouldering its way between the towers, heading our way. The street was too narrow. It pushed between the buildings, caving their walls in. It left a wake of collapsing structures, mountains of rockcrete falling against each other, breaking apart to rubble and clouds of dust. The crack and roar of shattering buried the screams of the thousands who died with every step. Rubble bounced off armour the colour of old blood. The wrecking ball limb smashed the walkways that blocked its path. Our balcony was level with its shoulders.

Its right limb was a cannon half as long as the stompa was high. The barrel came up. It pointed at the balcony.

We started to run.

The weapon powered up with a hum so great it shook the walls of the manufactorum. My teeth vibrated. I tasted blood.

There was a great flash. It tore the world asunder.

## 2. SETHENO

She was to the west of the gates when they were destroyed. Brenken was on the other side. The energy discharge of the tractor beams scrambled the vox in the immediate area, and Setheno lost track of the colonel. But the regiment responded quickly. It fought back hard. It made the orks pay.

Yarrick's voice rang from every tower. His call to action became the voice of Volcanus itself.

Heroic gestures. Handfuls of water scooped from an ocean. The fall of the hive had begun. Determination and luck might see the resistance hold out as much as another day. No more. She was in the midst of an effort grandiose in its futility. She could see the end coming with the certainty of nightfall and dawn. Not for the first time, she envied Yarrick. He was not blind. He could read the signs as well as she did. But he could hope, even when that hope was a form of denial.

She could appreciate the confrontation with the impossible. She valued the miraculous.

There would be no miracles in Volcanus on this day.

Even so, she fought. She battled the orks with as much fury as she would if she felt hope. She had a role to play on Armageddon. The planet must be saved, and she must follow the dictates of fate. She could not see where her path led, but it had brought her here. The crucible of another defeat might show the way. In loss there might be a key, as yet obscure, to victory.

So she killed the orks, and bought Volcanus what time she could. She was not hoping, but she was seeking, and that was enough. It was what had sustained her since the end of the Piercing Thorn.

She was still on the ramparts, firing down at infantry as it passed through the gap in the wall. She placed the bolt pistol shots with precision, drilling through the skulls of the greenskins. Many of the most heavily armoured orks wore no helmets. They were taller than any human. As if they feared no attack from above, only their throats and lower jaws were protected by huge, fanged gorgets. Setheno punished their arrogance, splattering their brains across their massive piston-driven armour. When they fell, their followers howled and fired wildly, disoriented by the sudden death of their chieftains.

She slowed the tide by an infinitesimal degree. But there were more of the beasts, always more, and the tide still rose.

A great thunder from uphill. A stompa had reached the Kasadya manufactorum. There was a flash, and a massive concussion blast. Then the long, rolling, escalating crash of an edifice falling.

Yarrick's voice was silent.

Something hit the wall behind her, shaking the ramparts hard. Setheno turned. One of the stompas had not ventured into the city. It was advancing along the wall, smashing more of it down with every step. For the moment, the orks were bottlenecked by the width of the breaches. The stompa was removing even that limitation.

Clarity. Her curse and her blessing. The ork menace was so vast, the developing war so gigantic, the contingencies too many. So much of her path was dark.

But not now. Not in this instant.

She holstered her pistol and ran towards the stompa. She prepared for each strike of the wrecking ball, adjusting her balance. She did not stagger or lose a step. She eyed the stompa's arms, evaluating. The confusion of the battle receded, the din and smoke fading to the rear of her consciousness, to resurface only in the event of a more immediate threat.

She moved through a crystalline series of elements. Her speed. The rhythm of the stompa's movements. The swing of the ball. The threat of the right limb, a flamer whose jets shot over the wall and drenched the faces of the hab towers with liquid fire.

She knew what she must do. She knew when to do it. This was her gift of perfect clarity, and before her were mere orks.

No, she thought, seconds now from her encounter with the stompa. Not mere. These orks were led by a power that, if it were not stopped, could shake the Imperium.

She was in the shadow of the stompa. Its wrecking arm came down. The spiked sphere slammed into the ramparts a few metres in front of Setheno. The crash was deafening. A storm of debris struck her armour, but she kept her footing. The ball buried itself deep into the wall. The surface beneath Setheno's feet heaved and cracked. Another collapse began.

Setheno leapt forward. She landed on the wrecking ball. Now a few seconds marked the difference between success and death. She took three steps towards the huge chain. It grew taut. She jumped again and wrapped her arms around a link.

The arm began to rise. She climbed from link to link. The arm lifted the ball free from the wall and it began its swing upwards. The chain flew outwards. It was horizontal. Then it was vertical.

She released the chain. She dropped towards the upper

segment of the limb. She hit, landing in a tangle of cables wrapped around a piston two metres thick. She seized the cables. The arm began its descent. She braced herself. Above her, orks on the stompa's shoulder turrets tried to shoot her down, but their vehicle's own movements made her too erratic a target.

The wrecking ball hit the wall again. The impact travelled up the arm. It shook her every bone. The mass of her power armour gave her enough inertia to keep her grip. If she had still been on the chain, she would have been snapped in half.

In the brief pause before the arm rose, she climbed. As the limb reached the horizontal, she stood and ran the rest of the length, balancing on the pistons. At the moment of descent, she made still another leap, and landed on the stompa's shoulder plating. The metal was smooth. She was on a slope. Her boots slipped. She dropped to her knees and in a single movement drew *Skarprattar* and stuck the blade through the plate. It arrested her fall. She yanked herself forwards and up, stabbed into the shielding again, and timed her next lunge with the lateral rocking of the stompa as it took another heavy step. Momentum propelled her to the top of the shoulder. A boxy turret rose from the surface of the shield. Metal struts supported it. Setheno used them to work her way towards the head. The turret's heavy stubber rotated back and forth, angling down, strafing the ramparts. Setheno paused at the right-hand strut, pulled out her pistol and fired into the stubber's barrel until her shells punched through, distorting the bore. The gunner kept shooting until the weapon exploded. The turret bulged along the seams from the force of an internal blast.

The head of the stompa was surrounded by a crown-shaped collar. Setheno climbed over it. A huge, grotesque metal face in yellow and crimson towered before her. In the centre of its jaws, on an elevated turret, an ork sat at the trigger of a cannon whose barrel protruded over the collar. The greenskin snarled when it saw her. She put three shells in its skull before it could bring the cannon around.

Sword and pistol drawn, she ran past the turret and through the gaping jaws of the idol. She entered a dim, clanking, superheated space overflowing with levers, valves and wheels, stinking of promethium and ork bodies. Beyond the weak light entering from the graven image's eyes and jaws, the only illumination came from sparking machinery and momentary jets of burning gas. In the centre, a greenskin engineer stood on a raised platform and roared orders at its minions. Menial orks and gretchin scrambled over the controls, rushing back and forth to pull levers, release pressure, throw switches and turn the grinding wheels. There was no sense to what Setheno saw. There was only a mechanical frenzy, an ecstasy of invention and violence.

The engineer saw her. It howled and pointed. The massive harness it wore, sparking with diodes and electrical coils, lit up, casting a shimmering force field around the ork. A horde of greenskins swarmed her. When the orks abandoned their controls, the stompa's movements became more jerky and erratic. The deck heaved back and forth. Setheno took a wide stance, shifting her centre of gravity with the wild sways. She fired her bolt pistol into the attacking crew, shooting to kill, but also to damage mechanisms. Orks fell. Control surfaces erupted. The engineer howled and stamped its feet with anger. She swept *Skarprattar* wide and gutted the clutch of gretchin that were trying to scuttle around her back. Two larger orks slammed into her, wielding wrenches big enough to crush a human skull with a single blow. The blows rebounded off her power armour, but they drove her back and to the side.

Something large, heavy, metallic and edged began to grind against her armour's power pack. The two orks were pushing her into the huge gears to the right of the idol's jaw.

Setheno drove her blade through the neck of the ork on her right. It gurgled and slumped against her. The other took a step back and charged. She shoved at the corpse and fell to the side with it. The attacking ork's momentum carried it over her and into the huge cog wheels behind. It screamed, eaten by the machinery it had served.

Before Setheno could rise, an explosion lifted her and threw her into a tangle of levers. The orks near her were torn apart by shrapnel. The engineer raised another grenade. She jerked free of the metal just as the frag weapon went off. The blast knocked her forwards, teeth of metal digging deep into her armour. She fired at the engineer. The bolts ricocheted off the force field and smacked explosively into the walls and gears.

Smoke filled the idol's skull. The stompa walked on, its rocking becoming more and more violent.

The engineer threw another grenade, killing more of its crew and setting cables on fire as it sought to destroy the invader. Setheno ducked around a half-exposed cog wheel that protruded from the deck and was almost as tall as she was. The ork hurled another grenade. She raced out of shelter and forward, inside the arc of the throw, charging the engineer with *Skarprattar* before her. The explosion at her back lit the crowded space with flame. Machinery screamed. The wild rocking of the stompa propelled her forward and she vaulted onto the engineer's platform. Her relic blade and her power armoured momentum crashed her through the ork's force field. The feedback of energy blew up the coils on the ork's back. Energy lashed out, surrounding the ork, striking every corner of the stompa's skull. The engineer's eyes widened in distress.

The blast smashed Setheno through the jaws of the idol and propelled her through the metal shielding. She slammed up against the teeth of the collar, all that kept her from taking a twenty metre fall. Before her, the skull blew up, the greatest force shooting straight up like an incandescent geyser.

The stompa was decapitated. Elsewhere in the huge body, orks still operated limbs and pulled triggers, but all direction was gone. The huge flamer spread destruction in a circle as the stompa whirled. The turrets fired in at every point on the compass. The wrecking ball went wild. Out of control, it came flying back at the body and battered its way through the stompa's midsection. The frame shook with more explosions. The rocking became even more severe. As they panicked, the orks created more and more extreme movements. The arms waved. The stompa took a step first one way, then another.

The balance tipped.

Setheno shook off the stun and pulled herself to her feet. The stompa leaned forward. She looked over the collar. The ramparts were below.

The stompa began to rock back.

She jumped, sliding down the front of the stompa's skirt. As she reached the level of its chest, she pushed out with her legs. She fell away from the stompa, dropping through the air. She hit the top of the wall and rolled. The battering stopped just short of shattering her bones. She came to a halt, straightened out of a ball of pain and forced herself to her feet.

She ran.

Behind her, the huge war engine screamed with madness

and anger. The shadow of the stompa loomed over her. It stretched further and further ahead.

The stompa did not rock back this time.

Explosions behind her. The shriek and crack of something very large and vital being severed. The shadow growing, spreading night.

She ran faster, ceramite boots cracking rockcrete with every step, racing for the edge of the shadow. It pulled further ahead. Through pain and raw lungs, she gasped prayers of faith and service to the Emperor. The prayers granted her the speed she needed. She ran out from the shadow moments before the stompa crashed down atop the wall.

The barrier held the body up for a few seconds. Then, weakened by blows and the gaps in its integrity, it collapsed. Stone and metal fell together, embracing their mutual destruction. Inside the stompa, power sources, munitions and fuel reserves were crushed and breached. Explosions wracked the length of the vast body. The largest bathed the wall in fireballs and hurled giant metal plates hundreds of metres.

Setheno staggered forwards until she reached the smashed gates. She looked around. The stompa was down, but the damage to the wall was enormous. More and more and more orks were storming into Volcanus. Tanks and stompas brought havoc to the streets.

She began to climb down a slope of wreckage. Below, the Steel Legion was leaving the wall for the interior of the city.

There was nothing more to defend here.

## 3. YARRICK

The stompa's cannon took out the front half of the manufactorum. Facade and walls and floors disintegrated. I had a wall behind me when the orks fired. That was as far as I had run in the few seconds granted to me. That was as much as I accomplished in the aid of my survival. The rest was in the hands of the Emperor.

The Emperor protects.

Force and stone hurled me forwards. Something splashed against my back. Beneath my feet, the floor dropped away. I moved forwards and down, a leaf of flesh in the grip of wind and gravity. Sound and flame filled my senses. I put my arms over my face and held my head. I did not fight my trajectory. My body went loose and took the blows, but my will was iron.

Do not die. Not now. Not here. Your work is not yet done.

My thoughts were not so coherent. They were a wordless roar of refusal. But it had meaning.

I flew and I fell through heat and dust and battering stone. I tumbled and bounced, dropping with the collapse of the manufactorum. Time shattered into nonsense. I fell for an eternity and for mere seconds. Then there was a blow that felt like a power fist to my spine, and I was still.

Several seconds of sheet lightning agony passed before I could draw a breath. I coughed. I spat out dirt-clogged phlegm. The air was thick with dust, but enough weak daylight reached me that I could see where I was. I had landed on a large, canted slab of rockcrete. Below me was a jumble of rubble sloping towards the street. Beneath it, hundreds of thousands of citizens had been crushed to nothing. I looked up and saw jagged floors and twisted rebar. The lower half of the Kasadya complex, reaching far into its heart, had undergone a total collapse. The upper tower still stood for now, but I could see it sway.

I sat up. I left a bloody smear on the slab. The blood was not mine. Somner, I realised. He had been a few steps behind me and been disintegrated by the blast. Of the tech-priest there was no sign.

The stompa took a step backwards. Then another. It was going to fire again and finish the job.

I stood and made my way down the rubble. I moved with speed that would have been reckless if hesitation hadn't been even more lethal. I leapt from slab to slab. I angled my way towards the feet of the stompa. I was placing my faith in the orks' skill. I was trusting them not to bring the tower down on their heads. It was a weak form of trust. It was the only move open to me.

The rubble shook with the tread of the stompa. The curtain of dust turned the stompa into a mountainous silhouette. I reached the ground. I became aware of other shapes in the dust running in every direction. 'With me!' I shouted. My voice was raw and cracked. Some of the shadows heard me. They followed, perhaps blindly, on instinct, obeying the first voice they heard. No matter. They might survive. I called again. More figures ran beside and before me through the maelstrom of grey.

The stompa's feet were a few dozen metres ahead. The monster stopped walking. Its turrets chattered in the gloom above, attacking the walkways that were still intact in the vicinity. The orks ignored the fleeing insects on the ground.

I was close enough. Still shouting, though it took precious breaths to do so, I angled to the right, where, beyond the stompa, I saw the dark path of a narrow alleyway between towers. I called once more before the cannon fired again.

The earth shook. The deep, harsh, broken shout of the dying tower washed over me. A huge wind blew, as from the throat of a mythical beast. The dust roiled, thickened, became blinding. I choked. I could no longer see the shapes of the other runners. My voice was buried beneath the monstrous sound. My alley goal vanished. I kept moving, slowing just enough to avoid breaking an ankle on the broken surface of the street.

The alley reappeared a few steps before me. I plunged into the shadow. Other bodies followed me. I moved in deeper, to where the dust was less thick. I stopped to catch my breath. Perhaps twenty civilians had joined me. There were also two Steel Legionnaires. They approached me and saluted, identifying themselves as troopers Wyda and Delschaft.

'The rest of your squads?' I asked. I coughed again, and envied the soldiers their rebreathers.

'We were trying to flank the ork column when the Kasadya fell,' Wyda said. 'We lost them in the dust cloud.'

'But you know where you were heading.'

'Yes, commissar,' she said.

'Then we have a direction. I need a working vox.' I turned to the civilians. They were dust-caked wraiths, clutching their lasrifles and staring at us, waiting for any hope we could offer. I gave them purpose instead. 'We will take the narrow passages,' I said. 'Do not engage with the enemy except on my command.'

We left the stompa and its rampage behind. The alley branched into others. Some were no more than accidental spaces created by the density of architectural growth. I took us uphill, deeper into the city, following the sounds of combat. I stopped a few times to listen carefully, wary of the difference between an ork column firing with impunity and an actual struggle. Sustained bursts of las fire called to me. So did the honourable boom of Leman Russ guns. It took very little training to distinguish Imperial cannons from the undisciplined, excessive concussions of ork weapons.

The alley curved ahead. An engagement was nearby. Las, solid rounds and ork snarls of rage echoed between the walls.

The las fire was coming from above. On our right, iron steps zigzagged up the side of the hab block, leading to the arch of a walkway.

We went up, the sound of battle covering the clatter of our footsteps. On the walkway, a full squad of the Steel Legion was firing down on a large column of orks. They had taken down numerous footsoldiers. 'Follow the example of your comrades,' I instructed the civilians. 'Whatever these warriors do, do likewise.' Twenty more guns joined the assault. Lack of training was no issue. The enemy was impossible to miss. All the citizens had to do was aim down.

I found the sergeant. His name was Reithner. I drew him and his vox operator aside and we crouched low on the walkway. While the trooper worked to contact Brenken, I asked Reithner what he intended.

'Kill the greenskins until their big guns arrive,' he said. 'Then we get out fast. Hit them again as soon as we can.'

'Good,' I said. I gestured to the civilians. 'These people are now under your command. As will be any others who join this group. You aren't just leading a squad now, sergeant. You have a company. Are you up to the task?'

'I am, commissar.'

'Glad to hear it.'

Reithner moved back to the parapet to resume command of the firefight. His trooper handed me the handset. 'The colonel,' he said.

'*Commissar,*' Brenken's voice was muzzy with static, but clear enough. '*I'm glad you're alive.*'

'I'm as relieved to know you are,' I said. 'What is the situation?'

'*We've lost the wall. We slowed them for a bit, but they have total freedom of entry now.*'

'You're moving to the interior?'

*'Yes. Street by street interdiction now.'*

'I'm afraid not, colonel,' I said.

*'You're siding with the canoness now?'*

'No. But we can't block their access to the hive. They will advance no matter what we do. So let them. Draw them in. The ways of Volcanus are narrow. The deeper they go, the more spread out they'll become. If they try to bunch together, they'll slow down. The tanks will be limited in their range. With the citizens of Volcanus in the fight, we have the numbers. Draw them in,' I repeated. 'Draw them in and grind them down.'

*'Do you believe this can be done?'*

'I believe it is what we must do.'

*'We're already having to break down into squad level,'* Brenken said. *'That will give us more speed and flexibility of movement.'*

'Have them lead groups of civilians where possible.' I was already seeing the multiplication of force that could occur.

*'Where possible,'* Brenken repeated, grim.

'I know,' I said. There would be hard decisions. There would be massacres. Endless massacres. They were unavoidable. The best we could do was make the orks pay with their own blood for the slaughter.

I have never enjoyed deciding how people will die. Neither have I turned from the necessity of doing so.

*'Well,'* Brenken said. *'The Emperor protects.'*

'The Emperor protects.'

As I signed off, Reithner shouted a warning. The ork tanks were here. We ran to the far end of the walkway, furthest away from the arriving heavy armour. The entrance to a chapel awaited us. We were barely inside when the guns took out the centre of the walkway. The entire span collapsed a moment later.

We were inside the Chapel of Sacred Obedience. Its base straddled the roofs of three hab blocks. We had entered the north side of the transept. At the eastern door to the nave, stairs led down the habs. Reithert gestured in that direction. 'We can reach the street that way.'

I shook my head. We were beside the steps leading up the north spire. More walkways led off it from the level of the bells. 'The orks don't hold the higher elevations yet,' I said. 'Use that advantage. We can pick our targets.'

And through a day of burning grey, and a roaring night, we did. We moved from point to point in Volcanus, hammering the orks' infantry at choke points, ambushing them from above and moving on. By the time they had brought their heavy weapons to bear, we were gone. Civilians stumbled from shelled buildings and joined us. Before dawn, our group was two hundred-strong. Our wake was bloody. Morale was strong.

And as dawn broke, I knew we had lost.

# CHAPTER 11
# REDEMPTION AND SHAME

## 1. YARRICK

The spires were coming down. Ghazghkull had tired of street battles. He wanted Volcanus to fall *now*. The orks are not a patient race. But they are also stubborn, and will persist in a task beyond all bounds of reason. The combination of those two characteristics makes them ferocious enemies, and their sieges are savage affairs. What was different and dangerous about Ghazghkull was his adaptability. His tactics were complex and fluid, and his armed might was overwhelming. If he wanted to bring the siege to an end, he had the means to do so.

And so the spires came down. The stompas became more coordinated in their assaults. They grouped in pairs, blasting the base of one tower after another. Any building where resistance was strong, or where there was even the potential for a real struggle, was felled. The dust clouds covered all of Volcanus. I felt the cannon blasts in my chest, and the vibrations of each collapse through my boots. Instead of fighting for control, the orks were simply razing entire areas of the city.

'I'm sorry, commissar,' Setheno said.

We were standing beside *Sword of the Wastes*. Brenken's driver had managed to negotiate some of the narrowest streets of Volcanus and keep the colonel's command post mobile and intact. Brenken had moved upwards with the flow of the war. Despite everything we could do, the orks had taken more and more of the city. Their tide had risen, unstoppable.

We were stationed in the lee of the burned out rubble of a hab block. The orks had already passed through. The location was a point of calm in the conflict, a purged wasteland. Brenken had called us here to face the unspeakable.

Less than a thousand metres away, the tower of Saint Pausanias, an Ecclesiarchal monastery, buckled and folded in on itself. Caryatids, stained glass and columns splintered like powdery twigs. Vaults gaped like screaming maws. Its base was three quarters of the way up the architectural mountain of Volcanus, and its spire had reached the cloud-brushing heights of the hive's peak. Its death brought an end to many other structures. The collapses multiplied. A great rockslide rolled down the slope of Volcanus, killing orks and humans alike, but many more humans than orks. Tens of thousands. Hundreds of thousands. The echoes of the fall had not faded when, further up and to the west of our position, another tower shook, battered by cannons and wrecking balls. It leaned. It leaned too far.

And down.

'I know you take no pleasure in this,' I said to Setheno. 'But I wish you had been wrong.'

'So do I.'

I was holding down the full scope of my frustration and rage. Two hives. Two defeats. I had known the odds were

against Volcanus. The end had been preordained. And yet…
And yet… We owed the Emperor the impossible. It was little
enough to give the Father of Mankind. I had succeeded in
doing so in the past. Now, when the need to do so was as
urgent as it had ever been, I had been found wanting.

Over the course of the night, the orks had taken away the
high ground. The squads of jump-packed greenskins had
flown to the walkways, laughing as they tore through the
defenders of Volcanus, knocking them over the parapets to
their deaths. What the jump troops ignored, the tanks blasted
apart. And then the felling of the spires had begun. Our every
strategy was countered by a gigantic response.

'If we had had the troops…' Brenken had muttered a few
minutes ago.

The thought was tempting and frustrating. There was truth
in it. Von Strab had crippled our response. Had he doomed
us from the start? Yes, he had.

But that was not a complete truth.

I should have done more. Somehow, I could have done
more.

I would yet.

Brenken called to us from the interior of the Chimera. 'I
have Mannheim,' she said.

Setheno and I boarded through the rear hatch as Kuyper
left, giving us privacy. None of Brenken's surviving captains
were present. They would hear of the orders that would
come out of this meeting. But only the four of us would
know what was said.

'How secure is the channel?' I asked Brenken.

She shrugged, her face lined with exhaustion and despair.
'The princeps is speaking to us from *Steel Hammer*. As secure
as possible, I would say.'

We could not rule out the possibility that von Strab had found a way to monitor even that frequency. That changed nothing of what we would say. We had run out of options.

We approached the vox unit on the tactical table. 'We're here, Princeps Mannheim,' Brenken said.

'*Volcanus is lost to us, then?*' Mannheim said.

I answered, speaking my shame. 'It will be by the end of the day. At best.'

'*And then the orks will come for Armageddon Secundus.*'

'I suppose they might amuse themselves with Death Mire for an afternoon,' said Brenken. 'They've already shown they enjoy the entertainment of slaughtering our hive militias.'

'What are the dispositions in Secundus?' Setheno asked.

'*Unchanged,*' said Mannheim. '*Entirely defensive.*'

I clenched my fists. 'That's madness. The orks will take Armageddon down one hive at a time. They have to be countered by a unified force.'

'*I don't disagree, commissar. But that is the situation we face.*'

'Not to be changed while von Strab is overlord.'

'*As you say.*' Mannheim's response was careful, avoiding outright mutiny.

I thought about the regiments cantoned at Infernus, Hades, Helsreach, Acheron, and Tartarus. I doubted von Strab had concerned himself with the minor hives and other settlements. I pictured the combined strength of the Steel Legion and the Legio Metalica. Would even that be enough against what Ghazghkull had at his command? I knew enough now to speculate. And the question was moot. Von Strab had sabotaged any such effort. 'We need help,' I said. 'We need the Adeptus Astartes.'

'*Von Strab has forbidden requests for aid,*' Mannheim said. '*And then there's the warp storm. But if you think the effort must be made…*'

'It must,' I told him, 'but not by you. We can't risk von Strab relieving you of command. Short of execution, he has nothing left to use against me.'

'*He might well do that.*'

'Let him try.'

'*You will come to Infernus?*'

'Yes.'

'*I'll do what I can to clear the way for you to the astropaths.*'

'Thank you, princeps.'

'I'll go too,' Brenken said. 'My command is ending with the regiment.'

'*You have my sympathy, colonel,*' said Mannheim.

'We'll be travelling by Chimera, if we're lucky,' I said. 'That will barely keep us ahead of the orks. We need time. We have been fighting a reactive war, and losing it. We need the space to make some moves the orks cannot counter. Princeps, can you arrange for a Valkyrie to extract us once we're away from Infernus?'

'*Should I speak to General Andechs?*'

'No,' Brenken said quickly. 'Where is Colonel Helm stationed?'

'*Hades Hive.*'

Further than ideal, but if Brenken trusted Helm, then so be it.

'Speak to him,' Brenken said. 'We'll contact you later with our location. If we lose the vox…' She looked down at the map. I pointed to a spot and she nodded. 'We'll make for the eastern side of Irkalla.'

The settlement had been abandoned for centuries. Records on Armageddon going back more than five hundred years were very unreliable. Much was missing, especially around 441.M41. Next to nothing was known about Irkalla beyond its name. The reason for its end had fallen into shadow. All that remained were the ruins of what had been a sub-hive city. But it was a landmark, and there was nothing there to attract the orks. It lay southwest of Volcanus, towards the Plain of Anthrand. Death Mire was northeast. We stood a decent chance of reaching Irkalla unchallenged.

I tried not to think of my course as another flight. I tried to think of it as a countermove. What my reason knew to be true, and what my soul believed were two very different things.

'Time,' Setheno said, musing. 'Armageddon needs time.' She nodded to herself. 'I think we can gain another day. Not for Volcanus, but we can hold the orks here a little longer.'

'What are you thinking?' I asked.

'Nemesis Island.'

I grimaced at the bleak humour of our situation. 'You're right,' I said. 'You aren't offering salvation for Volcanus.'

'I have no time for lost causes, commissar.'

'Armageddon is not one.'

'No,' she agreed. 'Not yet.'

## 2. SETHENO

She reached the docks in the late afternoon. Movement through the hive was more and more difficult. Many of the maglev tracks had been destroyed, and power had failed over most of the city. Setheno descended into the underhive for part of her journey, and in its upper reaches she found a train that took her several kilometres in the right direction. But even here, below the surface, the damage was severe. Tunnels had been compacted by the fall of towers. Foundations had pancaked.

On the streets, what the orks did not hold they had reduced

to rubble. Setheno stuck to the shadows, crossing heaps of wreckage, passing between burning towers. She went alone. She was beneath notice, a single figure slipping through the blasted landscape of Volcanus.

The dockside region was relatively intact. Warehouses had been incinerated by ork artillery, but the greenskin army was still concentrated in the centre, north and east of Volcanus. Most of the damage in its west end had been caused by panic. Not all the citizens had stood loyal to the Emperor. Hundreds of thousands, perhaps millions, had turned to flight as soon as word spread that the siege was going badly. And with the end looming, millions were joining the exodus. They streamed out of all sides of the hive, the shattered walls letting them out as they had let the orks in. The west, though, was the site of the first great panic. It was natural for people to run here, far from the initial greenskin breaches. There was a choice of escape: on land, circling south away from the enemy army, running up into the Volcanus Mountains; or by boat, into the archipelago in the great bay beyond the hive.

Most had chosen the mountains. There was something in the islands almost as frightening as the orks.

It was Setheno's destination.

The docks swarmed with activity. There were still thousands upon thousands of refugees here, seeking any means of escape faster than foot. Few of the berths still had ships. In the near distance, the hulls of overloaded, capsized ships lay in the torpid waters of the bay.

Setheno pushed her way through the crowd. She had removed her helmet, and the people who met her gaze shrank away. They felt her judgement. Good. They should be fighting. They should be dying to buy Armageddon one more second with which to prepare its retaliation against the orks. If time weren't the precious resource it was, she would have brought punishment to the cowards.

She strode to the far end of the docks, past freighters and oil tankers turning into passenger ships, past empty moorings, and through the haze and smoke and dust. There were no refugees on the westernmost pier. The ship there was not one they would ever willingly board, no matter how desperate their circumstances.

The *Iron Repentance* was a mid-sized transport. Its hulk was dark grey, rusted, its only adornment a massive relief sculpture of the fist-and-scales of the Adeptus Arbites. Two troopers stood guard at the foot of the ramp leading aboard. Setheno stopped before them.

'You remain at your posts,' she said, approving.

'Until our orders change, canoness,' said one. He was a small, thin man, bulked out by his armour. His partner, average in height, appeared much taller in contrast. Setheno towered over both.

'They have changed,' she said. 'You will take me to Nemesis Island.'

To their credit, they hesitated. They would not disobey her command, but she was not part of their power structure.

She relieved their uncertainty by gesturing back at the burning city. 'You have no other charges on the way. Your fellow Arbites are fighting and dying in the struggle against the greenskins. Honour their sacrifice. Honour the Emperor.'

They bowed, and led her aboard.

The crew worked fast. In a few minutes, the *Iron Repentance* left Volcanus behind. It steamed through the dense archipelago. The water depth varied wildly, the shoals were lethal, and the ship's labyrinthine route took it through narrows so tight, the hull brushed against sheer cliffs on either side. In the background, the bleak music of the war continued, the dull beat of guns punctuated by the harsh crack of falling towers.

Grey afternoon had become grey evening when Nemesis Island came into view. It was a brutal uprising of rock, thrusting straight up from the sea. Its high basalt cliffs had been, through the industry of machines and serfs, rendered smooth as obsidian. They could not be climbed.

At the top were jagged battlements of rockcrete and steel. On the south side of the island, a crooked inlet, no more than a crack in the forbidding mass of the cliffs, led to the tiny port. The pier had room for a single ship. The *Iron Repentance* was the only vessel that ever plied its dark waters.

The boat docked. Setheno disembarked. The pier, wide enough for hundreds of souls, ended at a massively armoured guard house. Beyond that bunker, an iron door was set into the cliff wall. It was thicker than the gates of Volcanus.

An enforcer emerged from the guard house to meet Setheno as she drew near. The woman's lantern jaw tightened at the sight of the canoness. 'Has the war come to Nemesis Island?' she asked.

'No,' Setheno said. 'Nemesis is going to the war.'

## 3. STRIBOLT

The Nemesis Island Penal Facility burrowed deep into the rock. In the centre was a huge circular space ringed by a hundred levels of cells. A warren of tunnels spread out from the central block. The prison was also a mining complex. The hard labour of the prisoners expanded the facility with every passing day. This was necessary, because even with the high mortality rate, the population kept growing. New inmates arrived on the *Iron Repentence* every week. The pits went deeper, the tunnels became darker, and in time there was no reason to go through the trouble of transporting the prisoners who worked the farthest ones all the way back to the overcrowded cells of the centre. The abandoned slept and ate where they worked. There was little food. Even less sleep. There was the back-breaking work using only the most primitive tools. There were the hours upon hours, sometimes multiple days, of digging ore from the walls and loading it into the carts. For those chained to the carts, there was the long journey hauling the loads to the vast bay where the ore would be transferred to containers awaiting transport by lifter to the mainland. For those left behind, during the brief periods when the guards did not use shock mauls to force them back to work, there was the brutal struggle for survival, the scrabble for food, for dominance, for the illusion of safety in the death of hated enemies.

Sometimes, new arrivals would try to conceal themselves in the ore containers. If they weren't crushed by rock, they were purged by the security procedures. On their way to the landing pad on the south end of the island, the containers passed through a great furnace. They and their contents were heated to a temperature just shy of molten. Nothing organic survived.

In the exhausted seams, inmates remained. Food and water came more rarely. The struggle for survival became more savage, and then exhausted, and then silent. Mummified bodies, crusted in their dried blood, lay in heaps in the corners of endless darkness.

Stribolt knew what happened in the dead seams. He knew to remain chained to the carts. As long as he was one of those who returned from the depths, he had his cell in the central block. It was a few metres on a side, and he shared it with ten other prisoners. They slept in shifts. They were among the fortunate of Nemesis Island.

Keeping his privileged position meant killing. Stribolt had no objection. He was good at killing. It was murder that had brought him to the island. There was nothing unusual about murder in the underhive of Volcanus. Nothing unusual about running gangs, either. But he had run too close to the surface. He had harmed those who would be missed. He had warred against larger gangs, whose leaders had sympathetic ears just that little bit further up from the depths of the hive.

He had been on Nemesis Island for years. He still had his cell and his limbs. By the standards of the facility, he was thriving. And he would strike down any challenger to his position. As he was doing now.

He'd had his eye on Platen for several cycles. The new arrival was a head taller and very muscular. He had the loud voice and swagger of a man who intended to carve out his place as fast as possible, before the prison eroded his strength. Today, in the basin of the central block, where the prisoners assembled to drag the carts or follow them, Platen had stepped in front of Stribolt and picked up the bracket at the end of a chain.

'Fits my chest better,' he said to Stribolt.

Stribolt punched him in the throat. Platen coughed and dropped the bracket. Stribolt picked up the chain, ducked around Platen and wrapped the chain around his neck. He hauled back. The big man bent backwards, choking. Stribolt pulled harder.

No one intervened. Nearby guards and inmates watched the fight with mild interest.

Platen reached back and clawed at Stribolt's face. Filth-encrusted nails gouged the flesh from his cheeks. Stribolt jerked his face away. Platen's gagging was sounding liquid.

And then the voice came.

It spoke from the vox-casters spread around the entire

block. The effect was not unusual. This was how the many announcements, pronouncements and sermons of the warden, Mierendorff, reached the ears of the inmates. The difference was the voice. It spoke with a chilling authority far beyond Mierendorff's fondest hopes. The first words froze Stribolt.

'*You are the damned,*' the voice said, and the truth hammered his chest with a spike of bone.

Stribolt staggered back from Platen. The other man fell to his knees, gagging, but he stared in the same direction as Stribolt. So did all the inmates in the central block. Midway up the height of the huge space, a platform projected into the air. It was attached to the warden's offices. Instead of Mierendorff, a warrior of the Adepta Sororitas stood at the platform's edge. She paused before speaking again. She turned her head slowly. Her gaze swept all the rings of cells, and all the prisoners on the floor. She was too far for Stribolt to see her features clearly, yet he knew when her eyes fell on him, and he felt her judgement. For the first time in his life, he felt shame.

'*You are the damned,*' she repeated, and despair drove Stribolt to his knees. '*But even the damned have their use. The Emperor calls, and you will answer. The orks walk upon Armageddon with impunity. You will rise against them. You will take up arms, and you will follow me into battle. You will seek redemption in the faithful death, and this is already more than you deserve.*'

The Sister of Battle's words scoured Stribolt's soul. She was a figure of grey terror. He would do anything. To mitigate the judgement of ice, he would seek the absolution of fire.


## 4. YARRICK


The refugees streamed through the south gates of Volcanus. We were among them. Defeat, rage, impotence – they were a single mass, a weight of molten lead on my shoulders. Breathing was difficult.

Brenken sat in the top hatch of *Sword of the Wastes*. I crouched beside her on the roof, holding the heavy bolter turret for stability. I had to see everything. I had to see the full extent of the loss. I had failed, and I would not allow myself any grace. I would not turn away.

The Chimera moved slowly through the countless thousands of civilians as we passed through the gates. We were concerned with stealth more than speed at this stage. We did not want to attract the attention of the orks. For the time being, they were ignoring the refugee columns. There was still enough resistance in the city to keep them interested. When the last of the combatants fell, the orks might well make sport in slaughtering these masses.

Not yet, though. The tattered remains of the 252nd and the Volcanus Hive Militia fought on. As did any citizen who wasn't fleeing. I looked at the refugees with pity rather than hate. They weren't cowards. There hadn't been time to arm every inhabitant of the hive. Millions fought. Millions more had a choice of deaths. Some had hidden, paralyzed with terror, in their homes. I couldn't guess how many were still alive, and how many had been crushed as the orks toppled the city. If they survived, they would become slaves. I knew what that meant. It was survival only in the most perverse sense of the word.

The masses that fled were looking at a future that was no better. They had no destination. There were no settlements within a few days' walking distance. The closest were too small to provide for such numbers. And there would be little desire to make themselves obvious so close to the ork army. Perhaps the refugees had the vague hope of reaching Armageddon

Secundus. It was the land over the horizon, as yet untouched by the orks. It was where protection could be found.

Illusions. Delusions. The people would die of hunger, thirst and exposure before they had traversed the Plain of Anthrand. They would never even reach the Equatorial Jungle. If chance and cruel fate took any that far, their journey would end in its dense, verdant, predatory dark. Von Strab was wrong about the jungle holding back the orks. Desperate, weakened humans were another matter. It would strip the flesh from their skeletons.

We left the wall behind. I turned around to look at it, as I had during the retreat from Tempestora. Smoke rose from a hundred positions, forming dark columns rising to the low clouds. The echoes of combat followed me, accusing, drawing blood from my spirit.

Brenken stared straight ahead. Neither of us had spoken since we had boarded *Sword of the Wastes*. 'Will we find forgiveness?' she asked.

'From whom?'

'From our comrades. From the Emperor.'

'We are doing what we must to save Armageddon,' I told her. 'Von Strab is the one who should seek forgiveness. He won't find it.'

She nodded. She looked as unsatisfied with my answer as I felt. She had left a question unspoken, and I had left it unanswered.

Would we find forgiveness from ourselves?

I didn't know.

Away from the gates, Spira manoeuvred the Chimera out from the edges of the crowd. We picked up speed.

The molten lead pressed harder on my back and on my mind. I spoke in answer to its constricting weight. 'No more,' I said. 'Not one more.'

'Commissar?' Brenken asked.

'No other hive that I defend will fall. By the Throne, this I vow.'

I might not find forgiveness, but I would bring an end to shame.

# CHAPTER 12
# THE NEMESIS CRUSADE

## 1. STRIBOLT

There was a lifter on the landing pad. This time, the containers it carried were full of live prisoners. It transported them to the docks of Volcanus. Stribolt was among them. His forehead still burned. A guard had branded him with the sign of the aquila as he had entered the container. The same mark was on all the other prisoners travelling with him. It was the sign of allegiance to the crusade, and of their fallen state. All who saw them would know them to be the damned on the final march to redemption.

Stribolt arrived at the docks ahead of the first load brought back by the *Iron Repentance*. The lifter came down vertically, turbo engines blasting at the ground. The massive clamps that ran the length of its fuselage released the tanks two metres above a wide expanse of rockcrete before the dockside warehouses. The containers dropped with a crash. The jolt of the landing would have knocked Stribolt off his feet if there had been room to fall. The prisoners were standing, packed so tightly he could barely breathe. Front and rear hatches popped open. Stribolt shoved his way out of the stifling darkness of the tank and in to the waiting grey of the Volcanus day. It was the first time he had been in the open air in five years.

The lifter was already flying back to Nemesis Island for the next cargo. Over the course of the next few hours, it would make multiple trips for each one the ship managed. The docks filled with thousands of inmates. They crowded the refugees off the docks. They were herded by enforcers. *We're an army*, Stribolt thought. Male and female, they were shorn of hair and wore the same ragged grey tunics. Stribolt saw the terror in the faces of the refugees as they beheld this army, and he grinned.

Setheno was visible, marching back and forth on the roofs of the warehouses. Word filtered through from the prisoners closest to the civilians: Setheno had ordered the refugees to fight or drown.

One, weeping, had begged the canoness to tell them how they should fight without weapons. Stribolt laughed when he heard that. No inmate would have asked such a stupid question. Hands, nails, teeth, feet – he had killed with them and nothing else on plenty of occasions over the years.

But Setheno signalled to an enforcer, who rolled up the door to the warehouse on which the Sister of Battle stood. The building had become an armoury. Stribolt guessed it had been stocked with whatever caches were nearby and still outside the zones of combat. He ran forward with the rush. There were thousands more prisoners than weapons, and they pushed and kicked their way ahead of the refugees. The lasrifles were gone before Stribolt could get through the doorways, but he grabbed a bayonet. He savoured the weight of a real weapon as he shoved against the flow of the mob and back outside.

Setheno made them wait until the docks could hold no more. *'We advance in a single mass,'* she announced, her vox-caster reaching out from the roofs, the command picked up and repeated until it had spread across the docks.

Stribolt waited, impatient, desperate for the fight, desperate to prove himself before the unbending, merciless saint that had come among them. Then the order came. Setheno leapt from the roof to the ground and led the charge into the streets of Volcanus. Stribolt lost sight of her. He ran to see her again. He feared to fall under her gaze, yet he was desperate for a blessing, however painful, however fatal.

He ran towards the absolution of fire.

Consumed by the terror of faith, the mob moved up the widest avenues towards the maelstrom of war. To the rear, the lifter and the *Iron Repentance* continued in their tasks. The charge picked up momentum, and Stribolt had a sense of the limitless force of the crusade. He raced past the dark windows of the hab towers. On another day, the inhabitants of those blocks would have hidden, driven mad with fear at the sight of tens of thousands of Armageddon's damned loose and rampaging. On another day, Stribolt would have shown them how justified their fears were.

But not today.

Today the only target was the orks. Today there was only the sacred fire.

Setheno took the crusade right at a major intersection. Stribolt heard the shriek of voices human and xenos, the chatter of guns, the rumble of engines. He took the turn without slowing. He ran straight into the full battle. Setheno had brought them against a large contingent of orks. There must have been thousands of ork footsoldiers. Stribolt saw only a solid mass of the enemy filling the street, and moving through them the ugly, savage bulk of battlewagons. The greenskin infantry greeted the swarm of humans with snarls of delighted rage.

Some of the prisoners broke and tried to run. So did a larger number of refugees. The grey saint had foreseen the cowardice, and placed enforcers at the rear of the column. They turned their shotguns on the deserters. They blew the heads off the first to run. The others, wailing, turned back to the fight.

The orks waded in with crude, heavy blades longer than Stribolt's arm. The tanks opened up with their turret guns and cannons. Their huge, articulated claws swung through the mass of combatants. Orks and humans both fell. The greenskins with armour heavy enough to save them laughed at the enormous massacre.

Stribolt howled to drown out the mockery. The bullets were thudding into the bodies ahead of him. He found himself in the midst of a confusion of orks and humans. There was no order, only the cauldron of struggle. He stabbed and slashed with his bayonet. He opened one ork's throat, then jammed the blade through another's rib cage. It stuck in the bones. The brute wailed but did not fall. It raised its own weapon. Stribolt leaped at the ork, sailing over the brute's cleaver swing. It snapped at him with its jaws, tearing a chunk of flesh from his right calf. He swung himself around its neck and jabbed his thumbs into its eyes. The ork shrieked. It waved the cleaver blindly, trying to slice him from his perch. He dropped down and rammed his shoulder into the orks' legs. It fell and was trampled.

A stream of blood splashed against the side of Stribolt's face as he snatched the ork's cleaver from its broken fingers. He turned. An ork with arms like tree branches had ripped the head off an inmate with its bare hands. It grinned through the fountain of vitae. It brought its huge shotgun to bear. Stribolt dropped low. The shot blew apart two inmates.

Stribolt lunged through their falling bodies. It took all his strength to wield the cleaver and he brought it down on the ork's wrist. He cut most of the way through the limb. The hand dangled. Startled, the greenskin dropped the shotgun. It stared at the wound, offended. It bent down to retrieve the weapon. Platen grabbed it instead. He shoved the muzzle in the ork's face and pulled the trigger. The shotgun exploded, shredding Platen's torso and face. The ork stumbled back a step, laughing at the mishap, and Stribolt slammed the cleaver through its throat. He sawed until the greenskin fell. Then the press of more and more and more bodies carried him forward.

Stribolt was part of a wave. The prisoners pressed against the orks and held them. The tanks were immobilised by the crush. They had no room to turn. Their cannon fire stopped as ork footsoldiers jumped aboard to beat down gunners with too indiscriminate an aim. Stribolt had a glimpse of Setheno atop one of the tanks. She cut a gunner down with her power sword and threw a grenade inside the turret. The melee obscured her from his sight in the next second, but he heard the explosion. He jumped onto the shoulders of another ork and brought the cleaver down on its head, bashing at the beast's helmet. On both sides, for thousands of metres in either direction, the street convulsed with struggling bodies. More orks were arriving to combat still more prisoners.

In this corner of Volcanus, the orks had ceased to advance.

The ork threw Stribolt before he could sink the blade in its skull. He flew through the air and came down on another ork that was spraying a cluster of prisoners with flaming promethium. The ork stumbled forward. Stribolt straightened from his landing and jabbed the blade into the fuel tanks. It stuck. Promethium jetted uncontrollably. He jumped to the side and pushed through the crush. Human and ork bodies shielded him from the worst of the explosion, but liquid fire splashed against his chest. He beat at the flames. They seared through his prison tunic. His flesh burned. The pain made him scream.

It was an ecstasy.

It was an absolution.

Vision smeared by agony, he lunged at another wall of green flesh. He clawed and beat at the ork, half aware of the shapes of fellow prisoners hailing blows on the same target. His eyes were filled with tears of pain and tears of fervour. Did the saint see? Did she see the sacrifice? Did she grant him redemption?

The ork went down beneath the fists and boots of a dozen humans. Stribolt kept hitting with all the fury of his torment. He looked about, blinking away the tears. Where was Setheno? He had to see her. He had to know if he had earned a new judgement.

A huge shadow fell over him. He looked up. The claw of a battlewagon reached down to gather and crush. In the final moment before the iron fist closed on him, he shrieked his plea for redemption.

'*Do you see me?*'

His answer was the darkness and the shattering of bone.

## 2. YARRICK

We spoke to Mannheim once on the journey between Volcanus and Irkalla. We let him know we had left the hive and were making for the extraction point. That was an hour after we had left the hive, when we were still in the rolling terrain before Anthrand. We could still hear the war. We could still smell the smoke. We could even hear the greenskin army, but we could not see it. We had put a horizon between ourselves and the enemy. So we spoke to Mannheim.

Once.

After that, we dared not. The orks kept encroaching over the horizon. Spira detoured as best she could while keeping us on track. All day and into the evening, we caught sight of infantry and heavy armour movements. None of it was towards Volcanus. On several occasions, a deep insect snarl drew our eyes skyward. Squadrons of bombers flew just beneath the clouds. Some headed northeast, in the direction of Death Mire. Others went due east.

'They're heading for Armageddon Secundus,' Brenken said.

'Or preparing to, at the very least.'

'How big was that space hulk?'

'Too big.' We were seeing more and more signs that Ghazghkull had committed only a portion of his forces against Volcanus. He had more, much more, at his disposal and was not being idle during the siege of the hive.

We maintained vox silence. Colonel Helm's pilot would know where to find us. We were a single vehicle travelling a landscape that had become occupied territory. If we were discovered, we were lost, and so, perhaps, was Armageddon.

Night was falling when Irkalla appeared before us. We saw it first as clusters of huge, broken silhouettes. They gathered definition and mass as we closed in, but not life. They were the ghosts of buildings: collapsed façades, eroded towers, chapels sunken in on themselves. Violence, its nature obscure, had brought history in Irkalla to a stop. Wind, the driving dust of storms and acid downpours were eating at the ruins. The city was a cemetery now, interring its own memory. Its homes and manufactoria were its gravestones and monuments. They were all crumbling. Eventually, a night would fall over Irkalla, and no dawn would find it.

Spira drove straight through. Even the echoes of the engine were muffled as if the walls they bounced off were soft, growing and insubstantial. The orks, as we had guessed, were not here. They were not as far away as we would like, though. We saw occasional flashes of light to the north and the east. We heard the distant growl of huge engines.

'Still laughing at us,' I muttered.

'Commissar?'

'Nothing.'

The roads of Irkalla were broken. Many were stretches of clay between buildings, all traces of pavement long gone. Others had become deep, narrow canyons. They were traces of the convulsion that had been the city's doom. We crossed Irkalla without incident, but it weighed on my spirit with the force of an omen. This was the future Ghazghkull sought to bring to all of Armageddon. I prayed Tempestora and Volcanus would rise again. If I kept my vow to let no other hive fall, perhaps they would.

I rejected the omen. Instead, I read Irkalla as a goad.

On the other side of the city, the Valkyrie was waiting for us.

'Helm is a good man,' I said.

Brenken nodded. 'Mark him down as one to trust.'

'I shall.'

The pilot's name was Wengraf. He marched forward from his craft to greet us as we pulled up. 'Colonel Helm said I was to take you to Hive Infernus,' he said.

'To the staging ground of the Iron Skulls,' Brenken said.

'Yes, colonel.'

'We should take advantage of being in the air,' I said.

'True.' To Wengraf she said, 'We'll make this a reconnaissance flight. Take us as close to the enemy formations as possible. Carefully.'

Neither of us wanted to be shot down a second time.

Wengraf performed his mission well. The orks made it easier by being utterly unconcerned with concealment. Flames and bursts of energy lit up their encampments. The construction of their mad inventions continued without cease. Shields were piled upon shields on the vehicles. In the forges of the night, there were new weapons being born. Some would kill their creators. The ones that did not would bring grief to us. But on this night I was grateful for the greenskins' mania. Looking through the Valkyrie's viewing blocks, Brenken and I put together our most complete picture yet of the ork campaign.

There were some regions Wengraf dared not approach. He had to be wary of aircraft. And he gave a wide berth to stable, unmoving lights suspended many metres above the ground. We didn't need to get any closer to know those were the signs of immense war machines.

The worst thing we saw was, far to the northeast, a fiery glow on the horizon. Death Mire was already burning. Brenken and I exchanged looks. We said nothing. What use were words? We saw what we had known was going to happen. It had come sooner than expected. That was all. That was bad enough.

'There are several distinct armies,' Brenken said a few hours into the flight.

'Each strong enough to take a hive, or at least one without adequate defence.'

She snorted. 'And what is adequate?'

'More than what we were permitted on this continent.' I looked out the viewing block again. I saw a flash bright enough to be an ammunition dump blowing up. If it was an accident, it revealed an entire line of stompas. Whatever loss had just happened, the orks would regard it as nothing more than a stumble. 'They're much further towards Secundus than we had thought.'

'How long until they reach the jungle, do you think?'

I shrugged. 'I'm not sure. None of these armies appear to be on the march.'

'Camped for the night?'

'Perhaps, but all of them?'

'True, that doesn't sound like orks.'

'Nor does this level of coordination and discipline,' I admitted. 'But there it is.'

'So they're waiting,' Brenken said.

'For Volcanus to fall. Ghazghkull is going to take all of his armies through the Equatorial Jungle at once.' Then the deluge would descend on Armageddon Secundus. Every sight before us on this night had underscored the importance of our mission. I saw also a minute glimmer of hope. 'If they are waiting,' I said, 'the hours the canoness buys us will make a difference.'

'A tactical mistake at last?' Brenken said.

'I don't know. Perhaps not.' The strategic benefit of hitting Secundus with everything was obvious. 'It will be up to us to turn the decision against him.'


## 3. SETHENO


Setheno's crusade held the orks in the south-west quarter of Volcanus for hours. The greenskins sent infantry in greater and greater numbers to confront the prisoners. And meanwhile the lifter and the *Iron Repentance* continued to empty Nemesis Island of its charges. Inexhaustible numbers of animals tore each other to pieces. Justice was meted out in the midst of war, and minute after minute was gained for Armageddon's counterattack. Individual units of battle-weary Steel Legion troopers joined the battle. Their platoons smashed, they were driven ahead of the orks. Here they fought back, and around them the mob gained direction and focus. Desperation for honour, for redemption and for life fuelled the struggle, and the legionnaires, prisoners and refugees hit the orks all the harder.

And still: stalemate. Massive as the charge was, it could not drive the much greater force of the orks from the hive. But it drew the invaders' focus. It tied up resources. The orks could not resist the kind of challenge presented by the damned. The savagery was too familiar.

Setheno concentrated on the battlewagons. She moved from tank to tank, ducking under fire and then climbing aboard to strike down the vulnerable crews. She turned the heavy armour into flaming pyres. From their roofs, she praised the Emperor's name, amplifying her prayers through her helmet's vox-caster. She held *Skarprattar* high before each strike, so the prisoners who could not hear her would see her, see the light of holiness, and be called upon to renew the fury of redemption.

The battlewagons were inviting targets. The more the ork footsoldiers rushed to the fight, the more they hampered the tanks. The vehicles laid waste to all within the reach of their articulated arms. But barely able to move, they became fixed gun emplacements. They fell to her attacks. The streets roared with their flames.

The western sector of Volcanus was a tight, expanding, burning knot of war. Its density achieved a purity of murder. No step could be taken except through the flesh of an enemy. The grey of her armour was slicked with a wash of crimson. She waded through blood, she cut through bone, and she left a wake of fire and faith.

Where she walked, the prisoners howled prayers as they fought. They were deathbed conversions, but they had seen the truth she had brought to them. They felt the touch of her clarity. They embraced their sacrifice.

Perhaps they purchased some benefit for their souls. On that count, she had no insight. Nor did she care. All that mattered was the tactical value of their martyrdom. All that mattered was the hours they bought.

Time blurred. The battle was a storm of blood. Setheno's awareness of location faded. Her focus was on the next step, the next blow, the next kill. An ork came at her with a chain-axe. She shot out its throat. On her right, she sliced the fingers off another's hand before it could fire a rocket at point-blank range, and then she drove the power sword's point up through its chin and out the top of its skull.

But when the pounding of great footsteps began, the new necessity drew her attention to the wider view of the street. The stompas were coming. The stalemate was drawing to an end.

But not yet, she thought. Not just yet.

Two stompas appeared, one at either end of the avenue. They were as tall as the lower hab blocks, and so wide they blocked the streets completely. They were the walls of a vice, coming together with a steady, inexorable pace. Combatants fled from their heavy steps, but even the time between each slow stride was not enough. Running was impossible. Orks and humans were crushed beneath the massive feet. The stompas fired, but only with the shoulder turrets. The gunners were attempting some degree of discrimination in their targets. More evidence of the unusual discipline imposed on the greenskins by their prophet.

The discipline worked against the orks. Setheno was hurling an army against them that was destined from the first to be sacrificed. On these streets, the tactics of orks and humans were reversed. The greenskins had more interest in preserving the lives of their kin than did the humans.

The situation would not last. The orks' bloodlust would dominate, and their restraint would vanish.

A few more minutes. A few more small victories.

'We force the xenos to extremes,' Setheno announced. 'Strike now. Strike hard. Find redemption now or be lost to the Emperor's sight forever.'

Around her, the frenzy intensified. She saw the spiritual desperation in the eyes, and in the faces, and in the gestures of every human within the reach of her voice. They attacked the orks with the full fury that came of the fusion of spiritual terror and spiritual hope.

And they pushed the orks back. To Setheno's surprise, there was movement. It was possible to move forward, to pick up speed, to run. The orks were falling...

No. They were pulling back.

Even as she riddled more greenskins with bolter shells, Setheno looked up and down the street. She saw organised movement, not a rout. The stompas had reversed course. Even more slowly than they had advanced, they walked backwards. They left open space. The remaining battlewagons drove through the infantry battles towards the gaps. They mowed down many of their own troops, but the more valuable resource was preserved. The heavy armour disappeared, pulled away down the sidestreets. The footsoldiers followed. Orks in power armour, who had just arrived on the scene, disappeared next. Setheno had the impression of the sudden withdrawing of a tide. The withdrawal that precedes the arrival of a great wave.

Two more stompas appeared at the far ends of the street, and then two more. They went to work with cannons and wrecking balls. They resumed their strategy of the night before. They blasted at the base of towers. Tall ones. Spires that stretched for thousands of metres.

The work of destruction took seconds.

Instead of a warning, Setheno shouted a promise. 'Your reward comes now!' she pronounced, and pointed at the swaying tower before her.

The base disintegrated. The stompas disappeared behind the sudden billow of dust and rockcrete powder. Bracketed by other structures almost as tall, the tower began its fall. Its shadow fell over the avenue. The network of walkways shattered like icicles. Their fragments fell before the huge monolith. To Setheno's rear, the other tower began to fall towards its brother.

The prisoners and the orks still in the street froze before the vastness that came for them.

Setheno ran for the side of the street. She knew how long she had. She would not reach an intersection. She smashed through the nearest door without stopping.

Seconds slipping away. The shadow followed by the mass. A cracking thunder announced the end of the crusade.

She was in a hab. She turned left and banged open the door to the stairwell. She heard voices above and below. There were still people here, citizens crying out in terror.

She had used up her allotment of regret decades ago.

Final seconds. In her mind's eye, she saw the great eclipse of the joined shadows. She jumped over the railing. She dropped straight down the shaft formed by the spiral of the staircase. She fell towards darkness. She grabbed a landing three floors down, arrested her fall with a jerk, let go to plummet a few more, stopped herself again, dropped again, and then darkness swallowed the whole of the staircase. Millions of tonnes of rockcrete hit the street, and took everything with it.

The impact of her landing and the blows of the collapse knocked her unconscious. When she woke, Setheno was surrounded by the deep silence of vast death. The hab's roots went as far as the upper reaches of the underhive. She sat up. Her armour's servo-motors caught and whined. Waves of pain collided across her frame. But she could move.

She turned on her helmet's light. Where there had been a shaft, there was now a solid mass of rubble. The vault of the sublevel buckled. The groan of settling rubble disrupted the silence. Dust fell in steady streams on all sides.

The crusade was finished. She had done what she could. She had held the orks in Volcanus past its fall, keeping them anchored to the hive into another night. Whether that would suffice was up to Yarrick now.

She stood. She turned around until she spotted a grating in the floor. She tore it up. The drain went deeper into the underhive. Her path was clear: through the underhive to the docks once more, then commandeer the lifter back to Hive Infernus.

Above, the men and women who had followed her into combat had found their annihilation. Did they find redemption in the end?

That was not her concern. Her duty had been to push the condemned to seek absolution. She had done so, and they had met their final judgement.

# CHAPTER 13
# THE CRY

## 1. YARRICK

We reached Hive Infernus in a dim, crimson dawn. The Season of Shadows had begun. The winds of the Season of Fire had dropped, but now a deeper flame had kindled. In the Fire Wastes, the volcanic chains were in full cry. Their ash clouds joined the dust already blanketing Armageddon. The distinction between day and night was fading. We had entered a time of perpetual lightning, of a roiling sky glowing like a furnace, lit by the rage of the mountains. Our days and nights would now be shadows of red and black. We would be fighting beneath an endless fury.

Mannheim met us at the landing pad in the Legio Metalica's staging ground. 'We won't have much time,' he said as we walked towards the command block. 'If von Strab doesn't already know you're here, it won't be long before he does.'

'I know,' I said. 'So we won't try to hide.'

Von Strab's blind spot concerning the orks was immense. It was also one of his rare ones. His eyes were everywhere.

Whether his tools were human, servitor, pict-feed, one way or another, there were few corners of Armageddon into which he could not see, if he felt the need. Even in the underhives, he had his spies. But he couldn't look everywhere at once. The intensity of his surveillance increased in direct proportion to his presence. His physical safety was his paramount concern. This was followed by the need to know of anything that might conceivably offer a threat to that safety. Around his quarters, nothing moved without his knowledge. That was not my destination. The astropathic choir of Hive Infernus, housed in the control tower of the spaceport, was kilometres away from the administrative centre. But it was an important lever of power. I had no hope of reaching Genest, the master of the astropathic choir, without being seen by one of von Strab's creatures, organic or bionic.

'Your presence here will be notable,' I said to Brenken. 'If he sees you and Princeps Mannheim approaching, his focus will be on you. I'm hoping he won't hear what I'm up to until it's too late.'

'Should I have my pistol drawn?' Brenken asked, half joking.

'No,' I said. 'But keep it visible. Make him wonder.'

Mannheim and Brenken left the staging area a few minutes ahead of me. I gave von Strab time to notice them, and to busy himself with preparations for the encounter. Then I began the journey to the spaceport. I made good time. I took the maglev transports. There was no stealth to be had, but speed mattered.

It was all a gamble. I couldn't know if our diversion was working. I watched for von Strab's security forces. I watched the people around me. I had hopes that von Strab was in the dark about my presence. Even if he was aware of me, I didn't think he would order an attack. He had no reason to.

Not unless he guessed where I was going and why. I did not give him that much credit. Even so, I prepared myself for the worst. I was ready to kill anyone who tried to stop me from reaching the astropaths.

No one did. I was at the spaceport in less than an hour. In the tower, I rode the rattling lift up to the midpoint. It deposited me in a vast scriptorium filled with clerical clamour. This was where the messages to be sent were prepared, and the messages received were annotated. Distortions and misinterpretations were not unusual. The astropaths themselves were the ones who had the training and the knowledge to decipher and interpret the visions that reached them from the warp, and to encode the outgoing messages into the psychic forms that would travel the immaterium. It was the duty of this army of scribes to cross-reference, catalogue, contextualise and prioritise the communications. It was up to them to ensure the messages found their way to the right hands. The warp storm had cut message traffic to nothing, but there was still a large backlog to work through. Messages of vital military importance always received attention first. Trade queries and the like were dealt with in order, as time permitted. It did so now. There would be a great deal cleared. Assuming the orks left the scribes to work in peace.

I walked between rows of high standing desks. Few of the scribes even looked up from their data-slates and parchments. The air of the scriptorium was filled by the sounds of rhythmic tapping, the scratching of vellum, low whispers sounding out and discarding fragments of sentences, and sporadic coughs. There were perhaps a hundred scribes. Each individual seemed silent. Collectively, they created a constant susurration.

At the far end of the scriptorium was a pair of bronze doors engraved with the eye of the Adeptus Astra Telepathica. Two guards stood outside. They did not wear the uniform of von Strab's retinue; they wore the sashes of the Telepathica. Their loyalty should be to the choir beyond the door rather than to the overlord. On Armageddon, that meant little. It was entirely possible, even likely, they had been suborned.

I did not draw my bolt pistol as I walked up to them. I gave them the chance to show where their allegiance lay.

'I must speak with Master Genest,' I said.

On my left, the male guard said nothing. On my left, the woman said, 'He is meditating. He can't be disturbed.'

'He will have to be.' Was she lying? I was unwilling to guess. The guards looked at each other.

The male said, 'I will announce you, Commissar…?' He waited for my name.

I ignored the question. 'That won't be necessary. Let me in. Close the door behind me.'

They hesitated, then acquiesced. They pulled the doors open, then shut them with a clang after I passed through.

The choir was held in a nautilus spiral of depressions in marble. Each astropath sat on a small pew in a narrow cleft in the stone. Only their heads were visible above the surface of the floor. Their eyes were closed in a false semblance of sleep. The psychic energy in the room made my skin crawl. I forced my eyes to circle the spiral all the way to the centre. There Genest sat with his head bowed. I walked the circles, twisting and turning until I stood at the centre. I knelt and placed my hand on Genest's shoulder. 'Master Genest,' I said, 'the Emperor calls to you. More urgently than at any time of your life. Will you heed Him?'

I waited. After a minute, Genest raised his head. His eyes searched mine. 'What does He require?' he croaked.

'You tried sending a plea for help earlier. You must do so again, to specific recipients.'

'Which ones?'

'The Blood Angels. The Ultramarines. The Salamanders.' Those were the three Chapters who had forces close enough to the Armageddon System that they might be able to aid us in time.

'We have been unable to send or receive any messages since the warp storm began,' Genest said. 'You understand, commissar? The last thing to enter the system was the *Claw of Desolation*.'

'I understand, Master Genest. Before you tell me, I also understand that Overlord von Strab has forbidden any calls for help.'

'We are fortunate he didn't detect the one we sent on behalf of Princeps Mannheim.'

'And it is tragic no one else did.'

Genest's blank eyes stared straight ahead. The walls of his stone cocoon were inlaid with gold. The lines formed runes and occult patterns. They dragged at my awareness. I could only imagine how effective they must be in drawing Genest's consciousness into the folds of the immaterium. His eyes were blind, but I had no doubt the runes blazed before his inner vision. Genest said, 'How bad is it?'

'Very. The orks have conquered Armageddon Prime. They're on their way here. Von Strab's response has been disastrous, and there is no reason to believe he will suddenly show wisdom. Even if he did, the threat is far worse than I imagined.'

'You think we can't win.'

I hesitated, torn between my vow, my faith, and cold reason. I knew Armageddon could fall, yet I would not let it. 'We will win,' I said. 'We will win by doing what must be done. And we must summon the help of the Adeptus Astartes.'

'And if we can't send our plea through the storm?'

'You will. Because you must.'

Genest turned his head to face me. The white eyes seemed grey. His skull was brittle. The lines in his face were deep canyons. Wisps of colourless hair, insubstantial as hope, floated out from beneath his hood. 'You ask much.'

'I ask nothing. The situation demands this of you. Your duty to the God-Emperor requires it. And we have always owed Him everything.'

Genest nodded. 'Are there any details you hope to convey?'

'No. Keep things simple. This is a cry for help from Armageddon. That will suffice.'

'If we're interrupted…'

'I know. You won't be.' We both knew von Strab would stop the choir if he realised what was going on. I expected he would. Brenken and Mannheim's diversion would grant me only a limited head start. It would be my task to ensure Genest completed his.

I stood up. 'There may be noise beyond the doors.'

'We won't hear it. What's important is that we not be disturbed physically.'

'I'll see that you aren't. Thank you, Master Genest.'

'No, commissar. Thank you.' The corner of his mouth twitched upwards. 'I know you're right. Accepting the whims of the overlord as a necessity has been a burden. You've recalled me to the path of my vows. I feel the burden lift, and that is a gift. This is the form my war will take. I am satisfied.'

'You'll have earned your place in the song,' I said.

Genest laughed. The sound was dry, pebbles in leather. 'And will there be any singers left, commissar?'

'There will,' I promised, and left the chamber.

* * *

## 2. MANNHEIM

'I'm surprised to see you, Colonel Brenken,' von Strab said. He sat on his throne with the air of offended virtue. While expressing surprise, he was doing a masterful job of concealing it in his face. If he had been startled by Brenken's return, Mannheim thought, he had already moved on to calculating his response.

'You were expecting me to die?' Brenken asked.

'No. I just never imagined you would be capable of dereliction. But I expect you had bad advice.'

Brenken stiffened. Mannheim felt his own muscles lock in solidarity. On the way to von Strab's quarters, Brenken had spoken about what it had cost her to leave behind the tiny fragments of her regiment.

'What were your last orders to your captains?' Mannheim had asked.

'To fight as long as they could, then go to ground.'

'You're hoping for an extraction? Helm was lucky that single Valkyrie wasn't shot down. Von Strab was shouting about its flight minutes after it took off.'

'I won't have my troops thrown away,' Brenken had replied.

Now the colonel said, 'The 252nd has done all that was possible and more. I'm here to organise the rescue of my remaining troops, overlord.'

'Your return was unauthorised.'

'And,' Brenken continued as if von Strab had not spoken, 'I am here to report to you, in person, about the threat we face. Overlord, if we do not act, all of Armageddon is at risk.'

'Oh? What would you have me do?'

'A massive counterattack. Gather the regiments of the Steel Legion. March with the Legio Metalica. If we hit the orks as they're crossing the jungle, we can keep them bogged down until reinforcements arrive.'

'You agree with this proposal, princeps?'

'I do,' Mannheim said.

'So we should leave the hives undefended?'

'If we allow the orks to reach Secundus,' Brenken said, 'our defences will already have been breached.'

Von Strab smiled. 'But the jungle will not allow the orks to reach Secundus.'

'Overlord,' Brenken said, 'I assure you, they will cross the jungle. If they haven't begun the process already, they will very soon. I am as sure of this as I have been of anything in my entire career.'

'Given your lack of success in Tempestora and Volcanus, I'm sceptical of your judgement,' von Strab told her. He shrugged. 'But we can all be wrong. I have a better approach in mind. If the orks set foot on Secundus, they will find our cities well defended and they will be repulsed by the Legio Metalica.'

Mannheim blinked. The fate of the Iron Skulls was now in play. It had been torn from his grasp. His proud legion was suddenly the plaything of a petty tyrant's whim. He saw a new disaster taking shape. Von Strab was ready to repeat the mistake that had doomed Armageddon Prime. Piecemeal, he was engineering the loss of the planet. 'I must warn against such an action,' Mannheim said.

'Duly noted, princeps. My confidence in your abilities appears to be stronger than your own. No false humility, please. This is hardly the time.' Von Strab began to form his unctuous smile, then stopped. He frowned. 'What reinforcements?' he said.

'Overlord?' Mannheim asked.

'Colonel, you mentioned reinforcements.'

'Yes, because we need them.'

'We do not, and we cannot have them.'

'We do and we must,' she replied.

Von Strab stared at her. 'You're very certain.'

'I am. We–'

He cut her off. 'Did Commissar Yarrick survive?' He didn't wait for an answer. 'He arrived with you, didn't he?' Again, he didn't wait. He rose from the throne. His retinue clapped their gauntlets against their rifles. 'Get to the spaceport,' he ordered. He glared at Mannheim and Brenken. His face and scalp had turned purple. It was the first time Mannheim had seen him enraged. It was, he realised, the first time he had seen von Strab feel threatened. 'I will not be humiliated,' the overlord said.

'It is odd,' Mannheim replied, 'that you would prefer to be annihilated.'

## 3. GENEST

The rest of the choir had remained silent during his exchange with Yarrick. They had heard, though. And when Genest said, 'We have work to do,' the prayer that greeted his words was heartfelt.

It was a prayer for the strength to complete the task. It was a prayer of gratitude that they were taking meaningful action. It was a prayer for protection against what they would now encounter.

'Speak through me,' Genest told the choir. 'In the name of the God-Emperor. Be His words and His will.' He opened his inner eye. Slowly. Even before he began, the warp storm tore at him. It had become the fanged backdrop to his awareness, gnawing at his edges, waiting for him to turn its way, hungry for his mind and soul, and for the minds and souls of all the astropaths in his charge.

And now he turned.

Chaos raked him with claws. Pain stabbed into the core of his identity. It tried to pry him apart with lightning. A cacophony of half-formed ideas, broken language and molten dreams poured into him. His perception fell into a whirlpool, was shattered by eruptions, swept up in a hurricane. If he had been alone, his identity would have been whipped to shreds. But the choir was with him, and he with it. The telepathic song was a collective strength, a core that preserved. It held fast in the face of the storm, but Genest was just at its edges. He had to go deeper. He had to work his way through the vortex.

The message was simple. That was a mercy. It was direct, urgent, impossible to misinterpret. Genest forged a psychic impression as dense and focused as a bolter shell. It was as immune to distortion as any astropathic communication could be. Now that he was committed to this action, the message was vital to Genest. He shared the cry of Armageddon. He had not witnessed what Yarrick had in Secundus. But he felt the warp storm. He knew its corrosion. And he knew it was not a simple coincidence. Somehow, it was linked to the orks. They had not willed it into existence. That was impossible. But orks did have a psychic force of some kind. A threat as monumental as Yarrick described would have an effect on the materium. Perhaps the warp storm was one such effect.

Collective will, collective urgency, collective desperation. They gave direction to the choir. A unity of iron to pierce the chaos, to batter through the wall of howling disorder surrounding the Armageddon System. Genest directed the blows, and he was one with the blows. His identity had a single purpose, and the goal preserved him. The talons of unreality raked the flesh of his soul, the choir's soul. The choir bled, and he bled. The storm would tear them to tatters.

Forward. Deeper. And the storm reaching deeper into him. Entropy was insistent as acid.

Coming apart. Eroded. Disintegrating.

But though he was fraying, he held the shape of the cry. He forced it through the storm. Then he and the choir, mortally injured but fused in duty and need, hurled the cry to the galaxy and Armageddon's need shrieked across dreams.

## 4. YARRICK

In the scriptorium, I spoke with the two guards. The woman's name was Dreher. The man was Fertig. 'The choir is calling for aid,' I told them. 'The overlord will send forces to stop this message from being sent. Anyone who joins in that attempt is turning against the needs of Armageddon, and of the Imperium itself. I will use lethal force. Stand with me, leave, or fight me now. Decide.' I left my pistol holstered. I wanted their decision to be a truthful one.

'I am with you,' Dreher said. Fertig nodded.

'Good.' I turned to the ranks of scribes. A few of the nearest had raised their heads to watch our exchange. The others worked on. I raised my voice. 'I am suspending work in this chamber,' I announced.

A startled silence followed. An army of confused faces turned my way. Nothing in the memory of these faithful servants had ever interfered with their duties, least of all the commands of a military officer.

'Leave,' I told them. 'Immediately.'

They did, quietly, quickly, without question. They did not

understand, nor did they wish to. They believed their ignorance would shield them. Perhaps.

Even before the scriptorium was fully vacated, I began overturning the desks and benches. Dreher and Fertig joined in. We threw together two makeshift barricades, one in front of the elevators, and a larger one, over two metres high, before the bronze doors, with room behind it for us. The rest of the chamber's furniture we threw to the floor, denying any clear run to the doors to the astropathic chamber.

The lift clattered to life.

'Get ready,' I said. We took up our positions. We aimed bolt pistol and lasrifles at the elevator and through the stacked desks. 'Hold fire until my order,' I said.

The doors opened. Men wearing von Strab's colours collided with the first barricade. They climbed on top. There were a dozen of them, their weapons drawn.

'Fire,' I said.

We shot them before they had a chance to descend. We caught them in the open, vulnerable, surprised. They had not expected to be opposed. They had not believed it possible for anyone to fight the edicts of Herman von Strab. In those first few seconds, four of them were killed by their presumption. Two more dropped to the front of the barrier. They scrambled for non-existent cover. We took them down too. The others fell back to the other side, and they returned fire. Las burned though iron and wood. It chipped at our shelter, but couldn't reach us. Not yet.

'Stay down,' I told Dreher and Fertig. The pile of furniture was no barrier to my bolt shells. I aimed at the movement by the elevator and shot a man through the midsection.

We traded fire for a few minutes. Von Strab's men ran back and forth, making my shots difficult. Fertig took a hit to the right arm. His breath whined. He could no longer raise his rifle. He perched it on a broken desk and kept firing.

I killed two more, then reloaded. The elevator doors opened again, unloading reinforcements. Numbers gave the von Strab troops courage, and they changed their tactics. They pushed against their barricade. The heap moved forward along the floor for almost two metres before it collapsed. The overlord's faithful rushed us. They ran into our fire, and we took some down, but there were only three of us. Their shots kept us down, seeking the thicker portions of our shield. Dreher's luck ran out. Las came through a gap and seared her through her throat. I killed two more of the enemy, and they were down to ten by the time they reached the barricade. Half of them fired low into the desks. The others began to climb. I jumped up, held the leg of a chair and kept my feet a metre off the ground, avoiding the incoming fire. I fired up and through the barrier, spreading my shots. Bodies fell. Fertig tried to scramble up too, but his arm was too weak. Las took him down at the legs, and when he fell, he was burned.

I was alone against seven. I threw a frag over the barricade and jumped back. It was a short toss. It came down on the other side, too close to be safe. I crouched against the doors. The las-fire stopped as the grenade landed. There was a half-second of shouts of alarm, then the blast, the wind of shrapnel, and the screams. A portion of the barricade blew my way. Jagged metal and wood slammed against bronze. They cut through the back of my coat, lacerating my flesh. I felt a hard punch against my spine. It knocked me forward, but did not impale. I stood, turned and charged back, pistol firing and sword drawn. I plunged through the burning gap in the barrier. Splintered wood gouged my face and smoke enveloped me as I ran. On the other side, blood slicked the floor. Men with no faces and missing limbs writhed. One of the enemy, his uniform torn, his chest bleeding, lunged at me. I hacked at his neck with my blade. He staggered back three steps, vitae fountaining over me, and then collapsed.

Two left standing, still stunned by the blast. One raised his rifle. I blew the right side of his skull away. The other backed away from his gun, arms up. 'Your actions betray Armageddon and the Emperor,' I said. I shot him in the face, obliterating a traitor. Then I took my sword to the injured troops, finishing them off. I struck without mercy, but as punishment.

Silence, then, dusted with the creaks of settling debris. It lasted a minute before the elevator rumbled once more. There was no shelter now. I advanced to the doors and pointed my bolt pistol, ready to fire. The doors ground open. Von Strab stood with five of his retinue. Brenken and Mannheim were there too. I lowered my weapon quickly before his men had an excuse to shoot.

Another moment when I might have killed von Strab passed. I had not sought it, but the opportunity had been there. A squeeze of the trigger, one simple act, and we would have both been absent from the rest of the war. Let the chroniclers decide if my decision was the correct one.

I stepped back from the elevator. The guards emerged, rifles trained on me. Von Strab waited until they had me surrounded, then stepped out. 'Disarm him,' he said. His voice snapped with anger. His right cheek twitched. His mask of control had slipped. I was pleased. I had never seen a blow land against his power before, and I am human. I was happy to be the author of his discomfort.

His guards hesitated. I holstered my pistol and sheathed my sword. I stared at them, daring them to come for my arms. They stood fast, guns unwavering. They did nothing more.

Von Strab walked away as if his order had been obeyed. He kicked his way through the wreckage towards the far doors. 'I will not be defied,' he announced.

Brenken and Mannheim came up behind the guards. They said nothing. Their rank spoke for them. The guards took a step back from me.

Von Strab was a few steps from the door. 'You're too late,' I bluffed.

He looked back. 'You should pray I'm not.'

He was bluffing too, I thought. He walked forward again. He reached for the door.

The scream came.

It was a single voice and many. It was a mosaic of psychic pain. It wrapped itself around our souls. It savaged us with the shrapnel of minds. The guards dropped their guns. All of us clapped our hands to our ears as if we could keep out the cry. It rose, it twisted, it drew itself out to a ragged scraping of high notes. At the end, I thought I detected, buried in the horror, a note of triumph.

The cry ended. Von Strab had fallen to his knees. He stood up and hauled open the doors. We followed him into the astropathic chamber.

The choir was shattered. Several of the shapes in the marble cocoons were still. Others twitched, their mouths slack and drooling. A few wept. Master Genest turned his head at the sound of our arrival. Blood ran from his eyes, from his ears, and from a hole that had opened in the centre of his forehead, as if a predatory animal had gouged him with a claw. His face had turned white veined with rotten green. I wondered if he could hear us. Yet his blank eyes were trained on me. With a voice that seemed to come from the depths of the void, he whispered, 'It is done.'

# CHAPTER 14
# HADES

## 1. YARRICK

If Mannheim and Brenken hadn't been witnesses, von Strab would have had me executed. And even their presence would have been insufficient if Genest had been unable to complete the call for help. But Armageddon's silence was broken. Its plight was known. Von Strab had to factor into his political calculations the arrival of other parties. So he publicly washed his hands of me. He had his guards escort me to Seroff's quarters.

The lord commissar stared at me. 'Well?' he asked. 'Not enough greenskins out there for you? You felt the need to kill men engaged in the loyal execution of their duty?'

I snorted. 'Can't you do any better than that, Dominic? I was doing what you should have done.'

'You really believe that working at cross-purposes to the supreme commander of Armageddon's defence is helpful?'

'You really believe that following his lead is?'

'I don't have to answer to you.'

'No. But in the end, you will be called upon to answer for your actions. Whether or not any of us survive this war.' His new defensiveness was telling. He had to be uneasy about the conduct of the war. Seroff was no fool. I thought he was also uncomfortable about his alliance with von Strab. 'You're better than von Strab,' I said. 'We are beholden to the Emperor, not the corrupt.'

I had given him a way out. He refused it. His features darkened with his hatred of me. 'The disloyal have no lessons to teach about corruption.'

I shrugged. 'Very true.'

He took my agreement as an insult. Which it was.

'So?' I asked. 'What now?'

'I want you out of my sight,' he said.

But not dead, and not in prison. He had the official authority to see to those fates, but not the moral one, and he was conscious of Mannheim, and, like von Strab, of who might be on their way to Armageddon.

Seroff and von Strab had made their decision even before the guards had brought me to the lord commissar. They sentenced me to my original punishment. They banished me from the seat of power. And so at last I came to Hades Hive.

I flew out on the same Valkyrie that had brought me to Volcanus. Wengraf was heading back to rejoin Teodor Helm's command. I sat in the cockpit with him. At the first sight of the hive, I winced. My right arm throbbed again. I rubbed it, though the pain ran deeper than the muscles. My shoulder tensed as if caught in a vice.

Wengraf noticed. 'Commissar?' he asked.

I flexed my arm. The pain flared into a bright shock, jerking me to the right. Then it faded. 'I'm all right,' I said. 'An old wound on an old man.'

Through the armourglass canopy, I looked at Hades as I had not in the past. In the pursuit of my duty to the planet, as I endeavoured to become familiar with all of Armageddon, I had been to Hades before. Not for long periods, but long enough to know my way around. Like all of the world's great hives, it was a sprawling, mountainous concatenation of manufactoria and habs, each blending into the other. From this distance, spires and chimneys were indistinguishable in the shroud of black smoke. Hades was different from the other hives because of its decline. Its governor, Lord Matthias Tritten, had the least influence of any of his peers, and thus was one of the most beholden to von Strab. Hades' principle industries were mining and the refining of ore. Its output was measured in the millions of tonnes every year, but every year, the production decreased. One seam after another was exhausted. A massive, interconnected tapestry of mines spread from the city walls. The mixture of surface and sub-surface operations had turned the landscape outside Hades into a hollowed-out moonscape. The search for more deposits spread the mark of the hive ever further, but the last few decades had made it clear the richest reserves in that region of the continent had already been found. There was still work for millions of Hades' citizens.

And there was only desperation for millions more.

That desperation, I thought, would be useful. We were all desperate now, even if not every inhabitant knew it yet.

Hades Hive was distinct from the other hives in another way – its mountain of spires was hollow. The towers, manufactoria, chapels and winding, labyrinthine streets surrounded a structure so massive, it was the size of a small city on its own. The inner fastness of Hades was an indestructible relic of its history, of its former wealth, and of other wars, millennia past, on Armageddon. The hive had grown up around the great fortress. It was a squat, boxy monstrosity. It had been an attempt to create an entirely self-sufficient, unbreachable arcology. Ore refining, administration, worship, habitation – they were all contained within its gigantic rockcrete-and-iron walls. The fastness was a folly, suitable only to a state of war. Inside, there were more and still more barriers, a concentric retrenchment that envisioned the need to pull back and back and back, until only the most vital elements held out in one final keep. Life confined to its interior was intolerable. Even the governor's palace was a recent addition, built up on the fastness's roof. It was not a structure anyone inhabited or worked in by choice. For the hundreds of thousands inside, there was no choice.

On this day, I saw it with new eyes. I thought it was beautiful.

I looked down at the terrain, at the vast pits, the sinkholes, and the pinpricks of shafts. This was a network of hollowed out land that put the trenches of Volcanus to shame. I saw potential there too.

Wengraf descended to a landing pad inside the east wall. A wide road and rail network led to the main gate on this side. Transport vehicles and ore trains were still making their runs. They would do so until the threat was imminent. Inside the gates, the road traffic was re-routed around the tanks and artillery of the 33rd, 97th, 110th and 146th Regiments. Helm, overall commander due to seniority, had his troops on high alert, and his defence was ready for the enemy. The road would be the most inviting approach for the orks. I pictured the tactic used at Volcanus, and imagined the furious speed the battlewagons could achieve on that pavement. Helm had his heavy armour prepped to deny Ghazghkull this entry. As we landed, I saw plenty of activity on the walls. Good signs all.

A sergeant greeted me when I disembarked. 'Commissar Yarrick,' he said. 'Colonel Helm would like to meet you.' The soldier was an old veteran, long of arm and short of leg. His narrow face looked incongruous on his broad shoulders. He grinned as he saluted, and he kept grinning.

'What's your name, sergeant?' I asked as he led me from the landing pad.

'Lanner, commissar.'

'You seem amused, Sergeant Lanner.'

He nodded. 'Heard some good stories. Heard you don't put up with what that fat turd keeps shovelling our way.'

I managed to keep a straight face. Lanner's effrontery was astonishing. It was also bulletproof. I would be a hypocrite if I denied the accuracy of his evaluation of von Strab. I was also stunned any trooper would spout such blatant sedition to a commissar, never mind one he had just met.

I was caught off guard.

I liked the man immediately.

'I sense you're not one to conceal your opinions.'

Lanner chuckled. He tapped at his copious facial scars. 'I didn't come by all these in the battlefield, commissar. Amazing how many people object to a fellow being frank with them.'

'Amazing,' I said dryly.

His grin was huge now. 'It really is.'

The command tent was set up midway between the landing pad and the lines of tanks. Lanner pulled the flap back, announced me, carelessly saluted and sauntered away. I stepped inside to find Teodor Helm who was alone. Though younger than Brenken, Helm was old enough and not new to combat. He was wiry, of medium height, and had eyes of a grey so pale they seemed translucent. 'I'm glad to meet you, commissar,' he said. 'I thought it best we had our first conference on our own.'

'I agree. Let me begin with my thanks,' I replied. 'Those of Colonel Brenken too.'

'How is she?'

'As well as a colonel whose command has been thrown away by a fool can be.' If Helm had sent Lanner to greet me, it was clear we were going to understand each other.

'Has any of the 252nd survived?'

'In Volcanus? We've heard nothing. We can hope. The Emperor protects.'

'The Emperor protects,' he repeated, heartfelt.

I glanced around the tent. Its contents were minimal: a vox unit, a single chair, a table with maps of Hades and its environs. 'May I ask why you've set up command here?' There were plenty of buildings overlooking the traffic node he had turned into staging grounds.

'More central,' he said. 'When I have to move, I expect I won't have much time.'

'Very true.' Everything I learned confirmed Brenken's judgement of Helm.

Helm picked up a data-slate from the table. 'I have orders concerning you, commissar.'

'My guess is my original assignment as recruitment overseer has changed.'

'It has. Somewhat. I'm instructed to assign you as political officer to whatever company will be first out to meet the orks.'

'Those orders are subtle in their intent.'

'Quite. I am also to keep you far from the levers of command.'

'I appreciate your candour.'

He tossed the data-slate back on the table. 'I have no intention of following orders so idiotic.'

'Do they come from General Andechs?'

'Ostensibly.'

'You are showing little respect for the chain of command,' I reminded him.

'As a commissar, it is not just your right, but your duty, to remove unfit officers from their position.'

'It is.'

'By extension, and in the absence of said unfit officers, it could be argued it becomes your responsibility to set aside their unfit orders.'

'So it could be argued, yes.'

He spread his hands. 'Then the matter is in your hands. Commissar, I have reason to doubt the validity of these orders.'

We understood each other. 'Tell me where things stand in Hades Hive,' I said.

'I have integrated the Hive Militia with the regiments. That has gone smoothly. But based on what you saw at Tempestora and Volcanus, are we strong enough to repel the orks?'

'No.'

His eyebrows shot up. 'You think they will take Hades?'

'They will not. We will hold. And the citizens must fight with us.'

'As they did in Volcanus?'

'Yes. With full regiments and more time to prepare.' And my vow.

Helm nodded. 'Very well,' he said. 'We do not have the armoury of Volcanus.'

'We'll manage. What is your take on the governor?'

'That you should meet him for yourself.'

'I see. He's back, then?'

'Yes. Von Strab sent them all back to their respective hives yesterday. Governor Tritten is weak politically. The extent of the poverty here…' He shook his head.

'I know. And the underhive?'

'Tritten can barely keep a lid on it. He would quarantine it if he could.'

The situation had been bad when I had last been here. It had gone downhill since. I would find a way to use it all. I would fashion Hades into a weapon with which to smash the orks. 'You're right,' I said. 'I should see the governor.'

'Sergeant Lanner's squad will escort you. He's inspecting the battlements.'

'Will he rally the people?'

Helm grimaced. 'You should see him,' he repeated.

'I see.' I turned to go. At the flap, I paused. 'Colonel,' I said, 'Hades will not fall, because we will not fight a defensive war. We will go on the offence. This hive will be our counterattack.'

Matthias Tritten was not where Lanner had expected to find him.

The sergeant looked up and down the ramparts. There was no sign of the governor and his retinue. He asked the troopers stationed nearby. Tritten had left not long before, descending to the streets. They didn't know where he'd gone, but it couldn't have been very far.

'Not like him,' Lanner said. 'He likes to be visible, that one.'

'You're not new to Hades,' I guessed.

'Born and bred,' he said with rough pride. 'Underhive rat, me. I remember Tritten's father. Haven't been here that much since I was tithed, but enough. Wants everybody to know he's the great man, does our lord governor.' He snorted. 'When he's out and about, you always know where he is and where he's been.'

So Tritten's absence was significant. I walked to the inward edge of the rampart and looked out at the streets. They were crowded, too much so. The pedestrian traffic was interfering with the movement of military convoys. Tritten, or his proxy during his absence, should have already converted the entire hive to a war footing. I was seeing citizens attempting to continue with their lives. Already, this was a significant failure of leadership.

I put my displeasure aside. Where would a normally ostentatious governor go that would draw little attention?

I pointed to a large chapel about a thousand metres away, just visible between soot-blackened hab blocks. 'Let's try there.'

Lanner grunted in the affirmative. We made our way down from the wall and through the choking traffic to the Chapel of the Martyrs Militant. The church was a good symbol of the decay of Hades Hive. Its architecture was grand, and the grime that covered its facade was no different from what was the case in the other hives. But the rose window had lost many of its panes of stained glass. Some had been bricked up, but there were gaps too. Inside, the pillars and vaults were rough with layers of dirt and acid erosion. The floor crunched beneath my boots, the rockcrete flaking. The tapestries and banners had grown threadbare. The grime was so thick it obscured their subjects, and they gleamed slightly, as if slimy to the touch. The foul wind of Hades blew in through the gaps in the window, filling the nave with the sulphur-and-diesel stink of the hive. The banners moved sluggishly.

The chapel was empty.

Lanner said, 'Usually somebody here.'

I agreed. Even between services, it was very odd to see pews completely empty in any public place of worship. 'Unless they've been made to leave,' I said. I moved down the nave.

At the transept crossing, we heard the echo of footsteps on our right. We stopped and waited. The doors to the crypt were in the north transept. After a few moments, the lord governor of Hades Hive emerged through the doors, accompanied by a squad of his personal guards. They wore the deep blue Tritten livery. Their uniforms were stained, unkempt. They looked more like bored, hired guns than loyal servants of the family.

Matthias Tritten was a soft man. His contours lacked definition. Middle-aged, of average weight and height, his robes of office seemed too heavy for him. He hesitated when he saw us, then swept forward, doing his best to look imperious. He failed.

'I ordered the sanctuary cleared,' he said as he neared us.

Ignoring him, Lanner said, 'Commissar Yarrick, Lord Tritten.'

'We were looking for you,' I said. 'We understood you were inspecting the defences.' I made a point of glancing around the space of the chapel. 'How do you find them?'

I made no attempt to hide my contempt. Instead of trying to have me arrested, Tritten became defensive. His eyes jumped about the room, hunted prey. He had none of von Strab's deftness in calculation. 'I saw what I needed to,' he said. 'There are some aspects which Colonel Helm should see to, and I will bring them to his attention.'

'He'll be grateful, yes he will,' Lanner said. I shot him a look and he took a step back.

Again, Tritten did not retaliate. Instead, he said, 'Good.' Clearly, he did not feel himself to be in a position of strength. For a governor, that was pathetic.

My estimation of the man fell even further.

Tritten went on. 'I felt the need for prayer and reflection to prepare for the time of trial awaiting us.'

'Quite,' I said.

Tritten glared, and something cleared in his eyes. 'Yarrick,' he said. 'Overlord von Strab sent me word about you.' His master's voice gave him courage. 'I see you have already forgotten your place. We have nothing to say to each other.' He turned away, drawing his robes closer. He stalked off. His guards followed. They looked less bored than before, but uninterested in throwing their weight around in the defence of their lord.

'The roads are clogged with traffic,' I called to Tritten.

He stopped. 'And?'

'Play your role, governor. The citizens need direction. They are as much a part of the campaign as we are. Whatever you may hope, the xenos threat is coming here. The Steel Legion will fight to the end. And so must every citizen of Hades. Do you understand? Or do you expect to hide and pray and expect the Astra Militarum to make the nightmare go away?'

'I've heard enough.' He started walking again.

'Lead, and lead well,' I warned him.

'What makes you think you can give orders?' he snapped.

'What makes you think you can ignore them?'

He didn't answer.

I waited until the chapel doors boomed shut behind him and his escort. I made straight for the crypt stairs. 'We need to see what he wanted down there,' I said.

'Don't think he was praying?' Lanner asked, playing at innocence.

'Not for a second.' Tritten struck me as the sort who would plead to the God-Emperor with all his strength when all else had failed, but until then any expression of faith was a show. He was a coward, with a coward's pragmatic corruption. Something he valued greatly was in the crypt.

It didn't take us long to find his secret. One of his guards must have heard us enter the chapel, raised the alarm, and they had left quickly. There hadn't been time for proper concealment and the attempt that had been made only served to draw my attention. The lumen strips at the far end of the crypt had been destroyed. The dim lighting gave way there to pitch black. One of Lanner's troopers flicked on a torch. We walked down a narrow lane between the marble sarcophagi of ecclesiarchs. At the end was the largest and most ornate. It was the tomb of Saint Karafa. The details of the cardinal's heroism were part of the hidden period of Armageddon's history, but if it had been decreed that his deeds be forgotten, it had also been commanded that his name should be immortalised. The sides of the huge marble sarcophagus were carved into a tangle of shapes that suggested holy struggle without representing Saint Karafa's foes. The cardinal stood tall in the centre, radiating sanctity and the Emperor's light.

On the far side of the tomb was a door. Its outline was a rectangular seam cutting through the sculpture. I pushed. It swung open with the scrape of stone on stone. The tomb had been hollowed out. My jaw tightened at the sight of the desecration. In the glow of the torch, I could see the marks of tools and the damage done to the art. The work was not original to the tomb, yet it did not seem recent.

Inside the monument, a ladder descended a shaft. The beam of the torch could not reach the bottom. I crouched at the edge and peered down. No way to tell at a glance where someone starting down the ladder would end up, but the purpose of the shaft was clear.

Escape.

Lanner whistled. 'Doesn't do cowardice in half measures, does he?'

'He does not.' I straightened. 'We need to know where this goes.'

Lanner nodded. 'Gaden, Tetting, you're volunteers. Off you go.'

The two troopers began the long climb. We watched until they were just the sparks of two torches far below.

'What do you think, commissar?' Lanner asked.

'I think Lord Tritten was checking on a dynastic legacy.'

'Aye to that. Generations of cowards. Well, they were never loved, that family.'

'An escape route of this sort would have to be a last resort,' I reasoned. 'One to use when a shuttle flight away from Hades was impossible.'

'Must go far, then. No point popping up in front of the gates.'

'Yes. My guess is your men will find access to disused mining tunnels, and those won't surface until well beyond the walls.'

'As soon as they're back, we'll do some demolition.'

'No,' I said. 'This could be useful. Post guards, though. If anyone with a title tries to use it, shoot him.'

## 2. MANNHEIM

Setheno returned to Infernus, and she bore tidings: the orks were crossing the jungle. Mannheim was there in the throne room when she presented the news to von Strab. He was there to see the overlord's face when he heard what Setheno had seen from the lifter – the orks tearing through the natural barrier with fire and abandon, towering machines of war levelling trees, smashing a trail through for the rest of the army to follow. He finally saw terror etch its mark on von Strab's face.

*I have lived to see that*, he thought. It was not despair that made him think he would not live to experience much more satisfaction. It was realism.

'But the Equatorial Jungle *is* slowing them,' von Strab said, as if stating his wish with enough force would make it a fact.

'They were making good time,' said Setheno. 'The challenges of the terrain and the wildlife appeared to be inspiring them to greater efforts. They will arrive the stronger for their journey.'

'How long...?' Von Strab did not complete the question. Even now, he would not articulate what he had so vehemently declared was impossible.

Setheno finished the sentence for him. 'Before they reach Armageddon Secundus? A few days. Maybe less.'

'Well then,' von Strab said. 'Well then. I see.'

Meaningless words, Mannheim thought. Sounds made to buy some time, to save face, to pretend there was a simple solution to the catastrophe.

'Measures must be taken,' von Strab said, managing more than a two-word sentence. Then he looked at Mannheim. The next sentence he spoke was fully developed. It was articulate. It was full of meaning. And it was completely mad.

Now, walking across the vast pavement of the Iron Skulls' staging ground, Mannheim found he could not remember von Strab's precise words. Though he had expected them, the scale of their folly was so vast the rational mind refused to preserve them. He had to live the insanity of their meaning, though.

The stretch of rockcrete covered many square kilometres. It was beyond the outer wall of Infernus. The hive's density was too great for a flat, open space this vast. And it was home to colossi that towered over the battlements. Humans moving on foot were insects, their existence rendered trivial by the immense figures of war. The God Machines were motionless, statues of destruction rising to the sky. They were not silent, though. On all sides, Mannheim heard the powering up of reactors.

A wind of fire was coming into being.

Setheno and Brenken accompanied Mannheim on the journey to *Steel Hammer*. The Imperator's shadow fell over them, the twin cathedral spires rising from its shoulders pointing accusatory fingers back towards the heart of Infernus.

Brenken was swearing under her breath. 'Sending the Iron Skulls out with no support,' she said. 'He must know he's repeating the mistake that lost Primus.'

'He doesn't believe that was a mistake,' Setheno told her. 'It failed because of your incompetence. You did not carry out his orders as required. But now he uses his great weapon.' She spread her arms to take in the Legio Metalica.

'His,' Mannheim spat the word's bitter taste from his mouth.

'Your pardon, princeps,' said Setheno. 'That is how he views you, and all of us. Every soul on Armageddon exists for his benefit.' The cold, gold eyes looked at something beyond the horizon. 'Our tragedy is to have the truth of our debt to the Emperor so distorted. Its correct application would be our salvation.'

'What are your plans?' Brenken asked Mannheim.

'My orders don't give me much room to manoeuvre. We are to march to meet the orks. So we march.'

'But without any support...'

'I know.' His Titans would smash the crude ork machines. That was a firm article of faith. But the Legio Metalica represented one particular form of warfare. The God Machines were not designed to combat the mobs of smaller foes. They would inflict terrible losses on infantry and fast vehicles, but they could no more block their advance than a pillar could stop a tide. While they fought the ork gargants and stompas, they would be vulnerable to the waves of ork tanks.

'The orders are without merit,' Setheno said. 'They are given by a creature even more worthless.'

'But he is overlord, and I am no mutineer. I have given my oath of service, and I will keep it. If I break it, I am guilty of treachery and heresy.'

'Von Strab's command has no legitimacy,' Brenken said.

'On the contrary,' Setheno replied. 'Legitimacy is all it has. And there is a mechanism to remove that.'

Brenken picked up on the hint. 'Lord Commissar Seroff hasn't shown any interest in exercising that sanction.'

'I doubt he could even if he had the inclination,' Mannheim said. 'Von Strab is a miserable supreme commander, but he is very good at personal survival. His personal guard is good. His security precautions are strong. Seroff would have to be willing to die in the attempt.'

Brenken sighed. 'I'll try speaking with General Andechs, but he's beholden to von Strab.'

'I will pray for your success,' Mannheim said. They had reached the feet of *Steel Hammer*. Valth and Dammann, his moderati, stood at attention by the entrance to the right leg, waiting for him. 'I will pray for us all,' he said. 'The Emperor protects.'

'The Emperor protects,' Brenken and Setheno returned. They left him then, and he turned to *Steel Hammer*.

The elevator carried Mannheim and the moderati up through the leg and into the Titan's pelvis. There they walked through the corridor of vaulted metal, past rushing steersmen and tech-priests, to the core, and another elevator took them to the height of *Steel Hammer*'s head. As they rose higher, Mannheim felt the clammy grasp of Armageddon's politics slip from his spirit. He and his troops were about to live consequences of those foetid intrigues, but they would do so with honour and in the certainties of battle. If von Strab's lunacy was leading Mannheim to death and defeat, he would encounter both with honour. He would confront the inevitable, and do all in his power to send it fleeing.

In the skull, Mannheim stood beside the command throne for a few moments before beginning the linking ritual. He looked out of the armourglass eyes. Before him was the crimson and gold might of the Iron Skulls. The Titans stood in a wedge with *Steel Hammer* at its point. Three Warlords. Behind them, eight Reavers. Then a row of a dozen Warhounds. A respectful distance behind, but ready to race ahead if given the order, were the ranks of the Skitarii Rhinos. Valkyries sat on landing pads to the left and right. All the great engines of war faced the Imperator as if awaiting its inspection.

Everywhere the banners of the Legion flapped in the smoky wind of Hades. The winged skull on a field of red and the black aquila on yellow, side by side, the fury of the Iron Skulls fused to the cause of the Imperium.

The fury that could smash civilisations was ready to be unleashed.

The control of that power was still a new sensation. Mannheim was acting commander of the Iron Skulls. A new Grand Master had yet to be formally named. The previous one's sudden death gnawed at Mannheim. He had questions, all unanswered. He had speculations, all unsupported. Had the old man been assassinated? Had he defied von Strab in some way? Was Mannheim betraying his memory by remaining true to his oath? He couldn't know. He had no evidence, only hunches and a distrust of coincidences.

And he had his oath, his honour, and the unity he had preserved in the Legio Metalica.

'Let us begin,' he said to Valth and Dammann. He sat in the throne. Its mechadendrites uncoiled. They reached for the implants in his skull, his neck, his spine. Clamps held his arms and legs in place. In the last moment before the contacts were made, he bid farewell to the weak meat of his human self. He opened himself to the embrace of *Steel Hammer*.

He felt the wrench, a disorientation so great it was a perfect agony as his perception became that of a god. His body was in the cockpit, and it was also a hundred and fifty metres tall. His arms were human, and they were the instruments of final judgement. He was motionless in the throne, and he bore a cathedral on his shoulders. He was mortal, and he was the eternal embodiment of Crusade.

*Steel Hammer*'s machine-spirit fused with his consciousness. He and the Titan were both one and distinct. The rage of war became his passion, his one desire to strike the enemy with all the terrible force contained within his body. His reason was still Mannheim, and he checked *Steel Hammer*. He channelled its rage.

The actions of the crew were the circulation of blood through the great body. And in the cathedral, the tech-priests of the Adeptus Mechanicus prayed to the Omnissiah, and the work to preserve the soul of the machine began.

He opened a channel to the vox-network and the vox-casters that lined the spires. When he spoke, his voice was heard by every member of the Legion, and it became a thunder that rolled over the streets of Hades.

'Iron Skulls,' Mannheim said, 'the xenos threat hurries towards Armageddon Secundus. It is our sacred task to punish their transgression. We march alone, but who shall stand before us? We march alone, but the Emperor marches with us. So let us march, and shake the sky itself.'

The war horns of every Titan sounded, and the sky did tremble, blasted by a long, drawn-out fanfare of the end of worlds.

Then *Steel Hammer* moved. It turned. With each step a great blow upon a divine drum, the Imperator began the march.

# CHAPTER 15
# THE DEATH BARRENS

## 1. YARRICK

In the late afternoon of my second day in Hades, Helm sent for me. I expected to meet him in the command tent, and was surprised when Lanner brought me to one of the bunkers atop the outer wall. It was a hardened communications centre next to an artillery turret. Helm was alone once again, and he sent Lanner away. The bunker's slit looked out over the eastern approach to the hive. Inside, there was a stone bench built into the rear wall. A ledge, also stone, projected out of the right corner. The vox mic sat on the ledge.

Helm looked grim.

'What is it?' I asked.

'The overlord has sent out the Legio Metalica to take on the orks.'

'Without support.'

'Yes. Princeps Kurtiz Mannheim wishes to speak with you. You won't be disturbed here.'

In other words, we would be free to speak about subjects Helm suspected even he should not hear. 'Thank you, colonel,' I said, impressed.

Helm nodded and left. I sat. I reached to my right, to the vox bank on the wall and flicked the switch to open the channel. 'I'm here, Princeps Mannheim,' I said. 'Are you already within sight of the orks?'

*'Not yet. Our reconnaissance flights have spotted them. We will meet no later than early evening tomorrow. Commissar,' he said, 'it has occurred to me that of us all, you are best positioned to have a positive effect on the outcome of this war. You have the experience of Armageddon Prime. Based on what I know of Lord Tritten and Colonel Helm, you have greater latitude for action than von Strab expected when he exiled you. Yes?'*

'Yes,' I said. 'Hades will not fall while I live.'

*'Then I will ask you to bear witness to our struggle. I'll leave this channel open during the battle. I'll relay everything I can. May it prove to be useful.'*

'You don't expect to survive,' I said.

Mannheim didn't answer. His silence spoke for him. It spoke of insane decisions and of vanity taken to the point of treason. I seethed at the thought of all the Steel Legion regiments held idle at Infernus.

'General Andechs still refuses to stand up to von Strab, then,' I said.

*'Colonel Brenken tried to convince him to break with the overlord. He's hiding behind the chain of command.'*

Enough. The scale of Andechs' craven inaction meant I could finally do something to halt some of the madness. 'You'll hear from me again shortly,' I said. 'There is something I must do now.'

* * *

## 2. BRENKEN

She entered the general's quarters in the company of Setheno, Colonel Kanturek of the 167th Regiment, Colonel Vollbrecht of the 203rd, and Taliansky, one of Vollbrecht's vox operators. Taliansky looked nervous, as if he'd sensed being asked to accompany these senior officers was not going to be a simple honour.

Andechs stood up from behind his desk. He'd been studying a map of the western reaches of Armageddon Secundus. Envisaging the sites of the coming conflict, Brenken guessed. And little else. Andechs had not indulged in luxuries. The office he used in the administrative tower was large but spare. Shelves of maps and reports, a row of devotional texts, a personal shrine. The map on the desk was unmarked. There was no data-slate.

He was doing nothing.

'General,' Brenken said, 'we have come to urge you, once more, to order heavy armoured support of the Legio Metalica.'

'Our regiments are ready for immediate deployment,' Kanturek said. She and Vollbrecht looked like the tanks they commanded. They were solid, square, bull-necked officers and were as honest as they were stubborn. They lived for the forward momentum of battle and were straining against the leash imposed by von Strab, and held by Andechs.

'The overlord has made his campaign plan clear,' the general said.

'The overlord is wrong,' said Brenken. 'You know this, sir.'

Andechs sighed, tired of them all. He turned back to his map. 'There is nothing more to be said. Leave now.'

'No,' said Brenken.

Andechs looked up sharply. 'What?' he snapped.

'Taliansky,' said Vollbrecht.

The vox operator shuffled forward.

'Turn it up,' said Vollbrecht. There was no joy in his tone, but there was the satisfaction that came of knowing justice would be done.

Taliansky adjusted the volume. Static spat. Brenken said, 'You heard, commissar?'

'*Yes.*' Yarrick's voice crackled from the speaker. '*General, you are abdicating your responsibilities. In this time of war, that is desertion.*'

'Is this your excuse to have the Adepta Sororitas do your dirty work, Yarrick?' Andechs was staring at Setheno.

'I am here as a witness,' the canoness said.

'We are here to follow the laws of the Astra Militarum,' Brenken said. She unholstered her laspistol. She trained it on Andechs. She accepted what might happen yet, but she still hoped it would not come to pass.

'*This is your chance for repentance,*' Yarrick said. '*Will you deploy in support of the Legio Metalica?*'

'No. Colonel, lower your pistol. This is mutiny.'

'*No,*' said Yarrick. '*I am empowered to sanction any officer, of any rank, who fails in his duty to the Imperium. General Andechs, you are following the orders of a man who is manifestly unfit for command. If you continue to do so, you prove yourself unfit as well. For the last time, deploy your troops.*'

'Lower your pistol, colonel. That is an order.'

Brenken's aim held steady. The only sound in the pause was Taliansky's gasp.

Yarrick said, '*Colonel Brenken, I find General Andechs has failed in his duty, and turned his back on his oaths of office. Shoot him.*'

The las struck Andechs in the centre of his forehead. It

burned his brain to a cinder. He toppled forward. His head cracked hard against the edge of the desk on the way down.

'It's done,' Brenken said.

'*Colonel Brenken,*' Yarrick said, still speaking formally, still passing sentence. '*You are the senior-most colonel. In the absence of other generals, I declare you commander of the Steel Legion regiments on Armageddon.*'

'And so I have witnessed,' Setheno said.

'So witnessed,' said Vollbrecht and Kanturek.

Brenken holstered her pistol. To Taliansky she said, 'Go. Get a detail in here to remove the body.'

'What are your orders?' Kanturek asked.

'You know what they are.'

Vollbrecht grinned. 'We leave at once.'

## 3. MANNHEIM

At first, it seemed that a mountain chain advanced over the horizon and into the Death Barrens. At this distance, the gargants were conical silhouettes. They rocked from side to side with each step. The smallest were twenty metres high. The largest were as tall as *Steel Hammer*, but much broader at the base.

And there were so many.

Closer, and the details of the stompas and gargants became clearer. There were different colours to the armour, and different icons mounted atop the monsters. Most common was a deep rust associated with a horned symbol, but there was a foul yellow too, and icons of sunbursts and moons. There were several ork clans in the host before him, Mannheim realised. They were marching with a unity of purpose that was monstrous to behold.

'Are you there, Yarrick?' he said.

'*I am, princeps.*'

'You were right. We have never seen orks like this before.'

After the savage excess of life that was the Equatorial Jungle, the orks were now in a land of heat and ash and rock. There were no settlements here. There was no water and no life for hundreds of kilometres. This was the dead land, the great emptiness to which all of Armageddon advanced, year by year, as it was consumed by the needs of the Imperium. To attempt a crossing of the Death Barrens on foot was not an act of folly – it was an act of despair. It was suicide. But the ork infantry was a carpet spreading across the barren terrain. The footsoldiers swarmed between and ahead of the gargants and stompas. Even from this height, even from this distance, where the individual orks were insects, dots on the landscape, Mannheim knew that the infantry would cross the Death Barrens and reach Infernus not weakened, but hardened by survival and eager for war. He could see the monstrous energy of the greenskins in the movement of that carpet. The orks were running. They did not see a desert. They saw a wide, unobstructed path to rampage.

'They don't know despair,' he muttered, forgetting he'd left the vox channel open.

'*No, they don't,*' Yarrick said. '*As a race, they're incapable of it. Which isn't to say they can't lose morale.*'

'I will choose their outright extermination.'

Ahead, the battlewagons and warbikes raced past the infantry. The vehicles too were beyond counting. Mannheim turned his eyes from the tide of smaller enemies. In those numbers, they were threats too. But he could not let his focus be taken away from the gargants.

He changed vox channel and hailed Kanturek and Vollbrecht. 'How far are you?' he asked.

'*We are closing,*' Vollbrecht answered. '*We caught our first sight of* Steel Hammer *a few minutes ago.*'

'We are out of time,' Mannheim said. 'I suggest you begin your artillery fire now. We will provide you with coordinates.'

The orks were already unleashing salvoes, whether their weapons had the range or not. The biggest cannons did, though their accuracy was poor. Their shells chewed up the land before *Steel Hammer*, punching craters as if an invisible force slouched towards the Iron Skulls.

Mannheim looked straight ahead. 'The gargant in a straight line from us,' he said. 'Plasma annihilator.'

'As you command,' said Valth.

Mannheim's muscles flexed to raise his right arm. Held fast to the throne, it did not move. The Imperator lifted its right limb in its stead. The moderatus's will worked in tandem with his own, and the weapon charged, pulling directly from the Titan's reactor.

Blood from the heart.

'Fire,' Mannheim said, and the machine-spirit roared.

The plasma annihilator launched the rage of a sun. The red-tinged darkness of the afternoon flared savage white. The ork lines were etched with jagged shadows. The beam hit the core of the gargant.

'Fire,' Mannheim said before the glare had faded.

Drawing from the reactor, the plasma annihilator was capable of salvoes in quick succession, though speed came at a price. The energy feed to the Imperator's other systems fluctuated. *Steel Hammer* slowed in its stride. But the gun fired, and the great light came again, and the beam hit the gargant in precisely the same spot.

*Steel Hammer*'s blow could have punched through the armour of a cruiser. The gargant's explosion was so huge, and so bright, the ork lines vanished for a moment.

Mannheim savoured the beautiful illusion.

The Iron Skulls wedge spread out behind him. The Titans unleashed a salvo that would have reduced a hive to cinders. Volcano and melta cannons, multiple rocket launchers and gatling blasters, and more; the full range of the Imperium's greatest weapons of terrestrial war turned their anger on the orks. The greenskins, as eager and wrathful, sent a storm of missiles and shells and energy beams towards the Legion. The space between the lines of god machines became an inferno. *Steel Hammer* marched forward through the explosions and fire. The slow, rhythmic sway of its gait was untroubled by the holocaust. The Imperator was majesty itself. As ever, Mannheim felt the awe of the mortal before its sublime power, and he felt the wrath of the machine-spirit as it advanced towards its prey. The void shields flashed, spiking towards their limits. They held.

The intensity of the firestorm faded long enough for Mannheim to see the state of the battlefield. More gargants were burning. Several were smoking, blackened wrecks. One took one last step and succumbed to a chain reaction of inner explosions. Flames burst from the jaws of its idol skull, and it came to a halt, sixty metres of dead metal in the barrens. Craters were spread over the landscape, and Mannheim saw a dull gleam where the weapons had melted rock into glass. Countless ork infantry and smaller vehicles had been destroyed.

But there were countless more, screaming towards the Iron Skulls as if nothing had happened. The Skitarii Rhinos drove forward to meet them, but they were a sword blade striking at an avalanche. One Warhound had vanished, and a Reaver to the right was badly damaged on one side. Its left arm was twisted slag, and the left leg moved in fits and starts. The wedge was still intact.

The gargants and stompas marched past their wounded or destroyed kin. Behind them, still more arrived. And behind them were more shadows, silhouetted by the angry red throb of the sky. Mannheim now understood the scale of the battle. The orks had hundreds of their barbarous god machines.

After the two quick shots, he had to let the plasma annihilator cool. But the Imperator's shoulder-mounted missile pods were armed and ready. Mannheim raised the left arm. Its extremity was formed by the five barrels of a Hellstorm cannon. 'Dammann,' Mannheim said.

'Charging period complete.'

Then, into the breath between the two lines' salvoes, a devastating artillery barrage fell. It blanketed the ork advance. Battlewagons exploded. Bikes sailed end over end through the air, disintegrating as they flew. Huge holes opened up in the infantry.

The armoured regiments of the Steel Legion had spoken.

'*Princeps,*' Vollbrecht voxed, '*we will be with you soon.*'

'You will be welcome,' Mannheim said.

The inferno returned to the Death Barrens. The Iron Skulls advanced with measured, even relentlessness. The huge strides of the Imperator and the Warlords were timed so as not to outdistance the Reavers and Warhounds. The Legion was a single unit, its attack a precise, target projection of immeasurable force. The orks were a vortex, a chaotic burst of all-consuming destruction.

The Hellstorm fired. The gargant in the centre of its blast became a cascade of molten metal. It poured itself halfway to the ground before its armaments exploded, spreading the devastation still farther. The beam scythed stompas to the left and right of the gargant. They flew apart as they were caught in the death blast of their larger brother.

The vox filled with shouts of damage reports from the other princeps. The volume of ork fire overwhelmed void shields. It battered open the armour of more of the smaller Titans. Mannheim sensed a sudden wave to the right. His body registered the explosion as if the pressure and the heat were against his own flesh. The Warlord *Fornax Mortem* had exploded. Its plasma reactor, fatally breached, had melted down. Where the Warlord had stood, now a mushroom cloud rose, its anger a mirror for the crimson fury of the sky above. Somehow, the crew had managed to direct the worst of the blast forward, wreaking still more havoc in the ork ranks. It also incinerated several Rhinos. The shock wave crashed through *Steel Hammer*'s void shields. The shields tried to distribute the energy evenly, but even then it was too much and overwhelmed the system. Mannheim's teeth slammed together as the shields collapsed and the power feedback flooded back into the Titan, jolting the machine-spirit with agony.

The shields rebuilt, but before they did, ork missiles slammed into *Steel Hammer*'s torso. The armour held. Shells the size of tanks struck the left-hand spire of the cathedral. Iron and stone shattered. Mannheim gasped in pain and outrage. The rubble fell past the eyes of the Titan. The bodies of tech-priests, killed at prayer, tumbled by, bouncing limply off projections.

The war horn raged. The shields came back.

'*Princeps,*' said a voice from the torso of the Imperator. '*I have a damage report.*'

Mannheim barely listened. He knew it was not critical, except in the outrage committed. He thought of the scarred place of worship, of the dead above, and retaliated in kind. Plasma annihilator and shoulder rocket launchers ripped into another gargant. The lower half of its skirt disintegrated. The towering monster tottered, stability gone. It crashed to the ground, crushing hundreds of orks beneath it.

The artillery barrage continued. The precision of Vollbrecht and Kanturek's troops was exemplary. The rain of shells advanced ahead of the Titans, pounding the greenskin mechanised infantry. Some of the enemy forces had gone around the Iron Skulls' formation, coming up behind. They were hit by the tanks of the 167th and 203rd as they came closer yet to the battlefield.

The distance between the two lines of colossi diminished. Short-range weapons came into play. The speed of the battle and the intensity of the bombardments increased. The brilliance of destruction swallowed the armies. Mannheim marched *Steel Hammer* through an unbroken maelstrom of energy and projectiles. The light was blinding, obscuring, annihilating. He heard more of his troops fall. Some had time for a brief valediction before the silence took their feed, but two more, a Reaver and a Warhound, died as *Fornax Mortem* had. Those ends were sudden and destructive to all.

Far more gargants and stompas fell than Titans. The orks had more, and still more, but they were fighting the Legio Metalica on its terms. The Imperial fire hit what it was aimed at. The artillery and tanks prevented the other ork elements from tackling the Titans while they were engaged against the gargants.

The ork advance slowed. Momentum bled away. The gargants walked to meet the march of the Iron Skulls, but though their numbers were greater, they did not use the advantage to flank the Imperials. They converged on the conflict, and the storm of annihilating fire became ever stronger. Footsoldiers and vehicles went in circles, caught between the iron rain of artillery and the iron wind of tank shells.

More ork machines died before the Iron Skulls. The enemy

losses mounted faster than those of the Legion. The monsters of war were almost within striking distance of each other.

'Maintain formation and keep up the pressure,' Mannheim ordered. 'Coordinate fire. Our priority is always the nearest target.' The ork power fields absorbed punishing damage, flaring with emerald light. When they went down, though, they stayed down, and the gargants' armour was weaker than the Titans'. Their patchwork excess was no match for the divine forgework of Mars. As the range shrank, the orks brought more and more weapons to bear. The closer they were, the more dangerous they became. So keep them at bay. Blast them to slag, make their deaths destructive to others.

And still the wedge advanced. And still the gargants came, endlessly emerging from the smoke and flame, trudging behemoths in the shape of raging idols. In the aftermath of another blast of the Hellstorm cannon, when the destruction was so pure it cleared the air for a space, Mannheim saw the largest gargant in the middle distance. It was as tall as *Steel Hammer*, and was so wide it travelled on tracks. It was a tank grown to godlike proportions. Mannheim promised it a suitable end.

*I am coming for you*, he thought, and the machine-spirit rejoiced.

On the vox, voices screamed. There was something new in the field.

The artillery barrage stuttered.

The ork machines tightened the noose around the Iron Skulls.

## 4. VOLLBRECHT

Two waves of metal surged around the vast line of the Titans. Spotters called them in. Vollbrecht climbed out of the hatch of the Leman Russ *Reach of Morpheus*. He raised his magnoculars to his eyes. The Irons Skulls' formation was thousands of metres wide, but the expanse of the Death Barrens gave the ork tide all the space it needed to manoeuvre. The Titans had drawn the force of the foe inward. Now a command had been given, and the orks were flanking.

With claws.

The waves crashed together. They became a great crest. The foe came in such numbers that Vollbrecht had a momentary impression of iron insects scrabbling over each other. Then the scale registered. His throat constricted.

Not a stream of insects. A flood of degraded Dreadnoughts.

He was looking at a mob of armoured monsters. The smallest were three metres tall. They were cylinders on articulated legs, waving pincers and guns on the ends of arms almost as long again. They came in swarms, clustered together like iron maggots come to devour Imperial flesh. Pushing through the swarms were squads of much larger monsters. They were much closer in size to the Dreadnoughts of the Adeptus Astartes. They were in the form of orks, recreated as bellowing metal giants. There were even larger engines, walkers more massive than tanks, taller than Sentinels. Their claws alone were the size of the smaller engines. Vollbrecht had seen those walkers only once before. He had been present when concentrated shelling had killed one and torn it open. Impossibly, the giant weapon had been operated by a single ork.

So was every monster descending on the regiments. A mass of infantry, every soldier transformed into a battle tank.

'Taliansky!' Vollbrecht shouted into the interior of *Reach of Morpheus* to the vox operator. 'All tanks fire at the new threat. Basilisks, maintain support for the Iron Skulls.' The ork engines were too close to be tackled with artillery.

The cannons of the Leman Russ lines lowered their aim. Shells flew at the enemy. They ripped into the clusters of small walkers, each direct hit blasting the cylinders to shrapnel. The walking cans nearby stumbled away from the destruction, arms waving in panic. The bigger engines marched through the cannon fire. Some slowed when hit. A few stopped. The giants shrugged off the hits. The shells only dented their forward armour.

The wave was close now. The orks sprayed the Steel Legion with twin-linked stubbers, flamers. They did little damage and were not quite in range. The cannons and rocket launchers were much worse. A tempest of high explosives tore into the tanks. The world erupted on all sides of Vollbrecht. He climbed back down and slammed the hatch shut behind him. Bullets clanged off metal where his head had been moments before.

*Reach of Morpheus* shook as the cannon fired again.

'Tell me that's a kill,' Vollbrecht said.

'Yes, colonel,' said the gunner, Strobel.

'Good.' To Taliansky, he said, 'Tight ranks, fire forward, drive forward.' His driver, Koch, acknowledged. 'We'll cut their ranks in two.' Vollbrecht gave the order as if it were possible. He had to believe it was. 'Get me Colonel Kanturek,' he said after Taliansky had relayed his commands. The tank shook again, battered from outside. Vollbrecht felt like a stone in a can. The blow almost knocked him out of his seat.

'She's waiting to speak to you, colonel,' Taliansky said and passed the unit over.

Kanturek had issued the command to close the spaces in the formation. She was riding in *General Walpurga*, a hundred metres back from *Reach of Morpheus*. 'Vollbrecht,' she said, 'it won't work.'

'It's the only move we have.'

'*We'll be throwing the regiments away. We have to pull back. I can't see the other side of that force.*'

'The Iron Skulls–'

'Will be on their own if we are utterly destroyed too. We have to salvage something.'

Shattering explosions outside. Vollbrecht cursed his blindness. The gun boomed. 'It's too late,' he said. 'We can't–'

'Throne!' Kanturek shouted in alarm. 'Vollbrecht! Break right! Break right! Break–'

Koch had swerved at the same moment as Kanturek's warning. There was a huge crunch and Reach of Morpheus tilted onto its side. Armour plating tore. The walls caved in. Taliansky screamed, caught in the compacting interior. Vollbrecht lunged for the hatch. The tank tilted higher. A monstrous claw broke through the armour. Vollbrecht got the hatch open and started to crawl out.

One of the giant walkers had seized the tank. It was crushing the hull with its claw. It shook the Leman Russ like a Grox tearing into prey. The movement hurled Vollbrecht from the tank. He hit the blasted ground hard, snapping his left arm. He staggered up and away from the destruction. The ork flipped the tank over and pounded on the hull, caving it even as the explosions within jetted flames through the splits in the armour.

Flames and explosions everywhere. Disoriented, in shock, Vollbrecht stumbled on. His breath was a harsh echo in his rebreather. The ork Dreadnoughts were smashing the formation to bits. Kanturek had been right. But it was too late for anything. The small walkers clustered around crippled tanks, carrion-feeders. They ripped rents wider. They turned their flamers on the interiors or reached in to bludgeon the crews to pulp. One of the ork-shaped engines seized a cannon with two claws and squeezed at the very moment the gun fired. The front of the tank blew up. The walker waved its claws in joy, brandishing the severed gun like a club.

The ork engines were a mob, and it had stormed the Steel

Legion. It overwhelmed with numbers and power. Vollbrecht's disorientation ceased to matter. There was nowhere to turn. There was nothing to do. Monsters of iron rioted through the regiments. The tanks still fought. The air shook with the concussion of human and greenskin weapons. Ork walkers blew up. The smallest were crushed beneath Leman Russes. And none of the struggles mattered. There were always more walkers. The mob was without end.

Vollbrecht moved through a landscape of flame and embodied violence. Ork and human wreckage surrounded him. Tanks charged their opponents. Monstrous walkers welcomed them with stubbers two metres wide, shrieking energy weapons, and always the giant claws.

Beneath the cacophony of the battle, the rhythm of the Basilisks had continued. Now the rhythm slowed. Gaps opened up. Then it stopped completely. The mobile artillery had no defence against walkers.

Vollbrecht discovered he had drawn his laspistol. He squinted at it. He didn't know why he held it.

Something huge roared behind him.

He turned, raising the pistol because he must still fight. He fired at a crimson leviathan. It didn't notice his shots. It didn't notice him. It marched on, a wall of metal, its head unleashing howls of triumph. The wall loomed over Vollbrecht. It cast him into the night.

## 5. MANNHEIM

After the screams, the silence. All communication with the 167th and 203rd Regiments ceased. So did all supporting fire. It took only a few minutes. The Iron Skulls were alone on the field against the orks.

For a short period, the difference was minimal. The ork infantry and armour in the near vicinity of the struggle between gargants and Titans was caught in the crossfire. Anything on the ground was obliterated.

Even so, Mannheim foresaw the end.

'Yarrick,' he said. 'Are you still there?'

'*I am.*'

'The Steel Legion regiments are gone.'

'*I understand.*'

'I will do what honour requires.'

'*I know you will.*'

As he spoke, the end drew nearer. The Warhounds reported attacks by massed ranks of smaller walkers. The mobs destroyed the Skitarii Rhinos. They joined with the stompas and the gargants, and there were too many foes for the Warhounds. They began to go down.

The wedge formation became untenable. The Legio Metalica's advance stopped. The gargants came at the Imperials from all sides.

We came this far, Mannheim thought. He turned *Steel Hammer* in a ponderous circle. Valth and Drammann fired the Hellstorm and the plasma annihilator as fast as they could. The draw on the reactor was fierce. Mannheim gave the annihilator no time to cool. The risk of catastrophic overheating was real. He and the moderati knew there could be no sparing of the weaponry. Perhaps they also knew, as he did, that soon there would be no more risks to consider.

The Hellstorm beam overloaded one gargant's power field and disintegrated its top half. Two more leaned in to take its place. The tracked monster was close now. It flew banners and savage icons, a barbaric mirror to the glorious pageantry on the peaks of *Steel Hammer*. The multiple missile platforms echoed the towers of the cathedral. *Nemesis*, Mannheim thought. *I will see you destroyed.*

The giant gargant's missiles flew for the Imperator. A few exploded against other ork machines. Others lit up *Steel Hammer*'s void shields. Another gargant struck with a limb that had been fashioned into a chainsword twenty metres long. The void shields could do nothing against that weapon. It cut into the armour. Mannheim brought the Imperator around and slammed the mass of its own limbs against the gargant. The blow shattered the blade and hurled the gargant back.

More rockets hit the back of *Steel Hammer*. So did shells. So did energy beams. The shields collapsed. The damage stabbed deeper and deeper. Mannheim registered the damage reports as background. The Titan's movements became sluggish. The crew was dying. Flames shot through the corridors. The cathedral had taken so many hits it was a grand ruin, fire and smoke billowing from its broken walls.

The machine-spirit wailed its fury and its agony. It strained against the reins of Mannheim's control. He held fast. He directed its rage. He made its retaliation count.

Soon there would be an end to all doubt. In the small corner of his mind that observed the struggle with dispassion, Mannheim granted himself the luxury of final questions. He did not ask for peace or absolution. He would be satisfied with the conviction he had been true to his oaths, to the Imperium, and to the Emperor.

Should he have done more to stop von Strab's madness?

He could have. He could have turned the Legio Metalica against the overlord.

And in so doing, he would have broken his oaths. The oaths had sustained him and shown him his purpose his entire life. There were those who could bring judgement to von Strab within the laws of the Imperium. He would not harm that which he had devoted his existence to preserving.

Yet the doubts remained. So be it. Let them be his punishment. And let the Emperor judge his deeds.

The Father of Mankind would not have long to wait.

Mannheim brought *Steel Hammer* around to face the supreme gargant once more. It fired a huge energy weapon in the centre of its torso. The beam was a lightning helix of crimson and emerald. It struck the core of the Imperator before the void shields could recharge.

The chatter of tech-priests updating damage ceased. There was a ferocious power surge and Mannheim jerked in the command throne. Blood filled his mouth. It ran from his eyes and ears. The machine-spirit howled. There was a crack, a breach, a loss most vital.

Tocsins sounded. Breathing heavily, Mannheim shut them off.

'Princeps,' Valth said. 'The plasma annihilator...'

'I know,' Mannheim rasped. The primary weapons had both shut down, protecting their own systems from the building catastrophe. The reactor had received a mortal blow. It was going into meltdown. The radiation levels throughout the Titan were soaring. He felt his skin begin to burn.

The machine-spirit had gone mad. All coherence was breaking down. Mannheim's sense of the great body turned into a collection of fragments. There were legs. There were arms. There was a head. They had no relation to one another. He stared through armourglass at his killer. It was a mountain. Its armour was red, the red of blood, of the burning sky, of the pain that wracked his frame. The jaws of his huge skull were open in an eternal idiot grin.

'Nemesis,' Mannheim hissed. 'You die with us.'

His fraying awareness found *Steel Hammer*'s right leg. He lifted it. He jerked it forward. Sheet lightning tried to split his skull in half. The Imperator took a step. It rocked towards the gargant.

Rocket and energy blasts hit on all sides. More wounds, more fire. They didn't matter now. Mannheim sought the other leg.

He moved it.

Another step.

Almost there.

Time falling away, his skin reddening, his body failing, all strength turning to ash, flowing away to the Barrens.

He voxed whoever was still alive to hear him. 'Iron Skulls, these are my final orders. I command you to withdraw, if you can. Live to avenge the Legio Metalica. Live to preserve the Legio Metalica.'

He sounded the battle horn one last time as *Steel Hammer* toppled against the gargant.

And then, in the midst of the ork triumph, he became the heart of a sun.

# CHAPTER 16
# NEGOTIATIONS

## 1. YARRICK

Lanner and I went alone to the underhive. Helm was right –
we might not come out again. The risk was worthwhile. My
mission was delicate. It required a light touch, a nuanced
sense of the emotional and political currents, and the split-
second decision to kill. Each person who accompanied me
multiplied the possibility of error. I wanted Lanner, who knew
the territory, and he carried a portable vox unit. That was all.

I was searching. I didn't know who I was looking for, nor
where I could find them. I trusted they would find me.

We went deep, to the regions from which hope had long
since been banished. There was no true name for the spaces
we found. They were far below the foundations of any structure. Biological and industrial effluent formed their rivers.
There were tunnels that might have seen maglev trains in the
early years of Hades, or they might have been constructed for
that purpose but never used. There were the remains of mining pits, the last of their ore extracted many centuries past.

The larger caverns had walls and roofs that were mixtures of natural stone and rockcrete. I was in the land of detritus of all kinds. Especially the human form.

'Been a long time,' Lanner said.

'Since you were in the underhive or since you were the comms trooper?'

'Both.'

'Nostalgic?' I asked him.

He growled.

There were eyes on us during my entire journey. A commissar stood out in any civilian environment. The further down we went, the more of notice I became.

Good.

The awareness needed to keep from being ambushed held thoughts of Mannheim's loss at bay. I understood what had happened. I understood its import. I denied myself the hope that the cataclysm of Titan reactor meltdowns had diminished the orks' force. Hope was forbidden until Armageddon was liberated. So was despair. Until the triumph, there could only be determination.

We reached a zone of eternal night lit by wavering, scavenged glowstrips and burning torches. We pushed through crowds of the most desperate of Hades' denizens. In the narrower passages, they pressed together like maggots. They had the pallor of maggots too, where the colour of their flesh showed through the grime and the ritual scarification. We walked until the space opened up. A patchwork metal bridge stretched over a chasm into which sewage fell in a cataract. In the centre of the bridge I brought us to a halt. I rested my hands on my holster and the pommel of my sword. I waited.

It took less than five minutes for the first gang to approach. The bridge traffic thinned to nothing, then, from each end, a group of five men and women walked towards us. They wore crude armour fashioned from scrap metal. They carried axes and cleavers just as crude, but clearly effective. Their faces looked as if they had been caught in frag grenade explosions, the shrapnel still embedded in their cheeks and forehead after leaving long scars. It was a good illusion. I was sure it impressed many of their enemies and all of their prey. It made me optimistic that I was not wasting my time.

'Say and do nothing,' I warned Lanner.

The largest thug had embedded large metal fragments in his chest. He grinned, showing drill bits instead of canines. 'Trespassing, old man.' The hardware in his mouth gave him a lisp.

'I don't think I am. The Emperor reigns here as he does above, and I go where my duty takes me.' Before he could follow up with another taunt, I said, 'We don't have time for posturing. The orks are coming, and I have business with the gangs. All of them. So you need to prove to me that you're worth speaking to, or you fetch someone who is.'

The thug snarled and took a step forward.

'Excuse me,' I said. I pulled out my bolt pistol, whirled and put a shell through the head of the man who had been creeping up behind me. Then, to make myself clear, I turned back and shot a second thug, one standing just to the right of the leader and looking on with anticipation. The reports of the shots bounced off the walls of the cavern.

In these depths, pushed to the worst excesses merely to survive, humans began to resemble orks. And I understood orks.

'Now,' I said, 'I will repeat myself just this once. Prove you're worth my while.'

The leader's eyes had widened, and he had lowered his axe. 'Name's Beil. I speak for the Heirs of Grevenberg.'

Grevenberg. The family had been nobility once, or so the

legend went. The truth behind its fall was buried as deeply as the criminal who laid claim to the name. 'Good,' I said. 'There is war coming, and you have a role to play.'

He snorted. 'You think we care what happens above?'

'You will when the greenskins come to destroy what little you have and kill you for sport. The orks are coming to Hades, and if we don't stop them together, we will die together. Tell me, do you think the people of the hive above have what it takes to stand against the xenos?'

He laughed. So did the others. I had asked an absurdity.

'Then someone has to lead them,' I said. 'Someone who knows Hades well enough to use it against the greenskins.' What I said was the simple truth. The recruitment of the civilians in Volcanus had been necessary but insufficient. We had to keep the Steel Legion and Hive Militia units intact and focused. If the civilian forces could operate with something like effectiveness on their own, then their numbers might truly count for something.

And the gangs knew the subterranean paths of Hades. That too, was crucial.

The gang chieftain wasn't laughing now. 'Keep talking,' he said.

I smiled. I had told Helm I would turn the hive into a weapon. This was another step.

## 2. VON STRAB

The governor of Infernus walked with von Strab onto the upper spire landing pad. The shuttle was ready. There was a conversation von Strab was eager to have aboard. He had no interest in what Erner von Kierska had to say. But in a few minutes von Strab would be on his way to Hive Tartarus. He could afford the illusion of patience.

'I still don't understand why I must stay,' von Kierska said.

'You would abandon your duty?' von Strab asked, finding the right mixture of shock and implied punishment.

'Or course not. I just think in Tartarus I would be able to make decisions in a more sober fashion. Mistakes happen in the heat of the moment.'

The argument was almost plausible. Von Strab countered with one even stronger, and just as much a lie. He put his arm over von Kierska's shoulder. 'The people need you here, Erner. They need to see you standing with them. Leadership is from the front.' He smiled. 'If you try to leave, I'll have you executed.' He kept smiling until he was sure the threat had registered. Then he extended mercy. 'Don't think you're being abandoned. There is something I must do in Tartarus that will turn the tide of the war in our favour once and for all.'

'Really?'

Von Strab almost laughed at the idiot hope on Kierska's face. 'Yes.' This was very close to being the truth.

'How long will it take?'

'A few days, I think.'

'The orks will be here before then. What do I do?'

'You don't believe the Steel Legion will hold them back?' The outrage came so easily. It was a gift.

Von Kierska's fear of the orks overrode his fear of von Strab. 'No,' he said. 'I don't.'

They had reached the shuttle. The hull door was open, waiting. Von Strab put a hand on the ladder to the passenger compartment. 'Then it falls to you to be creative where Colonel Brenken fails.' Her name curdled on his tongue. Since taking over from General Andechs, she had wrested more and more of the control of the Steel Legion from von Strab's hands. Her death would be helpful to him. Based on what had happened to Mannheim, that death would not be long in coming. 'What is needed is a dramatic move. No one has tried negotiating with the enemy yet.'

'Negotiation?'

'It's a thought.' He climbed into the shuttle and slid the door shut against von Kierska's entreaties.

Inside was a squad of his bodyguards. Alayra Syranax sat in a seat close to the cockpit, next to the luxurious travel throne reserved for the overlord. Von Strab settled himself in it. 'Well?' he asked.

'They're almost ready,' Syranax said. 'The degradation over time has been considerable.'

'What does that mean?'

'Proper functionality cannot be guaranteed.'

Von Strab waved the problem away. 'Then we'll deploy them all. Enough will work.'

The shuttle's engines rumbled and the hull vibrated as it lifted off. Von Strab glanced through the viewing block. Infernus dropped away. Von Kierska was a forlorn figure on the landing pad. Von Strab thought about what he had said to the governor, and hoped von Kierska would do as he suggested. The longer the orks remained concentrated in the vicinity of Infernus, the better.

He felt no regrets. The only ones he had ever experienced involved missed opportunities. The campaign decisions he was taking came easily. As far as he was concerned, there was no such thing as a difficult choice. This was the mark of a born leader.

He turned back to Syranax. Time to work out the details of the orks' extermination.

* * *

## 3. WISMAR

Von Kierska called the mission an honour. Edgar Wismar had his doubts, though not his choice. The Arvus Lighter he piloted felt thin in a way it never had when he had flown the governor from one hive to another in the past. Then, he had been pleased by the political doors opened for him by the skills he had learned during his service in the militia. His days as a combat pilot had ended over half a century ago now. His family connections had been enough to find him a first position in the periphery of the Lord von Kierska's retinue. He had spent years establishing his reputation for discretion, loyalty and moral flexibility. He was a politician, but one who could fly on his own, if necessary. And discretely, if desired. Von Kierska had found him to be valuable, and Wismar had moved closer and closer to the inner circle. He had never thought about his training with anything other than pride.

Until a few hours ago. When von Kierska had approached him with the most important mission of his life, Wismar had thought for several minutes about blinding himself. In the end, he had lacked the courage. He didn't think he had the courage for what he was doing now. Only a sense of unreality was keeping him on course. This could not be happening. He wasn't flying west of Infernus. He wasn't really about to attempt this madness.

The Pallidus Mountains were off his starboard wing. He thought about turning north. He was beyond von Kierska's reach at this moment. No one could stop him. But where would he go? He pictured landing in the Fire Wastes, and how long he would survive after landing.

No. He had no choice but the mission. Von Kierska must see some hope in it.

Wismar saw the orks sooner than he had expected. They were so close. At most a day's march from Infernus. The army stretched further than he could see into the perpetual crimson night, a mass of soldiers and war engines no force could hope to stop. Wismar brought his aircraft in lower. He thought he should find somewhere to land.

Because he had to make a decision, and because he had to take action, his mind went blank with terror. His hands froze on the controls. He stared through the canopy as if he could arrest time and hold the landscape motionless. But it continued to move.

The aircraft dropped lower. The orks were closer.

Squadrons of bombers flew by, and he screamed. He screamed again when jump-packed orks streaked up from the ground. One landed on the canopy. It grinned at him.

For some time then, the only thing he was aware of was screaming. But his body must have remembered the necessary skills. He did not crash. When he stopped screaming, his aircraft was motionless and on the ground. It was surrounded by the jump troops. They were doubled over with laughter. He stared at them, and at last recalled his mission. He hadn't been shot down. The orks hadn't ripped the canopy off. His continued existence was cause for hope, though it was also a source of terror.

He raised the canopy. He climbed out of the cockpit and dropped to the ground. His legs collapsed under him. He grasped the landing gear to pull himself up. The gale of the orks' laughter was a physical blow. When he stood, he tried to take a step forward. He could not. His hand was welded to his craft's gear. The orks stopped laughing and stood in a semi-circle before him, grinning, waiting for him to entertain them again. These greenskins were different from what Wisbar knew of the xenos. Their armour and equipment appeared to be well maintained. It gleamed. The icon on their chest plates was a fanged skull over two crossed axes.

Wisbar cleared his throat. He cursed von Kierska as he prepared to end his life in a state of abject fear and humiliation. Now the moment had come, the ludicrous nature of his mission was apparent, as it should have been all along. But he had no course of action other than to follow this path until its end. He said, 'On behalf of Lord Erner von Kierska, governor of Hive Infernus, I have come to discuss terms.'

The orks waited, their grins growing wider all the time. There would be laughter again, and that would be an end to him.

Wisbar sobbed, and then he started to laugh himself. 'Of course you don't speak Gothic,' he said.

But they did.

## 4. YARRICK

'Who are your primary rivals?' I asked Beil.

'No one.'

I gave him the flat gaze I would to an insect pest. 'I have no use for the delusional.'

He looked away from my stare. 'The Rachen,' he said.

'Time for a parley. You're going to take me to them.'

'Why?'

I was honest. 'Because I am not making you lord of the underhive. And because alliances will be necessary. Whatever your conflicts are, they are now irrelevant.'

He said nothing, looking sullen.

I leaned towards him. 'Do it.'

He glanced at the other gangers. They were looking at me with a mixture of curiosity, respect and alarm. I was a mad old man, and clearly dangerous. I also had authority. I could do things for them.

Beil nodded.

I pointed at his troops. 'They're with us only to the edge of Rachen territory,' I said. 'We're already fighting one war. Anyone who tries to open a second front I shoot on the spot.'

Beil grimaced, but again he nodded. He was young, faster than I was, and stronger. But I would have killed him. He knew it.

We descended lower. We took forgotten shafts and crevasses between collapsed foundations. The stench and the darkness thickened together. The shadows of ruins became more jagged and less defined. We entered a world of refuse hills, swamps of waste, and the broken bones of the city's beginnings. We passed a heap fifteen metres high of gears, whose teeth were as long as my arm. Just beyond them, a huge wheel turned above our heads. It had lost its purpose centuries ago, yet it ground on, an idiot leviathan drawing on the power of the grid, even this far down. It marked a boundary. Beil's troops stayed on the other side.

The temperature climbed. An amber glow pushed back the night.

'What is that?' I asked.

'The leavings,' Lanner said. 'The Emperor grant the containment holds.'

'Doesn't,' Beil said. 'Not always.'

We moved on, and the source of the light became clear. The molten spillage of Hades' hundreds of foundries flowed down the channels to these depths, cooling but still liquid. It collected in reservoirs created by design and by chance. As we advanced deeper into the heat, I saw evidence of construction work on all sides. The reservoirs would fill, I realised, and there was no way to empty them. So the routes of drainage would have to be altered, channelling the lethal rivers to new containment ponds. For several hundred metres, we walked along the iron wall of one makeshift reservoir. It throbbed with sullen light. The sides were flaking. Lanner's concern was more than justified.

Past the reservoir we started down a narrow passage between huge plates of iron. They might have been intended to be the cladding of void ships. A cluster of shadows waited for us.

'Atroxa,' Beil said, in warning and acknowledgement.

The shadows moved into the beam of Lanner's torch. They were more degraded and more savage than the Heirs of Grevenberg. They were barely human. Things of grey and muck. Some had filed teeth; others had their mouths lined with jagged scrap metal. The tips of their fingers ended in rusted, curved barbs. Atroxa was a hulking figure coiled in muscles and barbed wire. Her lips were pulled back in a permanent snarl over iron fangs. Her face was a gargoyle of overlapping scar tissue, spikes and blades. 'Beil,' she said. She spoke with difficulty, and her voice was a harsh rasp, iron dragging over a tomb.

I have heard some, who should know better, say that the most degraded humans muddy the distinction between themselves and the orks. This is a lie. The difference is there, always. I was about to use it.

'Do you fight well?' I asked Atroxa. 'I think you do. Time for you to shed blood. The Emperor commands it.'

## 5. SETHENO

The vox-casters across Infernus were appealing for calm. They should have been calling for action. Instead, von Kierska's nasal voice intoned platitudes about faith in the Emperor, the time of trial, and the patience to see it through until the coming of the dawn.

Something was very wrong.

Setheno moved along the Avenue of Labour Repentant. It spiralled around much of the middle height of the hive, linking manufactoria. The traffic along its length was normal. Von Kierksa's speeches urged the citizenry to continue in its duties. There was no sign of the Hive Militia.

Setheno saw the shadow of Armageddon Prime fall over Infernus. The regiments at Brenken's disposal were insufficient. The destruction of the 167th and 203rd armoured was a grievous loss. There was also confusion among the officers regarding the chain of command. There had been unhappiness with Andechs's subservience to von Strab, but there had also been clarity. Now Brenken and the overlord issued conflicting orders. Von Strab demanded all regiments but one to depart for Tartarus. Brenken commanded they stay. The four remaining colonels split, each faction convinced it was serving loyally. The 46th and 73rd mechanised infantry had stayed.

Not enough. Not nearly enough.

Setheno had left Brenken and the outer defence preparations when she heard the vox-casts begin. She had been waiting, sceptically, to see what von Kierska would do to galvanise the population. What she now heard and saw was worse than she had expected. She was surprised. The sensation was an unpleasant novelty.

At last she spotted a militiaman. He was standing near the open gates of a manufactorum. He was being a visible presence of order for the flow of workers entering and leaving. Nothing more. Setheno strode towards him. When he saw her coming, he backed away until he was against the building's facade. She loomed over him. 'What orders are you following?' she said.

'We were instructed to stand down, canoness.' His voice was barely audible over the pedestrian and vehicular traffic. His shoulders were hunched, anticipating her blow.

'By whom?'

'Lord von Kierska.'

'You obey a coward,' she said. 'Or worse.'

Then she was running, making for the high-speed funiculars to the spires. She voxed the regiments. Brenken came on after a few minutes. 'Von Kierska has demobilised the militia,' Setheno told her.

'*Throne,*' Brenken swore. '*Why?*'

'I will know shortly. Von Strab's hand is in this, I'm sure. Be prepared for the worst.'

'*Which would be what?*'

Setheno didn't speculate. The possible answers were many, all of them bad.

An hour later, she was in the administrative spire. Even with so many of von Strab's personal staff gone since he shifted Armageddon's seat of power to Tartarus, the halls were too empty. The few serfs Setheno saw fled behind closed doors or down side passages as soon as they saw her. Von Kierska's weak gruel of a speech followed her from floor to floor. The content appeared to have looped to the beginning once more. Setheno thought she was hearing a recording, but then von Kierska coughed, cleared his throat, and resumed. The spineless hope was mind-numbing.

Setheno slowed as she walked down the main corridor of the governor's quarters. There was one person visible. He sat outside the council chamber. Setheno recognised him as a minor noble, one of von Kierska's coterie of sycophants.

His arms were wrapped around his knees. From his throat came a single, high-pitched keening note, a whining 'Eeeeehhhhhhhhhnnnnnnn.'

The man twitched at the sound of her boots. He scuttled to one side, arms up to ward off the world. Setheno drew her bolt pistol. 'What has happened?' she asked.

'He gave me orders,' the man sobbed. 'I followed them. That's all. I had a mission. He promised... He said it would all...' The cry began again, louder, more despairing, 'Eeeeeehhhhhnnnn!'

Setheno pushed through the door to the council chamber.

The entrance was at the bottom of an inverted amphitheatre. Concentric, narrowing curves of benches were laid out on a rising slope. The higher the seats, the greater the importance of the councillor. The governor's lectern was at the peak. Von Kierska was there, speaking into a vox horn. He read from a sheaf of vellum he held. His hands shook.

There were orks in the room, lounging on the benches, watching the governor squirm. There were three of them, one half-again as large as the other two. They wore light armour painted with double-axe icons.

As soon as Setheno opened the door they reacted, spinning and hurling cleavers at her position before they had even properly seen her.

They used the wrong weapons. The blades clattered against her armour. She charged forward and fired her bolt pistol at the largest ork. She blew off its right hand as it pulled a sticky grenade from its bandoliers. It snarled in pain and alarm and jumped away from its severed limb. The grenade went off with a blast of flame and oily smoke that hurled chunks of wood and stone across the chamber.

The other two orks trained their shotguns her way. They ducked behind benches for shelter. Setheno drew *Skarprattar*.

She fired to the right, suppressing that ork while she ran straight for the other's position. It popped up as she jumped onto the row of benches one down, and then leapt again. The report of the shotgun was huge. The burst hit her right leg, pitting the armour, striking with enough force to throw her jump into an awkward spin. She brought *Skarprattar* down and cleaved the ork's skull in two as she fell. She hit the ground hard enough to have broken the bones of an unarmoured human. The other ork fired its shotgun, keeping her down. The chieftain barrelled through the pews, unfazed by burns and amputation. Setheno waited. More shotgun blasts chewed through the weak barricade. The weapons were ferocious in strength. A few direct hits could well punch through her armour.

The shots stopped. Setheno jumped to her feet and brought *Skarprattar* up. She sliced into the chieftain's stomach with the power blade. The ork's eyes blazed with rage and frustration, then dulled. It slumped against her, almost knocking her over with its huge mass. She threw the corpse aside. She fired her pistol again. She had the luxury of time now, so she aimed carefully. The bolt shells first decimated the ork's cover, then its body.

Von Kierska was screaming. He had covered his face with his hands. The pages of his speech were strewn about the chamber. The vox horn was still on, relaying his screams to all of Infernus.

Setheno walked up the slope to him. 'What. Have. You. Done?' she hissed. Her only answers were screams. The governor's quivering servant on the other side of the doors had told her enough. The treason was believable in a creature so weak.

She reached the lectern. Von Kierska stumbled back, still with his hands over his face.

# CHAPTER 17
# WHAT IS NECESSARY

## 1. YARRICK

For the second time in days, I heard of the defeat from afar. First the Legio Metalica, then Infernus. I mourned the loss of Mannheim and the decimation of the Iron Skulls. But there was honour in that tragedy. The orks had suffered for that victory. I did not know whether they had paid enough to make a difference. I could not afford to be optimistic.

About Infernus, though, I felt only rage. Though vox contact with the retreating Steel Legion elements was sporadic, I had spoken with Setheno and Brenken. I knew what had happened. I knew of the treachery. I knew of the events of the rout. Ork commandos, given access to the city by von Kierska, opened all the gates. At the same moment, a rapid strike force of warbikes and battlewagons raced up the western highway. This time, Ghazghkull didn't even need to force the walls. The orks were inside before the Steel Legion could respond. Bombers flew out of the blood skies and hit at the same time. The battle was a rout long before the first stompas and gargants appeared. All that was left for Brenken to do was extract what she could of the regiments before they were annihilated.

The orks were sacking Infernus. Once again, refugees spilled out in desperate convoys from the city. Once again, they had nowhere to go. The Diablo Mountains were as inhospitable as the Ash Wastes and the Plain of Anthrand. Millions fled, and millions would die with or without being harried by orks looking for sport. What remained of Brenken's forces were heading for Helsreach. They were leaving the refugees behind, even those who had decided to travel in the same direction.

The cold pragmatism of the move was Setheno's doing. Brenken had been born on Armageddon. She was one of the finest commanders I knew, and she believed that when she defended the Imperium, she was defending more than an abstract concept. She was defending its people. Abandoning a third population must have been agony. Her instinct would have been to provide some aid to the people fleeing for Helsreach. Understandable. And wrong. Without exception, every human on Armageddon was a tool of the war effort. We were all only valuable to the degree we damaged the enemy. Brenken knew this. She also experienced doubts in a way Setheno could not. What was simple clarity for the canoness would appear as cruelty to others.

Today, that cruelty was necessary.

The events at Infernus precipitated another necessity.

I entered the Chapel of the Martyrs Militant. Lanner had sent me word that Matthias Tritten was there. He had been seen going in, though he had not, as yet, descended to the crypt. So he was still alive.

The chapel was empty of civilians once more. Tritten's body-guards were seated in the rear pews. They looked at me. I stared back. They turned their heads to face forward. They would see what there was to see, but they had no desire to interfere. I made a mental note of their apathy.

I found the governor in the chancel. He knelt before the altar, head down, hands crossed over his chest in a pious aquila. The great skull of the altarpiece looked down at him in judgement. He looked up at my approach. The brittle arrogance of the earlier meeting was gone. In its place was animal fear. He was sweating. He licked his lips every few seconds. Tritten was a weak man, easily broken. He was broken now.

'What are you doing here?' I asked.

He licked his lips. 'I didn't go down there,' he said. 'I didn't even try. I'm telling you the truth.'

'I know you are. Why are you here?'

'Praying for guidance.'

'And has the way to your duty been revealed to you?'

He nodded. He looked eager now. 'Yes. Yes it has, commissar.' He was still on his knees. 'I had a decision to make. I had to know if I could best serve my people by being far from the site of immediate danger.'

'No,' I told him.

'No,' he agreed, nodding vigorously. 'I can best serve them by removing the danger.'

'Which is impossible. We are at war.'

'Precisely.' He smiled. The smile was unhealthy. His eyes glittered with the ecstasy of desperation. 'We remove the danger by ending the war.'

I sighed. 'You hope to negotiate.'

'Yes!' Tears trickled from his eyes. 'I didn't think you'd understand.'

His gratitude was revolting. It was worse than his arrogant incarnation. 'I understand perfectly,' I said. My tone was level, neutral. I wanted him to be open with me. 'What stage have the negotiations reached?'

'They haven't begun,' he said, and he sounded ashamed. 'I told you. I was praying for guidance.'

'So you haven't sent an envoy.'

'No.'

'You have one selected.'

He nodded. He looked back at the bodyguards. 'Seitz,' he said. 'He volunteered.'

'I see. Come with me.'

'You know the best way?'

'I do.'

He followed me back down the nave to his guards. I said, 'Seitz.' The youngest, hardest-looking of the group looked up. 'Out,' I said.

The three of us walked out the doors of the chapel. The rest of the guards followed a few moments later.

Outside, Helm and the senior officers of the Steel Legion regiments waited just below the top steps of the porch. Below them were a few hundred troopers. A crowd of civilians had gathered. After hearing from Lanner, I had asked Helm to gather witnesses.

All of this was necessary.

Tritten blinked at the faces looking up at him. The harsh glow of the street torches turned them into pale skulls. 'Citizens of Hades,' Tritten called out. Then he fell silent. He didn't know how to continue.

'Tell them what you have planned,' I prompted.

'Yes, yes. Of course.'

Seitz's eyes widened in alarm.

'Citizens of Hades,' Tritten began again. 'I will spare you the terror of war and the misery of a siege. I will negotiate with the orks.'

He waited. He expected cheers. Instead, the civilians muttered anxiously. The legionnaires stood in silence.

'I...' he tried again.

'That's enough,' I said. I drew my bolt pistol.

'But...'

I raised the pistol to his face. 'Matthias Tritten,' I said, raising my voice so it carried down the steps and into the street below, 'you admit to conspiracy and treason. You are unfit to lead, and you deserve no mercy.' I pulled the trigger. Before the echoes had faded, I turned to Seitz and shot him too. Then I stood, bracketed by the corpses, and addressed the people below. 'Citizens of Hades, you are children of Armageddon. You know the easy path is an illusion. War is upon you, and the orks will be soon. You have been betrayed by your governor, and I have acted in accordance with my duty. My name is Sebastian Yarrick, I am a commissar of the Imperium, and having imposed the ultimate sanction on this traitor, it now falls to me to act in his stead.'

I let my last pronouncement sink in before continuing.

'Hades Hive will not fall,' I said. 'I have vowed this, in the name of the God-Emperor. Now I call upon you to join me in this vow. Hades will not fall. *Hades will not fall!*'

I paused. Helm led the troops in answering. *'Hades will not fall!'*

Then the people responded, swelling the choir. *'HADES WILL NOT FALL!'*

'The struggle will be hard,' I said. 'We will fight, we will sacrifice, and we will bleed. Every wound will strengthen our resolve. Every death will feed our vengeance.' I pointed to the corpse of Tritten. 'Every act of cowardice and thought of treachery shall be punished by immediate execution. This end is dishonour. But every death in combat will sweep you to the Emperor's Throne. That end is glorious.

'Tell me your vow.'

'*HADES WILL NOT FALL!*'

'Though the orks shatter the sky itself,' I said, knowing full well the gargants would appear to do just that, 'Hades will not fall!'

'*HADES WILL NOT FALL!*'

Over the course of the next few hours, I repeated my speech. It was broadcast over the vox network. I made sure it was heard in every corner of Hades Hive. When I spoke, I was burdened by the ghosts of Tempestora and Volcanus. Nothing I had said in either locale had come to pass. But this time was different. I knew what was coming. I had time to prepare. The orks stopped here.

## 2. VON STRAB

The vault was deep into the Ash Wastes to the east of hive Tartarus. Until von Strab had ordered its excavation, its precise location had been a secret guarded by his family. For generations, it had been regarded as the last resort. Usable only once, it was the tactic to be reserved for when the von Strab hold over Armageddon was under mortal threat.

Such as now.

Inside the vault, von Strab stood with Syranax in a vaulted gallery overlooking the main floor. The overlord gazed left and right. This was the first time he had set eyes on the means of his victory. He was awed and proud. The space was huge. He had not expected all the weapons to be in one place. 'Isn't this dangerous?' he asked.

'The question lacks meaning,' Syranax said. 'It ignores the decision that precedes it. Once the determination is made to proceed with this course of action, consideration of safety becomes irrelevant.'

'I disagree,' said von Strab. 'I plan on being very safe before, during and after the deployment.'

'As you say.' It was impossible to tell with her metallic rasp of a voice if she was being sarcastic.

Enginseers moved with reverent solemnity between the weapons. Their chanted prayers floated up to von Strab. The ones who were not part of the ritualistic parade toiled at work panels in the side of the weapons, mechadendrites coiling through the ancient mechanisms. The air roiled with incense.

'The orks are at Infernus now,' von Strab said. 'This is the moment to strike.'

'Impossible,' said Syranax.

'That was not a suggestion. Implementation within an hour of my command, you told me. I am giving that command.'

'With apologies, overlord, further complications have arisen.'

'When, then?'

'Another few days.'

Von Strab's mouth dried. How fast would the orks sweep east? Tartarus was the hive furthest away from the front. Could he count on wiping out the greenskins before they were at his door?

East of Infernus, Hades was on the north coast of Armageddon Secundus, with the Diablo Mountains between it and Infernus. Helsreach was on the south coast, across more level terrain. If the orks kept up with their established pattern of attack, they would lay siege to those hives, and then Acheron, before turning on Tartarus. That was good.

And Yarrick. Yarrick was at Hades; though stubborn, he had his uses after all. He might hold the orks' attention another day or so.

Yes, yes, there was still time. Von Strab breathed more easily. The victory was still his. The plan required some fine tuning.

'Very well,' he said to Syranax. 'Let me know the instant they're operational. We will be using multiple targets.'

## 3. YARRICK

The orks amused themselves for a few days at Infernus. When their forces moved on, they left behind a contingent at the hive, as they had at Volcanus. They were beginning their occupation of Armageddon. We received fragments of vox transmissions from the captured hives. One of those came from Captain Stahl in Volcanus. He still lived. There was resistance in those cities, though I feared it was more entertaining than threatening for the orks.

Helm sent out reconnaissance flights, and we learned the greenskin army had split into two. One force made for Helsreach, the other for Hades. Their advance was quick, but the geography of Armageddon came to our aid all the same. The orks could not defeat distance merely by willing themselves to their next target. They had to cross the mountains and the desert. We had some time. In Hades, we used it well.

We also spoke to the other hives. Or we tried.

In Tartarus, Colonel Yurovsky had command. In Acheron, Colonel Morrier. And in Helsreach, Colonel Rehkopf. In Helm's tent, we set up vox communication with all three.

'*I wish you luck,*' Yurovsky said. '*We will listen for your news with interest. But Overlord von Strab's orders are explicit. I will not challenge them.*' He had left Infernus after Brenken's takeover. Von Strab had rewarded his loyalty by giving him control over the combined regiments in Tartarus.

'General Andechs also chose not to challenge those orders,' I pointed out. 'We might have been spared this disaster if he had.'

'*Really? Things went better for Infernus under Colonel Brenken, did they?*'

'That is how you're interpreting what happened there?' Helm was floored.

'*I wish you all well,*' Yurovsky repeated. '*The Emperor protects.*' He signed off.

'*He has a point,*' said Morrier.

'Where?' Helm demanded. 'On his head?'

'*The chain of command is vital,*' she said. '*I shouldn't have to remind you.*'

'Agreed,' said Helm. 'The higher up the rot goes, the more urgently correction is required.'

'*Is that what you are doing, Commissar Yarrick?*' she asked me. '*Because what I see is a coup. Ordering the execution of a general and killing a governor involve very generous interpretations of your remit, don't you think?*'

'I act according to my duty, and I will do whatever I must to save Armageddon.'

'*Convenient that this mission of salvation means installing yourself as ruler of Hades Hive.*'

'Whatever is necessary, colonel.'

'*You mean whatever is* opportune, *I think. Lord Commissar Seroff was right about you.*'

I sighed. 'This serves no purpose, Colonel Morrier. The orks don't care about our political differences, though our divisions are paving the road to conquest for them.'

'*You're right,*' Morrier said. '*This serves no purpose. I will not be fuel for your ambition, Yarrick.*' And she was gone too.

'Colonel Rehkopf?' Helm asked. 'You've been very quiet.'

'*Just thinking. So Yurovsky and Morrier are leaving it up to us to stop the ork advance?*'

'So it would seem,' said Helm.

'*Commissar Yarrick,*' Rehkopf said, '*with the orks dividing their forces, do we have the means to stop them? We have many times the resources you had on Armageddon Prime.*'

'No,' I said. 'Ghazghkull used a fraction of his strength on Tempestora and Volcanus. Conventional means and conventional tactics won't be enough. Total mobilisation is necessary, and we have to hit the orks in ways they won't expect.' I grimaced. 'Like they've been doing to us.'

'*I don't understand how they keep surprising us, and I've fought my share of greenskins.*'

'We have an enemy who knows us better than we do him,' I said. 'We have to disabuse ourselves of the idea there are tactics too sophisticated for this warlord. Colonel, this threat is historic. We are defending more than Armageddon. We are standing between Ghazghkull Thraka and the Imperium itself.'

After a moment, he said, '*I believe you're right.*'

'I'm glad to hear it. Has there been any news from Colonel Brenken?'

'*Yes. She expects to be in Helsreach within the day. She has a few hours' advance on the orks.*'

'Not much,' Helm commented.

'*We haven't been idle.*'

'Assume the worst,' I told Rehkopf. 'Assume the orks will breach your walls. The terrain outside Hades gives us some advantages you lack.'

'*What do you suggest?*'

'The hive must be your weapon, colonel. Find its blade.' I thought for a moment. 'Your docks,' I said. The inspiration was grim, but it made me smile all the same. 'Your docks have powerful blades.'

\* \* \*

## 4. BRENKEN

*Not enough*, she thought. The gargants were already silhouettes against the red horizon. The war was closing in on Helsreach. Rehkopf had done well, and he was showing her what was being prepared on the docks.

'If the orks make it this far,' he said.

'When they do,' she corrected.

Rehkopf pressed his lips together, but he didn't contradict her. He rubbed an augmetic ear. 'When they do,' he said.

'I'm no defeatist, colonel.'

'I know you aren't.'

Not enough, Brenken thought again. She gazed at the piers, looking for more to do. Helsreach was prepared in a way Volcanus had not been. The defences were deep and strong, but so was the readiness for street warfare. The population was more than braced. Brenken swept her gaze over the piers. The echoes of Setheno's exhortations reached the water, and the canoness was igniting religious anger. The orks would be met by fanaticism.

Still not enough.

It was the cry of the millions of dead of Tempestora, of Volcanus, of Death Mire, of Infernus. It was the pain of the uncountable refugees, abandoned to their fates in the wastelands of Armageddon, dying of exposure, of thirst, of heat, or run down by the exuberant warbikers. She had heard the cries as the Steel Legion regiments pulled ahead of the southbound refugees. Were any of them still alive? Unlikely. The orks had come behind them, the great tide of boots and wheels and treads. Brenken pictured what must have happened: the huge sound of the approaching army, the panic, the hopeless flight. The trampling.

She had heard their cries, and she heard them still.

Not enough.

Setheno's brutal sanctity made her incapable of empathy. Brenken did not consider herself a sentimentalist, but prolonged exposure to the Canoness Errant's void of mercy had made her more conscious of the doomed populations. She would never let civilian concerns affect tactical decisions. At the same time, there was worth in saving the citizens of the Imperium where possible.

Brenken pointed to the great tankers that brought fuel and water to Helsreach. They were docked and idle. They should be useful instead. 'Colonel,' she said to Rehkopf. 'We need a civilian construction detail. I want those ships converted to take passengers.'

'For evacuation?' He looked towards the streets and towers where the rage to kill was being stoked.

'Anticipating a partial one. The people will fight, but not all of them can. If we wait until a retreat is necessary, it will be too late.'

'Where would they go? The Deadlands?'

Brenken shrugged. 'Perhaps nowhere. Perhaps they'll be able to return. At least they'll be out of the greenskins' path.'

Rehkopf nodded.

Brenken wondered if he could hear the cries too.

## 5. VON STRAB

He was dining in the company of Lord Erich Rittau, the governor of Tartarus, and Seroff when the message came from Syranax. A serf, one of the Rittau family retainers, entered the dining hall with apologetic bobs of the head. All the guards in the room were von Strab's. He nodded to them, and the

The troops were already in place, a company of the 97th mechanised infantry led by Captain Genath. Lanner was heading one of the squads. The legionnaires weren't alone. The Heirs of Grevenberg were part of the trap too. There were more than a hundred of them, headed up by Beil. They wore armbands bearing crude aquila designs, the sign that I had deputised them. The measure was provisional at best. The urgency of the moment was ensuring a guarded cooperation between the Steel Legion and the Grevenbergs. I could count on a united effort against the common foe. But I had a great task ahead of me. I had to forge the Grevenbergs and the other underhive gangers into something more coherent and more permanent. There was no chance of a quick victory against the orks. Our only hope, then, lay in a long campaign. That meant using the gangers. They knew the underground warren even better than the likes of Lanner. So now, while Helm oversaw the initial defence of the walls, I would be at the forward emplacement, ensuring the first joint operation of the Steel Legion and the underhive denizens was as lethal to the orks as it should be.

I descended into the crypt of the Chapel of the Martyrs Militant. The Tritten family's escape route had turned out to be much more developed than we had expected. It must have been expanded and refined over the course of generations. It seemed Matthias Tritten's duplicity and cowardice was bred in the bone. Not only did the tunnels at the bottom of the shaft lead to a network extending through the underhive and into the mining complexes outside the walls, a surprising number of corridors in the web appeared to have been built for this express purpose, rather than adapted from existing passages. It was possible to go from the chapel to any of a score of exit points, some far on the other side of the Eumenides River, without ever being seen in either the mines or the underhive. There was even a maglev track. Its train, no more than a platform with benches, could carry up to fifty passengers. The Trittens had planned to escape with a full retinue, whenever the time to run had come. The preparations were so involved, I was surprised they had never been used. I wondered if the last Lord Tritten's ancestors would be pleased that he had decided to remain in Hades to the last, or if they would be disgusted by his stupidity.

Now I rode their train. Rather than escaping, I was travelling towards war. The journey, a rattling, jinking trip through total darkness, took less than half an hour, and gradually headed uphill. I used the train's simple lever control to stop it at our ambush point, just to the west of the bridge.

I ran down mining tunnels until I reached the company and the gang. The troopers and underhivers eyed each other suspiciously, but they hadn't come to blows. More troopers than Lanner had their roots in the underhive. There was likely old and bad blood in the air. But no one was acting on it. I had made it clear anyone who chose a target other than an ork would become my target next.

The cave we were in was not part of the Trittens' private warren. It was part of the mine. It ended at a wide crevasse descending hundreds of metres into the dark. A rung ladder in the wall to my right climbed up a shaft to the surface ten metres above.

Captain Genath came to meet me. 'The charges are ready,' he said. He had to shout. The rumble of the start of the orks' passing was tremendous, and the long-range guns on the walls had begun their bombardment.

'Good,' I said.

'So we attack?' Beil asked.

'When we can do the most damage. Wait for my word.' I climbed the ladder. My right arm was still shooting with pain, but I moved fast, an old man energised by righteous war. The ladder ended at a hatch set at an angle into the rock. I slid it to the side.

I was looking out of a low rise towards the highway a few dozen metres away. Ork infantry and transports rolled by. My instinct was to attack at once. Even a single step the xenos took towards an Imperial city was intolerable. But these targets weren't important enough. Our attack had to count for more than a few battlewagons. I looked to my right, east along the endless stream of greenskins. As I waited for a worthy victim, I heard the chanting of the orks. They repeated the same guttural syllables again and again. A name gave rhythm to their march. Not Ghazghkull this time.

*Ugulhard. Ugulhard. Ugulhard.*

One of the prophet's lieutenants. A warlord strong enough to lead an army of this size. But not Ghazghkull. If I am honest with myself, I was disappointed. I wanted to come to grips with the orks' prophet. I wanted to destroy the beast that had brought devastation, humiliation and shame to Armageddon.

Emerging from the gloom, I saw the great hulks of gargants. They had cleared the bridge, though they were still some distance from our position.

A bright streak against the sullen red of the clouds caught my eye. Then another. They were arcing contrails. Whatever it was appeared to be heading towards Hades. I frowned. It did not come from the orks. The other end of the contrail disappeared beyond the horizon to the south-east.

Human missiles?

Launched from where? By whom?

Von Strab.

I slammed the hatch shut and climbed down the rungs as fast as I could. 'Missile attack!' I yelled. 'Get back down the tunnels! As deep as we can!' I jumped from the last few rungs. The company and the Grevenbergs were already moving. 'Vox!' I shouted.

I didn't know how long we had. Minutes at most, and the seconds were flooding away.

What kind of missile? What has von Strab been hiding?

We pounded down the tunnels, taking the first slope down. A vox operator caught up to me. I grabbed the unit and contacted Helm. 'Missiles incoming,' I warned him. 'Get to shelter. Get everyone to shelter.'

He was shouting orders before the connection broke.

We ran into darkness. The slope was steep. We put tonnes of rock between us and the surface.

I imagined the worst. I imagined a forbidden, lunatic deployment of Deathstrike missiles.

I had already underestimated Ghazghkull's intelligence. Now I had underestimated von Strab's madness.

# CHAPTER 18
# VON STRAB'S LEGACY

## 1. YARRICK

It would be months before I pieced together all the details of the horror. Some knowledge came quickly, though. I would realise the nature of the weapon when I first saw the aftermath of the bombardment. When I saw the swamp of liquefied flesh.

Virus bombs. That deluded, treacherous, megalomaniacal scoundrel unleashed virus bombs. Weren't the orks bad enough? Even they must have been taken aback. Even they stopped short of such suicidal folly. In the history of the galaxy, has any sentient being other than Herman von Strab unleashed an Exterminatus-level attack while still on the very planet being attacked?

And while having dinner, no less.

The origin of the vault to the east of Tartarus is lost in the shadows of Armageddon's history. It was there for millennia, and I am grateful for its great age. The Emperor protects, even when mankind does all it can to strip itself of His protection.

Von Strab ordered every rocket launched. The targets were the hives either captured or under siege. He reserved one each for Tempestora, Volcanus, Death Mire and Infernus, but he decided the greatest number should be hurled at the locations under siege, where the greatest concentration of the orks would be found.

I can follow his logic to that extent, mad though it was. If the virus bombs had functioned as designed, von Strab would have done more than end the war. He would have scoured Armageddon clean of all life. And he stood on a balcony to watch the launches. He stood outside, with the wind blowing against him. His survival on that day is one of the more malevolent quirks of fate of that war.

The Emperor protects. Not all the missiles launched. The enginseers working at von Strab's behest had laboured hard, but what he asked of them was impossible. There were flaws deep within the mechanisms thousands of years old. I wish with all the hatred I bear for von Strab that the faulty rockets had been the first to launch. When their engines ignited, they exploded. I don't know if it was one missile or several that malfunctioned. The result was the same. The fuel detonation incinerated everything and everyone within the vault. Von Strab might have been able to see the fireball from where he stood. If he did, he saw his burning salvation. The explosion destroyed the virus. In the region of Tartarus, the destruction was limited to the vault. Beyond it, all was ash. There was nothing there to kill.

The other missiles flew. The guidance of the one heading for Death Mire failed. It fell to earth in the Plain of Anthrand. Tempestora and Volcanus were out of range for the degraded engines.

The Emperor protects.

Infernus, Hades and Helsreach were hit. Those impacts would have been enough to destroy Armageddon, but it was not only the casing, mechanism and fuel of the missiles that had degraded. So had the virus. It was a faint echo of its original potency. And that was disastrous enough.

I heard the crump of the air bursts. The sound was deceptively faint. That it reached us at all through the rock meant the blast was massive. A deep thrum ran through the tunnels. In the light of our torches, dust fell from the ceiling. We knew nothing more of what was happening on the surface. We kept going down, and waited for word from Helm.

The missiles struck just to the west of our position. They spread their cloud for thousands of metres in either direction. A grey mist descended on orks and hive. At full potency, there would have been no protection against the virus, except being in a shelter completely sealed from the outside world. But the Emperor protects. The payload of at least one of the missiles was inert. Underground, we were safe. In Hades, most of the defenders were able to reach shelter before the blast. Most, but not all. Some were too far from a refuge, some were too slow, and others never heard the warning. For once, the corrosive nature of Armageddon's atmosphere was a blessing. Few of Hades' streets ever saw daylight. Much of the city was enclosed. The stink of industry was inescapable. The air was close to unbreathable even with filters and scrubbers at work. But it was enough. The worst of the virus fell against the walls and roofs of Hades, an invisible slick of death sliding down the facades. Where the virus did not find organic material, it died immediately.

It did find victims, though. Many. On the ramparts and in the streets, in gun turrets where the viewing slits were open, and wherever the wind could reach, the virus took its prey.

A cry rose from the rockcrete canyons of Hades. It ended quickly. All organic matter broke down. Flesh and organs and bone deliquesced. People convulsed in agony and fear. They had the time to know they were rotting inside and out. They had the time to experience the full horror of that end. Human beings turned into dark muck.

Orks did too. They had no shelter. In the region of the blasts, from the gates to a few hundred metres east of the ambush point, their casualty rate was total. Infantry on foot and in transports disintegrated into green sludge. The battlewagons stopped dead, turned into tombs for their passengers. A stompa caught at the edge of the cloud lost its crew. It kept walking until untended machinery blew up and it toppled over, blocking a portion of the highway.

It was here, then, at Hades, that von Strab's action caused the greatest enemy losses. He succeeded in destroying that portion of the ork army that I had decided was unworthy of the potential of our ambush. It was a contingent I knew the conventional defences on the walls could handle.

At least the ork dead outnumbered ours.

Helsreach was not so fortunate.

## 2. SETHENO

She was facing west, within sight of the outer wall. She was standing in the balcony of the Chapel of Sacred Mortification, in mid-exhortation. That was when she saw the contrails. The orks had begun the siege with their leading elements, but the stompas and gargants were still some distance away. Setheno called a warning. It went out over the full expanse of Helsreach. She saw troops and civilians scramble for cover, but there was too little time. She stayed where she was. The kind of blasts she expected would kill her or not regardless of whether she was on the other side of armourglass doors.

The explosions were something different. They unleashed clouds that reached like claws over Helsreach. The wind from the west pushed them far into the hive, away from the orks. The clouds descended, tendrils trailing over the streets and habs like the fingers of a sickly, murderous god. At their touch, Helsreach erupted with a wet scream that became a choking gurgle, and then a sudden quiet. The wave of the cry swept towards Setheno, and she knew what had come upon the hive. She left the balcony. She closed the doors behind her, and put on her helmet. There was no other precaution she could take.

She waited.

She could hear the rise and fall of the liquefying shriek through the armourglass. She watched the mist drape itself against the door. She breathed evenly, waiting for the end, and cursing von Strab for hurling Armageddon into defeat and extinction. The end did not come. The wave of cries moved on, fading. Setheno gave thanks her war for the Emperor was not finished. She did not move yet. There was something else to come. Though the virus had lost the potency that struck through all but the most hermetic seals, the death toll on the streets had been massive. Hundreds of thousands had perished. The roads were awash with the thick stew of broken down bodies. The air was charged with the instant decomposition's sudden release of gas.

The inevitable took almost a full minute to arrive. The orks nearest the gates had losses of their own, she guessed. They regrouped. The attack resumed. A shell landed over the wall. Its explosion was more than enough. The gas ignited. A wall of flame erupted before Setheno as the western region of Helsreach became an exploding caldera. The heat shattered the chapel's armourglass. The flames roared through the door-way. They swept through the gallery behind her, incinerating carpets and tapestries. The fire enveloped her. She stood her ground. Her power armour absorbed the heat, absorbed still more, and then its warning runes began to flash.

She withstood the heat. She stared through the inferno. The conflagration was more intense than the death of Tempestora. This was a single, raging eruption, all the fuel combusting at once. Setheno saw nothing but the roil of flame. Helsreach had vanished, consumed in light and heat.

Setheno walked forward through the fire, back onto the balcony. She advanced until she bumped against the parapet. She met the flame with the ice of her rage. Von Strab had doomed Helsreach. But there could be no further retreating. The fight for the hive was foredoomed, but it would be long. It would cost the orks. She would make certain of that.

'*Canoness?*' Brenken's voice came over her suit's vox. '*What is happening? We're seeing flames and I've lost all contact with the eastern division.*'

So the clouds had not covered all of Helsreach. There was a battle yet to be had. Good.

'We have lost the east, colonel,' Setheno said. 'Von Strab has taken it from us with virus bombs.'

There was a long pause during which Setheno watched the storm and billow of the flames. So much was burning there. So much had been burned. Her existence since Mistral had been a series of pyres, an endless purgatory where hope and illusion burned together, and in their ashes were revealed to be one and the same. And here was another pyre, another cremation, and did fate think it had anything left with which to surprise her? The fires were all one to her now. They had been since the one that had consumed the Order of the Piercing Thorn.

The flames were nothing. The screams had been nothing. The losses were just another vector in the flight of war.

'*Why are we still alive?*' Brenken asked finally.

'I can only speculate the virus has lost strength with age. The missiles were not launched from orbit, colonel. For von Strab to have access to such weapons, their existence had to be a secret, and so they must have been here a very long time.'

'*You're sure it was von Strab?*'

'Aren't you?'

'*Yes,*' Brenken said after a moment.

The flames began to die.

'Make ready,' Setheno said. 'The orks are coming now. There will be no siege.'

'*We're ready,*' said Brenken.

The shape of the city became visible again. So did what was at the gates. The gargants had arrived, and there was no one on the wall to oppose them. The guns were silent. Without slowing, the first of the gargants smashed through the gates. Its war horns sounded. They were the triumphant roar of a great beast. Behind it, more of the huge engines marched into Helsreach. At their feet, the green tide surged.

Setheno turned from the balcony. She descended the steps of the spire. Her path was as clear as it had ever been. She would douse the flames with greenskin blood.

# 3. YARRICK

We waited beneath the surface. The rumble of the missile blasts passed. The vibration in the stone did not return. After a few minutes, before restlessness set in, I started back. Both contingents followed. Captain Genath caught up to me. So did Lanner. The sergeant was grinning.

'You look pleased,' I said to Lanner.

'Just looking forward to what's next, commissar,' he replied.

'Why is that?'

'Won't be dull.'

I laughed. 'No, I don't believe it will.' To Genath I said, 'Have you had contact with the other positions?' Ours was but one portion of the ambush. The operation was a large one. We had been preparing it since the day after my arrival in Hades.

'I have,' Genath said. 'All but one company reporting back. They survived whatever that attack was.'

'Have them get into position.'

We returned to the near-surface cave. I climbed the ladder once more. I grasped the hatch. I listened. I heard the movement of troops once more. It was the first time in my life the sound of orks meant a danger was over. I opened the hatch.

The terrain was covered by a stinking, dark green muck. I recognised it as organic. Part of my mind understood what that meant, and filed that knowledge away for later wrath. The rest of my consciousness focused on the actions of the enemy.

The orks were marching forward with even more energy. They had been bloodied, and hungered for retaliation. They splashed through the morass that had been their fellows. They were chanting again – *Ugulhard, Ugulhard, Ugulhard*. Faster, louder, riding the energy of ferocity. More infantry, more vehicles. Mobile artillery too, pounding the walls with shells and explosive energy blasts. A fallen stompa was an obstacle to the advance, but a platoon of battlewagons was shoving it to the side with their siege blades. Other stompas were taking their ponderous steps towards the wall. To my right, gargants twice their size rocked forward. There were three of them, a mountain chain advancing earthquake by earthquake. Flames gouted from chimneys on their shoulders, distant torches in the eternal red night. I was an ant at their feet, beneath notice, irrelevant.

I smiled.

I climbed a few rungs down and called to Genath. 'Alert the other positions. It's time.'

I moved back up. With Lanner in the lead, troopers climbed the ladder behind me. I heard Genath giving orders. We were ready. More than ready. I watched the gargants, and they couldn't come fast enough. The orks loved war, but so could we. I drew my bolt pistol, and it seemed to me I was holding the lever of a huge machine.

The first of the gargants drew level with my position. I waited, my finger tightening on the trigger. Then the second. I counted the steps. I counted the seconds. Each huge boom of the gargant's strides was a pendulum swinging closer to vengeance.

I savoured those moments. I was not above bloodthirsty anticipation. I feel no shame in that memory. I take pride in it.

I raised my pistol. The target didn't matter. I gave myself the luxury of aiming at a chieftain standing atop a battlewagon driving on the highway's edge, keeping even with the gargants. The beast's armour was redolent of savage arrogance. Plates were piled upon plates. Joints sprouted saw blades. The ork wore a necklace of human skulls, and it had the temerity to leave its own unprotected.

The third gargant was one stride away.

'Now!' I shouted. I leaped out of the shaft and fired. The bolt shell blew off the top of the ork's head. The brute's eyes widened in surprise at the sudden loss of its brain. Rigid as a statue, the corpse toppled from the battlewagon.

A few seconds passed between my command and its effect. It had to be relayed. Actions had to be taken. Fuses lit. The blow came at the precise moment I had anticipated. That it occurred as the ork boss hit the ground was a pleasing coincidence.

In the caverns beneath the highway, clusters of meltabombs went off. Rock turned molten. A stretch of road hundreds of metres long fell into the earth, into the abyssal crevasse below. The demolition was colossal. We had planted bombs along the cavern walls too, making the collapse even greater, widening the gap into a canyon. The middle gargant dropped into the void. Huge as the war machine was, the crevasse swallowed it whole. It had taken centuries to exhaust the ore here. The fall was thousands of metres.

The first and third gargants were caught at the edges of the collapse. They teetered back and forth. On the weapon platforms, orks gesticulated in alarm. The crews inside panicked, as I had known they would. Instead of immobilising the gargants, they tried to move forward or back, away from the danger. Each gargant raised a foot. The loss of stability was fatal. Gravity won. They toppled to their dooms.

The colossus at the far end of the gap from my position somersaulted down. The sight of a construction so huge dropping that way was awe-inspiring. A mountain fell as if it were a tree. It pushed a strong wind my way. Then it too vanished. A cacophony of crashes and explosions accompanied it all the way down, the sound of a hurricane made of metal. The earth shook. Further tonnes of rock followed the gargant, widening the pit even more, crushing the dying machines below.

An even bigger explosion followed and the deep reverberation knocked me off my feet. I stood as the last gargant fell forward. The crevasse was not as wide here. The monster wedged itself partway down. It was lying on its side, tilting down, its head suspended over the pit. Its right flank and limb were still above the surface. The arm, a claw twenty metres long, flailed. The crew was trying to use it to find purchase, a futile attempt to raise that gigantic mass out of the trap. The movement created the disturbing illusion of life, as if a death world behemoth were struggling in the grips of a tar pit. The vast sweeps of the arm did even more damage to the enemy. Where it hit the ground, it caught infantry and vehicles. A giant scythe, it carried them over the edge and into the dark. Hundreds of footsoldiers and dozens of vehicles had fallen in the initial moments of the collapse, and the gargant's throes created a continuous rain of tumbling greenskins.

And as they fell, so we rose. On either side of the pit, the Armageddon Steel Legion burst from concealed mining shafts. Troopers took up positions behind the shelter offered by the boulder-strewn terrain. We lined the highway and caught the orks in a kill zone too long to flee. Enfilading las, stubber and rocket fire cut the greenskins down or forced them into the pit. Genath's company concentrated its fire on the gargant. A missile platform was partially visible from our angle. We fired down at the rockets, hammering them with hundreds of hits in only a few seconds. Either we damaged a launch mechanism, or an enraged ork did the most foolish thing in its power. The missiles fired straight into the canyon wall. The fireballs washed back over the gargant and a huge rock-slide pounded the machine, setting off more blasts. More and more of the wall fell away. The pit widened. Burning, venting black smoke, wracked by internal detonations, the monster finally dropped into the darkness. Its monolithic claw grasped at air to the last.

To the west, the forward elements of the orks were trapped between the walls of Hades and the pit where the highway had been. Even with stompas, they didn't have the strength to punch through the defences. This was not the fragmented force they had faced at Tempestora and Volcanus. There was no betrayal from within as at Infernus. Hades stood united and determined against the xenos invader. The entire 33rd infantry regiment of the Steel Legion, supported by the Hades Hive Defence Militia, punished the ork footsoldiers with a hail of las so intense it resembled a continuous barrage of sheet lighting. Earthshaker and Demolisher cannons combined their fire on first one stompa, then another. The impact of that many shells overwhelmed the stompas' power fields and blasted through their armour. The stompas died explosively, blown apart by our ordnance and their own. As each died, it took battlewagons down with it. Waves of flame rolled over the green tide.

At the ambush point, we directed our fire at the orks on the other side of the gap. They were caught in their own bottleneck. The Eumenides Bridge narrowed their formation, slowing the advance. Once over the bridge, they had to stick to the highway. The ground was treacherous. It was porous with mines and traps. Our defences there were simple – rough camouflage concealing deep gullies. In some spots, all that had been necessary was to sabotage the structural supports of shallow tunnels. The closer the mines were to Hades, the more likely they were to have been exhausted, but not before becoming highly dangerous. The orks wandering off the safe route of the highway fell prey to the dangers that had killed hundreds of thousands of serfs. Already, numerous greenskin tanks were caught, upended, wheels and treads spinning in helpless anger.

From behind the hive's wall, the Basilisks of all four regiments rained shells on the narrow strip of land. They cratered the highway, threw body parts aloft and turned vehicles into rolling firebombs. Our horizontal fire chewed into the advancing lines. The orks retaliated ferociously, but at last the advantage was ours. The smoke, fire, dust and bursts of the artillery blinded them. Their fire was wild, undisciplined, random. It was powerful, and it was devastating when it struck home. But we never let the orks zero in.

I was surrounded by weapons fire. The world was a violent mosaic of energy bursts, las scars and explosions etching the red blackness, a storm of fire raging in through a night made of war. My eyes were dazzled. When I blinked, I saw the negative image of the battlefield. The orks seemed to advance in a rapid succession of still tableaux. I found my targets all the same. I put shells into skull after skull. Every time I pulled the trigger, I exacted a measure of justice for the dead of Armageddon.

I was shouting too. In the roar of battle, only those nearby could hear. 'Strike with fury!' I cried. 'Burn the xenos with the justice of our guns. The Emperor's spirit marches with us. We have smashed the greenskins' idolatrous engines. Now smash the orks themselves. Drive them back into the void and the flame. Let them learn the price of defiling Armageddon.'

The miracle began slowly. At first, I didn't realise it was happening. I was too consumed by the slaughter. On the other side of the Eumenides, several kilometres distant, were the broad, conical shapes of more gargants. They had stopped advancing. And then, as I began to understand what I was seeing, they turned around.

Heedless of the enemy fire, I stood up and leapt to the top of the boulder before me.

'The enemy retreats!' I yelled. I pointed forward with my sword. 'Behold the works of faith and steel! Comrades, we have humbled mountains!' I jumped from boulder to boulder, racing after the orks as if I would harry them into the Eumenides gorge myself.

My actions in those moments were as conscious as they were driven by instinct. When I had executed Tritten, I had in effect taken his place as the ruler of Hades Hive. To do what had to be done, it was crucial that I be seen not just as the leader by default, but as the leader Hades needed. So I would make use of the power of the commissariat. I had to be the symbol to rally the people. When I spoke, they must obey.

To become the symbol, I had to be seen, and be seen to inspire.

So I stood tall in the face of ork fire. I led the charge, an old man transformed into retaliation itself.

So I knew what I was doing. But I was also transported. I was transformed. I had endured defeat and defeat and defeat. We had been outnumbered, outmanoeuvred, and outthought by Ghazghkull Thraka at every turn. Now, at last, we turned the orks back. At last, they tasted defeat. The burning air of Armageddon, the stink of fyceline and promethium, and the unrelenting gale of our fire pushed me forward. My age fell away. I had the strength of a Titan. I pursued the orks, and they fled before my wrath.

The enemy's covering shots dropped away as the army pulled further away. I stopped in the middle of the high-way, pistol out, sword held high. I was vaguely aware of dull throbs in my ribs and my shoulder, and burning on the side of my neck. I was injured.

A trivial fact.

The shelling and the gunfire stopped, but there was still a huge noise. It had a two-beat rhythm. It kept repeating.

It was a shout from thousands of throats.

It was my name.

# CHAPTER 19
# UGULHARD

## 1. YARRICK

We had a breathing space. Yet I felt time slipping away even more quickly than before. There had been many days between my arrival at Hades and the first attack. We had used that gift of time well. The trap had worked better than I could have hoped, but the great blow was not one we could replicate easily. I had controlled the narrative of the opening act of the siege. I had anticipated how the orks would approach, and despite the disaster von Strab had unleashed, used their tactics against them.

Now I had to envision the orks' counterattack, and how to block it. I didn't have days. I might have hours. But I didn't know. The orks had retreated out of sight of the walls, behind the curve of the hills of ejecta. The new eruption could come at any time. I had to be ready.

The breathing space was a lie. It was a held breath. An exhalation of fire was imminent and unpredictable.

I had to be ready. I was thinking more and more in those

terms: *I*. I had to plan. I had to anticipate. I had taken on a duty by executing Tritten, affirmed it by devising the strategy we had employed, and consolidated it during the ambush. I had control of Hades, and Helm was backing me by deferring to my tactical decisions. Any leader is symbolic, and a commissar is a symbolic leader even when the chain of command is intact and functioning well. My role in Hades was evolving rapidly. Capitalising on it was imperative. I had vowed Hades would not fall. Its responses to the ork siege would have to be quick, nimble, decisive, unified.

Tens of millions would have to act with one will.

My word had to be law.

I was taking steps to making this necessity a reality. I prayed I was moving fast enough. I feared I wasn't. I wanted to be everywhere. I could not.

After the ambush, I joined Genath and the other captains at the head of the Steel Legion companies. We marched back to the gates, triumphant. The victory was a brief one, I knew this. I did nothing to check the celebration. Not yet. I let the spirits rise. As we came closer to the wall, the voices of my comrades joined those of the defenders on the ramparts.

And there was my name again, turned into a chant, into a shout of defiance aimed at the enemy. I let that happen too. It was necessary. I had to become something greater than Sebastian Yarrick. The hand and the eye of Commissar Yarrick had to be felt at every height and every depth of the hive.

The celebration had spread far beyond the wall by the time I met up with Helm. He and his fellow colonels greeted me atop the main gate, where I was visible to as many troops and civilians as could gather in the streets below, and at the windows of the hab blocks.

'I wish the overlord had listened to you from the start,' said Helm.

I grunted. 'Though I've made my share of mistakes. I underestimated the enemy too. No more.'

'What now?' he asked.

'Now we prepare for much worse.'

Helm had ordered vox casters brought to our location without my prompting. He knew the value of the moment. He was taking an active role in the shaping, the creation of my myth.

I stepped up to the vox and looked out at Hades. I had spoken to all of Volcanus. Then I had been a veteran commissar. Now I was engaging in a wilful transformation.

*Whatever is necessary.*

'A victory,' I said. I sharpened my gaze. It was directed at every soul who could see me. *Yes. I am looking at you. I am judging you.* 'You witnessed a victory today, didn't you?

'No. You witnessed a reprieve.

'Are you looking at me, and at the heroes of the Steel Legion, and thinking that we have the orks well in hand? Are you? Then you are beneath contempt. You are abandoning your fellows, and Hades, and Armageddon. You are abandoning the Emperor.

'This was a reprieve, and a chance. You see what can be done. Know this now. You will stand with us. You will fight. In all the days of blood ahead, you will fight, or I will execute you myself. Do this, and victory will come. What is victory?'

I paused.

'What is victory?'

Again I waited.

'Victory is when all the greenskins lie dead on the soil they profaned!'

The cheer came. It began with the troopers, who understood

the battles, but it spread to civilians, to the streets, to the interior of the arcologies, to the manufactoria, to the chapels and cathedrals. The hive city called for blood.

In Volcanus, the people had been ready to fight. That was not enough. The orks had become an extension of their prophet's will. I made no heretical claims for myself. We were all bound to be extensions of the Emperor's will. But I would see his will enforced by any means necessary.

'Hades shall not fall!' I shouted, and the cheer became a roar.

Time slipping away, each unused second lost to the enemy. Each second, the orks were preparing. Each second, their second attack was closer. Were we using the time we had well? Was I?

When the seconds ran out, I would know.

We sent scouts out to the edges of the mines on all sides of Hades. They came as close as they could to the ork encampment. We knew where the greenskins were, but I would not assume they would attack along the same route. We watched, and we prepared. The citizens' militia grew. Each company was attached to a squad of the Hive Militia, and their sergeants reported back to the Steel Legion. The organised defence of Hades grew and grew. There would be no refugees. There would be no flight.

No sunrise, no sunset, no cycle of light on Armageddon now. Only the crimson dark, its intensity rising and falling by the whim of the wind and storm and eruption. Could I say a day passed? Thirty hours did. And then the orks came again.

The distant thunder of their march gave us ample warning. They were heading back down the main highway.

I stood with Helm on the wall. The enemy had not come into sight yet, though we could see the flashes of energy discharges over the hills.

'No change at all?' Helm asked.

'Something will be different,' I said. What, though? The pit in the highway was a major obstacle. The rocky slopes on either side were steep. There was no roof for the largest ork war machines to get around. Battlewagons and the small walkers would manage, but in narrow columns. They would be at a disadvantage against our wall turrets.

The leading edge of the orks came into sight. Helm squinted. He raised his magnoculars. 'What am I seeing?' he said.

He saw huge rectangular shapes transported by the vehicles at the head of the column. As far as I could tell, they were simply gigantic metal slabs.

'Shields,' I realised.

'What?'

'The orks are attacking on two fronts.' I turned to go. 'I'm taking Genath's company down below. Stand fast, colonel. Hit those shields and hit them hard. The Emperor protects.'

## 2. HELM

The ork artillery barrage began moments after Yarrick headed for the underhive. The assault was massive, though most of the energy blasts fell short of the wall. The damage to the hive and the defences was minimal. But the explosions filled the region immediately east. They were blinding. Helm could see nothing of the ork force beyond. The cannons had to fire in the rough direction of the enemy. The shots were best guesses. Helm couldn't tell if they were hitting the orks in any way that mattered.

The barrage was another shield, he realised. The orks were using annihilating force as a cover.

'Lower the aim,' he ordered. 'Fire at our near approach.' He would make the land before Hades a hell for any being trying to draw near.

The shells added fireballs and fountains of earth to the emerald screams of the greenskin artillery. The war became a spectacle. For over an hour, a battering storm raged that served no end, as far as Helm could see. Both sides poured destruction into a space that neither occupied.

The absurdity made him uneasy. The orks' tactic gave them the upper hand. They knew where the wall was. He had no idea where they were, or what they were doing. He hoped the Earthshakers had hit the shields. He had to assume otherwise.

His hands clenched. The monstrous pyrotechnics mocked him with failure. There was no action he could take except to continue his own bombardment, aimed at nothing. He prayed Yarrick was faring better.

He realised he was counting on the commissar's success. He understood Yarrick's political strategy. He approved and supported the moves. But there was more. The success of Yarrick's ambush inspired awe. Three gargants had fallen to human infantry. The immensity of the sight had almost driven Helm to his knees. Hades needed Yarrick. Armageddon needed him.

The artillery bursts stuttered for a moment. Helm saw through the gap. The orks had erected the metal slabs as blast shields on the near side of the pit. One of them was destroyed, revealing the greenskin tactic.

Using dozens of siege ladders, the ork infantry was descending into the crevasse. They were opening a second front underground.

* * *

## 3. YARRICK

War in the underhive: a battering of sensations so utter it eroded reality itself. Flashes in the dark. The shriek of energy and the boom of gunfire bouncing off walls. Shrapnel, bodies and wreckage flying through the air, hurled by the wind of battle. We fought by instinct. If we stopped to reason, we would die.

Yet reason was necessary. If we fought the orks on their terms, savagery for savagery, we would lose.

The Heirs of Grevenberg were already fighting when I arrived with Genath's company at the level of the pit. Beil tried to kill the orks as they descended the walls of the pit, but he didn't have enough guns or troops.

'Lure them down,' I ordered. 'Lure them down all the way.' To the domain of the Rachen and all the worst vermin. 'We have to keep them together.' Once the orks started spreading through the underground warren, we would never get them out. They would infest the foundations of the hive. But if we could keep them bunched together, there was a chance to purge the city of them.

The legionnaires opened fire, spreading the shots wide, drawing the attention of every ork on the ladders.

They pursued us, and we moved down. We maintained a constant fire, whether there were orks in sight or not. We were the moving target, the bait.

The Grevenbergs took the lead, taking us through mining tunnels, tilted ventilation shafts wider than a Leman Russ, and passageways formed by the random encounters of collapsed walls and sunken foundations. We put some distance between ourselves and the horde. The orks were having to feel their way through the labyrinth, but our clamour gave them direction. I had full confidence in their ability to find us.

My faith was justified. We reached the Rachen's hills of detritus. By the boundary of the great wheel, we began the fight in earnest. The legionnaires formed tight squad formations with overlapping rows of fire. The Grevenbergs spread out along the flanks, disappearing into the heaps and angles of the dark world.

'Rachen!' I shouted. 'I've brought you a worthy enemy.' There was no answer. I took their presence on faith too.

It was a day that rewarded the faithful.

The orks spilled out of multiple conduits and tunnels in a wide arc before us. They plunged, roaring into the pathways between the heaps. We cut them down as they appeared. The Grevenbergs hit them from the sides, leaping from the dark with weapons as crude and lethal as the orks'. Squad by squad, we retreated into the amber hell of Rachen territory.

Atroxa's monsters attacked once the orks were past the wheel. Improvised explosives blew out the sides of the heaps. Metal fragments as a big as a man hurtled across the pathways, slicing orks in two. Rachen burst from the rubble-strewn ground, driving blades and claws into greenskin throats. The struggle turned into a savage melee. Gretchin swarmed over the heaps like vermin, overwhelming gangers with their numbers.

The orks were much larger than the human brutes, but the gangers were just as savage. During the slow butcher's journey towards my goal, I saw Beil wield his blade as both sword and axe, disembowelling and splitting skulls. Atroxa punched eyes out with spikes embedded through her palms, then tore throats out of her blind prey.

I noted them both. If they survived this day, they would become more and more valuable in the struggles ahead.

I was with Lanner's squad. We backed up beyond what appeared to be a low wall. It fell, releasing a wave of brackish, debris-filled water. The torrent foamed through the narrow passageways, knocking the orks down, drowning the armoured greenskins while the Rachen swam for the surface.

Many of the Grevenberg drowned too. If they saw the tactic as a betrayal, they showed no sign. They continued their flanking attacks, two or three or more attackers working in concert to take a single ork down.

'Spread the word,' I said to Lanner's vox operator. I ducked as ork bullets whined over my head. They ricocheted off the shattered metal and rockcrete. 'Move towards the glow. Find high ground. And I want rocket launchers ready.'

Lanner said, 'Commissar, you're mad.'

'Objections, sergeant?'

'None.'

Flames erupted forward and to the right of our position. They squeezed through narrow gaps in the heaps and filled a tight passageway. Humans and orks screamed. More humans than orks. The greenskins with flamers were pushing forward, purging their path of enemies. I took a frag grenade and sent it bouncing around the corner with the flames. We backed up quickly. The grenade's explosion became a larger fireball, then another, then more, a chain reaction of death. Following each other too closely, the flamer orks blew up in sequence.

The blasts toppled a pile of girders. A cluster of brutes turned from the flames and ran through our lines, their shotguns chewing up legionnaires and troopers. I shot one through the mouth. Teeth and grey matter exploded. We retreated faster. I couldn't see the rest of the company but I trusted they were moving in the right direction too.

I looked behind, towards the glow. The terrain was as I remembered it. We were about to pass through a triangular arch formed by two sunken foundations leaning against each other. Beyond that, there was relatively open ground before the right half of the reservoir receiving the molten cast-offs. On the left-hand-side were unstable-looking mounds, bristling with edges and spikes. They were death traps. On the far right was an almost vertical wall. Ten metres up, a wide ledge gave access to more tunnels. A slope of smaller debris lay in the corner formed by the wall and the side of the reservoir. It would do.

'With me!' I yelled. 'Climb or die! Judgement is at hand!'

The rush to the wall was disciplined, even with three disparate forces. The fighting retreat gave me hope. We had order even here. The Steel Legion company assembled at the base of the slope. Each squad as it arrived provided covering fire to the other elements. The archway and the narrow passageways kept the greenskins bunched together. Our guns were more effective while they were unable to use the advantage of their numbers. The gangers scrambled up the slope. The Rachen went up it like arachnids, reminding me this was their home. I was surprised by how many emerged from the dark and flew to safety, already disappearing down the tunnels. Atroxa, though, remained on the ledge, the beast surveying this region of her lair for the last time.

Some of the Heirs of Grevenberg, either through impatience or hostility towards the Rachen, broke left and climbed the other heaps. They paid for their error, impaled and sliced wide open by the vicious edges and points. A few made it to the top, perching like vultures.

The Steel Legion squads were next. The troopers were slower, weighed down by their weapons and uniforms. The orks shot back with ferocity, blasting troopers on the ground and on the slope, and gangers on the ledge. Heavy bullets chewed up the debris on the ground. They slammed into the reservoir wall, and I winced. The painful heat at my back seemed to increase. It was an illusion, and it was a reminder of how little time separated massacre from victory.

I was among the last to climb the slope. I moved up with the troopers carrying the missile launchers. I scanned the floor of the cavern. There were still humans locked in struggle with the orks. I was sorry for them. They were beyond our help, and I could not delay.

Pushing forward against our las, the orks spilled into the open space. In moments, the volume of their fire would overwhelm ours, and then they would wipe us out.

The troopers were above me. The rockets were ready. I was a few metres yet from the top. Ork bullets chewed at the debris and I slipped back. No more time and no choice. 'Fire on the tank,' I called.

One trooper hissed through his teeth, unable to believe the folly of what I had asked him to do. But he launched his rocket too. I was obeyed without pause. The missiles streaked into the tank and the cavern lit up with the blossoming fireballs. With a great cry of dying metal, the reservoir released its flood. A cataract of molten ore burst into the cavern. The breach was a hundred metres from me. The heat and light stabbed my eyes and face. I held up my arm as a shield, but I watched. The ore hissed and roared as it hit the floor. It carried the scrap metal before it. The orks stopped firing. They saw the wave of liquid fire rushing at them. They tried to run, but the rest of their force was still trying to push through the archway. There was milling chaos.

The wave hit. I savoured the screams. I had toppled the arrogance of the ork power with the gargants. Now I finally heard greenskin pain. It was a good start.

The ore covered the floor. It ate at the debris. The slope

trembled. I snapped out of my fascination and climbed the rest of the way to the ledge. I stood. I pointed at the writhing, burning, drowning orks. 'We will purge the xenos from Hades,' I shouted.

Across from us, the debris mounds collapsed and were swept away by the hell torrent. The gangers clutching to the peaks shrieked. They thrashed in transcendent pain, and disappeared beneath the bright death.

The killing wave crashed against the archway. It flowed through, submerging the orks beyond. The tide of fire rose and rose. Searing daylight filled the underhive. Death spread farther and farther. The orks had come down into the ground by the thousands. Now, crowded in narrow, twisting paths through high walls of metallic ruin, they blocked their own escape. The cries rose, almost drowning out the roar of the cataract. More hills fell, and then came a deep, loud, crumbling crack. The archway trembled. I watched calmly. There was no time to run. If the end was coming for us as well as the orks, then it would find me standing tall. Undermined by the ore, the leaning foundations lost their strength. They fell. With them, on the other side, came millions of tonnes of rockcrete. The rumble was as vast as worlds in collision. A god's fist smashed the rest of the orks to nothing. The contrast with the molten light of the ore was complete. Night itself had extinguished the region beyond the open cavern.

A new reservoir had come into being, and we were inside. The ore rose, lapping at the wall. The heat, already intolerable, shrivelled the lungs. My eyes were dry as stones. It was time to leave.

I did not hurry. I turned around. I faced legionnaires, Grevenbergs and Rachen. They stared at me as if the metal and stone had answered my will alone. I regarded them all in silence, then marched through the ranks and took the first tunnel I reached. Inside, I found Lanner, Genath and a vox operator. I saw awe even in Lanner's eyes. Then I saw the terror in the vox operator's eyes, and realised the looks I saw in these three had another source. 'What is it?' I asked.

'They're calling for you on the wall,' said Genath.

'Who is?'

'Everyone,' Lanner said. 'The people. The army.' He swallowed. I hadn't seen him nervous before. 'The orks.'

The chanting grew louder as I neared the wall. I ran through a battle of fanaticism. On this side of the wall, our forces were calling my name. As I climbed the steps to the battlements, I heard the countering cries of Ugulhard from the orks beyond. And at the top, just to the south of the gate, I heard a guttural, booming, inhuman voice snarl, 'Yarrrrick.'

I stepped into a tableau of suspended war. The ramparts had been battered. Smoke rolled over the wall. Several cannon turrets had been demolished. On the far side, the ground was a patchwork of overlapping craters filled with the wreckage of ork guns. Thousands of ork foot soldiers crowded forward to climb siege ladders. The defenders destroyed the ladders as they appeared, and the orks fired upwards, clearing the way for more ladders to rise.

A stalemate.

A few orks had reached the top of the wall. I found myself in their midst. Before me, barely more than five metres away and striding back and forth on the section of the battlements he had claimed for himself, was the giant who roared my name. He was summoning his rival to combat, and he had already dismissed Helm as being unworthy of that claim. The colonel was slumped against the wreckage of a cannon just on the other side of the warboss. He was moving, but weakly. His right arm was hanging at a strange angle. Blood soaked his face. Orks lined both ends of the warboss's territory, echoing each of his shouts.

I knew what beast this was, and I spat his name back at him. 'Ugulhard.'

The warboss turned. His pistol was larger than a heavy bolter. His right arm was encased in a power claw. I recalled seeing this ork leading the first charge on Tempestora.

Did silence fall over the battlefield at that moment? I don't trust my memory on this point. All my focus was on this foe. But I have a sense of orks and humans pausing as two symbols clashed.

I knew what was at stake. I'm sure Ugulhard did too. He looked down at me, and I saw disappointment in the glitter of those red eyes, ridiculously small in that giant skull. Ugulhard had come to fight the leader who had destroyed his gargants, and found a human no larger than any of the others, and much older. He snorted contempt.

I drew bolt pistol and sword.

Ugulhard grinned. He raised his claw and stepped forward to crush me with a single blow. I charged him, coming in under the blow. The claw punched and missed. I fired bolt shells into his chest plate and stabbed to the right, jabbing my blade into the meat of his gun arm. Ugulhard snarled and staggered back a step. He turned the gun on me. I fired straight into its barrel. The massive pistol blew up. Ugulhard hurled the twisted mass at me and it smashed my shoulder hard enough to spin me around. I moved back, putting some distance between us. He watched me, and his grin was pleased. I was giving him a fight.

The ork's ruined pistol had struck my left shoulder, but it

was my right that ached. The throbbing was back, worse than ever. It threatened to dull my reactions. And when Ugulhard advanced again, each step had a dark familiarity, as if our every move had been choreographed, and I had seen it all before.

Reaching out from a century and half, the winds of Mistral blew against my neck. I felt the grip of the daemon Ghalshan-nha tighten around my soul. I had lived these moments before. In fragments and premonitions, they had stabbed into my dreams. Now the mosaic was coming together.

Ugulhard swung his claw again. He was slow. I jumped back and stepped to the left. His swing pulverised a crenu-lation. His momentum kept him turning, and now his back was to me. It was too heavily armoured. I raised my blade to cut through his left arm again.

There was a blur, and Ugulhard whirled around, laughing. His sluggishness had been a ruse. He seized my sword arm with the power claw.

Dream and physical agony merged. I convulsed and dropped my sword. Ugulhard straightened to his full height. He stretched out his arm to show my dangling body first to one army, then the other. He roared his triumph. He clamped down.

My bones cracked. Blood burst from between the halves of the claw. My lips drew back in pain and hatred. My teeth ground together. I hissed in rage, and did not cry out. Laugh-ing, Ugulhard held my left shoulder with his other hand. He cocked his head, waiting to see that I had understood what he was about to do.

He pulled. He crushed. And I came apart.

The pain flared white and ultraviolet. At its centre, as muscle shredded and bone splintered, there was an uncanny libera-tion. The moment in whose shadow I had lived since Mistral had come, and it could wear at me no longer.

The light of the pain turned to darkness. Unconsciousness came for me, but I rejected it. I had nothing now but my will, and with it, I would kill this monster.

Ugulhard dropped me. I fell into a crouch. Blood jetted from my right shoulder, soaking my flank. The warboss examined my mutilated limb in his claw. I was beneath his notice.

My sword was within reach. I seized it with my left hand. I grasped the steel. I took my pain, and all the agony of burning Armageddon, and I forged them into a single action.

I rose. 'Ugulhard!' I shouted. He looked down, surprised. I thrust the blade between the rough seam of his armour and all the way through his throat. His eyes glazed with shock. His knees buckled. I sawed the blade back and forth. His wet choking gave way to the powerful spray of vitae. It fountained over me. Still I sawed, cutting through gristle and bone and my pain and weakness.

I cut all the way through.

I could no longer feel my body. My fingers were growing clumsy. But I held off the black. I dropped the sword and seized the huge skull. I carried it to the edge of the parapet. Now I held my trophy high, brandishing it before the orks.

'I am Yarrick!' I shouted in the greenskins' barbaric tongue. 'I look upon you and you die!' And then in cleansing Gothic, I howled my defiance of the great enemy. 'Do you see, Ghazghkull Thraka? Hades will never be yours! Armageddon will never be yours! Here is where we stop you! Here is where you fail!'

I hurled Ugulhard's head from the wall. The orks cried out.

And they turned.

And they fled.

And then, at last, I let the dark come.

# EPILOGUE

Months now. Months of fighting above ground and below. Hades burned. It bled. It screamed. But it stood. It would continue to stand. I had vowed it would, and my vow is iron.

I moved through the disused ventilation shaft with Lanner's squad and the Rachen. There was a nest of orks close by. Their snarls reached us through the wall of the shaft. The maze of the mines and the underhive was a weapon for both sides of the conflict. We moved beneath their camps. They infiltrated the hive.

We had come to punish their temerity once more.

I stopped walking and listened. The orks were just on the other side of the curved wall of the shaft. 'Remember,' I whispered, 'leave one alive.'

'Why?' Atroxa grumbled.

'So it can spread the tale.'

I raised my right arm. My powerful arm. Ugulhard's claw. With a single blow, I punched through the metal and burst through the pipe. The orks reared back in alarm. The monster had come upon them.

Be the symbol. The needful role of the commissar. I learned that lesson early. But in Hades, I had to be more.

Be the legend.

And now I knew that my name must have meaning for the enemy as well. The orks had their prophet. I would be something else.

I crushed a greenskin skull with the claw. I glared at the stunned brutes.

And as my eye blazed with killing ruby light, I became their nightmare.

# ABOUT THE AUTHOR

**David Annandale** is the author of the Horus Heresy novel *The Damnation of Pythos*. He also writes the Yarrick series, consisting of the novella *Chains of Golgotha* and the novels *Imperial Creed* and *The Pyres of Armageddon*. For Space Marine Battles he has written *The Death of Antagonis* and *Overfiend*. He is a prolific writer of short fiction, including the novella *Mephiston: Lord of Death* and numerous short stories set in The Horus Heresy and Warhammer 40,000 universes. He has also written several short stories set in the Age of Sigmar. David lectures at a Canadian university, on subjects ranging from English literature to horror films and video games.

# THE
# LAST WALL

### DAVID ANNANDALE

**WARHAMMER**
40,000

An extract from

# THE LAST WALL

Human and ork tanks fired at each other at point-blank range. Every shot hit. The vehicles of both forces disintegrated in flames and tearing metal, their deaths savaging nearby infantry. The losses mounted, but the greater human numbers made the difference. The advance slowed, but it did not stop.

'Faster!' Gattan ordered. 'Get us through!' The Chimera's armour wasn't as thick as a Leman Russ'. It had already taken one hit that would have incinerated Gattan if he hadn't ducked down the hatch the second before the shell struck. He was back up again the next instant, making himself visible to both orks and humans. Let one fear him, he thought, and the other take heart from his defiance.

Forward still, with more and more of the ork Battlewagons down. Gattan could see past them to the open gate itself. Then a huge shape emerged from the entrance. His eyes widened. 'Hard right!' he yelled. 'Evasive–'

He couldn't hear his words as the enormous gun of the ork battle fortress roared. The shell blew up a Hellhound close to Gattan's left. He turned his head away from the heat of the flames as the vehicle's ignited promethium reserves splashed outward, immolating human and ork alike.

The new ork tank was immense, four times the size of any other vehicle on the field. Its main gun looked like it belonged on a cruiser. The ork foot soldiers hooted their derision at the humans as they swarmed past their monster. The battle fortress moved forward slowly. Each shot was a high-explosive bomb, and each killed another Imperial tank. The few that missed made huge craters of human flesh in the infantry.

'Surround it!' said Gattan. 'All vehicles concentrate fire on this target!'

Clicks of acknowledgement on the vox, and Gattan had a moment to wonder when the overall leadership of the attack had fallen to him. Then there were no thoughts but the destruction of the monster. Leman Russ, Hellhound and Chimera encircled the battle fortress. Its gigantic turret moved with a sluggish laziness and picked them off one at a time. Their shells were pinpricks against its armour.

Gattan prayed that the accumulation of pinpricks would be enough.

The turret gradually moved his way. The Chimera kept circling, but the gun moved closer, each terrible blast consigning more of Terra's regiments to oblivion. Fernau's curses were cut off by a vox-squeal as his Chimera vanished.

But the miracle happened. Gattan saw cracks appear in the battle fortress' flanks. The fissures glowed red, then orange, then white. Even as he shouted to keep firing, that they were besting the monster, a terrible thought came to him.

He realised that this was too easy.

He realised too late.

The battle fortress exploded.